THE FACE AT THE WINDOW

Todd sighed. He pushed a fingertip between the iron slats that covered the window and pressed it against the pane, feeling the summer heat. The voices inside him groaned collectively.

Focusing on his finger, Todd willed it through the glass. In his mind, he saw the digit burst through the pane and the ragged glass edges slice off the tip of his finger. He wondered if someone could bleed to death that way, if *he* could bleed to death that way. A clacking sound redirected Todd's attention, and he glimpsed over his shoulder to see Russell gone and the door closed. When he turned back to the window, he let out a short gasp. He no longer saw his own reflection but a large white face gazing back at him. The sight paralyzed him, fascinated him, that vertical mouth, the dark, empty eye sockets.

Guardedly, Todd removed his finger from the window, stood on tiptoe, and peered through the slats to the ground two stories below. The head had no body, no physical framework on stilts. The head simply floated.

Todd lowered himself slowly, and the head drew closer to the windowpane. . . .

FAMILY INHERITANCE

DEBORAH LeBLANC

LEISURE BOOKS  NEW YORK CITY

To Mom, Dad, Dee, and Cobe,
for all that might have been.

A LEISURE BOOK®

August 2004

Published by

Dorchester Publishing Co., Inc.
200 Madison Avenue
New York, NY 10016

ISBN 0-8439-5347-0

Printed in the United States of America.

ACKNOWLEDGMENTS

Many thanks go to my friend and agent, Lynn Seligman, who took a chance and believed; to Don D'Auria, my editor, who made the seemingly impossible happen; to Leah Hultenschmidt for her hard work and vision; to Leisure's sales force for making the world revolve; to Nancy Eannace for her undying support; to Jay Burnside, for his invaluable attention to detail and constant encouragement (No, Jay, Saucy can't come back!); to the crew at CCSI, who kept the cogs turning; to Ro Foley and Monica Simon for reading, re-reading, and reading again; to Bill Thompson, who not only graced me with his friendship and support but taught me that less is indeed more; to Danelle McCafferty, who helped me untangle an obstinate web; to Jude, Teresa, Gerard, Elizabeth, Anne, and Mary for always being there; to Dave, Michelle, Rebekah, and Sarah, for their love, support, sacrifices, and understanding; and last but certainly never least, to my people, the Cajuns, who gave me a heritage larger than life. *Bien merci avec tout mon coeur.*

FAMILY INHERITANCE

Tomorrow never comes soon enough
For yesterday's mistake
And today passes too quickly
For its memory to fade

—The Book of Deliberations

Prologue

Neither of them moved. Standing shoulder to shoulder, they stared at the aging structure in front of them. Its weathered clapboards, wide and paint-chipped, seemed to hang on the building by sheer determination. The roof consisted of corrugated sheets of rusted tin that bowed inward toward the middle. In the center of the forty-foot span stood a single wooden door, which looked ridiculously inadequate for the expanse of building it served.

Taped to the door frame was a yellowing sheet of paper with one word stenciled across the middle: KNOCK.

Roberta reached down protectively and stroked her bulging stomach. The baby kicked. "Are you sure this is the right place?" she asked her friend. "I mean, look at this setup."

"Yeah, positive. We followed the map exactly,"

Sharon said, looking at the torn paper bag she had written the directions on. She slapped at a mosquito on her arm. "Maybe this wasn't such a great idea. You sure you want to do this?"

Roberta shifted nervously from one foot to the other, tasting the musky, fecund odor of a nearby bayou with her every breath. She was usually game for anything, but this place gave her the creeps. She glanced back over her shoulder at Sharon's husband's new '66 Mustang and hoped the weeds and sticker bushes hadn't damaged the paint job. Glen would be gargantuanly pissed.

She looked at Sharon again. "Yeah, but let's just hurry up and get it over with."

Sharon nodded, stepped forward, and quickly rapped on the door.

An eternity's moment passed before they heard a deep, scraping noise that sounded as though someone wanted to give them access by gouging through the door with a heavy object. The women looked at each other anxiously.

Although the door began to open slowly inward, they stepped back from it. It groaned arthritically as the opening widened. Five inches . . . eight . . . a foot and a half. The door stopped, leaving enough room for someone to enter sideways—someone who wasn't eight months pregnant. Sunlight stumbled into the room like a drunk entering unfamiliar territory, and they were able to see the cracked, wooden floor.

"Hello?" Roberta called out, her tongue feeling thick against the roof of her mouth.

"Hurry up!" A woman's voice boomed from behind the door.

Roberta jumped, and grabbed Sharon's arm to keep from falling over.

Sharon squeezed her hand, then patted it. She stepped forward, pressed through the entrance sideways, then stopped. She reached out tentatively and pushed the door open wider.

An elderly woman, as weathered and colorless as the clapboards hanging outside, stood just beyond the entrance. Wrinkles, deep and purposeful, ran from mouth to ears then eyes to chin, forming a haphazard tic-tac-toe on her face. Her small brown eyes were pinched between sagging eyelids and veiled with cataracts. A faded, Hawaiian print dress clung to her thick body.

The old woman peered nervously at the open door and frowned at the time and space it took Roberta to enter. As soon as Roberta made it inside, the woman slid a thick, bolt-action lock into place.

More apprehensive than ever, Roberta moistened her lips and shivered. It took a moment for her eyes to adjust to the darkness inside. When she could finally see, she blinked, surprised at the size of the room. It was no bigger than a walk-in closet. A hot, stuffy closet that smelled of sweat, Vicks VapoRub, and mildewed clothes. The walls were constructed from sheets of split plywood that had never seen a coat of paint. Light and air did manage to filter through the room, but only in small quantities.

An eight-by-ten picture of the Sacred Heart of Jesus hung lopsided on the far right wall. Above it rested a narrow shelf that held a ceramic cherub, a cactus plant, and a thumbtacked picture of Elvis. On their left stood a faded floral couch covered with a sheet of clear plastic. A young, black woman, her eyes swollen and red, sat on the sofa with her arms locked tightly around a small boy perched on her lap.

Against the back wall was another door, directly opposite from the one they had entered. The old woman waddled to it.

"Stay here," she said, her voice sharp, its Cajun accent thick. She didn't look back at her guests. "It's not you turn." She opened the door and shuffled through it, leaving a cloud of dust suspended behind her.

Sharon exhaled loudly. "Is she always this cheerful?" she asked the seated stranger.

The young woman stared straight ahead, not answering Sharon or even acknowledging her existence. The boy on her lap smiled.

Sharon gave Roberta a *get-a-load-of-this* look, then shrugged. "You'd better sit," she said, her voice loud in the small room.

Although the strange woman made her nervous, Roberta wanted to get off her feet. She sat, settling herself in as comfortable a position as she could manage. "There's room," she said to Sharon, patting the sticky plastic beside her.

Sharon smiled and leaned against the wall near the crooked Jesus. "That's all right. This'll work."

"Dat's a baby?" the boy suddenly asked Roberta. He looked to be no more than four years old, and the stained T-shirt and mismatched shorts he wore did little to hide his too-thin body. Dirt caked his bare feet in neglected layers. His eyes, although too large for such a tiny face, were a brilliant black and riveted to her stomach. He glanced up at her.

Roberta felt gooseflesh rising on her arms. "Yes, it is," she answered, forcing a smile. She pushed a sweaty clump of bangs from her forehead.

Breaking eye contact, the boy looked down at her stomach again. "I can hold it?" he asked. His head cocked sideways for a moment, then he flashed her a smile filled with tiny white teeth.

Roberta meant to chuckle, but what came out sounded more like a croak. "Uh . . . not yet," she said. "It has to be born first."

While the boy continued to stare at Roberta's stomach, he slowly pulled a thin arm out from the young woman's grasp and stretched out one finger.

"No!" the woman shouted, making Roberta gasp in surprise. Until now, the woman had seemed oblivious to everything happening in the room. "No!" She grabbed the boy's arm and pulled it to her.

Just as suddenly as the woman's animation switch had come on, it went off, and she returned to her catatonic gaze. She tilted her head forward and stared blankly, as if intent on watching every scene of some internal movie.

The boy frowned, waited a moment, then, just as smoothly as he had done seconds before, like a tiny Houdini, he released an arm from her grasp and extended his index finger. This time he managed to press it against Roberta's belly. The baby kicked hard and abruptly shifted to one side, causing Roberta to inhale sharply.

A look of naked terror fell over the young woman's face, and her arms flailed wildly as she pulled the boy's hand back to her. Roberta pressed herself farther into the corner of the sofa and watched in shock as the woman's mouth opened and closed silently, frantically.

The boy didn't put up a fight. Instead, a look of quiet frustration moved across his face, and he allowed her to pull him away.

Roberta was struggling to get up from the sagging couch, away from the strange little boy and woman, when the door at the back of the room opened and the old woman toddled through.

"It's you turn," she said, nodding to Roberta. She held on to the door edge with both hands as if expecting a blast of wind to yank it from her.

"But they were here before us," Roberta said, nodding toward the woman and boy, who were now both sitting stiff and silent.

"Don't matter," the old woman huffed. "He wants to see you first. Hurry up! He don't got all day, ya know."

Roberta tugged against the arm of the couch, working her hips forward. She waved a hand toward Sharon, who quickly stepped forward, grabbed it, and helped her to her feet.

"What's up with the girl and kid?" Sharon whispered.

"Hell if I know." Roberta glanced back at the young woman, whose narrow face dripped with sweat.

The woman's eyes suddenly flicked over Roberta, Sharon, and the old woman. She then lowered her head apologetically, placed the boy down on the floor in front of her, and stood. A sucking sound came from the plastic cushion as it released the back of her thighs. Grabbing the boy by an earlobe, she pulled him closer to her, and both stood quietly, watching the three women.

The boy's eyes never left Roberta's stomach, and his grin slowly reappeared.

The old woman pointed a threatening finger at Roberta. "You ever go to a gris-gris man before?" she asked loudly.

Before Roberta could answer, Sharon stepped in front of her. "No, she—"

"Did I ax you?" the old woman shot back.

"No, but—"

"Den shut up." The old woman peered around her to Roberta. "Whas da madda, you can't talk?"

"Yes, of course," Roberta said, stepping alongside Sharon. "She was only—"

"You always let her stick her nose to you business?" the old woman asked. She lowered her finger and tugged at the waist of her dress, hoisting either underwear or a slip higher on her hips. She shook her head, not waiting for Roberta to answer. "I'm gonna ax you again. You ever go to a gris-gris man before?" She scowled at Sharon as though daring her to speak.

"No," Roberta answered quietly. She glanced back at the woman and boy still standing in front of the sofa. The woman stared straight ahead, her eyes soft and detached. The boy's gaze remained glued to Roberta's stomach, and his grin widened when she looked at him. She noticed thin rivulets of liquid running over the couch's edge where the young woman had sat.

"Den why you come now?" the old woman asked impatiently.

Roberta, wondering if it was sweat or piss making dark splotches on the floor, cleared her throat. "A friend of ours said he could tell me if I was going to have a boy or a girl."

"And you tink dat's true?"

"I don't know. I mean, I've never been to one before."

"You tink dis is a game?"

"Oh, no," Roberta said quickly, "I didn't say that."

" 'Cause if you tink dat, you need to go home. He got no time to mess wit people dat don't believe."

Sharon took a step closer to Roberta, and the old woman harrumphed.

"I said, I didn't know if it worked because I've never been to one before," Roberta continued. "I didn't say that I didn't believe."

The old woman chuffed. "Der's no need to get snippy, no. I ax everybody dem questions." She plucked at her waist again, then stretched out a hand. "Well, if you comin' in, dat's gonna be forty dollars, and you have to pay right now."

The air in the next room felt at least ten degrees cooler and smelled musty and tainted with old motor oil. The sun, fighting its way through uneven board walls from the back of the room, washed through the vastness in smoky streaks. Rays of light fell over Roberta's face like hot ribbons. She squinted, tilting her head to get a better view.

"It's a garage," she said, and flinched at the echo.

Only there were no cars here, just a huge, dark space with an alcove set aside for the closet room. Roberta pressed closer to Sharon and peered nervously about. She saw nothing but open space and shadows.

The old woman shuffled ahead, motioning for them to follow. A deep laugh came from the back of the room, its author obscured by the light in their eyes. Sharon reached for Roberta's arm and pulled it tightly to her as they mirrored the woman's choppy gait.

A sofa, similar to the one in the tiny waiting room, but without the plastic, came into view. A man sat on one end and looked to be in his late forties or early fifties. His hair, blondish white and scraggly, hung down to his shoulders. His thin body was clothed in dirty jeans and a sickish gray thermal shirt, sleeves long despite the heat. He had one hand draped over the back of the couch, and his long, twisted fingernails tapped softly against the worn material. His other hand clutched a glass knob that topped a cane.

On either side of the ragged divan, like ebony sentinels, sat two large Dobermans. They might have easily been mistaken for cast-iron statues had they not blinked each time the man tapped his cane against the dirt floor.

"Come," he said, his voice deep and strong. His accent, like the old woman's, was heavy. He smiled, revealing teeth that were chipped and stained dark yellow. He raised one finger from the cane and crooked it. "Come here to Samuel." He watched intently as Roberta and Sharon moved slowly toward him.

The baby kicked and pushed hard inside Roberta, as though trying to force her forward faster. She reached down and rubbed gently.

Samuel's bright blue eyes locked onto her, and he let out a short laugh. "You betta sit down," he said, nodding toward the opposite end of the couch, "before dat baby knock you down."

Roberta glanced over at Sharon, whose face had turned the color of a bleached sheet. The dogs weren't even blinking now. They sat staring straight ahead, canine versions of the young woman they had met in the waiting room. She gulped and turned back to Samuel.

"Uh," Roberta said, "we have, uh—a friend who, uh—uh, well, someone told us—"

"I know why you here," Samuel said. He dropped his hand from the back of the couch and reached into his pants pocket.

Panic tap-danced against Roberta's spine. The baby was kicking incessantly, and her heart beat so hard and fast she had a hard time drawing a breath.

Samuel pulled his hand from his pocket and opened it, revealing a thick wad of money. After taking the two twenties from the old woman, who stood next to him, he laid them on top of the stack, folded it again, and tucked the stash back into his pocket.

"Don't be afraid of dem dogs," Samuel said. "Dey not gonna hurt you unless you hurt me." He scratched the dusty cushion next to him with a fingernail. "Come, sit over here. I'm not gonna hurt you either. I know I ain't too purty to look at, but I'm not gonna hurt you."

Roberta stepped forward, then sat, pressing herself against the opposite arm of the couch.

Samuel stared into her eyes as though they were

the only two in the room. "You want to know about you little baby, huh?" he asked, leaning toward her. His breath smelled of mustard and cigarettes.

"Yes," Roberta answered. She pushed farther back on the couch. "I'd like to know if it's a boy or a girl."

"You know, I can tell you if dat's a *healt'y* boy or girl," Samuel proclaimed. His eyes brightened mischievously. "Dat is, just in case you want to know."

Roberta sucked in a breath. *Can he read minds, too?* She had been worried about the baby inheriting any one of her family's health problems: diabetes, heart murmurs, extra toes and fingers, not to mention the mental breakdowns and depression that floated around in her gene pool.

"Can you *really* do that?" Sharon asked, walking toward them.

Samuel glared at her, keeping her at bay with his gaze.

The baby kicked Roberta hard, causing an "oomph" to escape her lips. She rubbed her stomach and smiled cautiously at Samuel. "It's been a little excited today." Her eyes flitted over to Sharon before settling into his gaze. "Yeah, I do want to know if it's healthy, too. What do I have to do?"

"You don't have to do nuttin'," he said, reaching into his front pocket again. Scissoring two fingers, he pulled out what looked like a metal plum-bob the size and color of a nickel. Its globular top was fat and solid, and it curved thickly into a dull point about one-third of an inch long at its end. A sturdy chain was attached to the tiny hoop at the top of the plum-bob. The other end of the chain dangled free.

"This won't hurt my baby, will it?" Roberta asked anxiously.

"No, no," Samuel said. "All you have to do is lean back a bit. I'm gonna put dis over you stomach. If you gonna have a healt'y boy, it's gonna swing back and fort'. If you gonna have a healt'y girl, it's gonna go in a circle. If it gonna—"

"What if something's wrong with the baby? What will it do?" Roberta spread protective fingers over her abdomen.

"I was gonna tell you, but you don't let me finish. If something is wrong wit de baby," Samuel said, giving a nodding glance at the pendulum dangling from his thumb and forefinger, "well, it just ain't gonna move."

His last statement made Roberta cringe. "I don't know . . ." she said, her hands beginning to rub in tight circles. She *was* eager to see what would happen, but a prickly feeling had started at the back of her neck, suggesting that maybe some things were better left alone.

"You don't have to go through with this, Bert," Sharon said, her eyes wide and worried.

"I know," Roberta said softly. What had started out that morning as no more than a dare and bet between friends was turning into a creepy sideshow. Roberta knew, however, if she didn't go through with this now, curiosity would drive her back tomorrow or next week to try again.

"You want to go home?" Sharon asked, a hopeful note in her voice.

"I'm not sure."

"Look, all bets are off. If you want out of here, we're gone."

Roberta chewed on her bottom lip for a few seconds. "Hold on, okay?"

Sharon sighed heavily. Soon she began to fidget from one foot to the other and looked around for the old woman, who had seemingly disappeared into thin air. "Sam, you have a bathroom in here?"

Samuel didn't answer. He stared at the pendulum, frowning. Although he had yet to place it over Roberta's stomach, it had started a methodical, albeit slight, metronomic swing.

Roberta was about to concur with Sharon's bathroom request, when she spotted the movement. She watched closely as its stiff back-and-forth movement picked up momentum.

"You have to tell me, now. What you wanna do?" Samuel asked, his eyes never leaving the pendulum's rhythm. "You baby's soul is—is strong. Real strong. And it be different, more different than any I seen before. Dis baby already know what it wanna do."

"Damn, just when I've gotta go!" Sharon said, squirming. "Sam—the bathroom?"

"You gonna shut you mout' over dere or what?" Samuel snapped at her. "Can't you see I have to pay close concentrate to what I'm doin'?"

Sharon's eyes sparked with anger, but she pursed her lips and crossed one leg over the other.

Encouraged by the unauthorized movement of the pendulum, Roberta asked, "Okay, Samuel, what do I do?"

"Lean back," he said. "You don't have to raise

you shirt or nuttin' like dat. Just lean back so I can put dis over you belly. And take you hands off."

Roberta leaned against the arm of the sofa and placed her hands on either side of her hips.

Samuel leaned forward on his cane and positioned the pendulum an inch above her abdomen. As soon as it neared her stomach, the pendulum's nodding seemed to take on purpose. It pushed forward and paused for a few seconds, its point frozen in midair as though for emphasis. Then it pulled backward again, the point pausing at the end of the swing.

"Don't be afraid," he assured Roberta. "All I'm gonna do is ax le Bon Dieu to take care of you baby, and I'm gonna ax da good spirits to show us if you got a boy or a girl. I t'ink they trying to tell us something already."

As the metal bob picked up speed, Roberta watched Samuel lean his cane against the sofa and stretch his hand over her stomach. His eyes closed, and she heard him begin to mumble something in Cajun French. Although she was fluent in the language, he spoke too softly for Roberta to make out what he was saying.

"It's a girl! It's a girl!" Sharon cried. "Look, it's moving in a circle now!"

Roberta felt a smile spread across her face and tears prick her eyes. "A girl," she whispered.

Abruptly the swinging stopped, as if someone had grabbed the pendulum on the downswing and held tight. Roberta's smile melted from her lips.

Samuel's eyes flew open, then narrowed with concern. He pinched harder at the chain with the tips of his thumb and forefinger. His left hand stayed suspended over her stomach.

"What's the matter?" Roberta asked, worried. "What's wrong, Samuel? Why did it stop?"

Ignoring her questions, Samuel focused on the pendulum and began to bellow loudly for God's protection. *"Mon Bon Dieu, je supplier vous votre protection pour cette femme et sa bébé!"* He struggled futilely to hook the chain with the middle and ring fingers of his right hand.

"Samuel, please," Roberta cried, "what's going on?"

It was no use. Samuel would not or could not hear her. Roberta tried to get up, to move away from the metal point aimed at her abdomen, but couldn't. Her body felt glued to the couch. "Sharon!" she screamed.

"Hey, get away from her!" Sharon yelled. Her hands doubled into fists as she swung and twisted her body. "What the—" She jerked hard to the left. "I can't move my feet, Bert! They won't budge!"

The dogs that had been sitting obediently started to growl. The low rumbling in their throats quickly rose to sharp whines as both dogs tried to stand. Thick muscles rippled along their backs, haunches, and chests, but they remained seated, their heads fixed straight ahead. Only their eyes shifted wildly from left to right.

Samuel's voice kept building, filling the room with overlapping echoes as he begged God to show them mercy. *"Oh, Bon Dieu, mon Bon Dieu et Saint-Esprit, donner pitié sur tout le monde dans la chambre!"*

The pendulum suddenly began to vibrate violently. The chain stripped itself through Samuel's fingers, and the point of the bob plowed into Roberta's stomach, bringing a piece of her blouse in with it. It started to corkscrew, trying to twist its way in deeper.

The shock of the assault delayed Roberta's scream, but not for long. From deep within the core of her, for the child within her, Roberta screamed.

Sharon, witnessing the horror, joined her.

The dogs' whining reached an ear-piercing level, and both began to shiver uncontrollably.

Cold sweat poured from Samuel's face. He shouted above the women's screams and the dogs' whining, creating a cacophony of terror.

"Oh, my God! My God!" Sharon screamed, twisting her body hard from side to side. "Take it out! Take it out!"

Roberta howled. *I just wanted to know! God, I'm sorry! I just needed to know!* Her mind felt like a frayed electrical wire, shooting sparks in every direction and threatening to short out a whole power system.

The pendulum twisted relentlessly, a maniacal drill trying to punch its way through her. Turning—turning. The hole it had torn open in her flesh widened, and blood soaked her blouse. The baby wasn't moving now.

Roberta felt something tear in her throat as she yelled. She twisted, thrashed, prayed to free her hands so she could pull the pendulum out. Nothing worked.

Samuel, with his head raised to the rafters, shouted

at the top of his voice, *"Dans le nom de Bon Dieu et Jésus Christ et le Saint-Esprit!"*

The pendulum's drilling stopped immediately, its point wedged about a half-inch inside Roberta's abdomen. Finding his hands mobile, Samuel cautiously reached for the chain, looped his hand around it, and pulled. The bob popped free with a sickening squish.

Both dogs fell with a loud thump to the ground, blood pouring from their noses and ears.

Roberta sat silent. No screams, no pain. Nothing. Her mind locked into the whirling darkness behind her eyes. Her hands were free, part of her knew that much, but she didn't move.

Neither did Sharon, who stood with her mouth open and urine streaming down her legs.

Chapter One

As Jessica LeJeune entered her home, a thin band of sweat formed across her upper lip. Three hours ago her world had changed for the better, and that scared the hell out of her.

Smile, she thought. *Just smile.*

"Hey, Mom, do we have any leftovers in the fridge?" Jake asked, dodging past her.

"Leftovers?" Jessica wiped the perspiration from her lip and kicked off her new blister-inducing pumps. "How can you possibly be hungry after everything you ate at the banquet?"

Jake grinned back at her before disappearing into the kitchen.

"If he eats any more tonight, he'll burst," Jessica said to her husband, Frank, who was busy locking the front door behind them.

He chuckled. "Didn't you read the warning label

they put on him in the hospital the day he was born?"

"Label?" Jessica smiled through a yawn.

"Sure." Frank sauntered up to her and planted a kiss on her forehead. "It said: Beware, male children are prone to hollow legs and tapeworms, especially upon reaching age ten. They cannot be satiated by a mere three squares a day."

"All that on one label, huh?"

"It was written in shorthand."

She laughed softly and kissed him. "Well, at least try and stop him from eating the hindquarter in the freezer while I take a shower."

"I think I can manage that." Frank licked his lips. "Mmm, you know I've never been kissed by the general manager of a corporation before. Not bad."

Jessica waggled her eyebrows playfully. "Play your cards right, bucko, and you never know, one day you could be tonguing a president." She bumped him lightly with a hip, then turned and headed for their bedroom.

The moment she was out of Frank's sight, Jessica felt her shoulders slump and smile fade. Here she stood, a thirty-five-year-old female, who had only tonight managed to squeak past the glass ceiling of one of the largest plastics manufacturers in the South, and she wanted to cry. Not with happiness, but in anticipation of what she had long ago labeled "the falling anvil," that damned black weight that always seemed to loom over her, waiting to crush any positive thing that happened in her life. Logically Jessica knew the feeling of foreboding made no sense, but she couldn't make it go away. And thirty-five years of experience had taught her that it wouldn't go away until it was damn good and ready. Until then, she would have to do what she always did—smile and act as though it didn't exist.

With a sigh, Jessica made her way into the bedroom and to the dresser, where she pulled out a pair of terry-cloth shorts and one of Frank's T-shirts. She gave only a fleeting glance to the circles under her eyes in the dresser mirror before going into the adjoining bathroom.

After setting the adjustable showerhead to pulse, Jessica quickly undressed and stepped into the hot spray. She turned her back to the water and closed her eyes. The last few weeks had taken a toll on her, but she figured it had been worth it. The long hours, little sleep, and countless meetings had finally secured the forty-million-dollar government contract Sternco Inc. had been salivating over. As soon as Joseph Tomas, Sternco's CEO, got word they were being awarded the contract, he'd thrown a party to celebrate. Done up in the simple Memphis tradition of barbecue and country music, the party had been the venue Tomas used to announce her promotion. She'd been surprised by the news and overwhelmed by the accolades from her coworkers. Tonight had been undeniably special; she knew that, she only wished she could feel it.

Jessica opened her eyes, not wanting her thoughts to go any further. She grabbed a bar of soap and quickly washed. The one thing that bothered her more than the falling anvil was thinking about why she had such a hard time finding more than a moment's delight in her own successes. Why nearly every pleasure she experienced in life felt tainted with an ulterior motive or a pending reproach. If she dwelled on those things too long, memories came, and they were far worse than any anvil.

Once she had dried, dressed, and brushed her teeth, Jessica went back into the bedroom and found Frank already propped up in bed, both hands tucked behind his head. After fourteen years of marriage, his long, lean body, now clad only in boxer shorts, still made her heart thump a little faster.

He let out a soft wolf whistle when he saw her. "My little Cajun beauty. I swear you get prettier every day," he said.

Jessica struck a pose. "It's the outfit." She trailed the back of her fingers over the T-shirt that hung down to her knees. "Oscar de la Frank."

"My compliments to the designer." He patted the pillow beside him. "Why don't you come closer so I can get a better look, maybe feel the material? It looks exotic."

"Oh, it is," she said, ambling closer. "Made from the finest cotton and hand-stitched by virgin maids in New Orleans." She climbed onto the bed and stretched out alongside him.

"There're virgin maids in New Orleans?"

"You said exotic."

Frank smiled and slowly traced the side of her nose with a finger, then her lips and chin. Jessica sighed as her body began to relax.

"Jake in bed?" she asked.

"Um-hmm." His finger trailed down the side of her neck. "Why? Got a particular, no-children-allowed activity in mind?"

"I'm thinking of one or two."

"Yeah? Well, with your one or two and my ten or eleven, this could get interesting." He leaned over, nipped the knob of her chin with his lips, then stared at her intently. "I was very proud of you tonight, Jess."

She stiffened briefly, then ran a hand through his thick brown hair. "Thanks, but do you think we could get back to those one or two—"

He kissed her firmly, then said, "It's okay to feel good about what you've accomplished."

"I know, but I don't want to talk about that right now." Jessica pressed her body closer to his. "In fact, talking wasn't something I had in mind at all." She lowered a hand past the waistband of his shorts.

Frank moaned. "You're not playing fair."

"So sue me."

Grinning, he teased the neck of the T-shirt down over her left shoulder and lowered his lips to her bared skin.

"Mom?" The sound of Jake's muffled voice was quickly followed by a knock on the bedroom door. "Can I come in?"

Frank rolled onto his back with a groan. "What timing."

"He probably has a stomachache." Jessica sat up and pulled the T-shirt back into place. "Come on in, buddy," she called to her son.

The bedroom door opened slowly, and Jake stuck his head inside. His usually cheerful face was pinched in a scowl.

"What's up, champ?" Frank asked him.

"I don't feel so great."

"Stomach?" Jessica asked. She got out of bed and went over to her son.

"Huh-uh. My head hurts real bad."

Frowning, Jessica touched Jake's forehead, then his cheeks. "You don't seem to be running any fever." She smoothed his black, curly hair. "Why don't you scoot on back to bed, and I'll be right behind you with a couple of aspirin and water."

Jake nodded and ducked back out of the room.

"Want me to see about him?" Frank asked.

"I'll go," she said, already heading for the bathroom medicine cabinet. She glanced back at him and grinned. "You just start thinking about twelve and thirteen."

A couple of minutes later, with headache supplies in hand, Jessica went into Jake's room. He was stretched out on his bed with an arm thrown over his eyes. The baseball-shaped lamp on the nightstand beside him glowed dimly.

"Sleeping?" she asked quietly.

Jake lifted his arm and squinted up at her. "Huh-uh." He propped himself up on an elbow.

Jessica sat on the edge of the bed and handed him two aspirin and a cup of water. "Must be a whopper of a headache for you to keep the lights down that low."

"A double whopper," Jake said. He took the pills, popped them into his mouth, then downed the water in two gulps. He handed her the cup and lay back on the pillow.

She leaned over and kissed his forehead. "Close

your eyes," she said, and placed a hand on his head. "I'll stay here for a minute or two to make sure the aspirin kicks in."

Jake nodded, yawned, then turned toward her and curled his short, thin body into a ball. He closed his eyes, but a grimace remained on his face.

Jessica studied her son, the soft peach fuzz on his cheek, the way the end of his nose curved up slightly. Except for the black hair and the raspberry-shaped birthmark on the nape of his neck, both of which he'd inherited from her, Jake was a miniature copy of Frank. Down to the sparkling hazel eyes that always seemed to look upon the world in perpetual wonder. Both of them shared the same love of football, car races, and hot-fudge sundaes sprinkled with crushed graham crackers. She hated to see either of them ill or in pain, even if it was only a headache.

Slowly Jessica slid the pad of her thumb between Jake's eyes. Immediately her mind's eye filled with a vision of small, interwoven blood vessels, hundreds of them. A few of these capillaries seemed to draw nearer, growing clearer in focus as though begging for her attention. They throbbed fiercely, constricted, clearly desperate for blood flow and oxygen. Jessica trained her attention on these, and soon a tingling sensation, like the vibrations from a low-voltage electrical source, began in her thumb. It traveled into her hand, up her arm, then moved across her heart before shooting up to her head. The moment it registered in her brain a stronger resonance started to flow in the opposite direction, moving from her brain to her heart, down her arm, then through her thumb to Jake's forehead.

She didn't really understand what was happening, just that it was something she had to do, like sneezing when the urge hit you. It was a need she'd experienced quite a few times in her life, even in childhood. But, like the anvil, she often hid its existence. Only when it came to her family did the urgency get so strong it overtook her, and she was left with no alternative but to respond. When that happened, she usually disguised it with medication, like she'd done with Jake and the aspirin. She concealed it not only because she didn't understand it but also because of the inconsistencies. Sometimes it worked, sometimes it didn't, and she could never understand why one way or the other. Hiding it also eliminated expectations and disappointment. Not that she thought Frank or Jake would hold her to a performance standard, but she suspected others would. And life was complicated enough.

Jessica moved her thumb ever so slightly to the right and saw the constricted vessels begin to expand. When they were finally free-flowing with blood, the tingling ceased, and Jessica removed her hand from her son's head. She kissed him again and got up from the bed.

Jake blew out a breath and turned over on his back. "Thanks, Mom. The—uh—aspirins must've worked, 'cause I feel a lot better."

"Good." She bent down and tweaked his nose. "Get some sleep now, okay?"

He nodded and snuggled deeper into his pillow. "Mom?"

"Hm?"

"Will I be able to do that one day?"

She stared at the open curiosity on his face and hesitantly asked, "Do what?"

Jake tilted his head to one side and frowned briefly as if the question confused him. His eyes locked onto hers, and she saw indecision in them. Finally he smiled and said, "Be a boss of a big company someday, like you. Or maybe own my own business like Dad."

Jessica nodded slowly, suspecting her son had just danced around what was really on his mind. She decided not to press the issue. "Absolutely. You can be anything you want to be, buddy. Most times it takes a lot of hard work, but all of it's possible."

"Even if I want to be an astronaut?"

"Yep."

"Or one of those guys that drives a train?"

"You mean a conductor?"

"Uh-huh."

"Of course you can."

"What about a—"

"What about you get some sleep now," she said with a chuckle. "We can talk more about this tomorrow morning."

"Okay, but Mom?"

"Yes?"

"For my birthday on Friday, do you think I could get a book on how to be a doctor? I think maybe that's what I'd like to be when I grow up."

Jessica nodded toward the model airplanes cluttering his dresser. "What happened to becoming a pilot?"

"Oh, I figure I can do both," Jake said earnestly.

"See, that way if one of my patients needs to get to a hospital really fast, I can fly 'em there."

She pursed her lips, feigning serious consideration of his plan. "Well, makes sense to me," she said. "I'll see what I can do about that book."

Jake's face beamed. "Cool." He pulled the corner of his pillow up close and closed his eyes. "Night."

"Night, buddy."

Jessica left her son's room and hesitated for a few seconds in the hallway, wondering what had just transpired between them. She shook her head. *Leave it alone,* she thought. *If he knows about this—this thing you do with your thumb—and wants to ask about it, he will.*

Confident she'd chosen the best course of action—or inaction, for that matter—Jessica took off for the kitchen. She wanted to surprise Frank with a glass of Chardonnay, something to fan the fires of romance that might have dwindled somewhat after their little distraction.

Her bare feet slapped across the cool tile floors as she made her way into the kitchen and flipped on the light. Squinting against the brightness, she went to a cupboard and pulled out two wineglasses.

After collecting the Chardonnay from the refrigerator, she placed the glasses on the counter, then wrestled the cork from the wine bottle. Jessica topped off the first glass and had the second glass half-filled when she heard a thump against the window near the breakfast nook. She glanced up in time to see a sparrow bounce off the pane. It immediately took flight, disappearing into the darkness, then a second later it slammed against the pane again, breast first.

Un titisse cogner la mort arriver. The old Cajun axiom came to Jessica unbidden. *A sparrow hits, death will come.* At that very moment, she saw herself not in her own kitchen but back in Louisiana and in Grandma Aleda's sitting room. She'd been six years old, playing bourrée for matchsticks with her grandmother, when a sparrow had flown into a nearby window.

Grandma Aleda gasped. "La nom de Père et du Fils et du Saint-Esprit," *she said, crossing herself. She repeated the sign of the cross twice more, never taking her eyes off the window.*

"What's wrong, Grandma?"

Aleda put the cards she'd been holding down on the coffee table and reached for the rosary beads she always carried in the pocket of her housecoat. "You see what that bird do?" she said. "Not a good sign, non. *He's warning us somebody going to die soon."*

"Who?"

Aleda shrugged. "Don't know for sure. We got to watch the bird. He hit one time, that mean a friend going to die. Two time, cousin maybe. If that bird hit the glass 'til he kill himself, that mean close, close family."

Jessica shivered, remembering how her grandmother had found that bird dead on the lawn below the window. Two weeks after that, lightning had struck Uncle Numa in a cane field, killing him instantly.

Downing one of the glasses of wine, Jessica

watched the sparrow strike the kitchen window a third time. On the fourth collision, instead of bouncing off the pane as it had done before, the bird seemed to hang suspended against the glass for a couple of seconds. Then its head flopped to one side, and it dropped like leaded weight out of sight.

Jessica grabbed the second glass of wine and drained it quickly. "Just what I need," she mumbled. "A clairvoyant bird to go with my falling anvil."

Chapter Two

Eli swung his feet over the edge of the swaybacked porch and dangled them over the murky water. He gazed down the length of a westbound slough to the horizon. He loved the swirling hues of sunset over the Atchafalaya. Violet and tangerine, milky pink and rust, the colors brought him peace, something he desperately needed.

All around him, swamp creatures gave voice to the dying day. The resonating, high-pitched *uhmmmp, uhmmmp* of baby alligators, the deep, hollow grunts of bullfrogs, the chitter of insects too numerous to count, and the splash, gurgle of croakers and mullets slapping against the surface of the water. A family of nutria scurried across a nearby grassy island while a loggerhead turtle, as big around as a dinner plate, settled lazily over a floating log. Overhead a barred owl screeched noisily from a tupelo, and herons and egrets swooped and glided around Eli's small shack toward their nests.

He watched and listened with a heavy heart. All of his life, Eli had felt as much a part of the bayou as any one of these creatures. Now all that was changing. Lately he didn't feel part of anything. Not the swamp, not even the human race. He felt used up, spent. He barely slept anymore. His dreams, which seemed to be growing more horrid over the last three months, barely allowed him two hours of rest a night.

Eli drew in a deep breath and dipped a toe into the water. While he watched the ripples slowly widen and spread toward a cypress tree, he heard the faint whine of an outboard motor. He cocked his head and strained an ear to gauge its distance.

Two miles, maybe two and a half, which meant the boat was just outside Fosey Point, a finger inlet normally clogged with floating mats of water hyacinth. Hundreds of jagged cypress stumps jutted up through the hyacinth like old rotted fingers. It was a boater's nightmare, and few attempted to cross it for fear of propeller damage or never finding their way back. This one, however, sounded determined, drawing ever closer, which could only mean Johanson was headed his way.

Eli dropped his head wearily.

Thin and seemingly older than moss, Johanson had been a part of Eli's existence for as long as he could remember. Although the man lived inland, he showed up at the shack every so often in his beat-up skiff and had been doing that since Eli was five years old. Back then, Johanson would bring supplies in from town, then take time to teach Eli about the swamp. They would hunt and fish and, most important, talk, something Eli's mother rarely did with him. Johanson wasn't his father—that much Eli knew because the old man had told him so when he'd asked. The two weren't even related. Eli had always been too afraid to question Johanson further about why he came around if they weren't blood kin. Maybe the man felt sorry for the young woman and boy who fended for themselves in the swamp without help from anyone. Eli didn't know and really didn't care. So what if Johanson's reason for coming was pity? He just never wanted the old man to stop visiting.

Although their relationship continued to grow and strengthen over time, it had taken on an abrupt change after Eli's twelfth birthday. Eli woke up that particular morning expecting to find an apple propped on the foot of his cot, the usual birthday gift from his mother. Instead, he discovered his mother sprawled across the floor, ten feet away, dead. When Eli had gotten up enough nerve to get out of bed and investigate, he found bluish-green foam pooling onto the floor from her lips and a half-empty can of drain cleaner near her body. Saddened but not surprised that she'd taken her life, Eli had waited a few hours before dragging the petite woman's body out of the house and onto the porch. He rolled her body into the water and allowed it to float away. It didn't go very far because of the tangle of water lilies and tree stumps, so he'd just watched her caramel-colored face bob up and down until the cloudy waters swallowed her.

Soon after Eli left the watery grave, he went to a nearby island to check on nutria traps. Normally his mother ran ground traps, and he ran the water traps and catfish lines. Now, with only himself to depend on, he'd have to learn how to do both.

Eli's first ground-trap lesson nearly cost him a foot. Still thinking about his mother, he'd walked across the line run without paying proper attention and wound up stepping into a trap that had been hidden under a blanket of moss. Fortunately the contraption had been old and rusted, and when the metal teeth snapped around his foot just above the ankle, it punctured skin and muscle but didn't crush bone.

After an hour of struggling with the trap, Eli finally freed his foot. The moment it was released, an overpowering urge to spit on the wounds came over him. So he spat—and the puncture wounds closed instantly. For some reason Eli was never able to explain, he had been no more surprised by the healing than he had been about his mother's death. What did surprise him, however, was what followed.

The incident with the trap seemed to be a catalyst for change that reached beyond the bayou. Once Eli mentioned the healing of his wounds to Johanson, the old man started coming around more often and bringing other people with him. Sick people. People with wounds that oozed vile, smelly fluids. Some had external tumors the size of oranges. Children and elders were often carried onto his porch in makeshift beds, their bodies riddled with diseases that ate flesh from the inside out. A few were brought to Eli tied with rope, their minds demented or lost.

Often these sick people brought him gifts of food and clothing. They would light candles on his porch and call him "rasaunt." Johanson had explained to Eli that a rasaunt was a rare person, a person more powerful than a local traiteur. Johanson also told him that a traiteur healed with prayer but that their powers were confined to small ailments, like a toothache or sunstroke. A rasaunt was a mixture of healer and dispeller of demons. The rasaunt *was* the prayer.

Eli hadn't understood much of what Johanson meant back then. And now, even at thirty-nine years old, it still wasn't much clearer to him. All Eli knew was he didn't want to do this anymore. He was tired of fighting the sickness demons that showed up on his porch every day. Too often they stayed with him, lingering around in his head, confusing his thoughts long after the healed person went home.

Spotting an arrow of light just beyond a grove of trees not far away, Eli reluctantly got to his feet. He went into the shack, removed a kerosene lantern from a shelf above his cot, and lit it. By the time he placed the lantern on the wooden crate that served as his dinner table and went back outside, Johanson was mooring his skiff to a porch post. When he spotted Eli, he nodded but offered no smile.

Eli leaned against the rough-hewn siding of his shack and quietly studied the two other men sitting in Johanson's boat. One of them sat with his back against the bow in jeans and a light blue, blood-stained shirt. He had rumpled blond hair, a thick, square-jawed face, and appeared to be middle-aged. Long, fresh scratches marred his cheeks. Between his legs sat the second man, a younger, smaller version of the first but with auburn hair. A thin rope had been wrapped around his wrists, binding them together. The man whipped his head from side to side and mumbled incoherently.

Drenched in sweat, Johanson finally stepped out of the boat and onto the porch. His long white hair clung to the sides of his face. As usual, he wore a ragged pair of brown pants, a gray thermal shirt, and rubber boots. He walked up to Eli and laid a hand on his shoulder.

"Dis one be bad," Johanson said with a slow shake of his head.

Eli nodded.

Johanson gave Eli's shoulder a little squeeze, then released him and signaled for the men in the boat to stand.

The man in the blue shirt quickly got to his feet, pulled the bound man up with him, then leaned over and picked up a small carton from the boat's bench seat. Johanson helped them onto the porch.

When the strangers stood before Eli, the man in blue said, "Uh, I'm Earl and this—this here"—he threw a glance at the bound man—"is my brother Shank. You're, uh, I, uh—you're the rasaunt?"

Eli stared at him.

With a confused, frightened look, Earl peered over at Johanson.

"He be the rasaunt," Johanson said quietly. He motioned for Earl to give Eli the carton, which he did.

"It ain't much," Earl told Eli. "Just eggs. I hope it'll do."

Eli took the carton of eggs from him and placed it

on the porch railing. He turned back to Earl and said wearily, "Bring you brother in my house and wash all his face. Water's in de tub by de wood stove."

Frowning, Earl looked back at Johanson.

"Do what he say," Johanson said.

Still frowning, Earl took Shank by the shoulders and steered him toward the entrance of the shack. Before he could get his brother across the threshold, however, Shank swung around and spat in Eli's face. Then he let out a loud, hoarse laugh that echoed across the bayou. More than a dozen birds fluttered away from their perches and soared toward farther, safer branches.

"Sorry—sorry," Earl said, grabbing Shank by the arm and pulling him away. "My brother's been sick bad. The doctors say—"

"Don't matter what the doctor say," Eli said. "Now go. Wash all his face like I say."

As soon as the men disappeared into the shack, Eli turned to Johanson. "Dis de last one," he said. "Don't bring no more."

Johanson's narrow shoulders slumped, and he looked up at the darkening sky. "No use you say don't bring no more. It don't work like dat."

"How you know how it work?"

Johanson glanced down at him. "I just know." Without another word, the old man turned away and went into the shack.

Eli waited a few minutes, then grudgingly followed him. He knew it wouldn't do any good to press for a clearer answer because Johanson always did things in his own way and in his own time.

When the man felt a more detailed explanation was needed, he'd give it. Until then, Eli had no choice but to wait.

When Eli entered his house, he found Shank sitting in a straight-back chair with his arms secured behind him. His chin rested on his right shoulder, and he kept blowing puffs of air as if a slew of candles needed to be extinguished. Earl paced nervously nearby, and Johanson was at the washbasin, rinsing off the back of his neck. The lantern cast a muted yellow glow over the room and its occupants, but to Eli, the only thing it truly illuminated was pain. The pain hidden in Shank, the pain soon to be his.

"Do I need to, uh, do anything?" Earl asked, folding and unfolding his arms over his chest.

"Best you wait over dere," Johanson answered. He pointed to Eli's cot, then grabbed an old rag from a peg and dried his neck. "And no matter what happen here wit' you brother, stay dere. Understand?"

"Yeah—okay." Earl eyed Eli anxiously before going over to the cot, where he sat and began chewing on a thumbnail.

With Earl out of the way and settled, Eli walked up behind Shank and quickly pressed the pad of his thumb between the man's eyes. Immediately Shank reared his head back and bucked in the chair. Eli pressed down harder, making sure he didn't lose contact while hot bolts of energy shot from his thumb into Shank and from Shank into him.

The image that forced its way into Eli's mind weakened his knees. He wasn't prepared for this. Not the large, white, bulbous face—the dark sockets void of eyes—the thick, cracked lips that outlined a vertical mouth. Not the long, thin tendrils that protruded from both sides of its head, each one piercing through and weaving deep into Shank's brain. It was Maikana, the spirit of madness, the face from Eli's most recent nightmares, the face he had often seen reflected in his mother's eyes. Eli suddenly felt like a minnow in the path of a hungry alligator, frightened, helpless, and way too small.

Shank stomped a foot against the floor, then abruptly slumped in the chair. "Ah, so you do recognize me, you pathetic, obnoxious worm," he said with a laugh. Though the man had never spoken to him directly, Eli knew this wasn't Shank's voice but that of Maikana. The wet, raspy sound of it made him shudder.

Eli glanced up at Johanson. The muscles along the old man's jaw contracted rhythmically, and worry creased his brow. Instead of meeting Eli's gaze, Johanson turned away and walked out onto the porch.

Unnerved by Johanson's disappearance, Eli moistened his lips, and his palms began to sweat.

"Nervous, are we?" Maikana said. "Well, you should be, you impotent mongrel. Though I must say it is positively quaint that you would presume yourself to possess the significance of strength to do away with the likes of me. How droll, how utterly preposterous."

"Sh-Shank?" Earl's petrified voice fell flat in the small room. Eli heard the metal legs of his cot squeak, and he held up his free hand, warning Earl to stay put and remain quiet.

Thunderous laughter erupted from Shank. "Oh,

why not allow the man an opportunity to experience a taste of my cunning. The more the merrier, I say."

A trickle of sweat ran down the side of Eli's face as he pressed down even harder on the spot between Shank's eyes. Instead of the energy flow between them growing stronger, however, it waned.

Shank lifted his head and glared at Eli. "Oh, come now. Persistence may be a virtue by transient standards, but this is absolutely absurd."

Eli peered down into Shank's face, the reflection of his enemy clearly evident in the man's eyes now. More than anything, he wanted to release Shank and join Johanson outside. But he couldn't. To stop now, with Maikana exposed, would mean instant death for Shank—and possibly for Johanson and Earl as well. Eli knew his death would be a given, though that didn't concern him as much as harm coming to Johanson. He tightened his lips and willed a sharper, clearer focus of energy into Shank.

In his mind, Eli immediately saw two slim tendrils extract themselves from Shank's brain. Hope surged through him. He concentrated harder, his body shaking with the power of it.

Shank's eyes closed, then his lips fluttered with an exasperated sigh. "Very well," he said. "As you wish, little man."

Suddenly Eli felt as though steel pokers were skewering through his head. With an involuntary whimper, he braced himself. Though he knew absorption of pain was part of the process, never had he felt it so strong before. Wild, erratic visions consumed him: faces that wore elongated masks of sorrow and torture, many with twisted, pitted features. Some faces had no eyes, some had mouths but no lips, and those mouths yawned and gaped as though determined to chew through him. He saw gun muzzles pressed against his temple, knife handles protruding from his jugular, then gigantic spiders and panthers, demons and snakes, all poised, ready to devour him. Eli felt his body slump, then sway with the enormous weight of it all. Fear was no longer an emotion, but a living, breathing entity inside him.

He clung to the back of the chair, resolving to remain on his feet. His determination was short-lived, however, as a larger image suddenly took precedence. It was that of a delicately featured woman. She stood with her back to him, a birthmark, the size and shape of a berry, prominent on the back of her neck. Her body began to split in half, as Eli knew it would, for she too had been part of his nightmares, as she would be the reason for his salvation—or possibly the basis for his ultimate death.

Chapter Three

The next morning when Jessica walked across Sternco's lobby to the bank of elevators, she thought she'd hyperventilate with nervous energy. She felt as she had on her first day with the company, excited and eager for the new challenge.

She couldn't help grinning with pleasure as she stepped into the empty elevator and pressed the button for the fifth floor. She had started with Sternco as a marketing executive when they were located in Baton Rouge, Louisiana. On her one-year anniversary date with the company, the board of directors made the decision to move Sternco's headquarters to Memphis and had encouraged her to follow. It had taken many late-night discussions with Frank before they decided to make the move to Tennessee. Frank's software consulting company, LeJeune & Associates, was well on its way by that time, with loyal clients established in many cities throughout the south. They knew moving his office would be a royal pain in the ass, but not detrimental to his business. Jake had just turned six and was getting ready to start school, so the timing was perfect. Undoubtedly her new promotion proved it had been a great career move.

To hell with falling anvils and dead birds, she thought. *I won't let them spoil today. I won't!*

The elevator stopped with a soft thud, and Jessica walked out into the reception area still carrying her smile.

"Well, good morning, Ms. General Manager," Marie Thornton, the stocky, blond receptionist said with a wide grin. She removed the phone's headset, stood up from behind her oval desk, and gave Jessica an exaggerated bow.

Jessica laughed and offered a slight curtsy in return. "Why, thank you so ever much, ma'am. I'm truly honored, truly I am." She walked over to Marie's desk and gave her a quick hug. "How's the morning treating you?"

"Usual busy," Marie said, sitting back down.

"Phillip doing better today?"

"Much better." Marie gingerly placed the headset back over her bouffant, then pointed to the picture of her twelve-year-old son that sat on the corner of her desk. He'd recently experienced his first real break in baseball—his leg. "He's still hopping around on crutches but loving the attention."

Jessica chuckled. "Send him my best, will you?"

"Oh, I will. He—" The telephone panel emitted a

sharp beep-chirp, and Marie gestured for Jessica to wait while she answered it.

"He loved the baseball cards you sent him," Marie continued after transferring the call. "And you should see his cast now. I don't think there's room for one more signature. He even got the mailman to sign it. That boy's such a ham."

"Aren't they all?"

"That's for sure." Marie *tsk*ed suddenly and shook her head. "Look at me yakking away here. First day in your new position and all, I bet you've got a million things to take care of."

"Well—now that you mention it, I could use your help with something," Jessica said.

"Anything."

"Would you please send out a memo to all the department heads, letting them know there'll be a meeting at two this afternoon?"

"No problem."

"Great. We'll use Conference Room—" A stab of pain, sudden and blue-flame hot, struck Jessica in the middle of her forehead. Bile raced up her esophagus and filled her mouth. Her eyes watered rapidly, and she grabbed onto the edge of Marie's desk.

"Jess!" Marie yelped. She jumped up from her chair and reached across the desk. "What's wrong?"

Jessica squeezed her eyes shut, then opened them slowly. She couldn't seem to focus on Marie's face. Everything around her blurred and wavered in kaleidoscopic ribbons. She attempted to look around for a trash can—something, anything to get rid of the foul liquid in her mouth—but any movement, even shifting her eyes, made the vertigo worse. Jessica heard her name being called, but the sound was like listening to a long-distance phone call with a bad connection. She reached out blindly, searching for the tissue box Marie normally kept on her desk, and heard the clatter and scatter of pens and paper clips falling to the floor.

No tissue. Jesus, no tissue, and I'm going to puke.

"Jess?" a faraway echo called. Only, it sounded like "JJJeeesss?"

A humming started in Jessica's left ear, low at first, then quickly building to a high-pitched screech. It sent electrical shocks through the fillings in her teeth that ricocheted up to her brain. She stumbled backward, involuntarily swallowing the acrid bile.

A man's voice, loud and distinct, suddenly penetrated the excruciating screech. "Poor girlie girl. Standing there with your face all scrunched up like you just swallowed a mouthful of shit. Didn't you like my little trick? I've got more, girlie. I've got a lot more." The man laughed, a wet, thick sound that made Jessica's stomach churn and heave.

Abruptly, the screeching and the voice stopped. The pain ebbed, leaving Jessica with a dull throb behind her eyes. She squinted up at Marie, whose eyes were wide with concern, then looked around, slowly moving her head so as not to initiate another bout of whatever had just happened. No one else was in the room.

Who the hell was the man?

She turned back to Marie. "Did you hear that?" she asked. Her throat burned as though it had been scraped raw.

"Hear what?"

Jessica knew there would have been no need for Marie to ask that question if she'd heard the man's voice. She thought better of making an issue of it.

"Jess?"

"A humming noise, that's all," Jessica said offhandedly. "Must have been my ears ringing or something."

"You okay?"

"Better. Just a headache that caught me by surprise."

"Looked like a pretty serious one to me," Marie said, leaning over her desk to get a closer look at Jessica's face.

"Kind of like an ice-cream headache times a thousand. Just came on suddenly." Jessica rubbed her temples and glanced around the reception area again. "Was someone else just in here, Marie?"

"Huh?"

"Another person." Jessica pressed her fingers against her eyelids. "Was there another person in the room just now?"

"Another person?" Marie looked around quizzically. "No, Jess, just us. Why?"

Jessica looked at her through splayed fingers. *Who the hell was the guy?* "Nothing. Just wondered how many people I'd made a fool of myself in front of." She attempted a grin, but it didn't quite make it to her lips. Smoothing the front of her blouse, she asked, "Would you have any Tylenol?"

"Yeah, you bet," Marie said. She sat back in her chair with a plop. "Boy, you scared the heck out of me. I thought you were having a heart attack or something." She opened the top drawer of her desk and pulled out a small cylindrical container. "Here, keep them. You look white as a ghost, Jess. Maybe you should see a doctor, huh?"

"I'm already feeling much better," Jessica said, reaching for the Tylenol with a shaky hand. "Really." Marie frowned, and Jessica had to admit she was a little worried herself. Blurry vision, auditory distortions and hallucinations, sharp pain in the head; those were not symptoms of an ordinary headache. She wondered about the possibilities of a brain aneurysm or a tumor. *Get a grip, Jessica. You're going over the edge here.* She took a deep breath. "Anyway, I had a checkup about six months ago, and everything looked fine. Maybe it's eyestrain, and I need glasses." She uncapped the cylinder and shook out two caplets. "So you'll let everyone know, right? Two o'clock. Conference Room Five."

"Sure," Marie said hesitantly.

"Thanks."

Jessica walked to the water cooler near the corridor leading to her office. She pulled a paper cone from the holder and filled it. She could feel Marie watching her as she drank. Her body felt heavy and sluggish, as if she'd gained fifty pounds in the last five minutes. She tried to remember the date of her last period.

Why is it whenever something goes wrong with a woman's body, the first thing we think of is a damn period? she mused. *Okay, quick inventory. The headache—yes, but not* that *severe. Sluggishness—yes. Strange voices—nope. Not a part of the monthly cycle unless it's a new form of PMS: Pre-Menstrual*

Spook! She crumpled the cone and squared her shoulders. *Get ahold of yourself, girl. That red, red robin came bob-bob-bobbing along two weeks ago.*

"Morning, Jessica," a voice said behind her.

She swung around quickly. *Not the same voice, chill out.* The room did a lopsided spin. Attempting to appear casual, she leaned against the wall for support and was relieved to see Harold Kite, Sternco's chief financial officer. If it didn't have numbers or dollar signs attached to it, Harold wouldn't give it the satisfaction of existing in his world. Tall and thin, with a black pencil mustache and a nose that hooked to the right, he reminded Jessica of a silent-movie villain. Harold intimidated several people with his calculated coolness, but Jessica wasn't one of them.

"How are you, Harold?" she asked.

True to form, Harold reached around her for a cup, never noticing, or choosing to ignore, her near stumble. "How goes it?" he asked, leaning over to depress the blue water spigot.

"Good."

Harold swallowed the water and smacked his lips as though he'd just finished a tart lemonade. "I hear schedules are off."

Jessica looked at him steadily. "Slightly off. But we're establishing a plan that should put us immediately back on track." She bit the inside of her cheeks, a trick she'd learned a long time ago that kept her face from responding to her environment inappropriately. Right now she wanted to scowl. She knew Harold would love nothing more than to gloat in an executive board meeting that the woman they'd chosen as GM could not rally up the troops and meet objectives. He loved being the bearer of bad news, especially when it involved women. Jessica had always refused to get caught up in Harold's political barbarism, and he hated that she wouldn't play the game.

A conniving sneer spread across Harold's face. "I'm sure you will. Exactly *how* far off are we?"

"Not enough to affect revenue or net profit percentages this month," Jessica said. The ache behind her eyes began to spread to her temples. She painted a smile on her face. "There's a meeting at two. You're welcome to join us if you'd like."

Reddening slightly, Harold wadded up the cup and started toward the elevator. "Can't. Too many projects going on," he said, never looking back at her.

"Right," she called back to him, then, under her breath as she headed down the corridor to her office, "asshole."

The clicking of her heels on the marble floor kept time with the throbbing that grew in her head. She entered her office, closed the door, and leaned against it. She looked at her desk and groaned. Reams of computer printouts and folders covered the top of the mahogany surface. She just wanted to go home and lie down.

Forcing herself around the desk to her chair, Jessica let her body fold into the leather and closed her eyes. The burning in them had stopped. She felt she needed to check them out to see if they were bloodshot, though. They *felt* bloodshot. But she didn't have the energy to move.

Maybe I should get another checkup, she thought. She listened for a moment to the steady hum of the fluorescent lights above her. She wasn't one to go to the doctor for every sniffle. In fact, getting an exam once a year was a commitment she adhered to only because of Frank's insistence. But hearing weird voices had nothing to do with the sniffles. Something was definitely wrong. She opened her eyes and felt prickles of fear whisk through her as she thought back to the sound of it. So menacing, so angry and degrading.

A knock at the door made her jump and sent her pulse racing. The door opened without invitation, and a thick mane of curly black hair popped through the opening.

"What's up?" asked Lisa Daigle, Jessica's closest friend and marketing director for Avid.

"Close the door, okay?"

"Girl," Lisa said as she entered the room and pushed the door shut behind her, "Marie was right. You do look like shit."

"Thanks a lot."

"No, really," Lisa said emphatically. "Your eyes are all puffy and red, and your face is awfully white." She walked up to Jessica's desk, shoved a stack of papers to one side, and perched a hip along the edge. Her eyes narrowed behind her red-rimmed glasses. "I mean, you look absolutely wasted. If I didn't know any better, I'd swear you'd sipped a few for breakfast." She pulled her glasses down to the end of her nose and peered intently at Jessica. "Spill it. What's up?"

Jessica sat up slowly and made a halfhearted attempt at straightening the chaos on her desk. She debated on how much to tell Lisa. She'd known her for what seemed like three lifetimes. They'd played together as kids and roomed together in college. She'd even helped Lisa get the job with Avid, which was a subsidiary of Sternco, just as they were relocating to Memphis. Since the only thing she'd had to worry about uprooting was Hombre, her cat, Lisa jumped at the opportunity. Still, even with all the history between them, Jessica couldn't bring herself to a full confession. The whole incident was just too weird, too funny-farmish.

"Well?" Lisa asked.

"Just a headache. No big deal."

Lisa snorted loudly. "Hey, it's me you're talking to, remember? For Marie to bring it to my attention, it had to be a big deal."

"I'm fine, really. It was just a big-ass headache."

"All right, Mother Teresa," Lisa said, pushing her glasses back into place. "You trying to be some kind of martyr? You're so damn hardheaded about stuff like this, Jess. It's okay to be sick, you know."

"You sound like your mother."

"Tough."

Jessica grinned. "Look, I've already decided if it happens again, I'll have it checked out."

"Promise?"

"Girl Scout's honor."

"You were never in Girl Scouts."

"Okay, Miss Charmine's School of Ballet's honor."

"We only went to one class. It doesn't count."

"What are you doing here, anyway? I thought today was your first day of vacation?"

Lisa hopped off the desk. "Yeah, I thought so, too. But there was a *situation,*" she said, crinkling her nose like she'd just bitten into chalk. "I had to come in and handle it." She grabbed some files that were threatening to fall from the desk. "You know you're a pig, don't you? That new GM title they gave you should stand for General Mess, not General Manager."

Jessica smiled and took the files from her. "Planning anything exciting during your time off?"

"Is this your way of getting me to stop lecturing you about your health?"

"Pretty much."

"It's not working."

"Pretend it is."

Lisa grimaced. "Okay, well—let's see. I plan to clean out my garage and Easy-Off the oven. You know, that self-cleaning crap doesn't really work."

"Sounds productive."

"Yeah, I thought so."

"Want to come to dinner tomorrow?" Jessica asked, leaning back in her chair.

"Depends."

"On what?"

"What you're cooking," Lisa said with a snicker. "You're not exactly the Galloping Gourmet."

"Probably gumbo," Jessica said. She was feeling more like her old self. Her brain felt heavy, but at least the Tylenol had taken the edge off the pain.

"In July?" Lisa asked, her voice pitched with false incredulity. "Sounds good. What time?"

"Around se—" Jessica's intercom buzzed, and Marie's voice filled the room.

"Jess?"

"Yes?"

A heavy, expectant pause, then, "You may want to take me off the speaker."

Jessica looked up at Lisa, who waggled her eyebrows. She picked up the receiver. "What is it, Marie?"

"There's a Deputy Nunez on the phone, and he asked if we had a 'Jess' working here," Marie said in a whisper. "Says he's from Louisiana."

At the mention of her home state, Jessica's heart began to thunder. She immediately thought of the sparrow she'd seen the night before. "Thank you, Marie."

"No problem. He's on line one."

Jessica glimpsed the on-hold indicator light on her phone. It became a miniature beacon, flashing a warning in Morse code: *Caution! Stop!* She tapped the button quickly. "This is Jessica LeJeune."

"Uh, Ms. LeJeune?" a congested voice said on the other end. "This is Deputy Nunez from the Lafayette Parish Sheriff's Department. That's in Louisiana, ma'am."

"Yes, I know, Deputy. I'm originally from the area." Jessica looked up at Lisa, who whispered, "Deputy?"

"Oh, sorry." He cleared his throat. "Figures you would be with a name like LeJeune and all. Anyway, ma'am, I'm callin' to find out if you might know a Todd Guidry?"

Fear slammed hard against Jessica's chest, and her throat constricted. "Yes, he's my brother."

Lisa, who was now almost stretched out across the desk, mouthed, "What? What?"

Jessica shooed her away and mouthed back, "Hang on!" To the deputy, she asked nervously, "What about my brother? Is he all right? Where is he? How did you find me?" She could almost hear the sparrow beating itself to death against her kitchen window.

The deputy let out a hacking cough. "Excuse me—summer cold. Your brother, uh—Ms. LeJeune, right?"

"Yes, yes, Jessica LeJeune." Jessica stood up. "Is my brother okay?"

"Well, somewhat," the deputy answered. Then hurriedly: "Oh, he's not dead or anything. No, ma'am. He's fine that way. We've got him here in the parish jail, though. Seems like he had some trouble keeping his clothes on."

"What?" Jessica sputtered, dumbfounded.

"See, we got a call from a woman in Lafayette who said her ten-year-old boy had been playing near the old Middle Brook holding station. It's a place where they sit boxcars sometimes to unload freight. You know, feed, fertilizer, stuff like that. Don't know why that lady let her boy play out there, though. Can be a dangerous place. A real dangerous place. Just last year some kid got stuck—"

"Deputy," Jessica interrupted sharply, "my brother?"

"Oh, sorry. Anyway, the boy came back and told his mama there was a naked man in one of the cars. She called us. We went to check it out, and sure enough, your brother was sitting naked as a jaybird in one of the old freighters. His head was a little banged up, but we had a doctor check him out, and he said the injuries weren't serious." Another wheeze, then a cough. "Anyhow, there was an old pair of pants in the train with him. We dug around in the pockets, looking for some identification, and found a piece of paper with the name Jess on it and a couple of phone numbers. No identification, though. It took him a while before he could tell us his name."

"What do you mean 'it took him a while'?" Jessica paced in front of her desk, the phone cord spreading papers into further confusion.

"Well—uh—he wasn't exactly—collected. Thinking straight, you know?"

"Deputy!" Jessica fumed. "What are you talking about?"

Another hack, then a sniffle. "Your brother seems to be delusional, Ms. LeJeune. I can't tell you what's wrong with him. I'm not a shrink. But I can tell you we're getting ready to bring him to Municipal Mental. That's a small holding clinic in Broussard, just outside Lafayette. The state clinic is full, so we have to bring him to Municipal until state gets a bed open."

Jessica froze in midstride, her mind trying to grasp and decipher what she'd just heard. "Wait," she said finally. "Can you please just hold him until I get there? Please, just a few hours?"

"No, ma'am, I'm sorry. We're not allowed to keep anyone here—I mean, in the station, in your brother's condition. And besides, if you could see him, you'd rather he be somewhere where someone can be looking after him."

Nothing made sense to Jessica. She didn't know what to say.

"Hello? Ms. LeJeune, you still there?"

"Yes—yes, I'm sorry."

"Look, I'll give you Municipal's number. If you wait a couple of hours, you can call them and find out more about your brother." He rattled off the seven digits, then as an afterthought threw in the area code.

Jessica grabbed a pen and hurriedly wrote on the back of the first piece of paper she could flip over. "I appreciate the call, Deputy," she said, then hung up in the middle of his "You're wel—"

"What was that all about?" Lisa asked.

"Todd's in trouble. I've got to go to Lafayette."

The two women stared at each other for a moment. The silence was deafening; not even the fluorescent bulbs hummed.

"How bad?" Lisa finally asked.

"Bad."

"I can go with you if you'd like, or I can stay with Jake while Frank goes with you," Lisa offered.

"No, thanks. I appreciate the offer, but I'm not sure how long I'll have to be there." Jessica sat heavily in her chair. "Frank'll want to come, but there's a big project he's working on that he can't afford to leave. Besides, it's always better for Jake if Frank's there when I'm away."

"Yeah, but I'm on vacation," Lisa said. "I can just shoot out there with you, and if you've got to stay longer than my time off, I'll just head back. At least you won't be alone the whole time."

"Thanks anyway."

Lisa leaned over the desk, squeezed Jessica's hand,

then headed for the door. "Well, too bad," she said. "I'm going to take care of a few things here, and then I'm going with you, hardhead. What do—"

Jessica's eyes started to burn fiercely. This time there was no accompanying headache, but it felt like someone had taken lighter fluid to her eyeballs, then struck a match. Tears ran down her cheeks as she squeezed her eyes shut. A hollow pounding began in her ears, and the tone quickly changed and deepened, racing from one ear to the other. Abruptly, the plangent ruckus ceased and was immediately replaced with raspy, labored breathing. Terror pulled every nerve taut in Jessica's body. She strained to open her eyes, but they felt seared shut. The breathing grew louder, stronger, pushing through her veins as though determined to replace the blood that flowed in them. Her body vibrated with the sound. She tried to open her mouth to call out for Lisa, but her lips wouldn't move.

Dear, God, I'm going to burst! her mind screamed.

The pitch of the asthmatic inhale–exhale–inhale pushed through her body with such force that she thought she was going to lose control of her bodily functions. Her mind could barely formulate the words *STOP! STOP!*

It did stop. So quickly, in fact, the effect nearly pitched Jessica forward. She threw her hands out in front of her and found the desk.

Pop! A sound like someone slapping air from a plastic bag came from behind her. Before she could even react to it, a deep voice, *the* voice, sour and malignant with hate, shouted, "Hey! Pay attention now. Toddy's fucked up, girlie girl, and it's all your fault."

Then, just as before with Marie, everything abruptly went quiet. Jessica opened her eyes cautiously. Through thin slits she saw Lisa at the door. Her face was a pasty mask, and a thin trickle of blood ran from her nose.

"Did you hear that?"

Jessica studied Lisa's face. This *wasn't* like earlier with Marie. This time she wasn't the one who'd asked that question. Lisa had.

Chapter Four

Todd Guidry was crouching naked on the floor in the corner of a padded room. His eyes were shut so tight, sparks of white light sprayed the backs of his eyelids. The pain was good. He bit his lip hard and tasted blood. The pain was very good. It drowned out the voices—some of them. He hated the sounds, the harsh, deep whispers that he couldn't quite make out, and the sudden ranting shouts that scared the hell out of him. The worst part of it all was that the voices knew his name. They tricked him. Occasionally they would speak softly, tenderly. Then, when they had his attention, they would tell him to do things, terrible things. He could be passing someone on the street, and demon voices would force him to look into the person's face and tell him to gouge their eyes out. A pleading from inside him, small and muffled, like a child hidden away in a box in the back of his brain, would stop him from acting out on what he'd been commanded to do.

Part of him knew the voices weren't supposed to be there. Out of nowhere they had started a year ago, and he didn't know why he couldn't make them go away. What he did know, however, was that they were real. Very, very real. He tried over and over to stop them, to regain control, but it was like fighting the battle of Armageddon in his mind. He'd cried out to God so many times, scared and confused. But the voices were always the ones who answered. They tried to trick him. They sounded like God. And he didn't want to disappoint God.

Todd shivered, gooseflesh rising like dwarfed moles over his body. *They* had put a hospital gown on him when he was first brought in, and he'd ripped it off. *They* had put thumb clamps on him to keep him from taking it off again, but he'd maneuvered out of the gown anyway, rolling it into a ball around the four-inch plastic cord that connected the clamps. It was the snaps. Todd was certain they had put small transmitters in the snaps of the gown. *They* didn't know he knew their tricks.

Lights were another gimmick they used. He'd been careful to shield himself from the luminous infiltration produced by the two strips of fluorescent bulbs embedded in the ceiling eight feet above his head. They didn't know he was aware of the CIA and certain militia groups listening to him—to his every thought, through that light. But he knew. Oh, yes, he knew, and he'd learned how to fool the bastards. If he concentrated hard enough, he could create a reflector in his brain that would send the thoughts from the CIA back into the air and straight to the militia, confusing them.

Todd's legs ached and complained in their unaccustomed position. He lowered himself gingerly and stretched his legs out in front of him. Cocking his head to one side, he listened attentively. For now, God and the CIA were silent. A shudder raced up his spine, as did a feeling of being utterly exposed. More than exposed—opened, like some frenzied pathologist had perfunctorily sawed through his cranial cap, then tossed it aside as useless. Exhaling slowly, quietly, he scooted backward, working his legs up and down as inconspicuously as possible until his back felt support.

The walls that surrounded him were four-foot panels of dingy padding. The mural of stains across them had been drawn by past tenants in blood, spit, and one large, darker spot where he assumed a John Doe had crapped in his hand and used it as finger paint. The floor was covered with inch-thick canvas that looked like it hadn't been cleaned in years.

The sour smells didn't bother Todd. Clothes bothered him. Light bothered him. The angry, accusing voices in his head bothered him. Occasionally he'd have seconds of peace, like now, but he knew they were only false breaths of hope. Sometimes, during those respites, a series of pictures, like the quick snap frames from a slide projector, would go through his mind. Pictures of a strong, young man who looked very much like him, only clean and happy. Those visions reminded him of a time when the world had been filled with infinite possibilities. A world where he could laugh and dream and love and be loved, where no one looked at him in fear or revulsion. Each time he'd tried to name that world, to make it part of himself again, the voices would come back and make all of it irrelevant.

There were only two voices Todd wasn't afraid of: the Informer's and the Protector's. He didn't hear them often, and when he did, it was like background noise. He'd only started hearing the Protector a few days ago, a whisper he had to strain to hear. "Someone coming—coming—bad—soon." That was all the Protector ever said. Todd didn't understand what it meant, but at least he had a sense that someone watched his back.

The Informer, on the other hand, sounding very much like his uncle Wallace after too many rum and Cokes, had been around for a while. He told Todd things that no one else knew—important things, chemical things, electronic things—that could destroy the whole planet. Todd Allen Guidry had been given explicit instructions on how to use this knowledge just in case things turned bad and he needed a way out. A way to rid the world of all its human maggots. Oh, yes, he was getting ideas from *the* source, intelligence far greater than the damn CIA had access to.

Todd knew no one believed he was privy to such exclusive and valuable data. Not even Carlisle, and he'd known stuff, too. The lanky, stoop-shouldered man had found Todd hiding in an alley behind a bar and grill on Southpark Avenue and brought him to the train. He had trusted Carlisle immediately. Todd could tell the man knew how to keep gamma rays and transmitters, which seemed to be every-damn-where, from getting to his thoughts. Carlisle always walked around with one hand on top of his head.

"They watchin' you too, huh?" Carlisle had asked when he first spotted Todd.

It had been night, so Todd was able to keep his eyes wide open. He looked at Carlisle and thought, *If you're one of those FBI bastards, then you will be able to hear me right now and tell me what I'm thinking.*

"Well?" Carlisle asked again. "You'd better do somethin', buddy. You're in the open, and they're gonna find you for sure." He quickly exchanged his right hand, which had been clamped to the top of his head, with his left. "They got rays shootin' out everywhere. Look at you, your head's not even covered."

Todd followed Carlisle to the boxcar. The walk there produced an exchange of first names and talk of the government's infiltration into every American's mind through subliminal messaging. They even determined that the traffic lights were codes used by the FBI. Green was the signal that another mind was being controlled. Red was the signal that an attempt had failed. That would have been the signal for Todd and Carlisle; they were sure of it. When Todd tried to explain to him that he had exclusive information from the Informer about how certain things worked, Carlisle listened. Had even nodded his head that he understood, but Todd knew he didn't *really* understand. He could only hope the transmitters were not finding their way into Carlisle's head through his fingers. There was just something about the look that Carlisle had given him that made Todd suspect that that could be happening.

The men talked until the sun washed dawn into the boxcar. They'd determined by that time that there was surely a plot being orchestrated by the militia groups to poison both of them since they had been so clever in avoiding thought transference. They didn't take any chances. The thread used to bind the seams of their clothing together was the only logical place the poison could have been placed, so all clothing was removed.

Todd's voices came back louder and harsher as the day's heat shriveled the protective covering from the boxcar. He'd beaten his head repeatedly against the ribbed walls, trying to stop, or at least garble, the sounds in his brain. The next thing he knew, the car's sliding door was shoved open. They'd found him, and, worse still, Carlisle was no longer there. Todd was sure *they* had disintegrated him.

Now the bastards had brought him here and were trying to get to him. To get the information the Informer had given to him, then disintegrate his ass. *No way! No damn way!*

Todd eased one eye open—testing. The frequencies were down, he could sense it. *The sonofabitches must be sleeping.* He grinned. The small triumphs always felt good. He turned his head casually, looking around the room through squinted eyelids. A brown speck scurried and snapped at his peripheral vision. His heart rate accelerated off the Mach scale. *They caught me! They're going to beam that brain thing right through the slit in my eye! Direct access!* He squeezed his eyes shut and swallowed hard.

"Todd," a hollow voice whispered in his left ear. "Open your eyes, boy. I've brought you something.

Something to make you smarter, sharper than them."

Todd's breathing grew rapid. He opened his eyes reluctantly. His eyelashes, like hundreds of spider legs, filtered his view. It could be a trick. The voice sounded like the Informer, but sometimes the voices were hard to tell apart. He raised his head and through tightly controlled eye slits saw the brown speck settle in the crack of two wall panels to his right. His eyes teared as he filled with excitement and gratitude. He had discerned right. It was the Informer's voice, and he'd sent help.

Thrusting his back firmly against the wall, Todd turned his head and pressed his cheek hard against the smelly canvas. He closed his eyes reverently and stuck out his tongue like a Catholic awaiting communion. He waited patiently, his mouth watering as his tongue tipped the musky pad.

"You knew I would come, didn't you, boy?" the voice asked, its tone boastful and strong.

Todd didn't move. *Yes!* His mind answered hungrily, anxious to please, anxious to be worthy. The back of his tongue burned as he forced it to its farthest length.

"Take what I've sent to you. It'll make you stronger."

As the first microscopic breath of movement touched his tongue, Todd let the tears slide down his cheeks. He had been sent help—finally. There was a scurrying sensation at the tip of his tongue that stopped as it reached the middle of his mouth. Todd pressed his teeth together carefully.

Sensing its demise, the cockroach began to scuttle

furiously from molar to molar. Clamping his lips together, but being careful not to bite down too hard, Todd let the gift cleanse him. Cleanse him of all the poisons he knew *they* were trying to force into his body through the lights and air vents overhead. He felt the wire-thin legs pinch against the meaty cushion of his tongue and the hard shell of his gift pop and jump against his palate. He wanted to tilt his head back and open his mouth. He wanted to pull his lips outward and stretch them beyond capacity so the insect could clean every crevice of him. But he knew better. *They* would snatch his gift away. He had to trust that the Informer gave these benefactions special powers to cleanse every possible place the poisons could get to, even if the gift could not physically touch it. Todd trusted and allowed it to run over the back of his teeth and gums. He raised his tongue cautiously so the priceless gift could at least get to the tender flesh beneath, if it wanted to.

The roach threw itself at the back of Todd's throat, causing him to gag. He squeezed his lips together tighter and swallowed. The scratching in his throat was short-lived as the bug slid down Todd's esophagus. Heat seemed to regenerate every nerve in his body.

Now come and try to get me, you sonofabitch! Todd's mind screamed. *You thought you were winning? Well, fuck you! You hear me, you communist spy sonofabitch? Fuck you!*

Todd opened his eyes wide and stretched his arms to work out a kink in his right elbow. His mind felt stronger, more powerful, almost invincible. He watched the hospital gown billow over his lap as he lowered his arms. It didn't matter that the snaps were exposed now. He'd been given protection.

No whispering. Thank God, no whispering. He stared at the opposite corner of the room. He was afraid to think. He never knew how long the silence would last or what would trigger the other voices. His stomach gurgled, and his bowels cramped, then relaxed. He was tired—so tired that his skin felt like a lead drape.

Suddenly two sections of wall to Todd's left yawned open and a thick man with bristly black hair appeared. Todd froze.

"Well, I'll be damned," the man said in amazement. "How in the hell did you get it off?" He walked into the room, and the door closed behind him with a heavy, thick sound. He strolled over to Todd, a circlet of keys jingling in his right hand, and glared at him suspiciously. LEROY JOHNSON was stenciled across a name tag attached to his blue jacket, and below it, in smaller letters: ORDERLY.

Leroy twirled the ring rapidly around his index finger, then shoved the keys into his coat pocket like a gunslinger holstering his weapon. "How in the hell did you get out of the gown?"

Todd looked through the man. He thought of his gift and made the man disappear from his mind—from the room. Even though he'd heard him speak, he wasn't there. Todd could make him go away. He knew things—important things.

"Damn fruitcakes," Leroy mumbled. "Don't I have enough to deal with around here than having to look at your ugly ass?"

Todd sat motionless.

"You like showing off that noodle, huh, fruitcake? Huh, fruity?" Leroy asked, his voice becoming a husky whisper. "You like it when old Leroy looks at that skinny noodle of yours?" He squatted down beside Todd. "Come on. Show old Leroy what you hiding in there."

Leroy moved the gown up from Todd's lap and hesitantly slid his right hand under it. "That's it, fruity. Let Leroy see how big a boy you really are," he murmured, starting to stroke Todd. "And if you're good, Leroy's gonna show you how big a boy he is. Might even let you touch it. Whatta ya say, fruity, hmm? And you know, fruity, little tooty-fruity, it don't matter if you tell anybody." His eyes closed for a moment, as though relishing the feel of silk in his hand. "Who's gonna believe a fruity? Huh? Who's gonna— SHIT!"

Todd lodged his teeth firmly into Leroy's right forearm.

"Let me go, you goddamn fruitcake!" Leroy yelled, grabbing Todd by the hair with his free hand.

Todd held on, his teeth locking deeper into the dark skin. Leroy hit him on top of the head, then over his right ear, his words accentuating each blow. "Let—me—fucking—go!"

A click sounded from the door, and Leroy quickly snatched his left hand to his side. "Help! Get him off me!" he bellowed.

A woman in a stiff white uniform hurried into the room. "Hold still," she yelled, rushing toward them.

"Get him off! Get him off!" Leroy shouted.

She unzipped a nylon utility bag she wore around her waist and pulled out a syringe. She uncapped it and, with the movements of a prize boxer, swabbed and stuck Todd's arm.

"Get him off me!" Leroy screamed, his voice cracking.

"Just a second. He'll let go."

"Just a second! I could get some kinda fuckin' disease from this guy!"

The woman pursed her lips, paused a few seconds, then said, "Pull your arm away, slowly."

Leroy pressed his arm down against Todd's jaw, and Todd allowed it to fall slack, releasing him.

After placing the syringe back into her bag, the woman glared at Leroy. "Now, go to my office," she demanded.

"Hey, the guy's gown was off when I got here. I didn't do nothin', honest. I was just tryin' to put it back on him when he up and bit me."

"I meant your arm, Leroy. I'll take care of it in my office," she said tersely. "Where were you, anyway? I've been looking for you everywhere. Didn't you hear me paging you?"

"No, ma'am," Leroy said. He clasped his hand over the bite on his arm. "I didn't hear a thing."

"Well, you're supposed to be with me on rounds. You should know that by now. Don't disappear on me again, understand?"

"Yes, ma'am."

"Good. Now wait a minute. Before you go, help me dress this man," she said, eyeing Todd. "He should be quiet for a while."

As though his body had been awaiting her command, Todd's chin dropped to his chest and he began to fall into a quiet darkness. He'd taken care of the *real* fruitcake and could handle the crap they pumped into his body. He was safe for now.

Hands suddenly appeared out of the black veil that plumed over Todd's thoughts. He watched curiously as they moved closer to him. The palms were turned upright, the fingers curled inward, like a mother's hands beckoning to her child. He had no fear of them. He watched the arms come into view, then the torso. The last thing he saw before the Thorazine took him beyond the darkness was the face. Shoulder-length hair the color of roasted walnuts embraced it.

He called to it longingly.

"Jess."

Chapter Five

Eli felt the heat of a near-noon sun on the back of his neck and wished it would go away. The last hour had been the only sleep he'd managed to get after Johanson, a cured Shank, and a baffled Earl left the night before. The moment they departed, Eli had stretched out on the cot, exhausted. Solace never came, however, because the nightmares began almost immediately. They eventually chased him out of bed, then finally out of the shack altogether. He wound up on the slope of a nearby levee, where he sat elbows to knees, his face in his hands. This position didn't stop the dreams, but it seemed to limit their ferocity.

Each dream had been a slight variation of the same basic theme—his destruction. The woman with the birthmark would appear on his right and Maikana to his left, each of them determined to annihilate the other. For one to get to the other, though, they had to physically go through him. How they managed to do that was the variable. Most often they tore through his flesh. Then, just before either of them reached muscle, Eli would wake screaming. Even more horrible than witnessing the mutilation from a dream-state were the sensations that accompanied it. He'd been able to feel each layer of skin being ripped from his body as though it were actually happening.

Eli knew he couldn't go on this way. Night after night, dream after dream, torture after torture. If something didn't change soon, he would have no choice but to follow in his mother's footsteps and take his life. By his own hand, at least death could come quickly, and so would peace.

Slowly, Eli lifted his head. He didn't even have the energy to be startled when he saw Johanson standing beside him.

"How long you been here?" Eli asked. His tongue felt thick and grainy, as if coated with wet sand.

"Twenty, thirty minute maybe." Johanson squinted over the bayou. "You stay to the levee all night?"

"Pretty close."

"Gator coulda climb up here wit' you, you know."

Eli struggled to his feet. "It don't much make a matter to me. It's near time I be done wit' anyways."

Johanson snapped his head to one side. "I don't want to hear you talk trash like dat no more no. You hear?"

"Why, if it's true?"

" 'Cause only de good Lord knows when you be

done wit'. All de rest is not you business. Dat's His business."

Eli sighed and leaned against a pine tree. "Well, He need to make up His mind, 'cause I can't go no more." He tapped his forehead. "It feel like Maikana stay wit' me here most all de time now. And her, too."

Johanson frowned. "She stay too?"

Eli nodded. Johanson already knew about the nightmares he'd been having, but he filled him in on last night's version. When Eli finished, he asked Johanson, "Now, you could live like dat? Wit' all dat in you head?"

The old man's mouth trembled before he answered. "N-no."

"Well, what I'm supposed to do?"

Johanson lowered his head, then hesitantly stuck a hand into his pants pocket and pulled something out. He held it out to Eli. "You—you supposed to find her. Dat's what you supposed to do. It's time."

Eli blinked at the broken necklace dangling before him. The pendant looked like an upside-down metal teardrop attached to a single length of chain.

"Here," Johanson said. "Take it."

"For what?"

"Dis gonna help you find where she's at."

"I already know where she at. In my head."

Johanson trudged over to a flattop stump and sat. He stared at the pendant for a long while, and when he looked back up at Eli, his eyes were wet with tears. "My boy, she's not just in you head. She's more real than me and you put together."

Eli's heart thudded loudly. Not because he'd just

discovered the woman from his nightmares was a real person, but because Johanson had called him "my boy." The old man had never done that before. It made Eli feel strange and warm inside. He wanted to hear it again.

"You understand what dis means?" Johanson asked shakily. "To go find her means you gonna have to leave de swamp."

The warm and fuzzies abruptly left Eli. "Leave?"

"Yeah."

Eli slumped to the ground in a squat. "But why I got to go find her? She already find me."

"You gonna know why when you get to her."

"But if she be like Maikana and—"

"She's not spirit like Maikana. She got bone like you bone and blood like you blood."

"Den how she get in my head?"

Johanson pinched the top of the pendant's chain with two fingers and let the rest of it dangle between his knees. "She just do."

"How you know her? How you know what she just do?"

"I just know."

Eli stood up quickly and pointed a finger at him. "What I'm supposed to do wit dat? You not tellin' me nuttin'!"

Johanson briskly wiped the tears off his cheeks. "I'm gonna ax you somet'ing, and you answer me true, you hear?"

Eli dropped the accusing finger. "What?"

"You trust dis old man?" Johanson asked, tapping his chest with a finger.

"Yeah."

"And you wanna get rid of all dis pain in you head, you heart—you soul?"

Feeling like he was being led down a crooked path, Eli hesitated for a moment, then answered, "Yeah."

"Den you gonna have to believe what I say now is true. Take dis." Johanson held out the pendant. "It gonna show you where she's at. De rest of what you gotta do is gonna come when you need it."

Eli stared at Johanson. It was true the man had never lied to him before, and although Eli trusted him with his life, he couldn't help but worry. Why wasn't Johanson telling him everything? Who was this woman? If she wasn't a spirit, why did she always seem to be connected with Maikana? If he found her, would he find peace? Was this woman the answer to stopping the nightmares and pain?

Tentatively Eli walked over to Johanson and took the pendant. He held it between two fingers and watched it sway. The movement felt heavy, and it made his fingertips tingle.

"If I go, you go wit me?" Eli asked quietly.

Johanson stood and laid a hand on Eli's shoulder. "I'll bring you to de landing past Fosey Point in my boat, but de rest you gotta do by youself, my boy."

This time Johanson's words of endearment didn't offer Eli comfort. He gathered the pendant into his palm, then scanned the sun-kissed bayou and the small, weatherworn shack in the near distance. From here, the house looked too small to have held so many hardships. Desertion. Loneliness. Fear. But it was home; his home. And deep in his gut Eli knew that leaving it now meant leaving it forever. Although that saddened him, he figured he had no other choice. For he was just as certain death would find him either way.

Chapter Six

Jessica wandered through Wal-Mart in a daze. She'd already run into two displays with her shopping cart, knocking over a stack of videos, then a pyramid of canned dog food. Most of the day had been that way for her, confused and disoriented.

After the incident in her office with Lisa that morning, she'd decided to tell her friend about the voice and all the physical ailments that preceded it. If anyone else had heard the detailed account, they would have probably awarded her front and center seating in Memphis's rendition of Municipal Mental. But Lisa believed her. She hadn't heard the voice, but had heard the popping noise, which she claimed started her nosebleed.

The hardest part had been convincing her girlfriend she didn't need to go to Louisiana with her. The truth was Jessica really did want her to come along. But a black fear kept tugging at the edges of her intuition. Though the trepidation seemed irrational, she'd been relieved when Lisa finally dropped the matter.

When they finally left her office, Jessica had forced herself through the rest of the day. She rescheduled meetings, informed her boss she'd be out tending to a family emergency for a few days, then stayed at her desk for hours, attempting to reach Municipal. The busy signals lasted until three. The woman who eventually answered the phone had been curt, harried, and informed Jessica that she couldn't speak to Todd. Yes, her brother was fine. No, the admitting doctor was not available to speak to her, and did she understand she was to bring a week's supply of clothing, pajamas preferable, and toiletries as soon as possible. Toothbrush, toothpaste, no dental floss or razor blades. No forks, knives, no medication from outside the facility, not even aspirin. Jessica had the feeling the woman was reading the instructions from an index card taped to her desk. She assured Jessica that there was no reason to rush out there that day, everything was under control. The next day would be fine.

How could anything possibly be fine or under control when your brother's in a mental ward? Jessica wondered, and gave the shopping basket a hard shove toward the men's department.

After picking up a few pullover tees, underwear, and a pair of jeans, she went to the pajama section. There she found a wide assortment of cottons and silks, some with cartoon devils printed on them or huge kissy lips. As Jessica thumbed through the packages, she came across a pair with little cowboys and Indians on them. She snapped her hand back as if it had neared a snake.

"Get—get a grip," she whispered shakily, and quickly grabbed three pairs of solid colored pj's and threw them into the basket.

Something felt ripe and ready to burst inside her. A gigantic memory pimple with enough purulence to drown her. Jessica hurried over to a cashier, paid for the merchandise, and left the store.

She sped all the way home with the radio cranked up loud, her method of avoiding thought. By the time she pulled into her driveway, Jessica had to force her cramped, curled fingers away from the steering wheel.

"Hey, there, good-lookin'," Frank called out the moment she walked into the house. He was standing in front of the stove dressed in walking shorts, a red pullover shirt, and a full-fronted apron with DARN GOOD COOK blazoned across the front. "Come and check out this masterpiece." He lifted the lid to a pot of simmering marinara sauce and grinned.

Jessica walked up behind her husband, wrapped her arms around his waist, and kissed his back. "Smells wonderful."

"What say we have a little salad, French bread, then some of this special LeJeune sauce over tortellini? Sound eatable?" He replaced the lid and turned to her.

"An absolute feast." Jessica rested a hand on his chest, then peered over her shoulder toward the living room. "Where's Jake?"

"Over at Evan Mitchell's house, planning a camping trip last I heard. He should be back any minute."

"Camping?" Jessica frowned. "Where?"

Frank hugged her. "Hang tight there, Mama Bear. They're only talking about a backyard jaunt the weekend after Jake's birthday. Should be relatively anaconda, cougar, and tarantula free."

"Okay, wise guy." She gave him a tired smile.

He studied her face, then cupped her chin. "Hard day?"

That tiny question hit Jessica hard in the chest, and she felt her bottom lip begin to tremble. She barely managed to utter, "Yeah," before the tears came.

Frank's brow gathered in concern, and he took her by the hand and led her to the kitchen table. "Talk to me," he said, pulling out a chair and motioning for her to sit.

Jessica squeezed his hand hard in an attempt to control her tears, then sat back and told him about Todd. She left out the details about her own episodes, however, because she knew he'd insist she see their family doctor before leaving town, and she didn't want to delay the trip to Louisiana any longer than she had to.

"Jesus, Jess, and you've been dealing with this by yourself all day?"

"Not all day. Lisa was with me when I got the call."

"You should've phoned me right away. I could've helped."

"There wasn't anything to help with, Frank. It's

only been one big frustrating mess so far. I hope when I get to Lafayette tomorrow, I can get some answers."

"When *you* get to Lafayette? Baby, I don't think you should be handling this one by yourself." Frank stood up, went to the stove, and turned off the burner under the sauce, then returned to her with a tissue. "I'm sure Mom would be glad to watch over Jake for a few days so I can go with you. All I'd have to do is give her a call and she'd be on the next flight here."

Jessica took the tissue and wiped her eyes. "I figured you'd say that, but there really isn't any need for you to come. Besides, you have that big McGregor project to finish."

"Steve can handle it while I'm away."

She shook her head. "He's your only employee. What if something else pops up while he's working on McGregor? How would he handle everything alone?"

Frank smoothed her hair. "He'd figure it out, Jess. You know, you're starting to sound like you'd prefer I not go with you."

"Not prefer," she said. "I just don't see any reason for it. And what about Jake?"

"What about him?"

"Having only your mom here might throw him off schedule."

"What schedule? Baby, he'll be eleven on Friday. It's not like he's still taking naps and drinking formula."

"I know, I know, but still—and what if I wind up having to stay in Lafayette longer than planned? What'll happen to his birthday party if both of us aren't here? He'd be so disappointed if we had to cancel it."

"Jake's a levelheaded kid. If something like that happened, I'm sure he'd understand."

Jessica looked away. "I know. You're right. It's just—"

"Hey." Frank lifted her chin with a finger and gently turned her face toward him. "If it's important to you to go by yourself, then do it." He shrugged. "I'd still rather go with you, if for nothing else but support, but you do what makes you most comfortable. We'll be fine here."

"You sure?"

"Positive. You go on and take care of Todd, I'll handle things here."

She let out a grateful sigh. "If I go by myself, I can—"

Frank leaned over and kissed her. "You don't have to give me the whys. The only thing I care about is what works for you. Just promise if it gets too difficult there, you'll let me come and rescue you, be your hero." He smiled softly.

"You'll always be my hero." Jessica stood up and folded herself in his arms. "Always."

The kitchen door opened suddenly, and a bright-eyed Jake burst into the room. "Hey, guess— Ah, man, if I would've known you guys were going to be doing all that mushy stuff, I would've stayed at Evan's."

Frank chuckled. "Mushy, huh? Wait until you get a little older, big guy. You'll be all up in the mushy stuff, too."

Jake wrinkled his nose. "Not me. I'm gonna be a

park ranger, and they watch for fires and bears all day. They don't have time for all that hugging and stuff."

"What happened to the doctor with the pilot's license?" Jessica asked while heading to the cupboard for plates.

"I'm figuring I can fit all three together," Jake said. "You know, if a fire breaks out and people get hurt, I can take care of them right there because I'm a doctor. Then, when the fire's out, I can fly to the hospital and do my other doctor's work."

"Whew," Frank said. "Mighty big job, don't you think?"

Jake grinned. "Yep." His eyes widened. "Oh, hey, guess what? Evan's dad got this new metal-detector thing. It's so cool! It's . . ."

While her husband and son discussed metal detectors, Jessica set the table for dinner. She listened to their enthusiastic chatter, smiled when appropriate, and ran a mental checklist of what she'd need to pack for the trip. Frank's understanding of her compulsion to go alone relieved her. So did his not needing to know why. Though she could think of a dozen excuses to explain away her desire to trek to Louisiana by herself, she couldn't think of one legitimate reason. As she had with Lisa, Jessica was riding on gut instinct, an intuition hampered by anvils and dead birds. Better to leave family and friends behind—in case, just in case.

She did her best to keep the conversation light during dinner, sticking to campouts and park rangers. All the while she struggled with thoughts of Todd and where he'd be sleeping tonight. By the time they finished eating, Jessica felt ready to collapse from mental exhaustion.

Once the dishes were washed and put away, and her family had settled into the living room for a little television, Jessica trudged to her bedroom.

Pack, bath, bed. She allowed those three words to spin through her mind over and over, hoping they would keep her brain busy. She sat down on the bed and closed her eyes for a few minutes. If she could just get through those three things, sleep would come. Then tomorrow would come, and she'd be in Louisiana and Todd wouldn't be alone.

Wearily, Jessica opened her eyes and got up. She went to the closet and was about to pull out her carryall when Jake came into the room. He stood inside the doorway and watched her solemnly.

"What's up, buddy?" she asked.

"Dad told me about Uncle Todd. Is he going to be okay?"

She paused, then shrugged. "I hope so. That's why I'm going over there, to make sure."

Jake looked down and twisted a foot sideways, making his sneaker squeak against the floor. "Are you—I mean—will you—" He glanced up at her and bit his upper lip.

"What?" Jessica coaxed.

"Will you bring Uncle Todd medicine like you do me and Dad when we're sick?"

Surprised by his question, she stared at him, silent.

"Will you?"

Jessica moistened her lips. "I'm not sure what's wrong with Uncle Todd, honey." She leaned over quickly to avoid his eyes and pulled out the carryall. "But whatever it is, I'm sure the doctors at the hospital are giving him something to make him feel better."

When Jake didn't respond, she glanced back and saw his countenance drawn and saddened.

"But they don't have your medicine, Mom," he said quietly, then turned away and left the room.

Jessica stood looking at the empty doorway for a long moment and felt a tear slide down her cheek. *Your medicine—your medicine—your—*

Briskly she wiped away the tear and went back to packing. She had to stay focused on reality, not some weird parlor trick she seemed capable of doing with headaches and stomach viruses.

As hard as she tried, however, Jessica couldn't stop thinking about what Jake said. All through folding and arranging, tucking and zipping, then finally bath and bed, his words haunted her. They eventually turned into a puzzle of sorts, becoming part of a whole something or other she couldn't quite put her finger on. It began to frustrate her, irritate her, the way trying to remember the name of an old movie or song did. The title sat right there on her tongue, waiting to be spat out, but for the life of her, she couldn't get it out.

Later, as Frank pulled her into the crook of his arm, ready for sleep, Jessica continued to struggle with the sense she was missing something. Something simple, yet significant. She tossed and turned, eventually got up for a drink of water, then went to the bathroom. When she stumbled back to bed, she covered her head with the comforter.

Finally, after two hours of restless agitation, exhaustion relieved her of the puzzle and she began to drift off.

Before long, sharp, short images flashed through her mind, like previews of dreams to come. Straitjackets, padded rooms, dimly lit corridors, and a dark, thin man—searching for her.

Chapter Seven

Samuel Johanson sat on an empty dock near Fosey Point, tossing small pieces of gravel into the water. He'd been there for hours, propped up against a lamppost, thinking about how he'd always dreaded this day—the day he'd have to send Eli out of the swamp. Now that it had come and was nearly gone, he didn't know what to do with himself. He felt like an empty glass, its contents drained and never to be replaced.

Plunk. Another bit of gravel hit the water.

For thirty-five years he'd been on a mission to return heart to heart and soul to soul. All he'd had to do was wait for the right time to make that happen. And today had been it.

Plunk. Plunk. Johanson didn't think there was enough gravel in the universe to help him think through what he was feeling right now.

He wondered, as he often did, about how different things might have been had he just ignored the incident with the pendulum and moved on with his life. For years he'd made a decent living working with the little talent he possessed as a clairvoyant. In actuality, he did better reading facial expression and body language than he did seeing the past or future. But overall he'd kept his clients happy. And he'd been relatively happy—until that day with the pregnant woman.

The event had started out innocently enough. At first, he'd sensed nothing different about the woman and the child she carried than he had with many of the other pregnant women he'd dealt with. As soon as he placed his hand over her stomach, however, all that changed. He not only felt the woman infected by Maikana, he felt a power coming from her unborn child that was different from any he'd experienced before. He knew then the child was the rasaunt. He didn't know how he knew, he just did. Until that time, he'd always thought the rasaunt to be a fable, a tale passed down through generations much like Santa Claus or the Easter Bunny or the feu-follet that was said to haunt the swamps. As was told, the rasaunt's healing power was far greater than any traiteur could possibly hope for, able to restore not only body, but mind, too. Able to battle Maikana.

Johanson knew he should have felt privileged to be in the presence of one so powerful. Instead, he'd been frightened and confused. For not only had he sensed the wonder of rasaunt in the belly of the woman, he sensed Maikana in there as well, as if the two masters, one of healing, the other of destruction, somehow lay side by side in the child. He couldn't understand how it was possible for the two powers to live in the same small space or how they had wound up there. It didn't make sense.

What made things even more confusing for Johanson was Maikana's attempt to kill the child with the pendulum. Why would he do that if he himself were part of the child? It was a question Johanson still couldn't answer. And as if all of this hadn't been enough for him to try and understand, much less deal with, Eli appeared soon after with his mother. The moment Johanson met the small boy, he sensed the same thing, rasaunt and Maikana, only not in embryo. Eli, too, carried both powers inside him.

Whether through a sudden surge in his clairvoyant voltage regulator or divine intervention, Johanson immediately knew that the boy and the unborn child were somehow connected, and that Eli wasn't meant to carry the power of rasaunt. As best he could figure, some kind of fusion accident had occurred between the children. Johanson also knew, as surely as he knew his name, that he had to play a part in the undoing or fixing of the accident.

From that day on, Johanson became obsessed with watching for signs that would indicate when it was time for the children to be reunited. Eli's most recent dreams had been that sign. The true rasaunt was ready.

There was still so much Johanson didn't know or understand. But he trusted God and the instinct he'd been given. They had brought him this far. If any more was required of him, he'd know.

Plunk. Ploop.

Johanson looked down into the rippling water. The lamp above him cast an arc of light over the dark waters. A few feet away, he saw two orbs the color and size of kumquats. They seemed to float in unison inches apart beside a flooded tree stump. They were the watchful eyes of a mama gator.

Plunk. The eyes submerged slowly.

"Really, must you persist with this irritating diversion?" a voice suddenly asked from the water below.

Startled, Johanson jerked upright. Then slowly, carefully, he leaned over the edge of the dock and peered down. He saw nothing but muddy bayou. Stray gravel fell from his hand and peppered the water.

"Come now. There is enough silt in these tributaries to last another millennium. There is no need to add more."

Johanson squinted. There, amid the ripples created by the falling gravel, appeared a large, white, distorted face just below the surface of the water. He sucked in a sharp breath and sat up quickly.

"You too late, Maikana," Johanson said firmly.

"How kind of you to offer such a warm welcome."

"Go. You got no business here."

"Oh, I beg to differ. And if I may remind you, it is your meddlesome behavior that orchestrated this outlandish adventure in the first place."

"What you mean?"

"Please, do try and keep up. Your simple mind causes me to exert far more energy than I am accustomed to."

Johanson huffed. "I don't got to listen to you

nohow." He started to get up, and the lamplight flickered.

"But you must stay. How else will you hear of your young friend's demise?"

Johanson sat back down heavily. "You can't do nuttin' to Eli."

"And what would cause you to make such a ridiculous assumption?"

" 'Cause what's suppose to be, suppose to be. Even you can't stop dat."

"Ah, then what shall be may surprise you, old man."

"You de one gonna be surprised, Maikana."

"Tsk. Still you refuse to accept the inevitable. Such futility, quite sad actually. You know, in reality you have spent over three decades mired in futility. Waiting all those years for the opportunity to reunite the ignorant with the befuddled. It would have behooved you to leave well enough alone."

"I do what I gots to do."

"Do you truly believe that sending that ignorant, illiterate baboon to her is going to make a difference? I assure you, it will not. I still remain in control of this situation."

"Dat's not true. De rasaunt gonna bring you down, Maikana, and you know dat."

"And how do you presume that will happen?"

Johanson pulled his legs up under him and didn't answer.

"As I suspected, you have not a clue. Well, allow me this reiteration in variance. Your friend will not make contact with this woman. He is, as you know, inherently predisposed to my influence. His mother belonged to me, as will he. Completely, totally, undeniably. And if I must, I will utilize every talent I possess to consume him prior to his making contact with the woman. They shall never reunite, and the purported powers to be shall, in fact, be no more."

Johanson waved dismissively. "Go, Maikana. Take youself back to de dark where you belong."

"You do realize you have signed your own death warrant by meddling."

"What you tryin' to say? I'm gonna die?"

"Correct, O brilliant one."

Johanson snorted. "So tell me somet'ing I don't know. What you 'spect? I'm eighty-four. Yeah, I'm gonna die. Everybody gotta die."

"That may be, but you will have the good fortune—or misfortune, depending on perspective—to expire by my hand."

"Yeah? And just how you gonna do dat? You don't got no hands!" Johanson leaned over and spat in the water. "I'm not stupid, no, Maikana. I know how you work. You make de mind sick, make de person see t'ings, hear t'ings until dey go mad and kill hisself or kill somebody. I know you can't do nuttin' all by youself. So right now, since it's just me and you, you like a boat wit' no motor, about good for nuttin'."

"What profound articulation."

"Go 'head, say all de big words you want. Soon de rasaunt gonna have de last say."

"Indeed. And what possible power do you suspect this rasaunt to possess that should concern me?"

"You know de power, Maikana. Eli already stop you before, and he only part rasaunt. De true rasaunt gonna stop you for good."

"Ah, but you forget, you worthless dolt, that a vast population awaits me. A countless number of minds plead for my care. The rasaunt proclaims to heal by touch, which in and of itself propagates physical limitation. I, however, am boundless, a zephyr seeking a hampered mind. Perhaps one damaged by a genetic blunder or altered via chemical misuse. There are so, so many possibilities, which brings me back to the case in point. I, you witless cretin, am far from concerned when it comes to this inconsequential human—this rasaunt."

Johanson blinked. He didn't understand much of what Maikana said, but he knew fear when he heard it. It talked big, it talked loud, and it talked too much.

"You afraid, Maikana."

A wet, boisterous laugh rang out over the swamp.

"Afraid? Preposterous! How utterly preposterous!"

"Den why you worry for? Why you bother wit' Eli and dis woman? If you not afraid, why you mad at me 'cause I sent Eli to her?"

Silence, save for the gentle sawing of crickets.

"I ax you a question, big mout'!"

The plop of a frog from bank to water.

"Uh-huh, dat's what I t'ought." Johanson nodded with satisfaction, then leaned back against the lamppost and closed his eyes. He waited a few minutes, listening, and when he didn't hear anything further from Maikana, he opened his eyes and dusted his hands across the front of his shirt. It was time to go home. His work here was done.

As he bent over to get to his feet, Johanson heard

the crunch of gravel behind him. He looked cautiously over his shoulder.

A stocky young man with a shaved head and red bandanna tied around his right forearm stepped into the semicircle of light beside Johanson. Dressed only in cut-off jean shorts and hiking boots, he sniffed and scratched his chin. "Hey—uh, bro', you got a dollar?"

Johanson glared at him, wondering what the man was doing here out in the middle of nowhere this late in the evening, and how much if anything he'd heard of his conversation with Maikana.

"So you got one?" The man shifted restlessly from one foot to the other.

"Didn't nobody teach you right, boy?" Johanson said. "You don't be sneakin' up on old people like dat."

"Uh, yeah, okay—sorry. So what about that dollar? You got one?"

"*Non.*" Johanson started to get to his feet, and the man clamped a hand down on his shoulder.

"Aw, come on, now. What about fifty cents? You got fifty cents?"

"*Non.*" Johanson shrugged off the stranger's hand and turned away.

"Okay, a quarter. Goddamn, you gotta have a quarter."

"Go back where you come from. I got nuttin' for you."

A pause filled with the rustle of leaves, the lapping of water, and a barely audible *click*.

Johanson glanced back warily and found himself

staring at a six-inch switchblade. Before he could react, the man plunged the blade into Johanson's carotid, then pulled up hard, ripping the artery open.

Horrified, Johanson tried to yell for help, but the only sound he managed was a loud gurgle. He groped at his throat. Blood—way too much blood. He felt its slick warmth, smelled its coppery pungency, heard it spew through his fingers. Slowly, involuntarily, Johanson slumped to one side.

The young man knelt beside him quickly and shoved his face next to Johanson's so they were nearly nose to nose. Then he widened his eyes. Reflected in them was a white, bulbous face with a vertical mouth. A laughing, vertical mouth.

Chapter Eight

At 8:45 the next morning, Jessica boarded Northwest Airlines flight 256, direct jet service from Memphis to Baton Rouge. There'd been a direct flight to Lafayette, which would have meant only a twenty-minute drive to the clinic, but it was shuttle service on American Eagle, and Jessica didn't do small planes.

She swung her bag up into the overhead bin, shoving it between a duct-taped suitcase and a Just Do It sports bag, then settled into her assigned window seat. No one was sitting in the middle or aisle seat yet, and she hoped they would stay vacant so she could be alone. She shoved her purse under the seat in front of her, then fastened the seat belt tightly around her waist.

Just as she leaned her head back against the seat, a young woman with a freckle-faced boy wrapped around one hip showed up. *So much for being alone.* The woman placed the toddler in the middle seat and, with deft fingers, managed to snap the seat belt amid squirming arms and legs.

The woman smiled at Jessica. "Hi, my name's Karen. This is C. J.," she said, tousling the boy's hair.

Jessica smiled courteously. "Hi." *Great,* she thought wearily, *a talker.* She grabbed the flight magazine from the stiff pocket on the seat in front of her and opened it, quickly feigning interest. Karen, evidently catching the hint, pulled out a paperback from the diaper bag she'd placed under the seat.

A bored female voice crackled over the intercom: "Please make sure your tray tables are stowed and your seats are in an upright—"

"O McDonyo had a farm," C. J. sang while flipping through a nursery rhyme book he held upside down.

Jessica closed the magazine and leaned her forehead against the narrow window. She watched as the plane backed away from the jetway, engine whining in full protest. Ground crewmen in khaki shorts waved orange batons, signaling in crisp arm movements: left—straight ahead—stop. They reminded Jessica of the crossing guard near Jake's school. She caught her reflection in the window and saw dark shadows under her eyes and lines creasing the sides of her mouth. *God, I feel old.*

She closed her eyes, feeling the rush and lift of the plane on takeoff. There had only been one other time when she felt this old, this inadequate. The day her mother died. It had been something she couldn't fix. Something she couldn't put a bandage on, give medicine to, reprimand, or encourage. Something that changed her life forever without her control or permission. It just was. She was afraid this issue with Todd was going to be another "just was."

"Life isn't a cakewalk, Jessica," her mother would have said. "You gotta eat what it dishes out and just hope you don't choke."

But you did, Mom. . . .

They had lived in Borrow, located a few miles west of Lafayette. The town was big enough, by south Louisiana standards anyway, to have one caution light and a Radio Shack on Main Street. A pea-graveled road, named Guidry Lane, flanked Highway 92 on its north end. The road had been named after her father. He'd owned most of the land down that one-mile strip and developed it by building shanty rent houses for low-income families. Her father had been considered the wealthiest man in Borrow, that endowment established by the fact that their house was finished in brick and not a rental.

Guidry Lane ran parallel to a coulee that meandered through the heart of the tiny town. Every house on the west side of Guidry had Washman's Coulee as part of its backyard. Its purpose, as far as the local residents were concerned, was local dump, sewer plant, and the best snapping turtle hole in the South. It was the primary reason ninety percent of Borrow was listed in the city hall records as a flood zone. The old folks used to say that if a mouse pissed in Borrow, it would flood. It certainly seemed that way. Especially during spring, when the season's showers would find every kid hauling floatees and beach balls to swollen ditches.

When the water in the coulee would get high enough, and its current fast enough to keep most of the debris out of the way, much less the floating turds, Jessica and Todd would take an old tractor tire tube and make believe they were Huckleberry Finn and Tom Sawyer. They would balance their legs along the rubber doughnut and push through the muddy water with broken broomsticks, imagining themselves on the mighty Mississippi.

Once, Jessica had gotten brave enough to dangle her legs over the edge of the tube and drag them through the water. When she'd pulled her legs in, she noticed a slimy, black leech stuck to her calf. It hadn't hurt, but it scared her to death, and she couldn't bring herself to touch it. Todd had looked at her with a mixture of curiosity and amazement and, without saying a word, yanked the leech right off. It was the first time she remembered feeling being taken care of.

The neighbors on Guidry had been a mixed lot. Some only stayed the length of their six-month lease, then moved on. Others, like Mrs. Delahoussy, seemed to have been there since the creation of dirt. Jessica always liked her. She was a warm, grandmotherly woman who always smelled of brownies and hugged like she really meant it. She kept a supply of Chiclets gum in a kitchen cabinet so Todd and Jessica would have a treat when they visited her with their mother. Todd always looked for the pink ones. He said they tasted like Pepto-Bismol, which was great with him. He would drink the stuff by the bottle if he could get away with it. Jessica liked the white gum squares. That was until she got older and discovered that Ex-Lax gum tasted the same way.

Then there'd been Mrs. Guilbeau, who lived on the far west side of Guidry Lane. None of the kids ever went there. During the summer, when it was too hot for a baseball game or the coulee was too shallow for rafting, they'd watch for her. Squatting behind the old pine tree across the street, they'd whisper and watch as Mrs. Guilbeau walked God-so-slowly to her mailbox. Her thin, bent frame seemed barely capable of withstanding the force of a breeze. Jessica always thought her to be just an old lady with wrinkly skin, but Linda Pellerin, who was in Jessica's third-grade class and lived two houses down from Mrs. Guilbeau, swore the woman was a witch. Linda claimed she'd seen strange lights going on and off in Mrs. Guilbeau's house at all hours of the night. It didn't matter if it was true or not. None of the kids was going to go over there to find out.

Catercorner to Jessica's house lived the Armonts. Their house was the only other nonrental on Guidry, and the four Armont boys made sure everyone knew it. Two of the boys, Robert and Markus, she'd had very few dealings with. They'd gone off to college by the time she was eight and Todd was five. That left Casey and Lyle Armont. Lyle, Jessica could handle. The only thing he ever did was shoot off his mouth about how they didn't have to rent from any Guidry while he picked boogers out of his nose.

Casey, on the other hand, was just plain mean. At nine years old, he outweighed both Todd and Jessica by at least fifty pounds. The fashion repertoire Casey used to enhance his self-proclaimed "coolmeister" image stayed consistent. It included a blond crew cut consistently oiled into quarter-inch spikes, horizontally striped pullovers that didn't quite hide his stomach, and a perpetual butt crack that peeped out from the top of his cutoff jeans.

Every time Todd played in the front yard, Casey would shout from his front porch, "Whatcha doin', stupid?" and throw rocks at him.

Things got worse with Casey after Jessica and Todd's parents divorced. They found themselves moving into one of the small rentals on Guidry because their mother couldn't afford the upkeep on the brick house anymore. Alimony and child support were nonexistent given that their father had taken off, address unknown. That was when Casey Armont went into full swing. He graduated from teasing Todd to pushing him around.

"Whatsa matter, bug-eyes? Now you gotta live like the poor people? Whatsa matter? Your daddy don't love you no more? Did you make him run away because he couldn't stand lookin' at your big, ugly bug-eyes?"

Todd would just stare up at him and never say a word. Tears would stream down his face, and he would clench and unclench his chubby hands at his sides.

One June afternoon, Casey crossed the line. Stepping right up to Todd, he shoved his potbelly into him, pushing him back. "Whatsa matter with you? You chicken or somethin'?" He let out a shrill laugh. "Now I get it, puke breath. Your daddy ran away 'cause you're a chicken." Casey stuck his hands under his armpits, then flapped both arms. "Pock, pock, can't love a chicken. Nope, ya can't love a chicken!"

Jessica walked out of the house in time to hear the taunts and see Casey hovering over her cowering brother. "Hey, leave him alone!" she yelled. Without thinking, she took off in a flatfooted run and plowed into the boy, shoving him away from Todd.

Casey stumbled backward, his large arms whirling to regain his balance. He grunted when he fell, his legs swinging high into the air, and his head snapping hard against the ground. He rolled left then right, like a turtle caught on its back, trying to get to his feet. Finally he rolled over on his stomach, pulled his knees up, and knelt.

"You piece of white trash!" he screamed.

Jessica pressed closer to Todd and put an arm around his trembling shoulders. He turned his face, almost tucking it under her arm.

"The baby's mama's gotta fight his battles for him?" Casey shouted, spit flying from his thick lips. "Whatcha gonna do, skinny? Beat me up? Ha!" He stood up and parked his fists on his hips.

"Leave him alone, you big tub," Jessica shouted back. "He's just a little kid." She felt Todd pull closer to her.

Casey swaggered over to Jessica, pulling his shorts up as he walked. A nasty grin spread over his face, and his eyes narrowed into slivers. "You talk big for a piece of white trash."

Before Jessica had time to react, Todd spun out from under her arm and charged headfirst into

Casey's midsection. The result was minimal. Casey kept his balance, and he charged back with fists raised toward Todd. Jessica jumped forward, her right fist cocked, and punched Casey across the nose. Blood gushed out of it immediately, shocking Jessica and sending Casey running home, crying for his grandmother.

To Jessica, protecting Todd from Casey had been easy. There were other things, harder things she'd had to insulate him from.

Before their parents' divorce, a nightly ritual of arguing would echo through the Guidrys' family room and carry down the hallway to Jessica's bedroom. As her parents' voices heated up, she would sneak into the hall and crouch in the corner created by the foyer and family-room walls. From there, she could hear everything and keep tabs on how serious things were getting. Her mother had been the screamer. Her father, low-toned or noncommenting, usually sat in his recliner, newspaper to nose, doing his best to tune out his wife's rage.

Jessica would hear the newspaper rattle as her mother poked it incessantly. She heard words like ". . . never pay attention to me . . . running around . . . lousy piece of white trash." That one Jessica was familiar with. The rest she hadn't been so sure about.

When the situation got out of hand, and their parents' shouts reached wake-the-neighborhood range, Todd would shuffle down the hall in his brown-and-white cowboy and Indian pajamas. He'd sit next to Jessica and rest his head on her lap while they listened together, each silently wondering what they had done to make their parents so angry.

"Don't they love us, Jess?" Todd would ask quietly, his small voice shaking. He already knew her answer, having asked this a thousand times, but he'd repeat the question anyway.

She would put her arm around his shoulders and rock her knees gently, humming as the angry voices crested, then fell. "Of course they do, Toddy," she would say to reassure him, but not really knowing for sure. Their parents never had much time for them. Both stayed wrapped up in their own worlds and their problems. In fact, there was only one thing Jessica had been sure of back then: "Always remember, we have each other, and I'll always love you, Toddy."

After their father left town, the nights were different. Jessica's mom yelled at her then. The newspaper wasn't there to rattle anymore, so she used Jessica's shoulders instead. Jessica just made sure Todd wasn't around when she sensed her mother's need for something to hit.

As bad as things were, the divorce took its toll on Todd. He started getting into fights at school, and his grades plummeted. The older he got, the angrier he became and the more he pulled away from his small family. Their mother, in alternating states of exhaustion and depression, simply gave up on him.

Finally, at seventeen and not long after Jessica got married, Todd took off, leaving only a note to his sister saying he would keep in touch. He did for a while. Collect calls came in once a month from Oregon, Michigan, or Florida, where Todd would cheerfully announce he was alive and well and just hanging out with friends. That was until two years ago when their mother died on his thirty-first birthday. Todd's calls became less frequent after that. The last time they'd spoken was five months ago, and she hadn't seen him since the funeral. In their last phone conversation, Jessica had tried to convince Todd to move to Memphis, to live with Frank and her, but he needed time, he said, "time and space."

The jerk and squeal of the plane's landing broke Jessica's reverie. She drew in a deep breath and glanced out the window once more.

I'm coming, little brother. I'm coming.

Chapter Nine

The dream unfolded for Eli in dazzling colors. He stood naked and knee-deep in the bluest water he'd ever seen. The shore lay less than a foot ahead, covered in sand so white it hurt his eyes to look at it. Birds with three-foot wingspans flew overhead, their feathered exhibition creating a medley of fierce reds, brilliant yellows, and shimmering emerald greens.

Smells, contrary to what his eyes beheld, wafted over him. Roasted turkey with corn-bread dressing. Melting cheese, fresh baked bread. Gasoline fumes and rotting vegetation.

His ears picked up even more contrariety. Instead of hearing the squawk and whoop of birds or the gentle lapping of water, Eli heard rumbles and sputters, clacks and ticks, all of which seemed to crest and then fall without an associated relevance.

The incongruities didn't bother him, but the fact

that he was sinking did. He strained to lift his feet from the water, but they felt mired in heavy, engulfing mud. Tiring quickly, he stopped struggling for a little while and wound up sinking deeper into the silt. Even now the water level reached him at midthigh.

While attempting to figure out how he would get out of this mess, Eli sensed someone watching him from the shoreline. He glanced up and saw her, the woman from his other dreams. Only now she looked to be around two years old. Same dark hair, same eyes. As though she knew he was sizing her up, she turned her back to him and allowed the wind to sweep the hair away from the back of her neck so he could see the berry-shaped birthmark. Once confirmed, she faced him again and offered her hand.

Eli hesitated. He wanted the help desperately, for he knew if he didn't get out of this bog soon, he would eventually be swallowed up completely. But she was so small, so petite, he was afraid if he took her hand, he'd wind up pulling her into the mire with him.

She leaned over slightly, signaling for him to hurry and grab on to her.

So he did.

Her strength surprised him, and he soon felt his legs being freed of the mud. He looked down, watching the liberation process in amazement. No silt or stain remained on his thighs as they slowly emerged from the water's surface. His knees soon followed suit. Then suddenly all movement, all progress, ceased.

Eli glanced up. The child smiled at him and pointed to their joined hands. Only then did Eli feel the tingling in his fingers and palm. Their skin had melded together, forming a solid mass of flesh. Within the mass, he felt muscle and bone merging, becoming one. Frightened, he tried pulling away but found himself stuck fast. The harder he tugged, the more he sensed himself being drawn into her, not only his flesh and bone but the very essence of who he was. He opened his mouth to cry out, to beg her to stop, but was unable to make a sound.

Then, from above them, appeared two wirelike tentacles. Both had points sharper than a finely honed needle, and they seemed to drop from the heavens without origin. Eli knew to whom they belonged, however. He'd seen these tentacles before, protruding from either side of Maikana's head. The child must have known as well, for she began to struggle violently. The more she fought, the faster Eli felt himself being drawn into her, devoured by her. Small tabs of skin began to peel away from the arm he had extended out to her.

The tentacles wavered for a few moments above the joined flesh, then without warning they speared into Eli's forearm, the sharp points traveling deep.

Eli screamed but heard no sound. He gritted his teeth, and just when he thought he'd die from the pain . . .

His eyelids fluttered, sending spasmodic messages of light to his brain—dream's over. Holding his partially fetal-positioned body still, Eli opened his eyes, inhaled deeply, gratefully, then felt a dull throb in his left forearm. He glanced down curiously.

The rat must have been gnawing on him for some time.

He lay quietly, watching it chew, watching droplets of blood fall to the cardboard that was his bed. He frowned as pain spread through his arm like hot oil. Inching his knees apart, he untangled his fingers that were pressed between them.

At the first whisper of movement, the rodent froze, its teeth still embedded in the dirty flesh. Before it could free itself, Eli snatched it up and held it squealing and squirming before him. He felt sorry for the animal. Slick and black, it could have passed for a wet kitten. *It's hungry,* he thought. Eli understood hungry. He hadn't eaten since yesterday morning.

He took notice of how wildly the rat's head swung about as though independent from the rest of its body. Its teeth were bared for attack. He lowered his hand to release it, then stopped, confused by the sudden hatred welling up inside him for the creature. Its eyes angered him, those shiny, ebony dots that bulged expressionless.

Eli tightened his grip on the vermin's neck, and the eyes protruded noticeably. Its mouth molded open, forgetting all notion of revenge. A shrill, wretched squeal tore from the animal as it begged for life, for air. Its hind legs wrapped and twirled in a desperate attempt toward freedom. Eli squeezed harder, his thumb crushing the miniature windpipe until the rat hung silent, blood spilling from its mouth.

The eyes looked the same to him in death as they had in life, blank—just like his mother's had been.

He threw the rat to one side, and when it thudded against a brick wall and fell to the ground, Eli frowned, his mind instantly blank.

Where'd the dead rat come from? Assuming some

cat had simply abandoned its morning meal, he shrugged and rolled over on his back.

He lay there for a moment, bringing his hands to rest on his stomach. The noises of morning sounded odd to him. Instead of locusts and croakers, he heard the rumble and sputter of engines, as well as voices and hurried footsteps, which swelled, then tapered off into echoes as people crossed the mouth of the alley where he lay.

Yawning, Eli sat up and twisted his body from left to right, working a cramp out of his back. Last night had been the first time he'd not slept on his moss-filled mattress or on the bank of some bayou, and he figured he didn't care much for the concrete and cardboard replacement. Nor did he much care for the world outside of the swamp. Too much was different out here, including himself. His brain felt cloudy.

After Johanson had dropped him off at the pier yesterday, Eli had watched the old man chug away in his boat until it was out of sight. Strangely enough, he'd felt no fear at being left alone to find his way through places he'd never been before. He'd simply taken out the pendulum Johanson had given him, dangled it in front of him, then walked the rest of the day, following its lead. Just as dusk fell, he flagged down a man in a pickup, who agreed to give him a lift only if he rode in the back. When the man dropped him off thirty minutes later, Eli had been too exhausted to move on. So he found a secluded area, a flat piece of cardboard, and rested. It took him a while to fall asleep, not so much because of the unfamiliar noises but because his mind seemed to be playing tricks on him. He'd feel a tickling sensation on his elbow, lift his arm to investigate, and find large pieces of skin hanging loose from his limb. Petrified yet curious, he'd reach out to touch it and find nothing there, his skin just as normal as it had ever been.

At first, Eli suspected Maikana might have had something to do with the strange visions, but he'd never known Maikana to induce hallucinations without also making some kind of grandiose appearance. Eli finally convinced himself that the gasoline fumes from nearby traffic were messing with his brain.

But where did the rat come from? Eli lifted his hands and squinted at them. He sensed some connection between them and the rodent, but his mind wouldn't clarify what that connection was.

Frustrated, he got to his feet and pulled the pendulum out of his pocket. Immediately it started to swing, nodding heavily toward the west. Eli sensed by the strength of its pull that he was getting closer to the woman. Johanson had told him that he would know what to do once he found her. So far, Eli still didn't even have a clue.

He lifted the pendulum to eye level to see if height would make a difference in its direction, and as he did, he spotted an inch-long flap of skin hanging just below his elbow. He swallowed hard and reached out with his free hand to touch it. This time it didn't disappear. This time it fell off in his hand.

Chapter Ten

Two hours after renting a Grand Am at the airport and making a phone call to Municipal for directions, Jessica was heading north on Veron Road in Broussard just as she'd been instructed. Three blocks down, past Rowen's Eye Clinic and Suire's Med Supplies, on the left, was the entrance gate to the clinic. She turned in, then drove almost another block to the back of the L-shaped building before she found the visitors' parking lot. It was nearly empty save for a blue Taurus with a busted taillight and crooked bumper parked in the south corner.

Jessica parked the car and killed the engine. She sat for a moment, both hands lying limp on top of the steering wheel, and surveyed the building.

The clinic was two stories of staggered pale bricks that looked as though it had been built in an age when architectural expression gave way to practicality and state budgetary constraints. The second floor featured spindly louvered windows framed in aluminum strips that had bled rust down the length of the structure.

The bottom floor had no windows, only a door at the end of either wing. Each was dressed with an overhead awning that jutted out like a worn bill cap. The canopy on the right sagged, looking apologetic in its attempt to shelter the metal door beneath it. A concrete bench with a jagged chunk missing from its seat had been placed at the far end of the right wing under a massive oak. The canopy off the left wing didn't look as pathetic as its brother. It hovered over a glass door that had the word EXIT stenciled across the middle from the inside.

Jessica suddenly realized that the only sound she could hear was her breathing. For such a huge place, it was unnervingly quiet. There were no hustling sounds of the busy. No sounds at all. Just an emptiness that echoed the oppressive silence of decay. A gloom pressed into her. *If all the loneliness in the world,* she thought, *every heartache, every anguish could be packaged and housed in one place, this would be it.* She started to feel light-headed and queasy.

"GO RIGHT!"

The shrill command startled Jessica, and she reflexively slammed a hand against the driver's-side window to keep the sound, or whatever had made it, from hitting her face. Through splayed fingers, she saw a couple of teenage boys racing on skateboards along the driveway of a run-down apartment building across the street.

Exhaling loudly, she tapped the window lightly with her fingertips. "Cool it," she told herself firmly. A trickle of sweat ran down the side of her face, and she rubbed at it briskly. With the engine off, the car had quickly heated up to what now felt like three hundred degrees. Her linen pants and blouse felt shrink-wrapped around her body. Jessica reached over the seat, unzipped her travel bag, and seesawed the Wal-Mart sack from it. *Should've put his stuff in a nice carry bag,* she thought. *Too late now.* She shoved her purse under the seat and got out of the car.

As she walked up to the glass door, she noticed there was a push bar on the inside to exit but no handle on the outside to enter. Just inside was a narrow vestibule floored in gray-and-beige-speckled linoleum. It dead-ended, after a few feet, into a windowless door. She sidestepped to the edge of the building and peered down its length. An uneven sidewalk ran parallel to the outside wall. A sign, fastened to a brick, read: "Visitors' Entrance." Beneath it, constructed from black electrical tape, was an arrow, that pointed back to the front of the building.

"Figures," Jessica said. She chuffed sharply and started down the long walk.

Her feet meandered around the concrete path's cracks and chips. *Step on a crack, break your mother's back,* she thought, then wondered what kid had thought up such a rhyme.

Maybe a kid whose mother swung at her butt and legs with the buckle of a belt just because the bathtub overfilled with water and wet the floor. Or maybe—just maybe because that kid accidentally knocked over a favorite knickknack that shattered into a million pieces. Yes, maybe when the beatings rode up high on her calves and back she'd sing that little ditty quietly, under her breath. And in the morning, with the welts and black-and-blue marks still stinging under thick blue jeans and a long-sleeved blouse, she'd walk along the school yard sidewalk, stepping purposefully on each open crevice and hum that little rhyme, that wish, that canticle of remorseful hope.

Jessica shook the images from her mind as she approached the front of the building. A bulky canister filled to overflowing with ash-colored sand and cigarette butts flanked the short flight of steps she took to the entrance.

Cool, peppermint-scented air welcomed her as she entered the foyer. A few feet beyond the lobby was a spacious waiting room, drab in its beige-painted cinder-block walls and void of furnishings except for an enclosed reception area. The cubicle looked like a giant box in the middle of an empty warehouse. Sheets of scratched Plexiglas formed the upper portion of the box. An arched opening had been cut out of the bottom.

A stubby woman stood inside the box near a collection of filing cabinets with her back to Jessica. She seemed preoccupied with stacks of manila folders that fanned out along a foot-wide cornice. Jessica watched for a moment as the woman flopped a hand lazily over an open file drawer. She picked up a folder, studied its tab like it held a subliminal message that needed decoding, then slowly put the file into the cabinet.

Jessica cleared her throat. The woman didn't turn around. She cleared her throat again.

"Yeah, yeah. I'll be right there," the woman said irritably.

Slightly taken aback and beginning to feel a little more than awkward, Jessica glared at the woman's back.

File up, look, twist, put in, turn back. File up, look, twist, put in, turn back.

Jessica tried again: "Excuse me, I'm looking for Todd Guidry."

File up, look, twist, put in, turn back.

"The *police* department told me to come here." Jessica hoped her enunciation of the local authority title would cause a reaction.

It didn't.

File up, look, twist, put in, turn back.

The sudden chirping from the phone did make the woman turn around—eventually. She wore white slacks and a matching tunic that zipped in the front. A large, plastic tag with the name MILDRED CARRIER stenciled across it adorned her breast pocket. Her hair, short and salt-and-peppered, was slicked back from a broad forehead that looked like it had never known a worry despite the fact that she must have been nearing sixty.

Mildred scowled as she picked up the phone, her gray eyes clear and suspicious and intent on Jessica's face when she placed the receiver to her ear. "Municipal," she said, the word sounding wrapped in thick mucus. It made Jessica clear her own throat. "Yeah, five o'clock." Mildred cast her eyes toward the ceiling. "Yeah, sure." She banged the receiver down on its bed.

"Yeah?" Mildred finally addressed Jessica through the plastic divider.

Jessica bit the inside of her cheek, then said, "Jessica LeJeune. I'm here to see Todd Guidry. The police department contacted me and said they were bringing him here." Jessica stepped closer to the scarred plastic, all awkwardness replaced with building anger. "Will you let someone know I'm here?"

"Are you a family member?"

"I'm his sister. My name is Jessica—Guidry—LeJeune." She wanted to add, "Is that family enough for you, you thickheaded piece of shit?" but didn't.

Mildred slowly dropped her eyes to a clipboard, and she flipped through the few pages attached to it. "Yeah, he's here," she said. She placed a thick hand on top of the counter and looked up, her face a sardonic mask.

Jessica bit down harder on her cheek, causing a sharp pain to shoot across the side of her mouth. She winced and released it. "Could you tell me where I can find him?"

"Sure, but it won't do you any good."

"And why's that?"

"Policy."

"Policy?"

"That's right."

Jessica drew closer until her nose nearly touched the divider. "Mildred," she said evenly, "what the hell are you talking about?"

Mildred's eyes became slits, and her lips tightened

like taut rubber bands. "Policy here is that no one—especially *family*—can have contact with the patient for at least one week." She let out a sarcastic huff and backed up a few inches. "Did you bring his clothes?"

"What do you mean I can't see him for a week?" Jessica asked loudly. She pressed a hand against the glass, inadvertently releasing the Wal-Mart bag. A clatter echoed through the room as a can of deodorant hit the floor and rolled out of the bag.

Mildred wasn't fazed. "I told you. Policy."

"I want to talk to someone in charge," Jessica demanded.

Mildred stared at her, amused.

"Do you hear me? I want to talk with your supervisor or the doctor in charge."

Mildred's expression became one of mild aggravation, as though Jessica were a gnat buzzing around her ear and needed to be swatted away. Picking up the phone, she pressed two buttons and waited. She wasn't glaring at Jessica now. That game had been played and lost.

Jessica folded her arms across her chest and widened her stance, watching as the woman barked to someone on the other end of the phone.

"Yeah, there's someone here who wants to see Todd Guidry. His sister. Yeah, Jessica LeJeune. I told her that. She wants to see someone in *charge*. Yeah—all right." She slammed down the receiver and scratched the back of her head.

Jessica lifted her chin, awaiting the verdict.

"Go through that door," Mildred said, tossing her head to the right, "when you hear the buzzer." Her hand reached under the counter. "Go down to the end of the hallway and take a right. There's gonna be a door straight ahead. That's the commons area. Someone'll let you in and talk to you there." She poked a finger hard against the glass. "You're gonna have to leave that bag up here."

Jessica was a bit surprised the woman had even noticed she'd carried one in. She picked up the bag, herded the deodorant can back into it, then looked for an opening in Mildred's cage. She didn't see one. Not up to another pissing contest, Jessica lifted the bag, flattened it as much as she could, then reluctantly pushed it through the hole in the Plexiglas. She had a strong suspicion that Mildred Carrier was going to do a thorough inspection of the contents.

"Please make sure Todd gets this."

"He'll get it," Mildred answered tartly, not looking at her.

Heading toward the door, Jessica looked back over her shoulder. "Thank you," she said, hoping the small offering of truce would at least allow Todd to get his underwear.

The buzzer sounded, and the door opened heavily when she pulled. She walked into the hallway, and a flutter rode through her. Twenty feet down the narrow corridor, the flutter became flat-out fear, and Jessica wanted to run through the building shouting Todd's name. Instead, she concentrated on the sound of her footsteps and turned right at the end of the hall.

She hadn't quite reached the door ahead of her when it swung open and a young, muscular man greeted her.

"How ya doin'?" he asked, a broad smile filling his face. He had blond hair trimmed short and combed stylishly away from a round, almost feminine face. He stood with his left shoulder against the door, holding it open at half-mast. An overlapping of whispers and grunts came from inside the room behind him. "Come on in. They called Dr. Rocheaux. He's here somewhere making rounds and shouldn't be but just a minute." He swept his right hand down and low. His white uniform, similar to the one Mildred wore, whispered a starchy crackle, and Jessica expected him to finish off with "After you, milady."

"Thank you—Russell," Jessica said, reading the tag pinned to his jacket.

His grin widened. Jessica returned it warily and stepped in front of him, feeling his eyes follow the top of her head as she walked by.

The room was of considerable size, windowless, and smelled of corn chips and stale sweat. The walls and floor were the same gray and beige as in the hallway, only with signs of much heavier wear. Metal folding chairs accompanied six tables that were lined up cafeteria-style in the middle of the room. Leaning over one of them was a heavyset, dark-skinned man, his face gleaming with perspiration. His nostrils flared and pulsed as he studied the face of his scrawny companion who sat across from him, shoveling through a family-sized bag of Fritos. The small man grunted heavily as he pressed more corn chips into his mouth, stretching his cheeks out farther and farther until he looked like a mutant chipmunk.

"He's gonna do it! He's gonna hurl! Gonna do it! Gonna hurl!" the large man chanted excitedly.

Feeling as though she had intruded on some secret ritual, Jessica looked away quickly and surveyed the rest of the room. Two card tables stood near the far right wall, both scarred with old cigarette burns. A middle-aged man with gray hair that clumped together in greasy ropes sat at one of them. When he spotted Jessica looking his way, he shifted hurriedly in his seat, folded his hands in his lap, and began rocking the upper part of his body. His pale, thin lips moved frantically, emphatically, as though in muted debate.

At the back of the room, a television sat high on the wall, the volume barely audible. Two women sat reticently watching the screen, one absently twisting strands of hair around her finger.

Against the left wall stood an enclosed cubicle like the one in the reception area, only smaller. In it were two women, one reading from a folder and the other hovering over tiny paper cups.

"You can sit here," Russell said, pointing to the first table near the door. He must have sensed her hesitation, because he added, "I'll be right here until Dr. Rocheaux gets here. Okay?" He glanced over at the guy with the puffy cheeks. "Hey, Ben, stop with the Fritos! You don't want me to take them away from you, do you?"

Ben grabbed the bag and pulled it tight against his chest, crushing most of the chips. His cheeks now a purplish pink, he looked up at Russell and shook his head.

"Sorry," Russell said, turning his attention back to Jessica. He pulled out a chair, sat, and folded his hands together with an exaggerated flourish. "So, your brother's here and you've come to see him?"

Jessica felt nearly every eye in the room turn toward her as she sat down. "Yes," she said. "I was contacted yesterday and told he was being transported here." She looked at Russell and felt a sudden need to explain the lapse of time in her arrival. "I live in Memphis."

Russell chuckled heartily. "I've been to Memphis," he announced. "A couple of years ago. Got to see the King's house and airplane and all. It was great! It must be terrific, getting to see it anytime you want to, huh?"

Jessica smiled politely. There was something openly innocent about Russell, and she knew he would be floored and filled with a thousand questions if she admitted she'd never been to Presley's house. The thought of going through a dead man's home and looking through his belongings and private life gave her the creeps. But she didn't feel like playing fifty questions. "Yes," she answered simply, then changed the subject. "Have you worked here long?"

"A bit over a year."

Jessica heard a chair screech roughly across the floor and looked up to see one of the television watchers making her way over to them. The young woman wore pink shorts and a red-and-blue plaid flannel shirt with the sleeves rolled up. Pink slippers with open backs flopped loudly against her heels when she walked. A black, lopsided ponytail hung over her right shoulder.

"Hey, Terri," Russell said to the girl. "How ya doin'?" He sat back in his chair, and Terri moved closer to Jessica. "Me and this nice lady are talkin'. Is there something I can get for you?"

Terri shuffled up to Jessica's chair and pressed her shins against the edge of the seat. "You got a cigarette?" she asked loudly, her eyes darting from Jessica to Russell, then across the room. "I can have a cigarette?"

Startled, Jessica leaned away from the girl. "I don't smoke," she said hurriedly.

"Now, Terri," Russell said, "you know there's no smokin' in here. You gotta wait for break time, and you'll get your cigarettes in the smoke room."

Terri didn't register understanding or caring at Russell's reminder of common-room etiquette. She fixed her gaze on Jessica and pulled at the bottom of her shirt nervously. "You got a cigarette?"

"I don't smoke," Jessica repeated louder. She looked at Russell anxiously.

He unfolded his large hands and smiled at Jessica. "Come on now, Terri," he said. "Leave the lady alone. You know you can't smoke in here anyway."

Terri started shifting from one foot to the other as though she meant to walk through the chair. Jessica stiffened. The girl was so close and her gaze so intense, it frightened her. She fought the impulse to jump up and bolt for the door.

Terri cupped a hand over her mouth as though intending to cough. She leaned closer to Jessica, then jerked her hand away quickly. "You got a cigarette?" she asked again, louder this time. Her emerald eyes blazed, and she began to wag her head from side to side. "Yeah, yeah, the bitch's got a cigarette. She ain't sharin'. She ain't gonna hand it over."

Jessica leaned back so far and hard against her chair that it wobbled, and she struggled to keep from falling over.

"Come on, Terri," Russell said, already on his feet and moving toward her. "Be a good girl. Go watch the soaps or somethin', okay?"

Terri plucked at the buttons of her shirt and tossed her head back, yelling, "You got a cigarette?"

Frito Ben pulled his chair closer to the table, and another teeth-clenching screech filled the room. As if on cue, his partner resumed his enthusiastic mantra. "He's gonna hurl! He's gonna hurl!"

Terri stepped back slowly as Russell approached her. She grabbed her ponytail and yanked hard. "Yeah, she got one. Look it, she got cigarettes. The bitch's stashin' 'em in her drawers. That's what she's doin', stashin' 'em in her drawers."

"Okay, here we go," Russell said, taking the girl by the arm and pulling her gently. She let go of her hair and crooked her arm around his. Russell glanced back over his shoulder at Jessica. "Be right back."

Jessica watched nervously as he walked Terri back to her seat and pushed down gently on her shoulders until she sat. The girl quickly snatched a strand of her hair and began twisting it around her index finger. Russell patted her shoulders, his smile broad and open.

Jessica stood up slowly, trying to be inconspicuous. Peripherally she noticed the man at the card table rocking harder now, his lips still moving in silent fury. Ben, who had evidently been distracted by Terri, turned back to his attentive friend and resumed shoving corn chips into his mouth by the handful. The women in the cubicle, who Jessica assumed were nurses, looked up only briefly to watch Russell with Terri.

A buzzer sounded, and the door next to Jessica clicked open. A balding man with wire-rimmed glasses walked briskly into the room. His eyes darted about before settling on Jessica.

"Ms. LeJeune?" he asked, marching up to her.

Jessica never thought five feet five was significantly tall for a woman. But now she felt like an Amazon as she stared at the pink wrinkles on the top of the man's head. "Yes, I'm Jessica LeJeune," she answered, holding out her hand.

He shook it limply. "I'm Dr. Rocheaux," he said. "I hear there's been a misunderstanding?" He took his hand from hers and tucked it beneath one arm.

"A deputy from Lafayette contacted me yesterday and said that my brother was going to be brought here," Jessica said. "I'd like to see him. Can you tell me anything about his condition?"

"Todd Guidry is your brother?"

"Yes."

Rocheaux unfolded his arm and leaned against the table. "No one explained our policy to you?" he asked, pushing his glasses up to the top of his head.

"When I called yesterday, the receptionist told me to bring clothes and toiletries. She never said anything about a policy." Jessica shifted uncomfortably.

Suddenly, a loud "YO!" and thump came from

the neighboring table. Jessica and Rocheaux turned simultaneously.

Frito Ben's face was now a vivid purple, and globs of pasty corn chips mixed with what looked like ham chunks and cottage cheese flowed out of his mouth in waves. Ben's rooting companion pounded on the table, his face bright with triumph. "I knew it!" he shouted. He leaned over, examining the clots on the table like they were precious jewels.

Before Rocheaux could get to him, the big man began to poke at the spongy lumps with a finger.

Russell, who had wandered off to chat with the nurses, shouted, "John-John, stop that! Stop it now!" His long legs giant-stepped their way to the table, and he snatched the man's hand away from the mess. The steady wall of vomit from Ben had stopped and was now spreading across the table in a voluminous pool.

"Russell," Rocheaux barked, his face paling dramatically. "Get that man cleaned up, now!" He glanced over at Jessica, who turned her head to keep from retching.

"Yes, sir, getting to it," Russell said. He'd already reached John-John and put his arm over his shoulders, nudging him toward the nurses' alcove. One of the women came out with a pan and towel. She took John-John, who was still grinning and claiming, "I knew it. I knew it!" and led him out of the room. Russell took the pan and towel and headed back to the undigested corn chips.

Terri jumped up from her seat and hurried over to Ben's table. She looked at the mess like it was yesterday's newspaper: something there, just not important anymore.

Rocheaux rubbed his eyes with a thumb and forefinger. "I apologize, Ms. LeJeune," he said, pulling his glasses back over his eyes. "I don't usually meet people in here. It's just that my office is occupied at the moment." His eyes didn't meet hers as he talked. He was busy watching Russell clean up Ben and the table. "There are reasons for the one-week, no-visitation policy." He turned and walked to the cubicle, where the remaining nurse handed him a stack of folders. He spoke up to compensate for the distance. "Once a patient arrives, there are many issues that need to be addressed. Stabilization is of the utmost importance, and, of course, there is the need to process the diagnosis, the medication needed, and the appropriate therapy." He cradled the folders and turned sharply, heading for the door. "Dr. Lee is the one responsible for Todd's case. You'll need to contact him regarding his condition. Now, if you'll excuse me—"

"Wait a minute, please," Jessica pleaded. "Can't you make one exception? I just want to see him, to make sure he's all right."

Rocheaux did a quick twist of the wrist and looked at his watch. "There has to be time for stabilization," he reiterated, reaching for the doorknob. "If we make an exception for you, we would have to make them for everyone, wouldn't we? I'm sorry, Ms. LeJeune, I really must be going." As if someone had fired off a starter pistol, he blurted out his remaining comments in rapid succession. "Like I said, Dr. Lee is your brother's doctor. Dr. Philip Lee. He's off today, but I know he will be glad to make some time for you to discuss your brother's case. Check at the information desk for an appointment time." A buzzer sounded. "Russell, would you please show Ms. LeJeune out?"

Jessica stood openmouthed as the door closed behind Rocheaux. She looked back at Russell, who was still wiping chips from Ben's shirt. Terri stood close by, observing.

"Let's go," Russell said cheerfully to Jessica. "I've gotta take the Frito champ back to his room for a change."

"Russell," Jessica said quietly, walking toward him. "Russell, I want to see my brother. Can you help me?"

Russell tapped Ben on the shoulder, a signal that brought the small man to his feet. "Don't worry, Ms. LeJeune," he said brightly and a little too loud. "Your brother is gonna be just fine. They take good care of people here." His eyes darted toward the cubicle as he maneuvered Ben toward the door. "I can't," he whispered to her over Ben's head. "They got him in lock-down right now, and I can't get in there."

Jessica couldn't believe what she'd just heard. "You mean my brother is locked up?"

"Shh! Please, Ms. LeJeune," Russell whispered sternly. He looked back nervously. "It's okay. They put most of the new ones in there to make sure they don't hurt themselves. I'll try to check on him for you. I promise."

"Hey, lady?" It was the man at the card table. He was standing now and leaning against the rickety table. "You gonna do me?" he asked, his eyes darting across the room, "You gonna do me, too, after the new guy?" The man's voice shook, and he began to cry. "Please, can you do me, huh? Please?"

Ben spun out of Russell's grasp. "Me, too, lady? I can be after the new guy, then after Roy there. Will ya? Will ya do me, too?"

Jessica looked from one man to the other in utter confusion. Their voices rang louder in unison: "Me, too, lady, me, too!"

Terri shuffled toward her. "You got a cigarette?"

"Please, lady, me, too! Me, too!" Both men were crying now.

"Got a cigarette?"

Everything churned in front of Jessica, nonsensical and impossible. She turned from face to face, not knowing whether to answer them or run. Russell made the decision for her. He pulled her by the arm and shoved her through the door.

Chapter Eleven

Jessica slammed a fist against the steering wheel. *What the hell kind of operation was that?* she thought. She had stumbled out of the clinic, stunned, and barely remembered getting into or starting her car. Her thoughts remained jumbled, racing helter-skelter for some portal of reasoning.

Slow down—think!

But she didn't want to think. She was afraid to think. There were too many old bones lying around inside her that had begun to stir. Coming to Louisiana had awakened them.

She grabbed her purse from under the seat and fumbled through it for a hair clip. Finding one, she jammed it between her teeth and worked her hair back into a ponytail. She clamped the barrette shut and was getting ready to put the car into gear when a horn blast startled her.

Behind the wheel of a green Oldsmobile that had pulled up next to her sat Lisa. She wore oversized sunglasses and signaled for Jessica to lower the window.

"What're you doing here?" Jessica asked before the window had lowered completely.

"It's good to see you, too," Lisa said, pulling the glasses down to the edge of her nose. She grinned.

"I mean—what—who's—oh, shit, Lisa, you know what I mean."

"Yeah, yeah, I know. Relax. Frank told me what flight you'd be coming in on. So I called Mom last night, gave her the CliffsNotes version of what was going on, and told her we needed backup. There was a direct flight to Lafayette this morning, so I took it, and she met me at the airport. We're all set to stay with her. Dad's offshore. It'll be just the three of us."

Jessica shook her head. "Trust me, you don't want to get involved in this mess."

"What involved?" Lisa jerked a thumb toward the building. "Hey, look, if you don't want me to stick my nose in there, no problem. I understand. But at least you'll have someone to talk with at the end of the day. You know, help sort things out. Anyway, what could possibly be better than coming back to my mom's cooking every night?"

Jessica rested a hand against her forehead for a second, then swiped it down the length of her face. She knew Lisa meant well, but she couldn't shake the feeling that her friend might be in danger here.

"Now, come on, let's get out of this heat," Lisa urged. "Mom's got a late lunch waiting for us, and I've got to get her car back to her. It's hair appointment day. You can fill me in on everything when we get to the house." She raised her car window before Jessica could protest.

Sighing heavily, Jessica reluctantly put the car into gear and followed Lisa out of the parking lot.

The house was small but well maintained. Lisa's dad, Glen, had always been meticulous about keeping it just so. The overlapping redwood planks were painted an immaculate white, and the window shutters trimmed hunter green. The window boxes still overflowed with artificial ivies, just as Jessica remembered.

She looked back from the plastic plants barely in time to keep the car from running into the garage door. She hit the brakes, put the car in park, and turned off the ignition. Glancing into the rearview mirror, she saw Lisa pull in behind her. Jessica got out of the car and was debating on whether to take her travel bag in with her when Lisa's mom burst through the front door.

"Jess! Look at you, just look at you!"

Jessica shut the car door with a hip and hurried over to her. "Miss Sharon, it's so good to see you."

Lisa walked up to the two women, grinning as they hugged and kissed each other repeatedly.

Tears stung Jessica's eyes as a heavy melancholy settled over her heart. It was the smell of her: Wind Song perfume and cigarette smoke. Sharon and Jessica's mother had smoked Parliament 100s for years. They had been loyal to their perfume and each other for just as long.

"You haven't changed a bit," Sharon said, her grin mirroring the one on Lisa's face. Her eyes softened. "God, you look more and more like your mom every time I see you."

Jessica lowered her head, a little embarrassed. Despite her serious issues, her mother had been a beautiful woman, much more beautiful than Jessica had ever considered herself to be.

"Oh, what am I doing?" Sharon said, shaking her head rapidly. "Come on inside. I bet you're starved."

Jessica nodded and followed Sharon into the house, making sure to wipe her feet on the doormat before entering. Lisa trailed quickly behind.

Sharon led them into the kitchen, where the table had been set for two. Jessica watched as she immediately began to maneuver food into plates. At sixty years old, Sharon still had hair as black as Lisa's. She was heavier than Jessica remembered, and her shoulders were developing a distinct slouch, but she still carried herself with the poise of a lovely, graceful woman.

"I don't have time to sit with you girls right now," Sharon said, patting the top of her tightly permed, although slightly mashed, hairdo. "Beauty shop day. But come on over here and eat and visit." She pulled a chair away from the table. "I hate leaving like this, Jess. Right after you just get here and all. But if I don't make this appointment, I won't be able to get another one for a week. And I can't take this mop looking like this no more." She laughed and leaned over to kiss Jessica's cheek. "I'll be back about four or so. We'll catch up then."

Lisa sat down at the table. "Keys are in the car, Mom. Tank's full."

"Thanks, sweetie." Sharon hurried past them. "Be back soon."

Within minutes, Jessica heard tires screeching out of the driveway. She grinned at Lisa. "Your mom's the greatest. She's hardly changed at all."

"She's something, all right," Lisa chuckled. She stood up and headed for the refrigerator. "Dig in. I'll get a couple of Cokes."

Jessica pushed the food around her plate with a fork. The steak and gravy were beginning to smell like corn chips.

"What's the matter?" Lisa asked. She handed Jessica a glass, then sat across from her. "You look a little green."

"I'm really not that hungry right now."

"Try to drink something at least," Lisa said, sprinkling Tabasco sauce over her steak.

Jessica took a sip of Coke. She realized she was trying *not* to look around the room—too many memories.

"Want to tell me what happened?" Lisa asked. She put her fork down and pulled her chair closer to Jessica's.

Jessica looked up at her and tried to get her mouth to move. All it would do was quiver. She bit the inside of her cheeks. It didn't help. Her eyes filled with tears, and she cleared her throat. She pushed herself firmly against the chair's back, hoping it would help her regain control.

"What?" Lisa asked gently.

"Uh—he—" Jessica couldn't get past the two words. She began to sob. She pressed on, however, telling Lisa as much as she knew. Even about the corn chips. The ache in her heart seemed to stretch wider with each sob. She hated losing control. It made her feel weak. But she could no more stop the tears right now than she could have turned herself into God.

Jessica's sobs finally slowed into hiccups. "It's like Todd's in a prison, Lisa. I just don't know what to do."

Lisa held her gaze for a long moment, then said firmly, "Yes, you do." Her eyes sparked with anger. "You're going to call that fucking doctor and demand to see Todd. That's what you're going to do. You've handled bigger shit than this, kiddo. Hell, you handle a company full of men, for God's sake." She swiped at the smeared mascara under Jessica's eyes. "You're going to get to the bottom of this. That's what you do."

Jessica took a deep breath.

"Go. Call the man and get your appointment set up. You can use the phone in my old room."

Jessica pushed away from the table and stood. A mental image of her feet in oversized boots, ankle deep in muck, came to her. All she had to do was tighten the laces and she could get through it. She took another deep, shaky breath. "You're right," she said finally.

"I know."

Jessica leaned over and kissed the top of Lisa's head. "Thanks."

"Go, girl," Lisa said. She picked up a fork and waved her hand. "You're getting slobbery on me. Down the hall, second door on the left."

"I remember. Is the phone still rotary dial?"

Lisa laughed. "Nah, the Daigles finally joined the twentieth century. Mom had it switched to touch-tone a couple of years ago. She kept the extension in my room so she could have some privacy when she and Aunt Helen talked. You know how those women can yak. Drives Dad nuts."

Jessica chuckled, then walked down the short hallway to Lisa's room and closed the door.

The room felt unfamiliar. It had been turned into an office of sorts. There was a daybed and a desk with a telephone on it against the right wall. A chest of drawers with a bouquet of silk flowers atop it stood against the left. The pink Priscilla curtains were all that remained of Lisa's old room.

Jessica walked over to the desk, picked up the phone book, and flipped through it. After finding the listing for Municipal, she grabbed the phone and punched in the number.

"Municipal," a male voice answered after the first ring.

"Yes, I'd like to speak to Dr. Philip Lee," Jessica said. She wondered where Mildred was. *Probably hiding in a hole somewhere like a groundhog, rooting through Todd's stuff.*

"May I ask what this is in reference to?"

"I would like to schedule an appointment with him. Todd Guidry is a patient of his, I believe, and I would like to get information regarding his condition."

"And your name, please."

"Jessica Guidry LeJeune," she said. "I'm Todd's sister."

"Hold, please."

The line went mute, not even elevator music interrupting the silence. Jessica looked at her watch, then glanced out the window. Nearing three o'clock, it was still brighter than noon outside.

"I'm sorry, Ms. LeJeune, Dr. Lee doesn't have any available appointment slots until next week. Will that be acceptable with you?"

Jessica sat on the edge of the bed. "No, it's not acceptable with me," she said, feeling the old piss and vinegar coming back.

"Excuse me?"

"I would suggest Dr. Lee take a hard look at his appointment schedule. I've already visited the clinic and found the conditions and staff deplorable. It will make no difference to me whom I will need to call, see, or persuade to get the answers I need. Even if that means going to the governor of this state. Do you understand? Someone who knows something *will* see me this week."

"Ma'am, there's no need to get upset. I'm sorry if you found our facility unacceptable. I'll make sure to relay that information to Dr. Lee." A pause, then the sound of shuffling papers in the background. "We can try to fit you in around two o'clock tomorrow, Ms. LeJeune. Dr. Lee's schedule is very hectic. He may not have much time to spend with you."

"Just put me down for two o'clock tomorrow."

"Fine. We'll see you at two."

"Yes, you will." Jessica hung up the phone. She knew the guy on the other end had taken the blunt end of her bitch stick, but she didn't care.

She decided to wait until evening before calling Frank and Jake. Dialing through to her voice mail, she checked for messages from the office. There was only one from her boss, saying he hoped everything was all right, not to worry about the office, and if she needed anything to let him know.

Jessica went back into the kitchen and found Lisa washing dishes. "I need some air," she said, grabbing a towel to dry.

"Want me to go with you?" Lisa asked, looking up at her through half-fogged eyeglasses.

"No. Thanks anyway, though. I just need to walk and think."

"Got your appointment?"

"Yep."

Jessica caught Lisa's smirk before she turned away.

"Going down Guidry Lane?"

"Yeah, I think so." Jessica gave Lisa a half-smile. "You know me too well."

"It comes with the deal. Here, give me that." Lisa grabbed the towel out of her hand. "It's changed a lot, Jess," she said, her voice softening. "You may want to hold off going over there right now. Took a walk there myself when I came down last Christmas. It's kinda run-down."

"I'll be okay."

"Yeah, I know. Ten feet tall and bulletproof. Well, if you have to go, the shortcut through Mrs. Gilbert's yard is still there."

Jessica remembered the opening in the hedgerow that led straight to Washman's Coulee. Every kid in the neighborhood had used it at one time or another, dodging through the azaleas and shimmying across the coulee on the two long planks that served as the commuter bridge between Guidry Lane and Sylvia Street where the Daigles lived.

"I don't know about those old planks," Jessica said, looking down at her shoes.

"You don't have to worry about that," Lisa said as she dried her hands. "It hasn't rained in a while, so the most you'll have to deal with is a little mud."

"No water?"

"Twentieth-century stuff again. City water, city sewage. Washman only gets rain runoff now."

Jessica started for the door, then stopped. "Are the Blanchards still living in our old house?"

"No, it's been empty for a while. Mom told me that not long after you guys sold it to them, Mr. Blanchard died. His wife went to live with her kids in Florida. The house has been vacant ever since."

Jessica walked over to the door and leaned against it.

"You sure you're okay?" Lisa asked.

"Yes," Jessica said quietly, then opened the glass storm door. She stepped outside and took a moment to get her bearings. Across the street, two houses over, was Mrs. Gilbert's place. She headed in that direction.

Sixty feet past a row of bare azalea bushes, Jessica spotted the muddy bottom of Washman's Coulee. The planks had been taken away, but Lisa had been right; there wasn't a need for them anymore.

Jessica edged down the embankment and hopped over the coulee's soggy middle. She braced her feet against some exposed tree roots and clambered up the other side. *I've really got to start working out,* she thought, panting. She looked down the length of the coulee. A russet strip ran down the ravine as far as she could see. Old tires and empty soda bottles were strewn everywhere. An abandoned stove rested on its side in the mud, accompanied by an assortment of metal pipes, three rusted dog pens, and an aqua-colored sink.

Turning back, she suddenly realized she'd crossed over the part of Washman that butted up against her old backyard. Her palms began to sweat, and a strange, heavy feeling settled against the inside of her chest. She walked through the yard with her eyes focused on the graveled road ahead.

Jessica never knew who had taken up collecting the rent from the houses on Guidry once her father left. It hadn't mattered to her then and mattered even less now. The neighborhood had turned into little more than a slum. The houses were so much smaller than she remembered. Many of the roofs appeared to be on the verge of collapse, and the windows were either covered with aluminum foil or broken. Overflowing barrels of trash landscaped most of the yards. A dilapidated tricycle stood in what was once Mrs. Delahoussy's front lawn.

Jessica could feel the house at her back. Her breathing became labored as she turned around and faced the deserted memory. It, too, was much smaller than she remembered. The once-ivory fascia boards were now a moldy lime color. Most of the bricks were mildewed or chipped. She walked steadily toward the wide living-room window and thought of something her grandmother had once told her on a trip to her old homestead. *Sometimes when you look through windows of where you been, it's like you lookin' backwards. That's not always a good thing,* non, *puppet. It's not you face reflected in that glass. It's the ghosts of what was.*

Pressing her face against the naked window, Jessica found that to be so true.

Her mother had been flitting around the house most of the day humming to herself. Jessica didn't know what was making her so happy. She wished she did so she could help keep the momentum going. She had kept a watchful eye on her anyway. Her mother was like an explosion always waiting to happen. No *matter what she saw now, Jessica knew it could change in a flash.*

She and Todd, already in pajamas, were starting a game of checkers when her mother waltzed into the living room. She wore a ruby chiffon dress cinched tight at the waist by a wide matching belt. Jessica thought she looked beautiful with her raven hair piled high on her head and crimson lipstick showing off sparkling white teeth. Her eyes, the color of honey, glowed with sparkles of gold and joy.

"Jess, go on now and get a bath ready for your brother. Daddy will be home soon," she said, brushing briskly at the front of her dress. "Patty is watching the two of you tonight. I put fudge pops in the freezer for treats if y'all are good."

"Okay, Mom." Jessica jumped up and ran down the hall to the bathroom. She hummed the tune she'd heard from her mother. She didn't know what the song was, but it didn't matter.

She raced to the tub, put the stopper over the drain, and turned the water on, keeping an ear cocked to hear if her mother was still humming. Jessica had left Todd to the checkerboard and wondered if he was cheating. She tried to remember the last positions of her red chips.

After pulling a towel from the linen closet, she placed it on the cabinet where Todd would be able to reach it, then hurried back to the living room.

Todd sat cross-legged on the floor, grinning mischievously.

Jessica stood in front of him, her hands on her hips. "Did you move anything?"

He giggled. "No, I didn't move nothing."

"Come on, Toddy. What did you move?"

"Cross my heart, hope to die, stick a needle in my eye. I didn't move nothing," he said with great animation.

"Keep it down in there!" their mother shouted from the kitchen.

Jessica squatted, and Todd scooted closer to her, giggling behind his hand.

"Shh," Jessica said quietly, trying hard not to laugh.

"Shh," Todd copied, giggling harder.

Jessica was getting ready to jump one of his checkers when she heard the pocket door that led from the utility room to the kitchen slide open.

Todd jumped up. "Daddy's home! Daddy's home!" he squealed, running for the kitchen.

Jessica got up slowly and picked up the checkers. She listened to the click of her mother's high heels as they quickened across the marble floor. Sounds safe enough, *Jessica thought, then went into the kitchen.*

Her mother was twirling like a ballerina on one

foot, the gauzy dress billowing around her slender legs. "Well? What do you think?" she asked her husband.

"You look beautiful," he said, Todd wiggling in his arms. He put the boy down and wrapped his arms around his wife's waist. "Looks like you're ready for a party or something." There was a teasing gleam in his eye that Jessica had seen only a couple of times before.

The phone rang, sending a chill into the air. Her mother's eyes clouded instantly.

"Whoever that is, just tell them you can't go," she said, slapping a hand against her leg.

Her father sighed deeply. "Don't worry, we're going to the party." He walked over to the corner of the snack bar and picked up the phone: "Hello?" To Jessica, it sounded like he said, "Yellow."

She held her breath and had already started moving backward toward the living room without realizing it.

"Why?" her father asked the caller. He listened for a moment, then sighed again. "Can't Louie handle it?" More silence. "Uh-huh, all right. I'll be right there." He placed the phone gently back on its cradle.

Jessica looked over at her mother and saw the storm clouds already covering her face. The brightly colored lips turned down in a deep scowl.

"Don't get upset," her father said, turning to his wife but avoiding eye contact. "I have to run out to the shop for a few minutes, twenty tops."

"I've heard that before," her mother said, doing an about-face and stomping off.

Jessica's father walked up to her and gave her a quick hug. She could smell motor oil and Old Spice. "Hey there, pumpkin," he said, kissing the top of her head. "Look here, I brought you guys something." He reached into his pocket and pulled out two rabbit's feet. One had been dyed blue, the other pink. He handed the blue one to Todd, the pink to Jessica. "There you go. It's for good luck."

Jessica ran an unsteady finger over the soft fur and wondered if the poor bunny had died after they cut off his feet. Touching the pink foot made her feel sick to her stomach, but she didn't want to disappoint her father. She hugged him. "Thank you, Daddy."

"You're welcome, sweet pea. Now do me a favor, will you? Tell your mom I promise I won't be long." He was out the door before Jessica could say anything.

Jessica looked at Todd, and they both became very quiet. That was the best strategy, the best plan: stay quiet. The quieter they were, the less likely their mother would be to notice them. They hurried into the living room and sat next to each other on the couch. The television was on with the volume turned down low. They would wait there until their father returned.

A moment later, Jessica heard a shriek coming from down the hall. She leapt to her feet and whispered sternly to Todd, "Stay here!"

"Jessica Lynn!" her mother screamed.

Jessica ran through the living room and into the hallway. She heard her mother's shouts coming from the bathroom. Oh, God, the water! *she thought fran-*

tically, remembering the bath she had started for Todd.

Her mother stood at the end of the hallway with her hands clenched into fists at her sides. Water gushed from beneath the bathroom door and lapped around her high-heel shoes. Her eyes were ablaze with a fire that would have made hell shiver.

Jessica sloshed through the water. "I'm sorry, Mama! I'm sorry!" she cried, cowering as she passed her mother. She wasn't quick enough.

Her mother reached out and grabbed a fistful of her hair, yanking hard. "Look at what you did!" she screamed. She slammed a fist into the side of Jessica's face, then jerked harder on her hair before shoving her into the bathroom door.

The door flew open and Jessica fell to her knees, water splashing into her nose and eyes. She slid toward the tub, her head striking the porcelain hard. The bathroom disappeared for a second, replaced with black and silver sparkles. Jessica got up quickly, pressed herself over the edge of the tub, and shut off the water. Oh, God, I'm going to die, *she thought.* She's going to kill me for sure this time!

Holding her small hands over the water, Jessica tried to calm the ripples. She willed the water below the tub's edge, willed the lapping waves down the drain and into the sewer, but all they did was lap and pour onto the floor. There was no other alternative. She would have to reach into the water and pull out the plug. Leaning over carefully, Jessica slid an arm through the water and yanked on the rubber stopper. Her foot slipped, throwing her off balance, and she nearly fell headfirst into the tub. A huge wave of water cascaded onto the floor.

Her mother was standing over her when she stood up. "Can't you do anything right?" she screamed, her face pinched. Her lipstick had smeared, and her mascara had run below her eyes, making her look like some macabre clown. "All I asked you to do was take care of your brother's bath! Was that so hard? Everything I do for you, everything! And this is how you pay me back? What the hell were you doing? And what—what's that?" She pried Jessica's hand open, and a soaked rabbit's foot fell to the floor.

"D-Daddy g-gave it to me."

Snatching it up from the floor, her mother screamed, "You don't deserve any presents. Nothing. You're selfish and spoiled enough as it is. What you let happen here is proof enough of that. Do you hear me?"

Before Jessica could answer, her mother whipped a hand through the air and slapped her face. "Get this mess cleaned up right now!"

Jessica hurried to the linen cabinet and grabbed an armful of towels. Her small body shook so violently, they tumbled from her hands and dropped to the floor, splashing more water over her mother's dress. Her mother's eyes narrowed, and Jessica looked down quickly.

She could feel the pain coming, smelled it coming, like the still, dank air before a hurricane. Without thinking, Jessica bolted. She slid past her mother, slipping and stumbling into the hall. Her wet paja-

mas clung to her like floppy skin, the pant legs heavy and dragging over her feet. She tripped over them, landing facedown. She jumped up in a panic, saw the water slosh against the baseboards, and ran.

"You'd better stop there, young lady!" her mother yelled after her. "You'd better stop!"

Jessica knew that her actions basically amounted to suicide, but she couldn't help it. She slid into the living room and hid behind her father's recliner, crouching down low.

Her mother stomped into the room, bypassed the recliner, and went into the kitchen. Seconds later, she returned with her fists clenched around a broom handle like it was a baseball bat.

Jessica heard Todd crying softly.

"I told you to stop, you ungrateful shit! Didn't I?" Whack!

Jessica felt the vibration against the chair as her mother struck hard against it with the broom handle.

Whack! Whack! Whack! The strokes intensified. The leather on the top of the chair creased deeper with every blow.

"Get out from behind there, now!" her mother demanded.

Whack!

Something in Jessica's mind clicked off. She crawled out from behind the chair and stood, facing her mother. She bit the inside of her cheeks.

Whack! The handle landed across Jessica's right side. She fell to her knees, a whimper escaping her.

Todd cried harder. "Mommy, stop!"

"Shut up!"

Whack! The next blow caught Jessica across the back. No sound escaped her this time.

"I could kill you!" her mother screamed. "You'd better pray, little girl! Pray to Mary—pray to Jesus I don't!"

Whack! Whack! Whack!

Yes, the ghosts in this place were indeed alive and well.

Chapter Twelve

A *different room. A different day?*

Those were the first thoughts Todd had when he opened his eyes. He stared at the pale walls across from him. *No pads.*

He remembered someone moving him, wrapping a scratchy blanket around his body and hoisting him into a wheelchair. And it wasn't the faggot, either—he remembered that, too. In fact, everything that had happened before the woman with the twelve-inch hypodermic needle seemed crystal clear. It was afterward that everything fogged up.

He turned his head to the left, trying to get a grasp of his new surroundings. The room was of an adequate size for the bed he rested on and the chair across from him. Anything else would have turned it into an overstuffed storeroom. A scant window slatted with metal bars allowed strips of light into the room. He watched the ballet of dust motes in the light, seeing them but not.

He looked up at the ceiling. He lay on his back with his arms and legs outstretched and secured by thick leather straps that were attached to the corners of the bed. Todd thought of pulling on the straps to test their durability but found he didn't have the energy to even uncurl his fingers. He thought of himself as prostrate before an altar, a sacrificial altar. *Hail Mary, full of grace—why have you forsaken me? So what else is new?*

The room smelled of old urine. An attempt had been made to freshen the air with some kind of peppermint stuff. It was like trying to cover a serious case of body odor with perfume.

Todd heard squeaky cart wheels and the scrunch of rubber-soled shoes outside the room. He lowered his eyes, watching the door and the knob. No movement. He watched and listened until the squeak, scrunch, squeak faded into a quiet echo.

He glanced over at his left hand, wrist bound and buckled. A long scratch marked the inside of his middle finger. The sting from it told him it was relatively fresh. *They should have just cut it off,* he thought. *I would've let them watch it grow back. Then they would've figured out who they were messing with.*

A thick voice seeped through the wall near his head. "It's that time. He's coming, and I warned you. You wouldn't listen, so all of you lousy mothers can eat shit and die!"

A flat scream, like a woman practicing vocal scales but sticking to only one note, followed. It sounded as if it were coming from another room, behind the wall to his left.

"I am the Christ!" the thick voice continued in bravado. "I am the instrument of universal power. Don't you see that? Hey, you in there. You can kiss my feet or kiss my ass, it's da same to me!"

The screamer ran out of steam just as the self-proclaimed messiah finished his speech.

Mumbling started inside Todd's head, whispers about covert operations that would be used to try and trip him up, to fool him into releasing information about things.

Todd moved his head sluggishly from side to side, straining to hear what was being said. They were whispering so low, so softly. If he could only make out what they were saying, he could protect himself from the evil they were planning against him.

He strained harder, fear building inside him like the blocks of a warped Lego set. No interlocking teeth, one teetering atop the other, all of it threatening to tumble into a pile of unrecognizable reality. Jagged, conspiratorial sentences cut through his brain. "He's going to . . . we can . . . burning . . . never know . . ."

He had to get out; had to move before they found him. Todd pulled against the restraints. There was strength in his arms, the strength of ten thousand. The strength of Hercules times ten thousand! He pulled harder, his body reacting slower than the rush in his mind. Adrenaline torched his fear, spiking it like squirts of gasoline to a flame. He pulled his arms and legs up and in as far as he could, every muscle in his body bulging and straining. His lips moved, trying to mimic the voices in his head. His heart pumped loud in his ears, blurring the words of the conniving demons even more.

"Stop the lies." The messiah's sermon started again. "Stop your denying and follow me!"

Bare feet steadily paced from the next room. Slap—slap—slap. The pace grew faster, more urgent.

A woman's cadence slid beneath the mesh of sounds and voices. "Take it off the wall. Take it off the wall. If you don't take it off the wall, it'll burn out my eyeballs." She made her claim with no more excitement than if she'd been announcing, "It's raining outside."

Todd's hands and feet locked into position, up and in, pulling against the straps. He tried to ignore the voices from the other rooms. They were not the ones he needed to be concerned with. The sonofabitches in his head were the dangerous ones. If he stayed this way, like a damn turtle stuck on his back, they would get him. They didn't know he could hear them, and that was good. That was very, very good. Thick beads of sweat, *or was it blood,* laced the front of his face. If he stayed perfectly still, maybe they wouldn't notice him. Just pass him by like a piece of furniture. The straps would eventually break. He was sure of that. Then he could get away.

The demon voices delayed and echoed. "Burning . . . to his breath . . . there will be no—"

Todd moved his eyes to the straps wrapped around his left wrist. *It's gonna come off. Just hold steady.* Another whispered thought came to him above the voices. It was not in sequence to what was happening, had no relevance to his fear. *If I reach out far enough, I can touch that chair.*

A clanging noise, like someone beating on a tin drum, permeated his brain. They were trying to get his attention. Bang! Clang! "Can't let him . . ." The voices grew clearer now.

Todd struggled harder to keep the straps taut. The room felt like the inside of a furnace, blazing with the refuse of half the world. He knew the most important piece of trash they'd burn was him. He had to get out, seek shelter, but the room was too small. It had no place for him to hide.

Maybe the window, through the metal bars. You can do it! Just get your ass out of these straps and shrink yourself through the slats. Oh, shit, oh, shit, too late. Too goddamn late!

Todd jerked his head to the right and strained to see the white underside of his shackled arm. A searing pain cut from his armpit to the inside of his elbow, and his lips moved quickly in silent prayer. He watched in horror as the flesh under his arm split into a maze of spider cracks. Tongues of flame soon rose and licked from each crevice.

Oh, Jesus, Jesus, Mary, they're burning me from the inside out! I won't yell, I won't. If I scream, they'll know for sure they've got me. I won't show them nothin'.

He felt the blood in his veins begin to boil, rolling like lava from his heart to his brain. The cracks in his arm widened, and the flesh suddenly burst open like the sunbaked belly of roadkill. Thick layers of fatty tissue curled over and into itself, exposing the stark white bone of his arm. Bright orange flames erupted from the wound, but nothing burned him. Instead, it felt like a thousand fingertips pressed into the meaty tissue of his arm. The pain of that sensation was greater than what could have been caused by any blaze, however. He would have preferred they mutilate his body, cut it into small pieces with a rusted ax, instead of them touching him this way.

Todd pulled against the straps and wondered how much longer it would be before the marrow in his bones would cook. Suddenly he spotted the pointed head of one of the conspirators in the flames. It had no eyes, just a gaping mouth filled with fragments of sharp yellow teeth. He watched as a swirling tendril slithered from the conspirator, searching for the hanging slabs of his flesh.

They're going to infiltrate! They're gonna stick that thing inside my veins and suck out my thoughts!

The fingertip touches pressed harder, opening him wider, and the flames spread farther. "No!" Todd pushed the scream from him with every ounce of breath he had.

The squirming tendril suddenly froze, as did the flames. They just stood in the ruptured part of Todd's flesh like a 3-D puzzle. The conspirator's head started to shrink slowly back into the hole in his arm.

"The gates of hell for you, boy! Can't you understand that? Don't you hear me?" the now-hoarse messiah yelled. Then his voice grew quiet with only enough volume to leak through Todd's wall. "They'll see. They'll see, won't they, boy?"

Todd knew that whoever was in the next room was talking to him. He knew he wasn't a messiah either, just some asshole making noise. But that was all right, maybe he could help him keep the demons distracted. Todd's eyes numbed in their position. He had to stand guard. He had to make sure they wouldn't try it again.

The flames stood motionless, resting in the hole of his exposed limb. Blue, thread-thin veins wound through the fatty mass of his arm, and Todd wondered what it would feel like to touch one. To squeeze it between his fingers until it burst. *Would the flame disappear then? Could it be extinguished that way?*

The door to his room opened suddenly, and Todd gave only a cursory glance to the two people who entered, then kept tabs on them from the corner of his eye. One was a tall, slender man with a band of brown hair circling the back of his head. A rooster comb of tufts lined the center of his scalp from front to back. He walked into the room on the balls of his feet, as though ready to sprint.

Closing the door behind them was a middle-aged woman in a white uniform, her face puffy and chalky white. A pink scalp showed through the tight kink of blond-white hair on her head. She shuffled through the small stack of folders in her hands. "Todd Guidry, Dr. Lee. Came in yesterday." She handed the man a sheet of paper.

The man pulled the chair away from the wall and placed it next to Todd's cot. He straddled the plastic seat, then cleared his throat. "Todd?"

Todd heard him from far away. His eyes darted toward the man, then locked back onto his arm.

"Todd, my name is Dr. Lee." An impatient rustle of paper followed. "Can you hear me, Todd? Do you understand what I am saying?"

Todd's eyes moved back to Lee's face. He knew he had to keep watch on his arm so the demons wouldn't come back. They could devour him whole next time. Take his skin from his body one layer at a time until they entered the very cavity of his being. Then all would be lost. All would be lost. Todd wished the man would quit calling his name.

"Todd? Want to tell me why your hands and feet are up that way?" Lee asked. "You must be tired of holding them there." He reached out to touch Todd's arm.

"No," Todd hissed. "They'll see you."

"Who'll see me, Todd?" Lee asked, his hand suspended in midair. "Tell me what you see."

It hadn't occurred to Todd that the man wouldn't be able to see the hole in his arm or the flames. Maybe it was a trick they were using to distract him.

More paper shuffling. Todd heard Lee telling the woman something but couldn't make out what it was.

"Todd, we're going to undo these straps." Lee stood. "Can you hear me? We're going to undo these straps and see how you do. If I undo them, will you put your arms and legs down?"

Play it cool, play it cool, Todd thought. *This is the only way you can get out of here. Focus, dammit! Focus!* He watched in amazement as the flames quickly shrank back into the fissure in his arm. The conspirator was gone now. He watched as his flesh unfurled and flopped back into place on its own accord, leaving behind thin black cracks on his skin.

Dr. Lee and the woman became irrelevant to Todd. He saw them and heard them, but his mind had difficulty putting their existence and purpose into perspective. He felt lost and afraid. It was as though Todd Guidry had suddenly ceased to exist and this *other* person had taken over. Nothing made sense, and everything made perfect sense.

The greatest part of Todd's fear was that somewhere, far below this pit he had fallen into, this Erebus of torment, was the someone he once was. And he couldn't get to him. No matter how far he stretched or how hard he tried, that person sank farther from his grasp. He saw it, heard the screams for help, yet could do nothing about it. All he could do was watch as that person—that Todd Guidry—died. The loneliness of that revelation was unbearable. He asked for death of the body but prayed fervently for death of the mind. To silence it forever, to snuff out all thoughts like the light from a candlewick drowned in melted wax.

Todd wondered what he'd done to deserve this. What horrible atrocity had he committed to be left alone to deal with forces greater than the creation of the world? There was no one he had harmed intentionally, no one he had tortured, to deserve such treatment. Todd wanted to cry. Cry with the pain of wanting to die and not being able to. He watched the cracks in his skin begin to squirm like worms frantic to find cover from light. Oh, yes, he wanted to cry. But the voices wouldn't allow it. They wouldn't allow a moment's rest from his having to watch. He thought of just letting go and letting them have him. But he knew that wasn't an option. Willingly letting these demons take his life would mean his very soul would be lost forever and that even in death he would experience no relief.

Todd started to laugh. Not in his eyes or facial expression, just in voice. His vision blurred, then cleared. Pale colors flitted in and out of his view but had no substance. He felt slight tugs at his wrists, then the straps removed. He heard a soft ping of metal striking metal, then a clatter from a far-off place. Two pairs of hands pushed his arms and legs down, and he let them, but he remained spread-eagled.

The woman, now standing at the foot of the cot, tossed a blanket over him. Todd watched with little interest as it floated over his bare legs. The hospital gown he wore had ridden to the upper part of his thighs, its hem twisted tightly beneath him.

"I need to ask you some questions, Todd, so we can give you the best care possible. Do you understand? Can you hear me?" Lee asked.

Yes, he understood. He had heard. But he had no energy left for answers. The laughing stopped. Todd looked at the doctor's face. It seemed kind enough.

"Todd? Do you know where you are?" Lee asked.

Silence, tempered with a blank stare.

"You're in the hospital. Municipal Mental Health. Do you remember how you got here?" Lee asked.

To someone else, Todd heard the man ask, "Can't find it—do you have another?"

Another quick shuffle of paper. The woman's voice droned on low and quick, the man's lower and rapid-fire.

Lee stood up, pushed the chair back against the wall, then patted Todd's arm. "I'll be back later to check on you," he said. "Miss Louviere, here, will be back in a moment with medication that will help you rest."

A muffled clack, a whisper of breeze as the door opened and closed, and Todd was alone again. He glimpsed at his arm. Only faint gray, stationary streaks remained. Suddenly he heard two sharp raps on the wall next to the cot. He shivered.

Rap! Rap!

Todd started to turn his head toward the sound, then stopped. *What if it's them? Maybe they snuck in when those people left. Maybe they'll gouge my eyes out or—or tear holes in my face and rip off my lips!* The raps grew insistent.

Rap! Rap! Rap!

He shifted his eyes to the right as far as he could before allowing his head to follow. Holding his breath, Todd swung his head quickly to the side, hoping to take whatever or whoever created the racket by surprise. Nothing there.

Rap! Rap! Rap!

He stared at the spot on the wall where the knocking seemed to be coming from. He tried looking through the wall. Nothing.

"Todd?" a gentle voice whispered. It was soft, like a lullaby before sleep. It brought tears suddenly and violently to his eyes. *Rap! Rap—rap—rap . . .* "Toddddd?"

The woman's voice seemed to pulse from behind the wall but at the same time in Todd's head.

"There's a way out," the voice murmured. "Will you trust me? Do you believe me?"

The direction of her voice or where she was didn't matter to Todd. His eyes fixated on the wall until it wasn't there anymore. Only the fact that she spoke to him mattered. There was something about it, something about that soft, musical voice that he wanted to hold on to, cling to, inhale and die with.

"Uh-huh," Todd answered dreamily.

"Good boy. Now listen carefully. I left a present for you, just for you. It's on the floor near your bed. Look over—you'll see it."

Todd didn't want to turn away. He was afraid if he did, she might leave. Excitement ravaged him, making him shake uncontrollably. He turned and stretched his arm over the edge of the cot and dangled his fingers to the floor. The linoleum floor felt cool under his fingertips as he tapped them around blindly. Other than dust collecting on his fingers, however, he felt nothing.

"Look—look. You'll find it," the voice cooed.

It was such music to Todd, tender strains that defied consonant and vowel. He pulled his arm back and gripped the edge of the cot. Rolling onto his left side, he let his head drop over the edge. Slivers of silver light shot from his eyes, and he had to steady himself to keep from falling out of bed. He squeezed his eyes shut, then opened them again. There, at the head of the frame, just beyond the edge of the thin mattress, lay his present. He snatched it up.

"Isn't it beautiful? Look at it. Touch it. Put it in your mouth." The voice was a canticle, rich and vibrant, filling the darkness of his mind with a tangible sustenance.

Todd rolled over heavily and raised the pen to eye level. He held the ends reverently. The smooth, black plastic tube had BROUSSARD'S INSURANCE COMPANY advertised in white on its side. But, to Todd, these words were but code to a higher knowledge. Something only she understood. And he would trust her. A thin metal band partitioned the pen in the middle, and a nub of metal at the top clicked the pen's point in and out, something Todd tested twice.

"Open it. Do what you need to do."

He twisted the pen halves quickly and pulled them apart. A small spring and plastic tube of ink fell onto his chest. He looked at the two empty halves in his hands.

"Go on, Todd. Do it."

"Who are you?" Todd asked, his voice cracked and hollow. "What am I supposed to do with this?"

"You know what you're supposed to do, Todd. It will give you relief and free you."

Todd looked at the tube halves. The tiny grooves and threads at the end of one seemed clearer, more in focus to him. He stared at the miniature ridges until they became mountains and valleys, ones that he could almost step into. He turned it, standing the pointed end on his chest. Wrapping his fingers around the tube to hold it in place, he pressed his right thumb over the threaded end. He pushed the tube harder into his chest.

If I press down hard enough, it'll go straight through my heart. Blood will squirt out of the top like a drinking fountain.

Although the thoughts flattered Todd's face with a grin, he knew it was not what the beautiful voice meant. That was not what was intended here. He lifted the pen from his chest and pressed his thumb firmly against the top ridges, watching his thumbnail grow red, then white, until he heard a crack. Pulling his thumb away, he studied the wedge of jagged plastic.

He dropped the top half of the pen to the floor and held the broken half in both hands. "Who are you?" he asked the voice again.

"Oh, you already know. Why do you want to confuse things? Look at it. Taste it."

Todd tilted the broken plastic to his lips. Closing his eyes, he stuck out his tongue and tasted. His mouth salivated at the bitter mix of plastic and ink.

"Look down and see. If it is so unclear to you, I'll show you. Look down," the voice whispered. It sounded as though her vibrant lips were but an inch from his left ear. He could almost feel their full, luscious touch.

Todd looked down at his legs, which were still splayed apart under the blanket. He frowned with uncertainty until he saw a jerk of the blanket right at his groin. Now he understood.

"That's right!" the voice said triumphantly. "I knew you would understand."

"Who are you?"

"One who will never leave you."

"Are you God?"

"No, not God." The voice laughed, the sound as pure as crystal chimes.

"Are you Mary? You know—Jesus's mother?"

Another tinkle of crystal. "I'm what you want. Take your present and get on with it."

Todd closed his eyes for a second, but only for a second. The other whispers in his head threatened to overpower the beautiful voice if he kept them closed too long. His left hand moved to the edge of the blanket and pushed it down. He arched his right foot toward his left leg and walked the blanket farther down until it was at his knees. The gown didn't cover his excitement.

He looked at the tube in his hand. *It will finally be over. This is the root of it all. This is the reason for it all. Do it quickly and get it over with.* He stared at the sharp ridges of plastic as he moved the pen's tube lower over his body. In his mind, he saw it already gone, detached, just a roll of flesh lying between his legs. Todd reached down to steady himself, knowing the instrument wasn't sharp enough to just slice right through it. He would have to saw it off.

Chapter Thirteen

"You should've seen the humma hummas on that babe," Markus Fontenot said, wheezing behind a bottle of Corona. It was early afternoon, and he was already on his eighth beer. "Edible ones for sure. You know what I mean, buddy?"

Eli stared at the greasy little man but didn't answer. They had been riding together for the last forty minutes, and the endless chatter exhausted him. Eli wasn't interested in humma hummas. He didn't even know what they were.

"Yeah, travelin' does have its advantages," Markus continued after a hefty belch. "Hell, just last month I was in Atlanta and stopped at the Rhino's Den to celebrate landing this big account." He chuckled with the memory, then sucked down the rest of the beer. "This cutie—no, not a cutie, more like a knock-a-man-off-a-bar-stool good-lookin', walks in with the sweetest little—"

Eli watched the white lines on the center of the highway zip by and wished the man would shut up so he could concentrate. Something was happening to him. Something bad. His mind had gone from cloudy to jittery. Thoughts skidded across his brain like rocks skimming water. His body ached terribly, and his flesh burned as though the blood trapped in the veins beneath it boiled. He examined his hands, which were folded in his lap. Angry red lines zig-zagged across his fingers and down his wrists.

". . . and that was the last I saw of her. Whoa, man, I gotta stop to choke the chicken or bust," Markus said, suddenly shifting in his seat. "Know what I . . . ? Hey, what's wrong with your face?"

Eli peered over at him.

"You're peelin' pretty bad," Markus said matter-of-factly. "Here, look." He reached over and flipped down the visor in front of Eli. The car did a sharp left-to-right swerve. "Whoa, boy." Markus put both hands on the steering wheel. "Go on, look. There's a mirror."

Eli glanced up into the reflective rectangle and barely recognized himself. Thin strips of dried skin hung from his cheeks. He reached up and tugged at one. It peeled off easily, leaving a pinkish splotch across the left side of his dark face. His eyes looked horrible, too, like day-old blood blisters. *What is happening to me?* Frightened and perplexed, Eli hurriedly flipped the visor back up.

"Probably some kinda psoriasis or something," Markus offered. "My cousin Bertha had it terrible.

Hell, I seen the skin on her arms peel off so bad they'd bleed. Mean stuff, that psoriasis. I hear it can drive a person crazy with the itching. Yours itch?"

Eli concentrated on the trees whisking by his window. The blurry green monotony helped to calm his burgeoning panic. "No," he said, "it don't itch."

"Yours ain't really *that* bad," Markus said. He reached over and put a hand on Eli's shoulder. "I seen a lot worse."

Wincing from his touch, Eli shut his eyes against the sudden images of the disease he saw ravaging Markus's body. His mind's eye stayed wide open, however, staring into something black and spongy, coating Markus's liver and lungs. Eli shook the hand from his shoulder. He didn't want to see any more.

"I'm dyin' here," Markus said, pressing down harder on the accelerator.

Eli looked at him curiously.

"If we don't get to a gas station soon, I'm gonna have a—"

The car jerked hard to the right, clipping off the rest of his words.

"Aw, hell," Markus said, gripping the steering wheel tight. "Blowout."

Eli pressed his hands against his knees as they swerved from side to side. A pickup raced by in the left lane, the driver tapping steadily on his horn.

"Hold on," Markus said. He strained to maneuver the car to the shoulder of the road, which was no more than a three-foot-wide path covered with reef shell. His right foot worked gingerly against the brake pedal.

The car slid, then finally came to a stop.

"Man," Markus said, combing his fingers through his thin hair. He held a trembling hand out in front of him. "See that? Steady as a rock. Who says you can't drink and drive?" He laughed and snapped his fingers. "Come on and give me a hand with the flat," he said, reaching for the car keys and opening his door. "It's the least you can do for the lift, right?"

Eli opened his door and pulled himself out. Every muscle in his body seemed to protest the movement. By the time he reached the back of the car, Markus had already opened the trunk and pulled out the spare tire.

"What's the matter? You're acting like an old man. Here, take this," he said, handing Eli a tire iron. "Pop the hubcap and break the lugs while I get the jack."

Eli grabbed the rod. He rolled it between his palms and watched Markus rummage through the trunk.

"Here it is," Markus said triumphantly. He raised the jack above his head like a trophy. His face resembled a sweaty pomegranate. "Now I gotta get the beer bottles out of the car in case a cop stops or something. I don't think it's likely; this road never has much traffic. But you never know. Hey, you gonna help out or what?"

Eli looked at him blankly.

"You do know how to use one of those things, don't you?" Markus asked, pointing to the iron.

He nodded slowly.

"Good, then let's get going." Markus snapped his fingers and headed for the beer bottles tucked under the driver's seat.

Eli wrapped his fingers around the tire iron and stroked it. A rush of wind from a passing semi pulled at his body, threatening to suck him into its path. He stiffened his stance and glanced at the red streaks on his hands. They had widened and blistered.

"Hey," Markus said, appearing with a paper sack. "That's not your dick in your hand, buddy." He laughed nervously and threw the sack into the trunk. He bent over to situate the jack under the bumper. "Come on now, let's get this over with."

Something in Eli's mind agreed. *Let's get this over with*. A sudden burst of white-hot energy flashed through him, and with neither thought nor intent, Eli swung the tire iron up and over, smashing it into Markus's skull.

Oh, God! What have I done? What—why—

The questions abruptly vanished from Eli's mind, and he yanked the rod out quickly before the body had a chance to fall over, then swung again, crushing the side of the man's face. He swung harder, again and again, destroying what was left of Markus Fontenot's head. Blood and bone fragments flew in every direction. A tooth grazed his left temple.

Finally exhausted and out of breath, Eli dropped the iron. He crossed the shoulder of the road, plucked two handfuls of grass and weeds, and used the mulch to wipe the blood from his shirt and pants. The gore on his clothes only smeared into a morbid tie-dye pattern. He threw away the makeshift rags and trudged back to Markus's body.

Ignoring the mutilated corpse, Eli picked up the tire iron, which now felt a hundred pounds heavier than it did earlier, then headed for the center of the highway.

Behind him lay miles of curving blacktop bordered by massive oaks and pecan trees. Ahead, more of the same. He noticed a couple of old houses about half a mile or so to the north. Far enough to obscure any tenant's view.

Satisfied with the apparent seclusion, Eli pulled the pendulum from his pocket, held it between two fingers, and waited. Instead of swinging wide toward the west as it had earlier that day, the pendulum jerked hard, pointing first to the south, then to the west. The interpretation came to Eli immediately. She was near. Soon he would be meeting the woman who tortured his dreams.

A car engine rumbled in the distance, startling Eli. He pocketed the pendulum and hurried for a thick grove of evergreens that stood back a couple hundred feet from the south side of the road.

He barely reached cover before a woman's scream pierced the air. The sound encapsulated so much horror, such mortification and panic, it drew an involuntary tear to Eli's eye. Absently swiping the tear away, he sat on his haunches beside a tree and rested the tire iron across his knees. Within minutes, he heard a car door slam and tires screech across the highway. He sighed, certain the screaming woman was going for help. He wouldn't have much time to rest and regain his strength.

Eli thought of the woman from his nightmares as he fingered the rod and rolled it over the top of his thighs.

Yes, he would definitely need his strength.

Chapter Fourteen

Jessica nervously tapped the face of her watch with a fingernail as the second hand swept past, marking another minute. Two thirty-seven. *So much for a two-o'clock appointment.*

She glanced over at the lanky guy with the bad haircut who stood inside the reception cubicle, doing his best to ignore her. At least he had been a little nicer than Mildred, who'd evidently taken the day off, by offering Jessica a chair when she arrived at Municipal forty minutes earlier. Her butt didn't appreciate the hard plastic, but at least it kept her from pacing.

"Ms. LeJeune?"

Jessica jumped up from the chair. "Yes?" she said, looking eagerly about for the voice's owner.

A middle-aged man in beige chinos and a maroon Hilfiger shirt bounded toward her from the back of the room. On the top of his head stood tufts of light brown hair that bounced along with him, giving him the overall appearance of a speeding Kewpie doll.

When he reached her, he shoved the folder he carried under an arm. "I'm Dr. Lee," he said, and extended a hand.

Jessica shook it firmly. "Thank you for seeing me."

"Not at all," he said. "My schedule's extremely tight, but I do need to ask you some questions. Let's go somewhere where we can talk, okay?" He spun about on his heels and hurried off before she had a chance to respond.

A bit nonplussed with his abrupt departure, Jessica blinked, then hustled after Lee, following him around the Plexiglas cubicle, then across the vast reception area to a room located in its far southwest corner.

After entering the room, Lee gave her a curt nod. "Please, sit down," he said, and closed the door behind them.

The small room held only a worn wooden conference table, surrounded by four ladder-back chairs. A large abstract painting hung on the wall to the right. Its tangle of multicolored swirls, dashes, and splotches gave Jessica pause. She wondered why a hospital, purporting to care for individuals challenged with reality, would choose to display something so loud and confusing. Just looking at the damned thing irritated her. She couldn't image what effect it might have on a patient—like her brother. Frowning, Jessica pulled out a chair and sat.

"Now let's see," Lee said, retrieving the folder from under his arm. He opened it, then removed a pen from his breast pocket. "You're Todd's sister, correct, Ms. LeJeune?"

"Yes, but please call me Jessica."

"All right." He sat across the table from her. "Before we get started, Jessica, I do want to apologize for what happened during your visit here yesterday. I heard from Dr. Rocheaux that things got a bit out of hand."

"That's an understatement."

Lee gave her a pained smile. "Again, I apologize. It's not customary for us to hold consultations in the commons area, but Dr. Rocheaux told me that his office was being used at the time of your visit, as was this conference room. The commons area is usually used only for family visits after the patient and his or her family become acclimated. But, from what I hear, you were adamant about seeing someone right away."

"I was." Jessica leaned closer to the table. "What do you mean by acclimated? Acclimated to what?"

"To the surroundings here, as well as to some of the unusual activities that may be demonstrated by some of our patients," Lee said. He scratched his chin thoughtfully. "The manifestations of certain forms of mental illness can be—well, unsettling at best."

"So I've witnessed. But what does that have to do with my brother? He's not mental."

Lee remained silent for a moment, then eyed her squarely. "Todd was certainly unsettled the day they brought him in, Jessica. He displayed aggressive and destructive behavior to himself and to others."

She jerked her head back, shocked. "What?"

"He arrived with injuries that, according to the police report, were self-inflicted. Nothing serious, just a few minor cuts and scratches. But he wasn't here an hour when he attacked a male orderly."

"Todd would never hurt anyone intentionally!"

"The orderly has the teeth marks to prove it."

"Then the guy must have deserved it," Jessica blurted angrily. She regretted the words as soon as they left her mouth. They sounded moronic and childish, traits probably not conducive to Lee's favor, which she needed if she had any hopes of seeing Todd.

Lee arched an eyebrow.

"Look, I didn't mean to—"

"Jessica, I can understand you wanting to defend your brother, but—"

"How can you be certain Todd did it?" Jessica asked. She pressed her palms against the edge of the table. "Did you actually witness this alleged attack?"

"Personally? No. But a nurse did. She walked into the room just as it happened."

Jessica drew in a deep breath, then let it out gradually as the reality of what he'd said sunk in and weighed down her heart. "I don't . . . why would . . ." She clutched her trembling hands together and forced them to her lap.

"What?" Lee asked.

"Todd . . . Todd's never done anything like that before. Attack someone. Bite someone." Perplexed, she shook her head. "I don't understand . . . what would make him do something like that?"

"He's ill, Jessica."

A tremor rolled through her. "With what?"

"Well, it's still early," Lee said. He waved a casual hand over the paperwork in the folder. "We haven't had much time to observe him. But I can give you my initial assessment based on the symptoms he's been manifesting."

"And that is?"

"I believe your brother is displaying signs of schizophrenia."

Jessica felt like she'd just been slapped. Wide-eyed, she searched Lee's face, hoping he would look at the file again and discover he'd made a mistake. His solemn expression did not waver, however.

He has to be wrong. He has to! Her mind flashed through old mental photos of her and Todd picking blackberries together, shooting marbles, bicycling up and down Guidry Lane. All recollections of a normal boy. If Todd had a mental problem, wouldn't she have noticed something back then?

"Jessica?"

"It can't be," she said, refocusing on Lee's face. "It just can't. What are the chances you might be wrong in your evaluation?"

"Less than half a percent," he said. "I work with people like him every day. This disease is relatively common, you know. It affects one in every one hundred people in the world."

"And that's supposed to make me feel better?" Jessica stood up and began to pace. *How could I have possibly missed this? Why didn't I keep closer tabs on him?*

"Do you know what schizophrenia is?" Lee asked.

"Just that it means someone has *really* lost it. Like

a split personality or something." She was getting dizzy from walking back and forth in the small room and getting angry with Lee for being so damn calm about the whole thing.

"No," Lee said firmly. "Split personality is a real condition but very rare. That's not what Todd has. Schizophrenia is a disease that makes it difficult for the person who has it to distinguish what's real and what's not. They have either auditory or visual hallucinations, sometimes both. Those hallucinations are as real to them as you and I having this conversation. Their thinking becomes seriously disorganized."

Jessica stopped pacing and stood facing the abstract, now an appropriate effigy for her own mental state. "How bad is he?" she asked.

"To be honest with you, he isn't doing well right now. But we're working with medications to get him stabilized."

"How long does it take to cure this thing?" Jessica asked the painting.

"It's chronic."

She spun around. "You mean it doesn't go away? Is that what you're saying?"

Lee's gaze remained steady. "Currently there's no cure for schizophrenia."

Her mouth dropped open.

"But," he added quickly, "with the proper treatment, many people who have it can lead productive lives."

"What do you mean, 'many people'? Not everyone who has it can be helped?"

"There are some acute cases that just don't respond to the medications we have available."

"And Todd?"

"I'm sure we'll find something that will help him. Like I said, it's still early. You need to give us time to work with him." Lee stood up and walked over to her. "Jessica, I'm going to give it to you straight. Schizophrenia is a tough disease. It's devastating to the person who has it and just as damaging to the family of that person. Todd's going to need a lot of support from all of you right now."

"There is no 'all of you,'" Jessica said. She rubbed the back of her neck. "There's only me. I mean, there're my husband and son, of course. But no other immediate family."

"Your parents are deceased?"

"Mother is. Has been for some time. We haven't seen our father in years and don't even know where he is."

"No other siblings?"

"No." Jessica walked over to her chair and sat down heavily. She felt small and abandoned. "It's just been the two of us for a long time. I guess I should have been paying closer attention."

With an adamant shake of his head, Lee sat beside her. "This disease is *not* your fault."

"No? Then whose fault is it? I've been taking care of Todd ever since I can remember. We lose touch for a few months, and he's . . . he's got this . . . this thing."

"It's no one's fault," Lee reassured her. "Look, the study of mental illness has come a long way. Why, only a few decades ago some people actually believed it was a result of evil spells. Others, including some doctors, thought bad blood or poisons induced it. We know better now, of course, but science still hasn't determined the specific cause of this particular illness or its cure. One thing we have discovered, however, is that people who suffer with schizophrenia also have a neurochemical imbalance."

Jessica looked at him quizzically.

"That means they are either sensitive to or produce too much of a certain brain chemical."

She pressed a hand to her forehead. "So you're saying he was born with it?"

"We're not sure, but that is a possibility."

"Why did it wait to show up now? He's over thirty. If he was born with it, wouldn't we have seen signs of it earlier?"

"Chances are that Todd experienced some mild symptoms off and on during his late teens and early twenties. The symptoms can vary in severity and type, so you may not have noticed anything. Why full-blown now? I don't know."

Dumbfounded, Jessica fell mute. She knew a million questions needed to be asked, yet she could not formulate even one. Intellectually she grasped Lee's explanation of Todd's condition. However, the news left her emotionally crippled, unable to disentangle fear from grief, anger from dread. Lee might as well have told her that half the earth had been destroyed two minutes ago. She doubted the magnitude and gravity of a situation like that would have had any greater impact on her than what she was experiencing now.

Lee glimpsed at his watch, then reached for the

folder. "Now, if it's okay with you, I'd like to ask you a few questions regarding Todd's history."

Jessica nodded and clutched her hands together once more. The first sign of a headache echoed along the base of her skull. *No, no, not now. Not the headache and that wacko voice yelling in my ear, please.*

"When was the last time you saw Todd?" Lee asked.

She wet her lips, then said quietly, "About two years ago."

"Did you notice any strange behavior from him then?"

"No."

"What about when he was younger? Anything out of the ordinary in his behavior?"

She thought for a moment, mentally scrolling through the past. "No, just Todd's usual clowning."

Lee scribbled a note on a page in the folder. "What do you mean by that? What kind of clowning?"

"Nothing weird or anything," Jessica said quickly. "Todd just liked to make people laugh, that's all."

Lee glanced up at her. "Is there any history of mental illness in your family?"

A sudden urge to laugh caught Jessica off guard. She bit the inside of her cheek and looked away. *Would you consider my mother's nervous breakdowns mental? What about the purse she kept filled with sleeping pills, wake-up pills, nerve pills, diet pills, pain pills, and, yes, lest we forget, laxatives? How's that? Is that mental? Oh, does throwing knives at her daughter and screaming, "I hate you, I wish you were dead," count as mental? Does it?*

"My mother had a nervous condition and took a lot of medication," Jessica finally confessed. "But nothing diagnosed or prescribed by a psychiatrist."

"Then how did she get the meds?"

Jessica studied her fingernails. "The town doctor was a friend of the family." Peripherally she watched Lee write in the folder, and a sudden thought struck her with the force of a pile driver.

"Dr. Lee, is this disease hereditary?"

He stopped writing and shrugged. "Candidly speaking, we're not sure. We recognize that the disorder tends to run in families and that a person inherits a *tendency* to develop the disease. That tendency can be triggered by environmental events, such as viral infections or highly stressful situations or a combination of both. Probabilities are that if you have one grandparent with schizophrenia, your risk of getting the illness increases to about three percent; one parent brings the percentage up to ten percent. If both parents have the illness, the risk percentage rises to about forty."

Jessica's head went to full throb. "What about my chances or my son's?"

"There are no guarantees," Lee said, then smiled tentatively. "But I wouldn't be concerned about it, Jessica. There are cases involving identical twins where only one twin develops the illness. The other remains perfectly normal. The children from both twins didn't develop the disease either."

"But Todd and I aren't twins."

"I know that, but the principle is the same. Just because Todd has the illness doesn't mean you or your son will have it."

A scowl abruptly fell over Lee's face. He leaned back in his chair and reached into his right pants pocket, where he withdrew a pager. His expression grew all the more somber as he studied the LCD. After thumbing a button on the device, he stood and stuck the pager pack in his pocket. "Jessica, do you know if Todd has any history of drug use or addiction? Pharmaceutical or illegal?"

"No. He didn't even take aspirin for a headache." She followed Lee's direction and stood. "Is there a problem?"

"What about any medical concerns? Surgeries? Chronic illnesses?"

Sensing she was about to be given the bum's rush, Jessica casually walked over and placed herself between Lee and the door. "Nothing more serious than swollen tonsils."

Lee leaned over the table and jotted down more notes. He closed the folder, picked it up, and clipped the pen to its center tab. "I'm sorry, but I'm going to have to end our meeting. There's an emergency I must tend to. We can reschedule for next—"

"Wait a minute." Jessica held up a hand. "When can I see Todd?"

"You can't."

"This isn't Alcatraz, Dr. Lee. I want to see him."

"That's not possible, especially today." Lee tried to sidestep her, but Jessica countered his moves.

"I'll get a court order if I have to," she said coldly.

His face reddened. "Jessica, you have to understand the system. The authorities are the ones who brought Todd in here. We're responsible by state law to assess his condition and take appropriate action. The courts have already given the institute its orders."

"So assess him. I won't get in your way. All I want to do is see Todd, talk to him."

"It isn't that simple."

"Why not?"

"Sometimes seeing a family member too soon into the stabilization process can throw the patient back a week or more."

"That won't happen with Todd," Jessica insisted.

"You don't know that for sure."

"There are no absolutes with anything, Dr. Lee, but I know my brother. I think if he saw me it would help."

Lee let out a frustrated breath. "All right. Give me a call in the morning, and we'll see how things are progressing."

"Does that mean you'll let me see him tomorrow?"

"I don't know—maybe. Just call me tomorrow, and we'll see. Now, please!"

Jessica stepped aside, and Lee rushed by, accidentally bumping her arm. The instant they touched a brief, horrifying image flashed in Jessica's mind—Todd, lying in a pool of blood.

Chapter Fifteen

Eula Mae knew something was different the moment she woke from her nap. Her eyes moved slowly around her bedroom, her heart beating and tripping in anticipation. Everything looked the same. It just didn't *feel* the same.

She sat up and listened intently, but all she heard was an occasional bark from a neighbor's dog.

"Lawd," she said with a sigh and reached for her glasses and teeth on the TV tray next to the bed.

The rocker across the room began to creak softly. Eula Mae pressed the black horn-rims firmly against the bridge of her nose and watched the wooden chair tip back and forth of its own volition. *Looks like company's comin'*, she thought. *Better go see who 'tis.*

Groaning, she pulled herself out of bed and headed for the kitchen. She barely gave the rocker a second glance as she passed it, and it creaked louder as though to protest being ostracized.

"Hush up, now," she said, making a special effort not to look back at the chair. "I heards ya already, and I get to it when I get to it." She decided to make her point by detouring to the bathroom first.

After freshening up, she went into the kitchen and turned on a small box fan that rested on an egg crate near the stove. She thought about opening the kitchen door so the air could circulate through the house, then remembered there was a sizable hole in the screen door behind it and changed her mind. It was still early in the day for mosquitoes, but she didn't want to take any chances.

She walked over to the sink, opened the cupboard above it, and pulled out a teacup and a coffee can with an aluminum foil lid. After placing both items on the counter, she reached over and turned on the water faucet. She waited a few seconds, then flicked her fingertips through the water.

"Needin' a bit hotter," she murmured, wiping her fingers across the front of her duster. She pulled the coffee can closer to her and carefully removed the foil. Reaching inside, she gathered a large pinch of coffee grounds with her thumb and middle finger. Her arthritis didn't care for the maneuver and pinched back. She grimaced but held her fingers tightly together until they were above the cup, then sprinkled the grounds over the porcelain bottom.

The steam rising from the water spigot fogged Eula Mae's glasses. She turned her head away from the vapors and rubbed the fingers of her right hand, attempting to stretch the ache out of them. Once her glasses cleared, she picked up the cup and placed the lip of it just inside the water stream until she approximated an inch depth. Then she turned off the water.

"Show to Eula Mae what you gots to show," she said, slowly pulling the cup to her.

As the swirling brew darkened and settled, she swiped the front of her teeth with her tongue. "Lawdy," she said in disgust. They tasted like they were coated with stale animal crackers. "I forgots to rinse 'em."

She lifted the cup and tapped a fingertip over the brown water. "Show to Eula Mae what you gots to show," she said again. Grasping the cup with both hands, she tilted it over the sink and slowly drained out the liquid. A few granules of coffee escaped with the flow, but the majority of the grounds clung to the sides and bottom of the cup.

Her first study of the black mosaic plastered to the porcelain made her breath catch. *It can't be,* she thought, adjusting her glasses for a better look. "Lawd, Lawd," she whispered. "It's for sure true. A rasaunt be comin'."

Her mother had told her about rasaunts a long time ago, but she'd always thought it was just a story, a tale to tell while they picked cotton or dug potatoes. The way her mother had told it, rasaunts were rare, only one born, usually somewhere in the South, every ninety to a hundred years or so. The thought of actually meeting one never occurred to Eula Mae, much less having one come to *her* for help.

She raised the venetian blind over the kitchen window so she would have better light to read the prophetic patterns. Eula Mae had always kept her clairvoyance a secret. Her mother's life had taught her all too well that the ability could be a curse more than a gift. People had followed her mother everywhere, never giving her a moment's peace. Blacks and whites had sought her out. "Tell me, Athena," they would say. "Tell me where to go, what to do, who to see, what to eat, where's the money?" And when her mother didn't tell them what they wanted to hear, they'd get mad and do bad things, like burn down a barn or kill one of their cows.

Why he comin' to me? Eula Mae wondered, swiping at her teeth again. Intuition tugged an answer closer, yet what it professed didn't make any sense to her. *Because the rasaunt is only half, not whole.* She didn't understand what that meant. The patterns clearly told her he was hungry and tired and right on top of where he needed to be, but not much else.

Eula Mae tilted the cup to the left and studied an arch starting to form in the grounds. "Lawdy," she breathed. "Maikana got a hold to this one's head. Lawd, Lawd."

She put a hand over the rim of the cup and closed her eyes to get a clearer picture of the evolving images in her mind. The rasaunt's face appeared first, thin and diseased-looking, with eyes that were sunken and red. The rest of him came seconds later and didn't look much better. Suddenly she saw his body and face splitting, like someone tearing a paper doll in half. *Half not whole.* She was beginning to get the feeling he'd been living half not whole all of his life and just didn't know it. But half not whole of what?

Eula Mae sighed heavily and opened her eyes. There was going to be no other way; she would have to physically touch him to figure it out.

Removing her hand from the top of the cup, she peered inside again and saw two thick rows of granules begin to merge into one. It was the first time in her ninety years that she'd seen anything like it. Her hands, already knotted and stiff, started to tremble uncontrollably. Maikana wanted to keep the rasaunt from his task, that much she understood. But here she viewed more anger and hate than she'd ever seen.

Before Eula Mae could read any more, the cup flew out of her hand and crashed to the floor. Coffee grounds splattered in every direction.

"Lawd, be merciful to you servant here," she said loudly. She kept one eye on the grounds while she reached for a dish towel. Bending over slowly, she lowered to her knees to clean up the mess. The towel barely touched the floor when the grounds began to take on a life of their own. They moved and gathered and slid across the floor in small circles, leaving fecal-brown trails across the cracked linoleum.

Eula Mae stood as quickly as her body would allow. "Gets outta here, y'all demons!"

The slithering mess stopped moving.

"Now," she said angrily, and tossed the dish towel over the grounds.

Resting a hand on the small of her back, she walked to the refrigerator. "Wonder if he like pork chops," she muttered. She was reaching for the refrigerator door handle when another image came to her. It made her heart shudder in her chest and shoulders slump with quiet resolve. "Well, I'm supposin' the Lawd's gonna get to it when He gets to it."

It took a moment before she could gather enough strength to open the fridge door and rummage through the small freezer. Inside sat one chicken covered with Saran wrap and two thin pork chops wrapped in foil.

"Lookin' like I won't be needin' these no more, anyways," she said, reaching for the pork chops. "No, siree. Won't be needin' these no more."

An hour later, Eula Mae was humming to the sizzle of onions and meat. She had cleaned up the grounds from the floor and tidied up the countertops. Although she sensed the rasaunt closer than ever, she felt ready, or at least as ready as possible. A silent determination had risen inside her, created by the simple confidence that God had a purpose for all things. She was damned strapped to understand what His reasons were sometimes, but that part wasn't for her to interpret. This upcoming visitor and the job God was giving her to do were, without a doubt, more than she bargained for. But then again, who was she to bargain with God? To her it came down to either choosing to accept what life dished out or not. What good would it do her not to accept it? It wouldn't change anything. Some things just were.

Eula Mae crooned softly as she spooned rice in mounded heaps onto a plate, then dressed the top of it with caramel-colored gravy lumped with onions and shriveled pork. She put the plate on the kitchen table alongside a glass of ice water, then absently wiped her hands on the front of her duster.

She shuffled into the bathroom, washed her face, and rinsed her teeth. After combing through her coarse, white hair with her fingers, she tightened the bun behind her head. She pinched both of her cheeks, pinking them slightly, then unbuttoned the front of her duster and shrugged it off her shoulders. She put on a blue housedress that hung on a hook behind the bathroom door and decided to keep her shoes off since they pinched her toes and made her ankles swell.

Before leaving the bathroom, Eula Mae decided that prudence superseded need, so she raised her housedress and backed up to the toilet. She'd heard somewhere that one of the first things to let go when someone died was bodily functions, and there was no way in heaven she was going to meet her Maker in dirty drawers.

Once assured that everything had emptied, she straightened her clothes and went into the kitchen—where she saw the rasaunt, standing just inside the door.

Chapter Sixteen

He had come *so* close, nearly to the bone. *Was it a bone? Was there a bone in it? Is that why they called it a boner?*

Todd laughed hysterically at his own joke.

"Shut up in there!" a man shouted from the next room. Thumps on the wall accentuated the demand.

Todd clamped a hand over his mouth and hiccuped. *If they would've just let me finish the job, everything would be better now,* he thought. The voices had told him to cut it off, saw the sausage, and don't touch it after detachment. He had been ordered to leave it on the floor for the janitor to pick up. Although Todd had worked diligently to comply with the command, he had not been successful.

"I could've done it, too, if that big sonofabitch hadn't shown up," Todd said, his voice sounding thick and slow in his ear.

An orderly, one Todd had never seen before, had walked in right as he bore down for the deciding slice. The man freaked when he saw the bed covered in blood. Todd tried wrestling the castration tool back from him, but the guy had been too strong. Within minutes, another man burst into the room. This one Todd remembered from earlier, someone named Lee or Leonard. Whatever the name, he'd injected Todd with medication that made the world and everything in it move way too slow.

With a grunt, Todd rolled over and sat up on the edge of the bed. Overall he felt pretty good. A little sluggish, but good. They'd stitched and bandaged him up, everything but his pee hole. "No permanent damage," they'd said.

If thine eye is the problem, then gouge it out. Better to enter heaven with one eye missing than to enter hell with your dick in your hand. Todd leaned over, nearly touching his head to his knees. The voices in his head were quieter than before, but still there. He listened to their musings while he tested the flexibility of his arm muscles, his fingers, his feet.

"I've already told them you're worthless, Todd, and that you had no business being alive. You were always worthless. You should have never been born, you know."

Todd waved a hand in front of his face. It appeared and disappeared from his field of vision in slow, jerky lines. *Maybe I'll cut this off instead,* he thought. *Don't really need it anymore. Going to need something bigger than a piece of plastic, though.*

"Hey, idiot, you listening? You're huff and puff.

That's the magic dragon, son, the demon of the underworld, the epitome of life everlasting, and the gnat-infested, crap-filled mouth of truth."

Todd stood up slowly, testing his feet against the floor. They felt tingly, and he imagined ants crawling beneath his skin. He put a hand against the wall and looked down at his legs and feet. Just hair and flesh; no ants, no demons in flames.

He took two wobbly steps forward, then stumbled and dropped to his knees. Pain ricocheted from his groin to his back, then up his spine. *Mother Mary pray for me—in the beginning was the word, then somebody forgot to read the rest of the book.*

"They're pumping nitrous oxide into this room, asshole. Haven't you figured that out yet? Next it's going to be sodium pentothal—then what're you going to do?"

Bracing a hand against the wall, Todd slowly got to his feet. Pain volleyed between his legs, as did an urgent itch. He reached down to scratch.

"I wouldn't mess around with that if I were you," a new, male voice said behind him.

Todd glanced nervously over his shoulder and saw a man standing near his bed with a dinner tray. He had a flawless face and neatly combed blond hair.

"Messed yourself up good," the man said, nodding toward Todd's crotch. "Good thing you didn't have anything sharper to work with." He smiled broadly and put the tray down on the bed. "My name's Russell, by the way. Thought you might be a bit too sore to make it to the cafeteria, so I brought your dinner to you. It's nothing fancy, but it smells good."

Hesitantly Todd turned around and studied Russell. The man looked harmless enough, but then again, the greatest demons wore masks of innocence. He walked stiffly to the cot and sat.

"Like I said, nothing fancy." Russell pulled the tin dome off the plate. "Some baked chicken, mashed potatoes, and carrots." Tapping a cellophane-wrapped cup, he said, "And juice, of course." He reached into the pocket of his lab coat and pulled out a plastic bag. " 'Cause of the, uh—accident, looks like you're going to have to manage with a plastic spoon. That's all they're going to let you have, and even then, I've got to hang around 'til you're done so I can bring it back with me." Russell took out the utensil and held it out to him. "Sorry."

Todd looked down at the plate of food, up at Russell, then back down at the plate. His stomach growled. He couldn't remember the last time he'd eaten.

"Need any help?" Russell asked.

Todd snatched the spoon from Russell, then tried to balance it across his fingers like a pencil, but his hand wouldn't hold steady.

"Don't worry about that," Russell said offhandedly. "The shakin'll stop in a bit. They gave you some serious meds for the pain."

"H-Hail Mary . . ." Todd mumbled. He needed to pray for the safety of his stomach. They could have poisoned the food. Even now, sodium pentothal might be soaking into the carrots. "Who—who art in heaven . . ." He moistened his lips.

Russell leaned over and patted Todd's shoulder. Todd flinched. "You tryin' to say grace?" Russell asked. He folded his arms across his chest and gave him a sympathetic look. "I'd be glad to help if you're havin' trouble with the words and all, but I'm not Catholic, so I don't know much about the Mary part. I can help with a good old, simple blessin' if you want, though. It's easy—thank you, Lord, for the day and food, amen. See?" He grinned.

Todd closed his eyes and saw the living room of his childhood home and his mother sitting in what used to be his father's recliner with an open Bible on her lap.

"Now you're going to be obedient little children, right?" his mother asked.

Todd and Jessica, kneeling on the marble floor on either side of her, nodded solemnly.

"And you're going to repeat everything I say, just like I say it, right?"

Silent, obedient nods.

"Good. Now, first we're going to thank the Lord for the day, then we'll thank Him for our food and for our clothes. Then we're going to pray especially hard that He brings your daddy back home to us. We're going to ask the Lord to let that man see his sinful ways and return here to his family. Understand?"

A unified "Yes, ma'am, Mama."

"Good. Okay, straight backs now, hands folded like I taught you."

And for two hours they would remain perfect little statues of piety, repeating the scripture verses read by their mother, replicating each Hail Mary, every Glory Be, every Our Father.

Todd opened his eyes, clutched the spoon in a fist,

and jammed it into the mashed potatoes. He didn't need any damn help with prayers. He knew them all.

His mouth watered as soon as his tongue tasted the creamy spuds. The first bite stuck in his throat, and he coughed.

"Be careful there," Russell said. "You might want to start out taking smaller bites."

Todd reached for a spoonful of carrots, changed his mind, and started to shovel potatoes into his mouth.

"Whoa there, buddy." Russell uncrossed his arms and frowned. "You'd better slow down, or you're going to choke again, maybe get a bad stomachache. There's no need to rush. No one's going to take your food from you. I'll stay right here and make sure of that."

Peering up at him, Todd continued to shovel through his meal. He needed to eat in a hurry—just because. He ignored the pain and itch in his groin and concentrated on the food and the taste it left in his mouth.

He felt his mood changing, becoming almost jovial. He wanted to toss the carrots into the air so he could catch them with his mouth like popcorn. But he didn't. He couldn't. If he did, the voices would figure out he was enjoying himself, and that would be the end of it, no more good meals. No chicken or carrots, no way. They didn't like for him to have stuff like that. They made him eat other things, like broken glass and cardboard, garbage, and even dog crap once.

Todd washed down the last bite of food with juice, then watched as Russell removed the tray.

"You did good," Russell said cheerfully.

Sliding gingerly to the edge of the bed, Todd belched softly, then gritted his teeth and stood. Immediately, his legs threatened to buckle, so he braced himself against the wall.

"Don't you think it'd be best if you rested for a while?" Russell asked. "Give your food a chance to go down proper?"

Todd ignored him and walked carefully to the window. The sun rode low in the sky, painting the horizon tangerine. He remembered walking along a beach once with a girl named Teresa. The sky had looked just like this, peaceful—lonely. Looking at it now made his chest hurt.

He backed away a little and spotted his reflection in the windowpane, especially the thin, pale scar that angled from the left side of his upper lip line to below his nose. The sight of it threw him violently into a memory.

Ten years old, playing football in the backyard with a couple of kids from the neighborhood. After catching a pass, Todd had raced for the goal line a few yards ahead. Along the way, he tripped and landed facedown on the edge of a shovel that lay buried under ankle-deep grass. The rusted blade sliced through his lip, parting it vertically, revealing teeth and gums. Pain flashed through him fierce and strong, as did the sound of the neighborhood boys screaming when they saw his face.

Scared and crying, he ran into the house, trailing a considerable amount of blood behind him. He made it as far as the hallway when everything around him began to spin.

Dropping to the floor, he screamed his sister's name. "Ess! Ess!" The syllable was all his mouth could manage.

After a loud clatter and a series of thumps, Jessica's bedroom door flew open and she bounded down the hall, almost running over him. When she spotted Todd, she reeled backward and all the color drained out of her face. Her lips moved, but she didn't make a sound. She stretched a hand out toward him, then quickly pulled it back.

His sister's hesitancy to touch him petrified Todd even more than the injury. His sobs built to near hysteria.

Jessica finally reached down and grasped his arm. "Oh, God—God! What happened?" Her fingers fluttered like nervous butterflies about his face, wanting to touch him but not.

"Uvel, uvel," he said, desperately trying to form the words.

"Aw, Jesus, don't talk! It makes it bleed more."

Jessica raced into the bathroom and returned with a towel. "Hold this to your lip," she said, thrusting it at him. Then she hurried toward the living room, and he knew she was going to call their mother at work. Not a good thing.

When Jessica returned, her face appeared grayer than ever, and she trembled. She sat on the floor across from him. "Does it hurt really bad?" she whispered.

He squinted and nodded.

"You don't have to talk." Jessica reached for his hands, squeezed them hard, then without another word placed one of her thumbs between his eyes.

Instantly he felt tiny pulses of electricity in his head. They seemed to be flowing from her thumb into him. Afraid, but trusting her completely, Todd closed his eyes, and the pulses grew stronger and harder. They carried a sound, a click, like the metal latch closing on his school lunchbox. Then his body felt weighted, and he had the weirdest sense that Jessica was *inside* his head, scooping up the pain as one would heavy mud.

When he'd opened his eyes to look at her, to see what was really going on, the pain in his face . . . just went away.

Todd sighed, wishing Jessica were with him now. He pushed a fingertip between the iron slats that covered the window and pressed it against the pane, feeling the summer heat. His bowels gurgled and his stomach cramped. The voices inside him groaned collectively.

Focusing on his finger, Todd willed it through the glass. In his mind, he saw the digit burst through the pane and the ragged glass edges slice off the tip of his finger. He wondered if someone could bleed to death that way, if *he* could bleed to death that way.

A clacking sound redirected Todd's attention, and he glimpsed over a shoulder to see Russell gone and the door closed. When he turned back to the window, he let out a short gasp. He no longer saw his own reflection but a large white face gazing back at him. The sight paralyzed him, fascinated him, that vertical mouth, the dark, empty eye sockets. It gyrated and bobbed behind the glass like a helium balloon on a string.

Guardedly Todd removed his finger from the window, stood on tiptoe, and peered through the slats to the ground two stories below. The head had no body, no physical framework on stilts. The head simply floated.

Todd lowered himself slowly, and the balloon-shaped head drew closer to the windowpane.

"Listen to me carefully," it said, sounding like a man with a phlegm-filled throat.

Todd took a small step back, suddenly very, very afraid.

"Time is of the essence, and you are taking entirely too long to complete your assigned task," it said. "I have been more than generous in supplying you with every opportunity and tool with which to accomplish this quietus, yet you linger still. Since I am quite familiar with your intellectual capabilities, I am confident it is not due to dim-wittedness. I must assume, therefore, you are choosing to defy me. Am I correct in that assumption?"

Mother Mary pray for—

"You will answer when addressed, you ridiculous, hypocritical religionist!" it roared.

Startled, Todd pushed away from the window. Before he could turn around, however, something grabbed him by the hair and smashed his face against the metal slats. He let out a yelp, and his head was jerked back again, then slammed forward once more, this time jamming his nose between the window bars, nearly breaking it. Blood gushed over

Todd's face, and before he could orient himself, a mauling blow struck his groin. He doubled over and fell to the floor, moaning, motionless, waiting for another attack. When it didn't come, he glanced up and saw the large white face still pressed against the window.

"You will heed my command!" it bellowed. The strength and anger in its voice seemed to penetrate into Todd's bones. "Die, you pathetic fruit of a whore! Be done with it and die!" With that, the head vanished.

Todd blinked, then rolled onto his side and began to laugh. What he meant to do was cry, to yell for help. He got up on his hands and knees and crawled to the door. Each movement drove spikes of excruciating pain through his groin, which only made him laugh harder.

Hours, days, months seemed to pass before he finally made it to the door. Todd curled up against it. "Be done with it," he said with a chuckle, and pressed a hand to his nose, encouraging it to bleed. He stretched his nostrils and twisted the bridge. *I may need to be done with it, you ugly fuck, but I'm the one who's going to say when and how! If thine eye is the problem, gouge it out—*

Todd pressed a finger to each of his eyeballs and wondered if his fingers would be long enough to reach into the middle of his brain.

Chapter Seventeen

Eli stared at the old woman, bewildered. This was definitely not the person from his dreams. She looked way too old, her skin dark like his instead of white. He couldn't have misinterpreted the pendulum, because it had pointed straight and steady toward this house. So why here? Why this woman?

"You opened both them doors?" the woman asked, trudging past him.

"No," Eli said. "It just do it by itself."

"Guess you got no udder measure but to come in, then." She pulled the screen door shut and latched it. "What they call you?"

"Eli."

"They call me Eula Mae."

While they stood scrutinizing each other, Eli wondered why the woman didn't seem to be disturbed by his appearance, which had grown hideous over the last twenty-four hours. After he'd left Markus and the woods, his body's deterioration seemed to accelerate with every passing minute. Most of his skin either cracked or peeled. The festering rifts that had started on his hands while riding in Markus's car, rapidly traveled down his arms and across his chest. In some places, the wounds opened wide and deep enough for Eli to see fatty tissue. Along the way, he'd found an old T-shirt near the side of the road and had torn it into bandages, wrapping the worst of the lesions. The mock dressings didn't help his chances for a ride, however. Passing motorists took one look at him, gawked in horror, then sped past. He'd had no choice but to walk the rest of the way. And walk he did, too many restless, sleepless miles, his body afflicted and weary, one thought pushing relentlessly at his mind: *Find her—find her—find her*. So why had he been led to this old woman?

"You hungry," Eula Mae said matter-of-factly. "And it don't look likes you doin' too good. Takes the chair at the table. I gots another one."

Eli sat at the kitchen table while she shuffled off to another room. A moment later, she returned, dragging a rocker behind her. She pulled it up to the table and sat across from him.

"I knowed you was comin'," she said firmly, and nodded at the plate of food on the table. "So eat."

"Den you knew more den me," Eli said. "I don't know why I'm here."

"You here 'cause you need Eula Mae's help."

"Help wit' what?"

"Feed you belly first, then I'm gonna tell you what you s'posed to know."

Obliging, Eli kept one eye on Eula Mae and ate greedily.

She watched him for a while and rocked. "How long it been since you et?" she finally asked.

Eli swallowed a mouthful of food. It lodged in his gullet, and he had to swallow twice more to force it down. "Don't keep track." A heat began to spread over his face, warm at first, like he'd been out in the sun too long, then escalating to fire hot. He peered down at the remaining food on the plate and decided he wasn't hungry anymore.

"You body look like it want to fall apart," Eula Mae said. "Like you be a young man with a old man's memory. How long you be like this?"

"Couple, uh, three days." Eli pushed the plate away.

Eula Mae nodded thoughtfully, then leaned into the table. "Well, I s'pose we best get about the business. Take the wrap off you hands so I can gets a good picture."

Eli shook his head. "Not much left of 'em."

"Don't matter. I gots to use 'em. All you life you touch most of what you sees. I gots to use the hand."

He caught his reflection in her glasses. It was someone he'd never seen before. Reluctantly, he removed the rag bandage from his right hand. "Why you do dis?" he asked.

Eula Mae shifted in her chair. "Why *you* do this?"

"No choice for me." Eli extended his hand, palm up.

"Neither for me," Eula Mae said, and reached across the table. The second she touched him the temperature in the room dropped twenty degrees, and his dinner plate flipped over, dumping leftovers on the table before tumbling to the floor and shattering.

Eli quickly pulled his hand back.

Eula Mae glared at the mess. "Don't pay no attention. Whatever it be, be bound and for sure to break all my dishes." She rapped her knuckles against the table and eyed him sternly. "The Lawd brung you here to me, and He gonna take care of the rest. Now, tell Eula Mae what you chasin'."

Eli placed his hand back on the table, and she pulled her glasses down to the end of her nose and peered over them. "You right," she said, examining his palm. "It just about gone." She found a spot on the fleshy pad right below his fingers that still held more than one layer of skin and pressed a fingertip to it.

"Lawd, Lawd," she mumbled, then sucked air in through her teeth.

Suddenly two cupboard doors flew open and a drinking glass shot across the room, crashing into the wall. Eli ignored the ruckus, concentrating instead on Eula Mae, who had her head bowed and eyes closed.

"What you see?" he asked hesitantly.

She scowled. "Hold on, now. It's all mix up. Wait 'til I sees better." With her eyes still closed, she tilted her head. "Look like you be from the swamp point, far back to the woods," she recited quietly. "That's true?"

"Uh-huh."

"And now you be out here chasin' a woman with a hard walk but a soft heart. She here in this town for sure. You be in the right place." Eula Mae frowned again, then opened one eye. "But you don't know why you be lookin' for her?"

Eli shook his head while he watched a patchwork rug zip across the floor, then levitate in midair.

Eula Mae sat back and looked heavenward. "Lawd, I can't be doin' my job if you ain't gonna hold 'em off," she said with exasperation.

The rug landed on the floor with a plop.

With a click of her tongue, Eula Mae began to rock again, her right foot slapping rhythmically against the floor with each downward thrust. "It's a mix-up story," she said, studying Eli. "So you gonna have to listen close."

He blinked, afraid to move, his heart pounding with eagerness. Finally, answers.

"Long time ago, when you be 'round three, four years old, you mama go to a gris-gris man to see if he can get rid of Maikana in her head."

At the mention of Maikana, a single, bombastic roar shook the tiny house. Eli jumped up from his chair and covered his head.

"Sit!" Eula Mae commanded.

Eli dropped to his seat immediately. "But—"

"Yeah, I know you know who Maikana be," Eula Mae said sternly. "He all over inside you head right now, but we gonna talk about that after a bit. Right now I gots to start from the beginning or get lost. So, like I say, you mama go to a gris-gris man and bring you with her. You mama want him to take Maikana out her head. The gris-gris can't do that, though, but you mama don't know that yet. While y'all be over there, another woman show up, a white one. She be big and pregnant. Big and pregnant with the true rasaunt, a girl rasaunt."

"What you mean true rasaunt?" Eli asked. "Johanson say I be de rasaunt."

"Johanson be the gris-gris man, *non*?"

He nodded.

Eula Mae stared past him. "Johanson don't lie to you, but he don't know all that's to know. You only part rasaunt, not true rasaunt like that baby girl." She shook her head as though to clear it, then harrumphed. "But you making me go ahead to myself again, and everything going to get tangled. So wait up."

She rocked harder and squinted, her eyes seeming to focus on a distant vision. "You touch that pregnant woman's belly," she said after a while. "And that girl rasaunt living inside the womb feel you, and she feel Maikana in you, too." Eula Mae made a quick circle in the air with a finger. "Now this be where everything get all mess up. The baby rasaunt want to heal you, want to take Maikana out of you, but because she not full ready yet in her power, something mix up. When you touch the stomach, some of her power go into you and some of Maikana that was in you, that you got from you mama, go into her. So y'all wind up half and half. You half rasaunt, her half rasaunt. You part Maikana, her part Maikana. You hear what I'm sayin'?"

Eli shivered. He felt fluid leaking out of his left ear but didn't bother to identify what it was. He remembered himself as a child, back in a place with two dead dogs, and suddenly understood more than what Eula Mae was saying.

"Dat's why she come in my dreams," he said. "She wantin' it back."

"It's more complicate than that," Eula Mae said. "While the rasaunt grow up, she know she different than other people, but she refuse to believe she got the power she got."

"Why?"

" 'Cause her mama sick with Maikana, and the rasaunt afraid she different 'cause she gettin' sick like her mama."

"You mean she can't tell no different?"

Eula Mae shrugged. "She been refusin' the rasaunt power for so long, she can't tell nuttin' 'bout nuttin'."

Confused, Eli stood and walked over to the kitchen sink. Shards of porcelain from the shattered plate pierced the soles of his feet. He ignored the pain. "How come if she don't want de power back den, she want it now?"

" 'Cause something had to happen to make the true rasaunt want to go past herself, go past what she afraid of."

"What's dat somet'ing?"

"Her brother. Her brother be real sick. That's why she come here. Maikana working on the brother hard and 'most through with him. When she gonna see her brother, her heart gonna hurt so bad, she gonna know it be time. Then she gonna want all her power more than ever before. You gots to be with her, Eli, when that happens so the two parts can go back to the whole. That's the reason you heart be sick all the time in the swamp. That be the reason why you dreamin' 'bout that woman, 'cause it's time to bring both the halves together. That's why the gris-gris man give you that necklace thing to come here. He knowed about some of this, not all, just enough to know he had to help put the two back when the time come to pass."

Eli slumped against the counter. What little energy he had left seemed to be draining out of him along with the fluid from his ear and the thick liquid now leaking from his right eye. "What gonna happen if I not be dere wit' her?"

Eula Mae clutched the arms of her rocker. "If you not go, then both halves of the rasaunt power gonna die. Maikana gonna be all that's left. She gonna die, you gonna die, the brother gonna die. And the boy, too."

"The boy?"

She sighed heavily. "I told you it be all mess up. See, this rasaunt be more different than the rest that come in the years past. All rasaunt before be men, this the first woman. 'Cause she be a woman, her power can pass on to her chil'ren. Only if she be whole, though. If she don't have all the rasaunt power before the boy come of age—and that gonna be soon. Maybe two, three days, I s'pose—there won't be no rasaunt power to be pass to him. Then he gonna have a empty place in his soul and in his head, enough so Maikana take him, too. Then he gonna die after not too long."

More perplexed than ever, Eli lowered his head and watched the blood pool beneath his feet. Not more than a yard away, he spotted the rug begin to inch its way across the floor.

"Eula Mae," he said quietly. "How come now?"

"I already told you how come now."

"But look at dis." Eli held up his hands. "My body wanna die right now. I can't even heal *me* no more. How I'm gonna give back to her what belong to her if I be dead? If de rasaunt power gone all out from me, what I'm gonna have to give back? How come my body be dyin' like dis now?"

" 'Cause you use the power of rasaunt you have all these years," Eula Mae said. "It flow through you, workin' most every day. That power got its own life force. The closer you get to her, the more it leave you to go to her. When it leave you, it drain the life force that s'pose to keep you body healthy."

Eli grimaced. "So what you say is eit'er way I'm gonna die. If I not go give it back to her, I'm gonna die. If I give it back to her, I'm gonna die 'cause dere won' be nuttin' left in me."

Eula Mae shrugged. "I'm not too sure. That's something I can't see too good. I think if she take all her power back before you lose everything, she can heal you, too, with her brother. She can heal you body and take Maikana out you head."

Tears sprang suddenly to Eli's eyes and made them burn. "Maikana be bad in my head now," he whispered. "I—I kill a rat wit' my hand. I didn't even know dat's what I do 'til way later."

Eula Mae placed a hand over her heart and nodded slowly. "And you kill a man, too."

Eli's tears fell harder, and he looked away, ashamed.

"Maikana workin' hard in you head, Eli. He don't want you to get to the woman. If she be made whole, he know she gonna help a lot of peoples. The more she help, the more power he gonna lose until he gone and can't hurt nobody no more. Maikana tryin' to use you to kill her. He want to keep you mind confused so when you meet her, you gonna kill her instead of giving back to her what belongs to her. You gonna have to fight hard to keep you mind about youself."

"How? How I can fight hard?" Eli cried. "I be too weak now. I barely made de walk across de yard when I come here."

Eula Mae stopped rocking and reached into the pocket of her housedress. "I gots some of this ready when I knowed you was comin'," she said, and pulled out a small glass vial. It contained a substance that looked like lavender salt. "This gonna give you a bit more time, bit more stren'th." Her eyes traveled down the length of his body. "Come more close to me. You too far."

Eli hesitantly inched his way closer until he stood beside her.

Eula Mae raised the small vial and flung some of its contents over him.

The instant the tiny granules hit Eli, his body began to jerk and convulse. He felt his eyes roll back in his head, and his hands slap at the air. He heard the cupboard doors behind him slam violently. He tried to brace himself against the table, but his body felt liquid, without muscle or bone, and he dropped to his knees.

He strained to cry out but couldn't, strained to see and wished he hadn't, for he spotted the refrigerator moving sluggishly across the kitchen floor on its own. It ripped up linoleum as it traveled. Within seconds the fridge door swung open, and a carton of milk flew out, sending a white spray across the room. Two eggs bulleted out of a plastic carton and splattered onto the floor while a container of cottage cheese hurled itself over Eula Mae's head.

A storage closet near the stove opened, releasing a dozen paper shopping bags that immediately took flight. The bags flew at Eli's face, then dove for Eula Mae's head, slapping at her.

"Gets out, you demon!" Eula Mae shouted, her voice shaking with anger. "You gots no business in this place. Get!" She flung out a hand, wildly sprinkling the remaining granules from the vial around her. Some of them landed on the food dumped on the table earlier. The leftover rice and meat liquefied and bubbled, filling the air with an acrid stench.

The paper bags soared for the ceiling, where they gathered to form a tight circle. There they stayed, suspended in midair.

Eli watched Eula Mae push down on the arms of her chair and stand, her face fiercely set, her eyes ablaze. "Gets out, you demon, by the Lawd God's name!" she shouted.

A roar, louder and more ferocious than the one they'd heard earlier, shook the house, and Eula Mae was slammed back into the rocker. Her bare feet flew out in front of her as the chair tipped backward, and her head banged against the wooden slats. She pitched forward again just before the chair went over on its back. Eli saw the bun resting near the nape of her neck pull upward, like someone had grabbed it and yanked hard.

"Yi, yi!" Eula Mae screamed. She leaned over and slapped at her head.

Suddenly she sat upright, and her bun flopped limply to one side. She looked over at Eli, her eyes wide and puzzled, blood trickling from the corners of her mouth. Gingerly she leaned back in her chair and pressed an unsteady hand to her chest.

Eula Mae blinked, and the paper bags fell from their airborne state, fluttering innocently to the floor. Her hand fell to her lap. She blinked again, slowly—and for the last time.

Trembling, Eli rose to his feet and hobbled to Eula Mae's side. He stood next to her, feeling a gentle resurgence of strength enter his body as he pondered all she had said. Because of Eula Mae, he now knew the purpose for his bizarre physical and metaphysical journey. Though the road promised little more than a dire destination, he had no choice but to keep going. There simply was no other direction for him to take.

As he gazed at her forlornly, another thought occurred to Eli. Surely with everything Eula Mae had discerned about him, she had to have known about her own impending death should she reveal what she learned. Still, this small, frail woman chose to help him, had opened her home and prophetic eye to him, had even shared her food. The depth of her selflessness humbled Eli, and he bowed his head respectfully.

After a long while, he tucked a few stray hairs behind Eula Mae's right ear, then left the house, lonelier and more afraid than he'd ever been in his life.

Chapter Eighteen

There they go again!

Jessica watched the flower arrangement on the dresser in Lisa's old room sway in its vase. She'd been on the phone with Frank only half an hour, giving him a summary of her visits to Municipal, and it was the third time she'd seen the flowers move.

She glanced at the window. Closed—the same position it had been in when she'd checked earlier. Even if it had been opened, she knew there wasn't enough of a breeze outside to flutter leaves. Perplexed, she peered up to double-check the light fixture. Same as before. Light on, no funny bulbs, no strange lampshade that could create an illusion.

"The place sounds like a circus act," Frank said.

"Huh?" Jessica asked, her eyes now riveted on the silk bouquet. It did a sluggish shimmy, then rose and fell in the crystal vase as though to straighten itself.

"I said, the place sounds like— Are you okay?"

She forced her attention back to her husband's voice. "What?"

"I asked if you were all right."

Jessica wanted to cry out, "No, I'm not! I've heard weird voices, had monster headaches, my brother is in some kind of Hitchcock nightmare, and now I'm watching a bunch of fucking flowers dance by themselves!" Instead, she said, "I'm fine."

A thin screech reverberated through the room as the vase began to slide slowly across the dresser. Jessica clutched the receiver tightly and gaped as the flowers twitched and jiggled, their container coming within a hair's width of the bureau's front edge before stopping.

"You don't sound fine," Frank said.

Her heart pounded, skipped, pounded again. *Keep it cool, keep it light.* "Uh—just uptight, I guess." Jessica wanted to tell her husband, *needed* to tell him what she'd just seen, but the words wouldn't come. She stood up from the daybed and inched toward the bedroom door. The phone cord stopped her after only five feet.

"I can understand why you would be," Frank empathized. "Did Lisa give you a break when you got in, or did she and her mother drill you for details?"

"They took it easy on me." She moved the receiver away from her mouth and exhaled shakily. Putting the mouthpiece back to her lips, she said with feigned casualness, "I think they could tell I wasn't up to sharing a blow-by-blow."

"That's good. Hey, you're not mad at me for giving Lisa your flight schedule, are you?'

"Of course not." She studied the dresser. All remained quiet on the floral front. "How's Jake?"

"Healthy and hungry, same as usual," Frank said. "He's spending the night at Brandon's tonight, then tomorrow Brandon's coming here. I'm thinking about taking off work early tomorrow so I can bring them swimming." He paused. "Jess, you know I want to be there with you, right?"

"I know, but I'm okay, really," Jessica said quickly. "You're helping me more by being with Jake. I feel better when he's with you instead of a sitter, less for me to worry about. Besides, don't forget about your project deadline."

"No deadline is as important to me as you, you know that. I'd just like to help."

Jessica loved Frank more than life, but right now she wanted off the phone and out of the bedroom. She worried, however, that if she rushed him, he'd suspect something more than she'd told him and jump on the next flight to Louisiana. That frightened her more than the self-propelled flowers, and she didn't know why.

"Look, I promise I'll call for my knight in shining armor if things get out of hand," she said, then thought, *Damn, how much more out of hand can things get?*

She heard Frank tap his front teeth with a fingernail, a habit he had when deep in thought, and knew that he was calculating the potential success ratio if he pursued the issue. Evidently assessing it to be zero to zip, he finally asked, "So what do you think your chances are that they'll let you see Todd?"

"Hard to tell. All I can do is keep my fingers crossed

until morning, then call and see what happens."

Frank sighed, filling in another long pause. "Have you eaten yet?"

"Yeah. Have you?"

"Not so fast, missy. Was it more than chips and a Coke?"

The top bureau drawer suddenly slid open about three inches, and the hair on Jessica's arms stood on end. "Yep," she said quickly. "Sharon cooked shrimp étoufee for supper." She didn't tell him she'd taken one bite and pushed her plate away. She pulled the phone cord taut. It only allowed her another inch closer to the door. "I . . . uh . . . I guess I'd better be going. I've had the phone tied up for a while, and Lisa's dad may be trying to call from offshore." She hoped the excuse didn't sound as lame to him as it did to her.

"Well . . . okay," Frank said reluctantly. "You know I miss that cute face of yours, huh?"

"Miss that cute butt of yours," Jessica said, barely able to give their good-bye ritual even a half-hearted effort.

"So that's why you married me, for my butt."

"That's right. Your butt and your cooking."

Frank laughed. "I love you, kiddo. Call tomorrow if you get a chance."

"Love you, too, and I will."

Jessica no sooner dropped the receiver in its cradle than the vase crashed to the floor. She let out a yelp and bolted for the door. Grabbing the knob, she twisted and pulled, but it slipped uselessly in her sweaty palm. Behind her, a bureau drawer groaned and creaked against its runners. The lights flickered twice, then glowed with the brilliance of a desert sun at high noon. In the time it took Jessica to squint against the glare, she heard an audible snap, and the lights abruptly died, burying her in an interminable black hole. A splintering crash erupted to her left.

Horror-stricken and nearly sightless, Jessica groped, clawed, and yanked on the knob. A scream swelled in her chest, and just before it burst from her lips, the door finally opened. She threw herself across the threshold, and the door immediately slammed shut behind her.

Without looking back, Jessica ran across the hall to the bathroom and locked herself inside. She leaned her forehead against the doorjamb for a moment, panting, unable to mentally grasp what had just happened. Logic tried to console her. The weird light show in Lisa's room might have been the result of a voltage irregularity, a quirk in the electrical current. Not being able to open the bedroom door could be chalked up to humidity, swollen wood, and a bad case of nerves. But what about the flowers and vase? The bureau drawer? Those unanswerable questions caused Jessica's chain of reasoning to break. She shivered, placed a hand over the light switch, then hesitated, debating whether to flip it on or not. At least in the dark, she wouldn't be able to see if the toilet lid started flapping up and down by itself or if the hand towels decided to choreograph their own waltz. She squeezed her eyes shut, forcing darker upon dark, willing her nerves to calm. She heard the *plunk-splat* of water dripping from a nearby faucet, footsteps pounding down the hall, then Lisa's frantic voice calling to her from behind the bathroom door.

"Jess? You all right in there?"

Jessica opened her eyes and felt them immediately well up with tears. "No," she whispered, her voice so low the word barely reached her own ears. "Definitely not all right."

"Jess?"

Not all right.

"Jessica!"

Reluctantly, Jessica flipped on the light switch and unlocked the bathroom door. "It's open," she said hoarsely, then went to the sink, turned on the faucet, and began dousing her face with cold water.

Lisa barged into the room. "Man, you had me worried! All that banging and slamming going on, I thought you'd fallen and . . . What's wrong?"

Jessica shut off the water and slid her hands wearily over her face. She peered into the mirror over the sink at the reflection of her friend standing behind her. How would she ever explain what she had seen without sounding deranged? The strange voice from her office had been bad enough, but add jiggling flowers and an animated dresser to the equation and the sum read lunatic. Maybe Municipal had committed the wrong member of the Guidry family.

"What?" Lisa pressed.

Instead of answering, Jessica pulled a washcloth from a towel rod and dried her face.

"You're weirding me out here, girl. Come on, what gives?"

Jessica neatly folded the cloth and placed it on the corner of the vanity before turning to face her. "Do me a favor," she said quietly. "Go and take a look inside your room."

"Huh?"

"Just go. Please. I need to know what you see in there."

"But what's—"

"Please?"

Frowning, Lisa did an about-face and left the bathroom.

Jessica balled her hands into fists and muttered a fervent prayer. "Please, God, let her see something in there so I'll know I'm not losing my mind."

She was on the tenth repeat of the invocation when Lisa returned a couple of minutes later.

"Well?" Jessica asked.

Lisa shrugged. "Nothing different but the phone. It's on the bed instead of the nightstand."

Letting out a long, shaky breath, Jessica sat on the closed toilet seat. "Flowers on the dresser? Drawers still in the bureau?" she asked tightly.

"Yeah—why wouldn't they be?"

Jessica bit her upper lip and looked up at the wide set of Lisa's dark, worried eyes, her clear, olive complexion, and the tousle of black curls that refused to be managed. The normalcy of it made her eyes fill with tears.

"Jess, just tell me—"

"They were on the floor," Jessica blurted.

"What was on the floor?"

"The vase, in a thousand pieces. And the dresser drawer, I heard—I heard it—break."

Lisa cleared her throat, her frown deepening. "I didn't see anything broken when I went in there."

Jessica searched her friend's face. "I'm afraid," she whispered. "I'm seeing stuff, hearing things.

Lisa, what if I have the same illness as Todd? What's going to happen to Frank? To Jake?"

With a look of incredulity, Lisa shook her head firmly and walked over to her. "Look, I don't know what happened in that room, but I seriously doubt if you have what Todd has, Jess. And in case you forgot, you're not the only one who's heard weird shit. Remember the popping noise in your office and how it made my nose bleed?"

"Yeah, but—"

"Huh-uh, no buts. Now come on," Lisa said, taking one of Jessica's hands and pulling her to her feet. "If you think I'm going to let you push yourself off the deep end like this, you're nuts—pun intended. We're going to go into that bedroom together and get to the bottom of—"

"I'm not going back in there," Jessica said, pulling out of Lisa's grasp.

"But I'll be with you the whole time," Lisa coaxed. "If there's any woo-woo shit going down in there, it'll have to impress the both of us."

"No."

Lisa blew out a loud puff of air. "Fine, okay, no bedroom." She leaned over and unrolled a handful of toilet tissue. "But we're at least going for a walk so you can get some fresh air circulating around that brain of yours, okay?" She waited for Jessica to nod in agreement, then handed her the tissue with a feeble smile. "Here, wipe up the snot. Last I saw, Mom was out in the garage boxing up canning jars, but she might be done by now. If we walk out there and she sees you've been crying, she'll play fifty questions or take your temperature or something."

Jessica nodded again, then took the tissue and blew her nose. She followed Lisa out of the bathroom and down the hall, averting her eyes from the bedroom as they passed it.

After they managed to get through the kitchen and out the back door undetected, Lisa led her around the side of the house to the driveway, then onto the graveled road.

They took a right and headed toward the dead end of Sylvia Street, about two blocks away. The security lamps illuminating the road cast sallow swatches over the neighborhood, and June bugs and mosquitoes flurried in their glow. The humid night seemed to add weight to Jessica's shoulders, and she felt them sag. She walked somberly, occasionally watching her feet shuffle through the gravel.

"Neighborhood hasn't changed much, has it?" Lisa asked after a while. She shoved her hands into the back pockets of her jean shorts.

Jessica surveyed the row of clapboard houses lining both sides of the street. Some looked dark and abandoned. Others, with kitchen or living-room windows brightly lit, revealed families eating supper or watching television. Every drought-stricken lawn had been sparsely landscaped. A meager hedge here and there, a few decorated with small, domed shrines of the Blessed Mother. The air here smelled of frying chicken and pine trees.

"Not much at all," she agreed.

Lisa gently nudged Jessica's arm with an elbow. "Hey, you want to talk about what happened back at the house?"

"Not now. Later maybe."

"Whenever you feel like it. I mean, I just don't want you to think I'm blowing off whatever happened to you."

"I don't."

"Good."

They strolled along in silence, Jessica listening to locusts whine and the crunch of gravel beneath her feet. The sounds began to sooth her and helped to chase away thoughts of ghastly flowers and self-destructing bureau drawers. A dog barked nearby, and she glanced back and saw a chocolate Lab bounding down the street toward them. Its lopsided gait and lolling tongue told her they were more likely to be slobbered on than attacked.

"Whose dog?" she asked.

Lisa, evidently lost in her own thoughts, looked up with a start. "Huh?"

Before Jessica could repeat the question, the dog was at their feet, barking and snorting and jumping excitedly.

Lisa scowled and made shooing motions at the dog. "Hershey, go. Go home."

Suddenly a woman's shrill voice called out from a darkened porch to their left, "Hershey, come here, boy!"

The dog stopped short and cocked its head, panting.

Lisa grabbed Jessica by the arm and pulled. "Girl, hurry. That's Mrs. Doucet. If she sees us—"

"Lisa? Lisa Daigle, is dat you?"

"Aw, man," Lisa whined under her breath, then out loud: "Yes, ma'am, Mrs. Doucet, it's me." She leaned into Jessica and whispered, "Keep going. If I introduce you to her, we'll be here for a month.

She'll want to know where you're from, who's your mama, who's your daddy—go." She gave Jessica a little push, then veered into the woman's yard with Hershey following close behind.

"You here visitin' your mama?" the short, round woman asked as she stepped out of the porch's shadow.

"Yes, ma'am. Just got in the other day."

"How's she doin'?"

"Just fine.

"Who's dat with you?"

"Old friend from out of town. How's Mr. Doucet?"

"Oh, his joints been achin' a bit. . . ."

Mrs. Doucet's voice faded into a low drone as Jessica headed farther down the street. She was only a hundred yards or so from the bramble bushes and trees that boxed in the end of the street, but she figured she would wait there until Lisa finished chatting with the neighbor.

The night thickened as she neared the dead end, and Jessica peered nervously behind her. She noticed that the last streetlamp she'd passed wasn't working. Hesitancy broke her stride. Her eyes narrowed, trying to discern shapes and the hint of any movement ahead. Not seeing anything, she pressed on.

When she was only a few feet from the prickly wall, she turned to see if Lisa might be heading in her direction. She wasn't. Jessica could still see her with Mrs. Doucet, who waved her hands about in animated conversation.

Assuming her wait to be a while, Jessica searched for a place to sit. There wasn't a lot for her to choose from: the graveled road, or a patch of grass in front of the thicket. She chose the grass but sat sideways. That way she didn't have to have her back to the trees, and she could still watch for her friend.

Jessica crossed her legs and leaned forward, keeping a peripheral eye on the road and the bushes while she absently plucked at blades of grass. A breeze came out of nowhere and kissed the right side of her face. Thirsty leaves shivered and whispered collectively. Before long her mind eased into the rhythm of the night, and she wondered what Frank and Jake were doing at this very moment. Jessica pictured them horsing around in the living room while they took a break from one of their favorite sitcoms. Another breeze ran across her back, and she watched the limbs from the bushes sway gently.

A tree frog leaped out from the underbrush, startling her. She let out a nervous chuckle when it hopped across the road. Her laughter quickly died, however, as the shrubbery to her right began to rustle. Her eyes drew anxiously to it. This time there was no related breeze.

Jessica glared into the thicket. *It's just the dog snooping around,* she told herself. Then her breath caught as two crimson orbs, like stained-glass eyes, appeared amid the tangle of branches. *Just the dog, just the dog*. Only, it didn't *feel* like the dog. Jessica rose slowly to her feet, and the eyes followed her every move.

She inched backward onto the gravel, and the quarter-sized dots seemed to float toward her. She stopped moving, and they held their position. Without warning, the eyes quickly disappeared, then reemerged a few seconds later, as though doing a slow blink.

"My soul is dying," a male voice said suddenly.

Jessica spun around, and her heart seemed to trip over her lungs, shortening her breath. The voice sounded like it came from behind her—beside her. She spun around again, back to the eyes.

"My soul almost gone."

Jessica dropped into a crouch and grabbed a handful of gravel, her only weapon if the man decided to chase her when she ran off. Once armed, she stood up and backed away slowly.

"If you run away, you brother gonna die," the voice said wearily. This time it came from the depths of the thicket.

She froze. "W-what?"

"Gonna die."

Jessica cocked her hand, ready to pitch her ammunition at the first sign of movement. "Who the hell are you?" she demanded.

Another slow blink. "Eli," the voice said steadily.

"And—and what do you know about my brother?" She stepped back a bit farther and tensed her throwing arm.

A groan, then: "Dat his soul gonna soon die, and you got to save it. You got to save him and me."

Most of the gravel fell from Jessica's hand. *This isn't real,* she thought. *Remember the vase, remember the voice in Memphis. This isn't real.*

"It be very real," Eli said in response to her thoughts. "Dis not Maikana playin' wit' you head like he been tryin' to before. Dis be very real. You got to get to you brother quick before Maikana finish him, and I got to go wit' you before Maikana finish me."

"Maikana?" Jessica directed the question more to herself than to him. She knew that name from somewhere, had heard it before—but where?

Eli groaned painfully. "Maikana a bad master spirit. He don't want what belong to you, whole. I got to fix dat. I got to give you back what belong to you so you can save you brother."

Jessica wet her lips. "Give what back to me?" She realized she had taken a few steps closer to the thicket.

"You got to save you brother. I can show you how. I give it back to you."

"Give *what* back to me?" Jessica asked.

"This," he said, his voice suddenly coarse and hard. The eyes blinked again, then widened.

Branches and twigs from the surrounding bramble began to crackle and snap like someone high-stepping through them. Jessica moved back cautiously and strained to see through the leafy tangle as the sound grew closer. The bushes parted two feet to her left, and a thin, black-on-black outline of a figure appeared. It moved slowly through the thicket toward her. Squinting, she noticed something raised over its head, something long and narrow and stiff.

A hand suddenly clamped over Jessica's shoulder, and she screamed and flung out what remained of her gravel ammo.

"It's me!" Lisa shouted, and ducked.

It took Jessica a moment before the familiar face registered.

"Good Lord, I didn't mean to scare you," Lisa said, shaking dust from her hair. "I've been calling you for the past couple of minutes, but you just stood here zoned. What's up with you?"

Dumbstruck, Jessica turned back to the thicket.

The red eyes and dark figure were gone.

Chapter Nineteen

A child's hand held the squirming fetus up to her. She saw tiny blue veins prominent beneath its pasty-gray skin, translucent eyelids, and a mouth so small it barely seemed capable of opening. It mewed softly, pitifully, and she reached out to take it from the child. This fetus belonged to her, having originated not from her womb but from her soul, and its purpose was to serve the world. This child had no business possessing it; some horrible mistake had been made.

"Careful," she whispered as her fingers stretched ever closer. "Careful, now—"

Abruptly the fetus was pulled away. "By the process of elimination and the laws of retribution, your lineage is no more!" a powerful, deep voice bellowed, and the child's hand quickly wrapped around the fetus and squeezed hard.

"No!"

Jessica bolted upright with a loud gasp. Her heart did a sputter, stop, sputter during the few seconds it took her to realize she'd been dreaming.

"Jesus," she muttered, and dropped back down on the pillow, trembling. The dream had been so vivid, so real, she could still see every detail clearly.

She turned on her side and pulled the pillow in close, trying not to think about it. The instant she closed her eyes, however, the images flooded back in Technicolor.

With a sigh, she rolled over on her back and glanced at her watch. Nine forty-five. "Crap." She scrambled to untangle the blanket from around her legs, then jumped up from the couch and rammed her knee against the coffee table. "Shit!"

She was hobbling around in a circle when Sharon, clad in bright yellow shorts and blouse, came strolling into the living room with a mug of coffee.

"Your morning wake-up dance?" Sharon asked with a grin.

"Got up too fast. My knee found the coffee table before the rest of me did." Jessica pulled up the left pant leg of her sweats. A red splotch about the size of a half-dollar marked the middle of her kneecap.

Sharon grimaced. "Oh, that must have hurt like the dickens."

When Jessica spotted worry lines growing on Sharon's forehead, she hurriedly pushed the pant leg down before the woman wound up calling for an ambulance and a staff of X-ray technicians. "It's feeling better already," she assured her. She nodded toward the coffee mug. "Is that for me?"

Sharon scanned Jessica's cloaked knee once more, then handed her the cup. "It sure is. Thought you could use a little caffeine to start your day."

Jessica forced herself not to limp as she walked over to her and took the cup. "This smells wonderful, thanks."

"You're welcome." Sharon propped a hip against the arm of the couch and patted the Naugahyde. "Now tell me something. Why on earth would you want to sleep out here on this old thing? You know you could've used the daybed in Lisa's room."

Since Jessica hadn't shared with Sharon the ominous experience she'd had in the bedroom—nor did she plan to—she opted for an easy out. She shrugged. "I like the couch. It's comfortable."

"So you slept well?"

"Um-hm," Jessica mumbled while taking a sip of coffee. *Considering it took me hours to finally fall asleep.* Most of the night she'd pondered over the red eyes in the bushes, that man's voice, his shadow, how he'd disappeared without a trace—if he'd ever really been there at all. Jessica hadn't told Lisa about the episode in the thicket because it sounded too far off the Prozac scales even to her. She'd explained away the gravel-flinging easily, telling Lisa she'd been deep in thought and had simply been surprised by her sudden arrival. The explanation had been a half-truth, but Lisa accepted it, although dubiously, then, thankfully, had left well enough alone.

"Good," Sharon said, then stood and ran a hand over the front of her blouse, smoothing nonexistent wrinkles. "I was hoping all the stress you've been under wouldn't keep you from resting. I know when

I've got a lot on my mind I can't sleep worth a lick. I break out in hives, too. Stress can do weird stuff to people sometimes."

"It sure can," Jessica said. *More than you know.* Wanting very much to change the subject, she took another sip of coffee and glanced at her watch again. "I didn't realize it was this late. I'm supposed to call Municipal this morning. They might let me see Todd today."

Sharon beamed. "Oh, that's terrific, honey!" She motioned to the phone sitting on a small, doily-draped end table near the recliner. "Go ahead and use that one if you want, since it's right here. I'll go back to making breakfast, give you some privacy."

Jessica gave her a grateful smile. "Thanks. Where's Lisa, by the way? Still sleeping?"

"Oh, no. She left about an hour ago for Mire's Garage. My car needed an oil change, and she volunteered to bring it in." Sharon patted her stiff upsweep and shook her head. "You know how men are. Glen was supposed to bring the car in before he left, but, of course, he didn't. And you'd think the man would know better. Why, just last week Mrs. Mouton from down the street had her car engine blow out because Mr. Mouton forgot to— Good heavens, listen to me ramble on like an old lady. Go." Sharon smiled and made a shooing gesture with her fingers. "Go make your call before I get cranked up again. We'll talk later." With that, she headed for the kitchen, her gold, plastic sandals slapping against the floor.

Jessica took another sip of coffee, then placed the mug on the coffee table. She waited until Sharon was out of sight before hobbling over to the phone. Her knee still hurt like hell.

She punched in the clinic's number, and after the fourth ring heard, "Good morning, Municipal. This is Russell. How can I help you?"

Jessica immediately associated the man's name with the face of the tall blonde who had escorted her into the commons area on her first visit to Municipal. "Russell, this is Jessica LeJeune. I—"

"Ms. LeJeune," he said brightly. "Well, if this ain't my lucky day. Here I was giving Suzanne a break from the phone—you know she's been taking Mildred's place. Do you know Mildred? She's the regular lady up front here, but she's out on vacation. So anyway, we're all kind of pitchin' in to help while she's out. But look at this, I pick up the phone, and I get to talk to you. Lucky, lucky day! How ya doin'?"

Jessica could almost see the smile wrapped around Russell's face. She wondered if he was naturally this perky or if he had a habit of pilfering happy drugs from a supply closet. "Doing fine, Russell. I'm calling—"

"About your appointment, right? Dr. Lee already left a message with Suzanne. It's right here on a Post-it note! You can come back this afternoon, same time as yesterday, two o'clock."

"He—he's going to let me see my brother?" Jessica asked skeptically. She'd anticipated continued resistance, not a preset meeting.

"Yep, looks that way. Dr. Lee's a nice guy, you know. Treats everyone here real good."

"That's wonderful—good—thanks, Russell. I'll be there at two."

"Sure thing, Ms. LeJeune. See ya then."

Jessica hung up the phone, perplexed. She still couldn't believe the ease with which she'd been given the appointment. After all she'd gone through to see Dr. Lee the first time, this seemed *too* easy. Jessica felt her falling-anvil paranoia slip into gear. What if this meeting had been set up only for Lee to reiterate that she couldn't see Todd?

Making a conscious effort to stay positive, Jessica made her way sans limp into the kitchen. She found Sharon at the snack bar busily filling two plates with scrambled eggs, bacon, and grits. A platter of hot biscuits sat nearby, along with two tall glasses of orange juice and a carafe of steaming coffee.

"Gosh, I hope you have a lot more company coming," Jessica said with a soft chuckle. The prospect of seeing Todd seemed to reclaim her appetite. She actually felt hungry now.

"Nope, it's just me and you," Sharon said.

"You're going to put ten pounds on me with all this good cooking." Jessica looked down at her sweatpants and T-shirt, sleeping attire she wore all year round. "Let me get some decent clothes on. I'll be right back."

"Don't be ridiculous! You're family and dressed just fine. You're lucky Lisa's not here, 'cause when her father's out of the house, she'll eat in her underwear."

Jessica laughed heartily and appreciated how good it felt. "I bet she would, too."

"You know it." Sharon pulled up a stool. "Now, come, eat."

"Thanks for all your trouble," Jessica said, sitting. "I really do appreciate your letting me stay here."

"Jess," Sharon said, hoisting herself atop a stool across from Jessica. "I meant what I said—you're family." She reached over, grabbed two biscuits, and placed them on Jessica's already overloaded plate. "And family does for one another no matter what. Whatever doing needs to be done, you just do it. So I don't want to hear no more about it, okay?"

"Okay."

"Now, eat before your food gets cold." Sharon waved a hand over the food. "Don't think I haven't been watching. You've hardly eaten enough lately to keep a hummingbird alive. Here, drink your orange juice."

Taking the glass obediently, Jessica drank. She wasn't a big fan of orange juice, but it was the least she could do for the woman. After emptying half the glass, she hefted a forkful of eggs into her mouth under Sharon's watchful eye. She couldn't help but sigh audibly as her tongue and palate savored the food.

Sharon's face lit up. "You like it?"

"You're the best cook on the planet," Jessica said sincerely, knowing there was no higher compliment to pay a Cajun woman than to praise her cooking.

"Aw," Sharon said, blushing. "Your mom was the good cook. She taught me most of what I know."

Jessica looked up, surprised. "Really? I didn't know that. I mean, I know Mom was a good cook, but I didn't know she'd taught you."

"You'd better believe it. I could barely boil an egg when I first got married."

They shared a smile, then ate in silence for a while. Jessica liked this: the smell of breakfast in a cozy kitchen, sun filtering through the window and washing the room with a new day, and talking with Sharon. It felt like a home, something she'd worked so hard to create in her own life. She inhaled deeply, wanting to record the moment to memory.

After wolfing down her last piece of bacon, Sharon blotted her lips with a paper napkin, then patted the thick roll of stomach hidden beneath her blouse. "Whew, I've gotta go on Weight Watchers!" She hopped off the stool and picked up her plate and glass. "Honey, if you don't mind, I'm gonna head up the street to Mrs. Comeaux's. I promised to bring her some soup."

"Need any help?"

"Nah, I have a couple of bowls to carry over, that's all. The poor old soul's got the flu, and you know how some of those old people are. They eat lunch in the morning and supper at noon." She uttered a series of *tsks*. "Can you believe not one of her kids has gone over there to check on her?"

Jessica shook her head in appropriate disbelief.

"If Lisa does that to me when I'm old and decrepit, I'm counting on you to kick her butt," Sharon said with a twinkle in her eye.

"Not a problem."

Sharon laughed and carried her dishes to the sink.

"Leave those dishes alone." Jessica got up and put her glass on top of her plate. "You go on and see about Mrs. Comeaux. I'll tend to the kitchen."

"Don't you touch a dish, young lady. You're comp—"

"Uh-oh," Jessica teased. "Were you getting ready to say company?"

Sharon blushed. "Okay, okay. So do the dishes if

it makes you happy." She walked over to Jessica and gave her a hug. Her face sobered. "So—they gonna let you see Todd?" she asked.

"Looks like it. Two o'clock today."

"You nervous?"

"A little."

"Mm-hmm, I probably would be, too. Well, you know if you need anything, I'm right here."

"I know."

Sharon eyed her steadily. "Jess, I'd like to give you something, and I hope it won't cause you to take offense."

"You couldn't do anything to offend me."

Sharon reached into the right pocket of her shorts and pulled out a rosary, its beads made of mother-of-pearl. She handed it to Jessica. "It belonged to my mama."

"Oh, Miss Sharon," Jessica breathed, overwhelmed by the woman's generosity. "I can't take this."

"Then borrow it. Every time I've gotten into a real bad jam, it's always helped."

Jessica touched the string of beads tenderly, then closed her fingers tightly around them. "Then I'll gladly borrow it—for Todd. He's in as bad a jam as you can get, I think."

Sharon hugged her again, then began flitting around the kitchen, gathering her purse and Tupperware containers. "Now the house is yours, so shower, make more phone calls, whatever you need. I'll be back later."

Jessica hurried to the kitchen door and pulled it open for her. "Thank you."

"What's family for?" Leaning over, Sharon kissed Jessica's cheek. "You de best," she said, then rushed out the door.

Memories of a childhood game came racing back to Jessica, one that Sharon had played with her and Lisa for years. Jessica volleyed back. "No, you de best."

Sharon, already halfway across the backyard, laughed. "No, no! You de best!" She walked faster and took a left past a storage shed, which obscured her from Jessica's view.

"No, no, no! You de best!" Jessica shouted from the door. Grinning broadly, she listened for Sharon's reply.

"No, no, no, no . . ."

As Sharon's voice faded away, Jessica gently closed the door. "You *are* the best, Sharon Daigle, without a doubt."

Before allowing herself to fall into a melancholy hiatus that might ruin her lightened mood, Jessica went into the living room and tucked the rosary away in her purse. She folded the sheet and blanket she'd used the night before and placed them neatly on the armrest of the couch. Checking her watch, she saw she still had a little over three hours before her appointment. Plenty of time to do the dishes, shower, and maybe go to a department store to pick up a small gift for Todd.

She went back into the kitchen, and as she gathered breakfast dishes a thread of hope stitched through her. If she had the opportunity to see Todd, talk to him, some of this horrible mess might be straightened out. She knew she'd be able to reach her brother, no matter his mental condition. Sure she had to consider what Lee had told her about schizophrenia, but didn't every rule have an exception? With a little patience and understanding from someone who knew him nearly as well as he knew himself, Todd could very well be that exception. He *would* be that exception if she had anything to do with it. Then they would toss this terrible mess behind them like some bad dream.

A fluttering recollection of the dream she had that morning came to mind, and Jessica quickly tuned it out. She concentrated instead on how she would talk Todd into coming to live with Frank and her.

With plates and platters stacked in both hands, she made her way to the counter near the sink and carefully put the dishes down. She grabbed a bottle of dishwashing liquid from behind the faucet, squirted a smiley face with the thick soap across the bottom of the sink, then turned the water on. As the sink filled with suds, she stared out the kitchen window, calculating bedroom and closet space in her home that could be used for Todd. Her hands sloshed lazily through the warm water as she daydreamed.

It was the sudden grimace on the man's face staring back at her from the window that made her realize he was there.

Gasping loudly, Jessica jumped back from the sink. She stared in disbelief at the drawn, diseased face. His eyes looked as if every blood vessel in his body had collected behind the irises, then burst. They reminded her of the eyes from the thicket.

The man stepped away from the window, his mouth opening and closing, his cheeks puckering, then distending like he was gasping for air. The rags he wore hung loosely on his emaciated body.

After the initial shock, Jessica didn't know whether to feel fear or pity. She moved cautiously to one side and threw open a couple of utility drawers. Finding only one with utensils, she pulled out the largest weapon she could find, a paring knife. *Just in case,* she thought.

Inching back to the window with knife in hand, Jessica caught sight of him still watching her. His large, blistered eyes seemed to beg for her to look at him.

"What do you want?" she shouted.

He blinked, then grimaced as though in so much pain.

"Do you need help?" *That's a stupid question. He looks like he should be in intensive care!*

The man swaggered forward and pressed his nearly skinless hand against the window screen.

Jessica jerked away reflexively. "What do you want?" she shouted again, louder.

He glanced at his hand pressed against the screen, then looked pitifully back at her as if to say, "Please, can't you tell?"

Torn between fear and compassion, Jessica visually checked the height of the window against the height of the man. There was no way he'd be able to get through the window without jumping up at least four feet and pulling himself through, and his body certainly didn't seem to be in any condition to do either.

Raising the knife so he could see it, Jessica reached up with her left hand and raised the window an inch. "What do you want?" she asked nervously.

The man blinked again, slowly—the blink of the eyes from the thicket. "You got to go," he said, his voice thick and low. "You brother—" His head began to twitch and spasm.

"You—you *are* him," Jessica stammered. "The man—that Eli man—in the bushes last night! You're him—you're real." She clung dizzily to the counter's edge.

"He don't have much—" Eli's body jerked as though in the throes of a seizure. His fingernails clawed at the screen. "You—the bridge—" His head snapped back and forth rapidly, and his eyes filled with fear and desperation. "You brother—not much long—will die—many will—you the—" His words were cut off as his body convulsed violently, then collapsed to the ground.

"Hey!" Jessica ran to the kitchen door, thought twice, then raced for the phone in the living room. When she reached it, her hands were shaking so badly she dropped the receiver on the floor. She snatched it up again and punched in 911.

Come on! Come on! she thought frantically, listening to the steady ring. She hung up and jabbed the three numbers again. The same unanswered ringing echoed in her ear. "Damn," she muttered, then hung up and pressed 0.

A nasally voice answered immediately. "Operator."

"I have an emergency," Jessica said, pacing blindly.

"Hello?"

Jessica looked at the receiver. "Operator, I have an emergency, and I—"

"Hello?"

"Hello!" Jessica yelled into the phone.

A click followed by a dial tone.

Jessica slammed the receiver down and ran for the kitchen door. Without thinking, she yanked it open, flew down the back steps, and into the backyard.

He wasn't there.

She stopped abruptly. The grass beneath the window where he'd fallen wasn't even depressed. She scanned the length of the yard.

"Where are you?" she called out.

When no one answered, Jessica sprinted to the west end of the house. "Where are you?" she shouted.

A bare-chested old man in boxer shorts stepped out of the house next door. "Something de madda?" he asked.

"Did you see a man out here just now?" Jessica asked anxiously.

"A man?" He looked about, scowling. "What man?"

"A black man," Jessica said, walking to the hedgerow that separated the two yards.

"A black man?" A flash of suspicion crossed the old man's face. "Wait, I'm gonna call de police." He turned back toward his house.

"Yes—I mean, no. Wait!" Jessica said. "He needs an ambulance, not the police."

The old man gave her a disgusted look and snorted. "I don't know nuttin' 'bout no sick nigga," he said, then scratched his potbelly and stormed back into his house.

Frustrated, Jessica spun about on her heels and examined the yard. *Where the hell did he go? There's no way he could've just disappeared into thin air . . . or could he?*

Her shoulders slumped suddenly, and Jessica lowered her head. *Hallucinations can do any damn thing they want to, can't they?* She walked wearily toward the kitchen window. *Face it, girl. Your mind is totally fucked up, and they're going to get a room for you right next to Todd's.*

Shielding her eyes from the sun's glare with a hand, Jessica looked up at the window and her pulse quickened. *Oh, please, please, just let it stay right there until someone else sees it.*

She reached up and gently outlined the embossed handprint on the screen with a finger.

Chapter Twenty

He couldn't run any faster. His lungs burned with every breath as his bruised, cut feet pelted the ground. Left, serpentine right—the direction didn't matter. The beating intensified across his buttocks, his back, and his calves. He gathered up enough courage to glance back but saw only his shadow. He was being pummeled to death by an enemy he could not see, which left him little chance for defense.

Dodging left through a grove of chicken trees and past a dilapidated utility shed, Eli pumped his arms hard and tried to ignore the fire in his chest. He jumped over a hedgerow and immediately found himself airborne.

Too shocked to do more than mewl, Eli soon wound up facedown at the bottom of a muddy canal. Spitting and gasping, he gathered himself up on hands and knees, crawled across the ravine, and grabbled for the exposed tree roots poking through the steep embankment. At the first tug, his hands radiated with so much pain his vision went bright white. Groaning, Eli rested his forehead against the six-foot dirt wall.

He ached to be out of this nightmare and back in the swamps, where he could be fishing for sacalait right now or setting nutria traps. Maybe even sitting on his porch, waiting for Johanson to stop by with store-bought bread and cheese. But Eli knew that wasn't going to happen. Not now, not ever again. He'd have to draw on whatever positives he could find right here, and presently that meant just being grateful the flogging had stopped.

Turning his head slightly, he scanned the opposite side of the canal. Waist-high weeds and pine saplings bordered its rim. There would be little chance of anyone seeing him from that direction.

Eli braced both feet against a ridge of dirt and peered over the edge of the embankment he clung to. A row of paint-chipped, clapboard houses stood about sixty feet away, each with littered and desiccated yards. Two chatty, middle-aged women hung sheets and towels along twin clotheslines three houses to his left. He lowered his head until his eyes were barely above ground level to make sure they wouldn't spot him. Just then, a short, pear-shaped man wearing orange overalls and matching cap came out of a nearby house. He carried a bulging plastic sack in one hand and an empty box in the other. After tossing both items into an already overflowing trash barrel, he called out to the two women, waved, then headed in their direction. Eli watched him for a moment longer before lowering himself to the bottom of the ravine.

He found a rimless tire, sat on it, then eased his fingers into his pants pocket and pulled out his metal guide. Holding the chain up with two fingers, Eli studied the motionless glob of iron attached to it. The stagnant pendulum confused him. Now that it had done its job and helped him find the woman, what was he supposed to do with it? Throw it away? Bury it in the mud? Keep it? He wished the pendulum could talk and give him clearer direction. Not only about its disposal but about the woman. Time was running out, and he still wasn't certain about what to do with her now that she'd been found. Twice he'd tried to reach the woman and twice failed.

Last night he'd come so close to her, had even smelled her scent through the bushes, but that other woman had shown up before they were able to connect. Surprisingly, the woman from his nightmares never said a word about him or their encounter to the other woman. She'd simply hurried away, visibly shaken, her friend trailing behind. After waiting a few moments to make sure neither of them turned back, Eli had followed them to a house that had an unlocked toolshed behind it. The shed served as a great hiding place, and he'd waited patiently there, watching for her through a pair of rivet holes in the building's tin walls.

It was well into morning before she finally appeared in the window. She looked different from the other times he'd seen her, though. In his dreams, in the thicket last night, her face had been taut with anger, fear, and frustration. This morning she appeared much more relaxed, softer.

Somehow he managed to approach the window without her noticing. When she did glance his way, she seemed to peer through him at first, blinded by some faraway notion. In that very instant, he'd been able to look into the woman's wide, dark eyes and see her soul. The sight had sent a wrenching pain across his heart. The majority of souls he'd seen in the eyes of people who had been brought to him in the swamp were egg-shaped, and they usually varied in color depending on the person's destiny. Pink for good, brown for bad, and a multitude of shades in between for those still to be determined. Hers, however, was silver and translucent, tube-shaped, with frayed ends like one of Johanson's hand-rolled cigarettes. He'd never seen a soul like that before. The very essence of it seemed to radiate a torturous ache, a searching and longing for something it never expected to find. And beyond it, making certain her soul's anguish stayed just so, was Maikana.

Seeing all of that within her had made Eli feel naked and ashamed. He wanted more than anything to help her then, to relieve her of the suffering he knew she bore, a suffering he felt responsible for.

Maikana made sure that didn't happen, however. When curiosity finally encouraged the woman to open the window, Maikana beat her to him. He'd descended on Eli in a rage, twisting and distorting his limbs until there was nothing left for him to do but smell the rot of his own body. He threw Eli to the ground, kicked him mercilessly, then yanked him to his feet. The beating that followed had been fast and furious, barely giving him the presence of mind to run.

Eli shoved the pendulum back into his pocket, deciding not to toss it. The sparse patches of skin left on the fingers of his right hand scraped off against the material of his pants, and he clamped his other hand over his mouth to keep from moaning aloud in pain. He listened for the chatter of the two women and man but heard only his breath being pushed and sucked through his fingers.

Gradually Eli became aware of something tugging on one of his ankles, then his left calf. He glanced down and froze at the sight of a snake, coiling its way around his leg. Transfixed, he could only stare as the serpent's body quivered and crawled, squeezed and flexed until its head finally came to rest on his knee. It hissed, and Eli whimpered. Before the woman and the dreams, before the pendulum and Eula Mae, he would have snatched the snake by the neck and whip-snapped it to death. But now Eli knew his hands were in no condition to attempt it.

The split tongue flicked at the air, and the snake's head wove hypnotically. Without warning, it recoiled and stiffened, its mouth springing open to reveal abnormally long fangs. The strike came fast and furious, and it sent a torrent of fire through Eli's leg. He cried out and grabbed his left thigh, squeezing as hard as his hands would allow.

With its teeth still embedded, the snake rapidly unwound its five-foot-long body and began to whip it about. Eli bit his bottom lip hard to keep from screaming as the fangs drilled deeper into his flesh, into muscle. They seemed to be trying to penetrate to the very marrow of his bone. Finally the fangs tore free from the viper's mouth, and the slithering attacker fell to the ground.

At first Eli thought it was dead, but then he noticed the crossbars on the back of its head growing wider and darker. It lay dormant for only another moment before coiling back into a strike position. Eli raised a foot to kick it, and the snake sprang upright to its full height, holding itself erect only by the tip of its tail. The toothless mouth yawned open.

"You pathetic excuse for a human," it seethed.

Startled, Eli fell backward, tumbling off the tire and smacking his head against the embankment.

"Did you actually think I would allow you to reach her?" The serpent held its body as rigid as a pole while the head shook emphatically. "Surely you cannot possibly be that moronic."

Eli's heart rate doubled, and he wondered what poison might be racing through his body. "Go away, Maikana. Dis not your place!"

Haughty laughter rolled through the ravine. "Not my place? Not *my* place?" The laughter came to an abrupt halt, and the snake inched closer to Eli, its black, piercing eyes riveted on him. "You have not possessed the wherewithal to restrain me in the past, and you never will, you ludicrous fool." The scaly head thrust forward with a dismissive snort. "It was I who sent you running in terror, not the other way around. You are nothing more than a meddling dullard who tends to affairs that are not of your concern. Why, you barely possess the power to defecate, much less command the likes of me."

Struggling to his feet, Eli glared into Maikana's masked face. "You afraid," he declared.

"Afraid? Look at who was cowering in the mud! Whom could *I* possibly be afraid of?"

"You afraid of me," Eli said. He spread his feet apart to keep balanced, and felt his left knee swelling inside his pant leg. "I can make de woman not half no more. Eula Mae told me you afraid of dat. If you afraid of dat, you afraid of me!" There was energy in Eli's defiance, and his mind raged with it.

The serpent's head cocked to one side. "You are referring to the old woman? That scrawny, half-cocked soothsayer?" Maikana grunted. "Everything she told you was pure conjecture. A farce, a down-right lie. Why, look at what happened to her. If she was as knowledgeable as she claimed to be, do you not think she would still be alive?" Instead of waiting for an answer, he hissed, "And look at you. What strength is there left in that pathetic body to take on the likes of me?" The black droplet eyes enlarged to twice their size. "You will die as did the old woman if you do not leave the woman and her sibling alone! Do you understand?"

Eli snatched at the slimy body and missed as it quickly recoiled. "I be de rasaunt right now!" he shouted. "And you gonna do what I say!"

"You are *no* rasaunt!" Maikana roared, and the snake's body wrapped around Eli's neck faster than a finger snap.

Eli clawed at the serpent frantically, uselessly, as the scabrous body squeezed against his larynx, cutting off all oxygen. And the noonday sky grew dark—darker—black.

Chapter Twenty-one

"I must reiterate that we're circumventing protocol here, something we rarely do," Dr. Lee said wearily. Dark, sagging crescents hung beneath his eyes.

"I understand," Jessica said. She tucked her hair behind an ear with a shaky finger.

"And the only reason we're allowing this exception is because you live out of state and Todd has no other local, family support system."

"Thank you for taking that into consideration."

Lee nodded, then drummed his fingers on the conference table through a long pause, studying her.

Jessica felt ready to explode with anticipation. "So do I get to see him now?"

The drumming stopped. "In a moment. But, Jessica, you need to be prepared for what you might see," Lee said.

"Prepared? With Todd?"

"Yes. It's important that you try to respond to your brother in as positive a manner as possible. This disease already causes great anxiety. Your reacting to him negatively could be detrimental to his progress."

"But why on earth would I do that? I *want* to see him."

"Remember the patients in the commons area the first time you came here?"

"Of course."

"Would you say your response to them was positive or—"

Jessica held up a hand. "I get your point. But anyone would have gotten a little freaked out in there. Some of those people had serious issues. Todd doesn't walk around stuffing Fritos in his mouth, then vomiting them up."

"That may be, Jessica, but Todd *does* have issues, as you call them. He has a mental illness."

"So you say, but—"

"Look, try viewing it from his perspective," Lee said, looking at her gravely. "Consider this. You're going about your normal life and out of the blue you begin to hear voices only you can hear, see things only you can see."

I just might know what you're talking about, Jessica thought grimly.

"After a while society begins to reject you because they don't understand your responses to those strange sights and sounds. You frighten them. You're terrified yourself. The visions and voices are stealing the world you once knew—your friends, work, hobbies, they're either gone or disappearing. And no matter how hard you try, you can't seem to bring them back. Get the picture?"

"Too well."

Lee leaned back in his chair. "Good. Now expand that scenario. You've wound up in a mental hospital and are being visited by the one person you think should care about you most—and the first thing you experience when you see that person is their fear or, as your mind will perceive it, their rejection of you. How do you think that would make you feel?"

"But I'd never reject Todd," Jessica said incredulously.

"Intentionally, probably not," Lee said. "But sometimes we do things or experience feelings that are purely reactive, just like the anxiety you felt toward the behavior of the patients in the commons area."

Jessica frowned and kneaded her fingers. "Those people were strangers, though. Todd's my brother, for heaven's sake. There's a big difference."

Lee folded his arms across his chest. "But you've never observed him exhibiting bizarre behavior before, have you?"

"Well . . . no."

"Jessica, you might see Todd talk to himself or ask himself questions, then answer them. He may laugh when the appropriate response would be to be sullen or cry when the response should be laughter. That alone may frighten you."

Perspiration dripped from under Jessica's arms. Her palms grew clammy, and her breathing short and shallow. Surely this man had to be speaking about someone other than her brother.

"When you see him, just keep in mind what we've discussed here. If he starts talking to himself or talking about something he sees or hears, don't get caught up in it. Don't feed it. Try talking about a lighter subject, like the weather or your family."

She attempted to moisten her lips, but her tongue moved across them dry and sandpapery.

"Something else you should be aware of. Todd's medication. We're working now to find the correct type and dosage that will be the most effective with the least amount of side effects. That's the difficult part sometimes. It's not like taking an aspirin for a headache. Every patient responds to the medications differently. It's a matter of finding the right balance. Some patients become lethargic. They may walk slow and stiff or have delayed responses to any form of stimuli." He paused, giving Jessica time to digest what he'd said. "You may see involuntary ticks in Todd's limbs."

Jessica's eyes roamed over Lee's face. *Tell me this is a dream, a joke. Come on, tell me.* The brown eyes that stared back at her remained solemn. No hint of a joke lay in them, no hidden prank soon to be revealed by a smirk. This was reality. This—thing, this disease, this phantasmal mind rape was as real as the chair she sat in.

"Another thing you'll notice—"

"Jesus, there's more?"

Lee cleared his throat. "Unfortunately, yes. Todd has tried to injure himself—seriously injure himself a couple of times since he's been in here. You'll see bandages on him. Well, the ones on the side of his head and his nose, anyway."

Jessica shifted to the edge of her seat, stunned. "You mean he tried to commit suicide?"

"More like self-mutilation. Sometimes patients take this destructive measure hoping it will stop the voices. Some do it because they claim the voices tell them to."

"What did he do? Where is he hurt? Jesus, aren't you people supposed to be watching over him?" Jessica didn't know how to position herself. Sit, stand, roll over. The room was closing in on her, and it felt as though all the oxygen had been sucked out of it.

"He tried to castrate himself and also came very close to breaking his nose. There are a few lacerations on his face, but nothing serious." Lee looked at her intently. "We do watch over our patients, Jessica. We're just not with them *every* minute."

"And that's supposed to be an acceptable excuse?" Jessica rose sharply, gripped the edge of the table and leaned toward Lee. "I want to see my brother," she said, glaring at him. "Now."

Lee scratched the top of his head briskly, then stood and carefully pushed his chair back under the table. Without looking at her, he walked over to the door, opened it, and called to the receptionist, "Page Trahan and tell him we're ready, please."

Jessica heard the whiny echo of "Russell Trahan, front desk, please. Russell Trahan, front desk" as Lee closed the door.

After a few moments of uncomfortable silence, Lee leaned a shoulder against the door and crossed one foot over the other. "So what type of business are you in, Jessica?"

She hated diversionary small talk, and Lee's attempt at it seemed especially stupid. What did business matter now?

"Plastics," she said curtly.

"Interesting. Manufacturing or sales?"

Jessica felt her jaw muscles tense. "Why didn't you keep a closer eye on Todd after he hurt himself the first time?"

A stunned expression swept over Lee's face. He uncrossed his feet and straightened his stance. "You're right. Normally, if a patient has exhibited self-destructive behavior, we put them into a secured environment to—"

"Secured? Don't you mean a lockdown facility, Dr. Lee?"

"To protect them," Lee continued as though she hadn't spoken. "Some people may consider it a lockdown, but it *is* used to protect the patient from him- or herself. Todd was secured when he was first brought here; I may have already told you about that. The next day he seemed much better, however, so we moved him to his own room. That's when the attempted castration occurred. After the incident, we changed his medication, and he seemed to respond well to it." He shrugged. "I didn't see any need then to move him back to a secured environment."

"What did he use?"

"Excuse me?"

"What did he use to—to—cast—hurt himself?"

"A broken ink-pen casing."

There was a light tap on the door, and Lee turned to open it.

Jessica quickly smoothed her hair and worked a smile onto her face. The phony grin disappeared, however, as soon as she saw her brother. Her chest hitched with the need to sob.

Todd shuffled into the room with his head down, wearing the blue pajamas she'd bought for him. The shirt was badly wrinkled and buttoned wrong. He wore an old pair of sneakers with no laces, and his dark hair was greasy, wildly unkempt, as though it hadn't been washed or combed in a month. Beard stubble spotted his cheeks, and a bandage lay across his nose and another one over his right temple.

"Well, hi there, Ms. LeJeune," the orderly who accompanied Todd said brightly. "Remember me? Russell?"

Jessica barely heard Russell. She wanted so much to run up to Todd and throw her arms around him, to hide him, cover him, protect him from this place, this weirdness.

"Hello, little brother," she said finally, and walked slowly toward him, holding out a hand.

Todd looked up dully and stepped away from her. "Shh!" he said.

"Huh?" she asked.

"Shhhhhh!" he said louder. "Shhhh!"

Jessica glanced over at Lee, who was rubbing the top of his head.

"Todd, why don't you have a seat," Lee said, with no more inflection in his voice than if he'd been addressing a dinner guest. "Your sister has been anxious to visit with you."

Todd's eyes loitered over Jessica's face, and he began to sway from side to side.

Russell rested a hand on his shoulder. "Come on, buddy. Have a seat."

Todd stopped swaying and threw his hands up defensively. His upper lip curled back in a snarl.

Startled, Jessica took an involuntary step back.

"I'm not gonna hurt you," Russell said soothingly. "You'll feel better if you sit for a while. Lookit, your sister came all the way from Memphis to see you. Isn't that somethin'?"

Todd frowned, then nodded slightly.

"Would you be more comfortable if I stayed in here with you?" Lee asked Jessica. "Or Russell?"

Jessica stared at her brother. She didn't know this man, this stranger with the hollow, drawn face. He looked dangerously lost, and there was a sense of desperation about him, an air around him that seemed charged with electricity. And it made her afraid. *This is crazy,* she thought, reprimanding herself. *This* is *Todd!*

"We'll be fine," she said, and pulled out a chair and sat.

Todd shrugged away from Russell's hand and stepped sideways toward the wall. Lee and Russell watched him guardedly.

"If you need anything," Lee said, "Russell will be right outside this door."

"Yes, ma'am. Right out there if you need," Russell said, then followed Lee out of the room and pulled the door closed behind him.

Alone with Todd, Jessica found herself unsure of what to do. She watched as her brother leaned against the wall opposite her and lowered his head, his eyes flitting back and forth from her to the floor. She placed her hands on the table and splayed her fingers. Her heart was beating too fast, and her face felt flushed.

She tapped softly on the table with a finger. "Come and sit with me," she said quietly.

Todd looked up sharply. "You can't trust them. It's nothing but traps."

Jessica swallowed hard.

He walked clumsily to the table, jerked the chair out next to hers, and sat in it hurriedly, like a kid vying for the last seat in musical chairs. He leaned close to her, and Jessica caught herself inadvertently pulling back. "They're going to try to use you to get to me," he spat. Sitting up rigidly in his chair, he slammed his hand down on the table.

Jessica started. "T-Todd." Her voice cracked. It was all she could think to say. Gradually she moved her hand toward his.

He jerked away before she could touch him and started rocking in his seat. "Don't make a difference, anyhow," he said, looking up at the lights, then around and across the walls. "They've got everything rigged."

Jessica left her hand resting on the table. She remembered what Lee told her about keeping the conversation light. "I see the pajamas I brought for you fit, huh?" *Damn, that sounds so lame.*

A sudden gleam filled Todd's eyes, and he mumbled softly.

"What?" Jessica asked. "I can't understand what you're saying."

Todd's lips moved faster.

"I can't hear you, Toddy. What?"

"Nothin', nothin', nothin'," he said, then turned his head sharply to the right and mumbled at the wall.

Jessica felt her eyes sting with tears. She quickly blinked them away. *Keep it light.* "Hey, you know what? Jake's getting ready to go into the sixth grade. Can you believe it?"

Todd slowly faced her, and his eyes softened. "Jake's smart."

A bubble of hope surfaced in Jessica. "You're smart, too. You always were."

Todd glanced up. "They put microphones in the lights, you know."

Jessica's bubble burst. She felt as if she were talking to two separate people, her brother and some guy from the planet Zorbo. She tried again. "Frank's doing good, too. His business is growing faster than he can keep up with it."

Todd's lips moved silently, and he traced the narrow crown molding around the ceiling with his eyes. His fingers ticked against his thumb like he was counting.

Jessica forced the conversation forward, ignoring his actions. "Things have been busy at work as usual. I'm working on some new projects that are—"

"Shhh!" Todd said loudly. He cocked his head to one side.

Jessica stiffened.

"Hear that?" he asked, his expression panicked. He looked ready to bolt. So much fear emanated from him, Jessica could almost smell it.

She found herself peering anxiously around the room. "What is it?"

"Listen," he begged. His body trembled. "Just listen!"

Jessica sat quietly. Other than their breathing,

she heard only a faint ring-chirp from a distant telephone.

"It's only the phone. See, there it goes again," she said, and smiled hesitantly. "Only the phone."

Todd's eyes grew wide, and his bottom lip quivered. He peered over his right shoulder with quick jerks of his head. "It's his voice—there!" he said. "Hear it? Say you hear it. Say you hear it!"

Tears began to stream down Jessica's face. She didn't give a damn about Lee's instructions. How in the hell was she supposed to talk to Todd about the weather? This was here and now, and that's all she could deal with. "Todd, I . . . what . . . who do you hear?"

Todd's tears matched hers now, and they reminded Jessica of the small boy she'd grown up with. The young, helpless boy who had once wandered off in a grocery store and gotten lost. The one who'd sat between the onion and potato bins, horrified and mute, until she'd found him.

"Who, Toddy? Who do you hear?"

Fixing his eyes on hers, Todd said quietly, "S-S-Satan. He's right behind you."

Jessica threw a reflexive glance over her shoulder, then turned back to him. "I don't—" Horror trapped her voice in midsentence. The face before her was no longer Todd's. It was a white, bulbous mass with a vertical slit for a mouth and hollow sockets where eyes should have been. The mouth parted with a lopsided smirk.

Gasping, Jessica flew out of the chair and stumbled across the room. She was about to scream for Russell when an uncontrollable quiver shook her body from the inside out. Before she realized what she was doing, Jessica spun around and jabbed a finger at the grotesque face. "Leave him the hell alone!"

Instantly, as though she'd simply swiped a thick cobweb from her line of sight, Todd's face reappeared, pale skin and all. He sat rigid and slack-mouthed in his chair.

Jessica rushed over and knelt in front of him. "Todd?"

He blinked.

"Toddy?" Instinctively Jessica lifted a hand and aimed the pad of her thumb at a spot between his eyes. Before she could touch him, Todd jumped up, knocking her over. He brushed violently at his face.

"Don't fucking touch me!" he screamed, towering over her. "You're one of them, aren't you? They do bad things here! There *are* bad things here. They want to punk my ass, and you're in on it too, aren't youuuuu?" The wail issuing from him seemed to make the whole room vibrate.

Terrified, Jessica quickly scooted away from him on her butt. Someone pounded on the door, then she heard Russell call out to her.

"Ms. LeJeune?" The doorknob twisted and jiggled. "Are ya'll all right in there?"

Todd's wails became a horrendous moan so mournful and lost, so pathetic, it made Jessica groan in pain. She lifted a tremulous hand. "Oh, Toddy, I want to help you," she cried. "Just let me—"

"Nooooo!" Todd ran and threw himself against the far right wall, knocking the abstract painting from its hook. As it crashed to the floor, Todd charged toward the opposite side of the room and once again slammed his body against the wall.

"Todd!"

Russell's pounding grew furious. "Ms. LeJeune, please, answer me! Something's wrong with the door, and I can't get in."

"He needs help, Russell!" Jessica shouted.

Todd let out a vicious roar, then tore across the room and threw his body against the door. His head cracked loudly against the jamb, and he stumbled backward, then sideways, then dropped to his knees.

"Stop!" Jessica scrambled to her feet, and Todd spat in her direction. A knot, the size of a golf ball, stuck out on his forehead. She forced herself to walk slowly toward him. "I'm not going to hurt you. Look at me. It's me, Jessica. I would never hurt you."

Todd's expression became one of pure hatred. "Don't touch me, you commie-sucking bitch!" Suddenly his eyes widened, and he whimpered. Without another word, he stood and shuffled stoop-shouldered to a corner of the room, where he pressed his back against the wall. He spread his arms out wide in mock crucifixion, and his lips began to move as though in silent, meditative prayer. Blood soaked the front of his pajama pants.

At that moment, the door burst open and Russell lurched into the room. "Oh, geez," he said breathlessly when he spotted Todd. "Ms. LeJeune, are you hurt?"

Jessica shook her head, mute with bewilderment.

Russell leaned back across the threshold and called out loudly, "I need that wheelchair in here, now!" He turned back to Todd. "You'll be okay, buddy. We're gonna give you something to help chill you out. I'll get you in some clean unders, and you'll feel as good as new." Russell eased up to him, put a hand on each of his arms, and pulled them down to his sides. Todd complied quietly, slumping against Russell's thick chest.

In a matter of seconds, a stout black man hurried into the room with a wheelchair. His steps faltered when he saw Todd.

"Over here, Leroy, hurry," Russell said with an edge of aggravation in his voice.

Leroy quickly wheeled the chair forward, slapped the brake bars into a locked position, then hustled out of the room.

Russell frowned and shook his head. "Can't get decent help these days, huh, buddy?" After positioning Todd in the chair, he released the brakes, turned the chair around, and pushed it past Jessica. "Now, Ms. LeJeune, don't you worry. He'll be fine," he assured her. "I guess maybe they were right after all. I guess it was just too soon." With that, Russell steered Todd out of the room.

Jessica remained motionless and stared at the empty doorway. Her brain felt incapable of forcing action from her limbs. *If you stay still, it will go away. The quieter you are, the better . . .*

She stuck a hand in the right pocket of her slacks and carefully pulled out the car keys. *The quieter you are . . .* She took extra care not to jiggle them as she left the conference room.

A petite woman standing behind the reception desk called after her as Jessica made her way across the lobby toward the double glass doors. The woman's voice sounded far away, from some other place, and belonging in someone else's life. The woman didn't matter. What she had to say didn't matter.

Too numb to speak and too drained to cry, Jessica pushed through the doors and labored down the steps. When she reached the sidewalk, she hesitated. She didn't feel right about leaving. Too much felt undone. *Maybe I should go and find Dr. Lee, talk to him. But about what? Todd? He tried warning me about his condition earlier. What more can be said?* She thought about the face she'd seen superimposed on Todd's, the one without eyes and vertical mouth. The voices, the flowers, the man in the window. There would be plenty to talk to Lee about—just not now.

With a shudder, Jessica headed down the sidewalk toward the visitors' parking lot. The path soon grew to an immeasurable length as partial images of Todd plagued her mind. His greasy hair, the laceless shoes, his tears, the fury in his eyes, his pain. Each vision seemed to add tonnage to her feet. She trudged on and on, lifting one foot laboriously after the other. She thought of herself walking through a river of heavy syrup.

Steen's Pure Cane Syrup at that, Jessica mused, and an unexpected chuckle escaped her. The chuckle repeated itself again and again, and before she knew it she was laughing uncontrollably and weaving off and on the concrete path like a drunkard. She spotted three teenage boys watching her from across the street, which made her howl with laughter all the more. Snickering and snorting, she staggered to the side of the building so she could lean against it. Her stomach ached terribly, and she had a painful stitch in her side.

As soon as Jessica's shoulder touched the bricks, the laughter withered, then died. A whirlwind of emotions took its place. Dread, sorrow, helplessness, hopelessness, anguish—all of them building to an enormous tower of Babel in the center of her brain. The sheer mass of it drew tears to her eyes and threatened to topple her over. Instead of falling, however, Jessica swung out and clobbered the side of the building with a fist. The masonry quickly became Todd's illness, their childhood, and the uncertainty of her own mental stability. She pelted the bricks over and over, crying and punching until her bleeding hand screamed for mercy so loudly she could no longer ignore it.

Panting and emptied, Jessica finally backed away from the building and wiped her eyes and nose with a forearm. She gave only a cursory glance to the bloodstained bricks before turning away.

By the time she reached the rental car, Jessica's head and injured hand throbbed violently. She fumbled with the car key, trying to fit it into the lock. It took four or five attempts before she mentally grasped that a small object blocked the keyhole, something round and worn and made of metal. It hung from a chain, which had been wrapped around the door handle. The object swung gently in the breezeless air and clanked softly against the car door.

Tink—tink—tink.

Chapter Twenty-two

Jessica finished cleaning away the blood and grit from her left hand in a bathroom located outside Sherwin's Pak-N-Sak. She didn't know yet how she would explain the injury to Lisa and Sharon. Lisa would probably understand her need to beat the shit out of a brick wall just because it happened to be in the right place at the wrong time. Sharon, on the other hand, would be more concerned with the wounds than the why. Although stiff and swelling, the damage wasn't that severe. Mostly scraped skin and a couple of deeper lacerations alongside her little finger, nothing a bandage wouldn't cure. But Sharon would take one look at the hand and start hyperventilating.

Checking her face in the mirror, Jessica scrubbed away mascara smudges from under her eyes, then smoothed her hair into place. Accomplishing these small but constructive tasks seemed to help corral her sense of control, and she felt stronger.

Satisfied that she at least resembled a human again, Jessica left the bathroom and went into the Pak-N-Sak for a bottle of water.

A few minutes later, she was sitting in her car downing Evian in huge gulps. After emptying the bottle, she tossed it onto the backseat, then started the car and drove out of the parking lot and onto Maynard Trail.

Years ago, Maynard Trail had been just that, a trail, located ten miles west of Borrow. The farmers had used the once deeply-rutted path to take their cotton crop to the market pavilion. Now Maynard was a two-lane blacktop with open ditches on both sides and the market pavilion no longer existed. It had been torn down years ago, replaced by a mini–strip mall that housed a We Care Hair Salon, Spanky's Pizza Parlor, and Bada's Shoe Repair. Just west of the mall, about a quarter of a mile down on the right, was Our Lady of Faith Cemetery, Jessica's destination.

She turned into the cemetery, drove past the wrought-iron gates, then parked her car in the shade of an oak tree.

Not giving herself time to change her mind, Jessica got out of the car and headed down the cemetery's central walkway. Multiple concrete sidewalks intersected the central path from either side, and she counted off three before detouring left. From there, she followed rows of crypts that had assigned numbers stenciled on square metal plates, which were embedded in the concrete along the edges of the sidewalk. Jessica soon found number twenty-three and veered right.

As she passed the first granite headstone, she lightly brushed her fingers atop it. It belonged to Arthur Soileau, who had been her eighth-grade math teacher, and the only person who had ever made algebra understandable to her.

Adjacent to Mr. Soileau were three, identical whitewashed tombs. They belonged to the Alleman triplets, and anyone who had ever lived in Borrow knew their story. Born in 1915, all three spinsters had died in 1995. Rumor had it, according to Lena Falcon, Borrow's vocal newspaper and postmistress, that Marion Alleman, the oldest of the triplets by ten minutes, had died of a heart attack. Lena claimed the other two sisters died simultaneously a half hour later because of broken hearts caused by the loss of their oldest sibling.

Two markers past the triplets sat a swirled marble headstone. Jessica stopped beside it and drew in a deep breath. She studied the three faded silk carnations that stood in ROBERTA M. GUIDRY's memorial vase. *Guess I should've brought flowers,* she thought.

Jessica sat at the foot of her mother's grave and stared across the field of tombs adorned with angels and crosses of varying shapes and sizes. Sepulchers of mortared brick lined the fence along the east end of the property.

"I don't really know why I'm here," she said quietly, her eyes moving steadily about. "It's not like you can do anything. Just thought you'd want to know . . . Todd's in bad shape right now."

Two squirrels squabbled over a pinecone twenty feet away.

"I—I don't understand . . ." A breeze played up the inside of Jessica's blouse, and she turned to face the name etched in marble. "Why couldn't things have been different, Mama?"

"I did the best I knew how," a familiar voice whispered in her mind.

"Yeah, but sometimes you have to try harder when the best you know isn't good enough," Jessica countered angrily.

"You turned out all right, even with my mistakes."

"After a lot of hard work. And let's face it, Mama, I'm still screwed up in a lot of ways."

"I don't see that."

"You didn't see a lot of things."

"Didn't you know I loved you?"

"I was never sure. Neither was Todd."

"I knew ya'll loved me, Jess."

"But that wasn't enough, was it? After Dad left us, nothing Todd or I did or said was ever enough."

"It looked that way because you saw me only as a mother, not as a woman who was hurting."

"You *were* a mother, and a mother's supposed to love her children, not beat them every time they turn around."

"I was a woman hurting, too, and it was hard to separate the two sometimes. Love had nothing to do with it. Jess, when life gets really stressful, different people react different ways. It's got nothing to do with whether you love someone or not."

Dingy rag clouds veiled the sun, and Jessica smelled rain in the air. She stood, squinted up at the sky, and thought about Todd and how "really stressful" things must be for him right now. How lonely and frightening.

Jessica dusted off the back of her pants. "Love's got everything to do with it, Mama. Absolutely everything," she said, and walked away from her mother's tomb, knowing she would never return.

Chapter Twenty-three

Aside from a tearful sniffle or two and an occasional "Oh, my" or "No way," Lisa and Sharon Daigle listened to Jessica recount her visit with Todd in relative silence.

"Then they wheeled him out," Jessica said. She let out an exasperated sigh. "I left after that. There wasn't much else I could do. Well—except for this." She briefly raised her left hand, which Sharon had already bathed in hydrogen peroxide, swabbed with Neosporin, and would have wrapped in enough gauze and surgical tape to eventuate mummification if Jessica hadn't insisted on Band-Aids. "Real responsible, huh? My brother has some kind of major breakdown, is chauffeured off in a wheelchair to only God knows where, and I'm outside punching bricks."

Sharon scowled. "Don't say that, Jess. You're one

of the most responsible people I know. You were upset, that's all. I wouldn't have known what else to do either."

"Yeah," Lisa said. "Considering all that drama, I think you managed pretty damn well. I'd have probably kicked the doc."

Jessica gave her a weary grin. "He wasn't around."

"All the more reason for me to kick his ass."

Sharon chuffed and got up from the table. "I'll get coffee," she said to no one in particular, and headed for the kitchen.

Jessica closed her eyes and kneaded her forehead. Reliving the details of her afternoon sojourn to Municipal had added tension knots to the back of her neck and made her head throb. For self-preservation purposes, she had not told them about Todd's facial metamorphosis. It was bad enough the event left a skid mark across her sanity scorecard. She wasn't about to share it. Jessica had also failed to mention her trip to the cemetery, but that had been out of respect for Sharon and the friendship she'd shared with her mother.

"So you going to fill me in?" she heard Lisa ask.

Jessica reluctantly opened her eyes. "On what?"

"On why you're being so goddamn stubborn."

"Huh?"

"This whole ordeal with Todd. Why won't you let anyone help?"

"With what?"

"You, Jess. There's no reason for you to be going through this by yourself. Frank should have been with you at that hospital today. Hell, I should have been there. I don't understand this 'I've got to do it all by myself' thing you've got going on. Nobody's asking you to play superwoman."

"I never said anyone was," Jessica said flatly.

"Then let us help. What's the big deal?"

Jessica sat back and absently traced a water ring on the table with a finger. She knew Lisa meant well and, as a trusted friend, deserved an explanation. But how could she explain a gut feeling? From the time the deputy had contacted her about Todd to now, Jessica carried the same sense of foreboding, one that strongly encouraged her to keep Lisa and Frank as far away from this situation as possible. She'd had no control over Lisa following her to Louisiana, but she could do her best to keep her corralled on neutral ground.

"Well?" Lisa asked.

"There is no big deal, Lisa, really. You and your mom helped me tonight just by listening."

"Oh, please," Lisa said with a quick snap of her head. "You might be able to feed that gratuitous crock of crap to someone else, Jessica Lynn, but I'm not falling for it. Something else is up with you."

Jessica frowned. She *hated* hearing her first and middle name together, and she knew Lisa knew she hated it. Through their many years of friendship, Lisa had only crossed that forbidden bridge during the direst tête-à-têtes, which had been all of three times. And this was the third. The other two occasions occurred years ago, when Jessica debated endlessly about marrying Frank, and when she'd found out she was pregnant with Jake. Back then she'd had serious doubts about her ability to be a good wife or a nurturing mother. Lisa knew better than anyone that Jessica's doubts sprang from a childhood well, where maternal influence had been anything but nourishing. Instead of offering gentle solace, however, Lisa had given her a severe tongue-lashing for even thinking she'd follow in her mother's footsteps. Jessica sensed she was about to get another thrashing.

"Now listen up, girl," Lisa said sharply. "It's time you—"

"Jess, honey?" Sharon walked into the dining room, inadvertently clipping Lisa's speech short. She carried a tray of steaming, mismatched coffee mugs and two miniature pitchers, one filled with cream, the other sugar.

Lisa shot Jessica a look that promised a later discourse.

"Ma'am?"

"If you don't mind my asking," Sharon said, placing the tray on the table. "What happens to Todd now?" She handed Jessica a mug, then gave one to Lisa.

"I'm not sure. All they keep telling me is that he needs to be stabilized."

Sharon nodded thoughtfully, then sat and collected the last cup of coffee. "Do you think it would help Todd if we went to visit him?"

Jessica set her mug down on the table. She'd been afraid Sharon would ask that question. "He'd probably enjoy seeing you, Miss Sharon, but after what happened today, it might be better to wait. And even then, I think the hospital limits visits to only immediate family."

"But maybe they'd let us go *with* you," Lisa said tersely, and reached for the cream.

Sharon glanced at her daughter curiously, then turned back to Jessica. "Well, if we can't visit him, then what about I cook something special, and you could bring it to Todd next time you go? A little home cooking might perk him right up. What do you think?" she asked hopefully. "Maybe steak, smothered in onions and some—"

"They're not going to let her bring food into that place," Lisa cut in.

"How do you know?" Sharon said. "She can at least ask. And what the heck's got you so snippy all of a sudden?"

"I'm not snip—"

"You're right, Miss Sharon," Jessica said, and threw Lisa an eye signal, warning her to back off. "I can at least ask if they'll allow outside food. Thanks for offering." She shifted tiredly in her seat and felt something sharp dig into her right thigh. "Damn!" She jumped up and swept a hand over her slacks.

"What?" Lisa and Sharon asked in unison.

"Something just jabbed the hell out of me." Feeling a knot in her right pants pocket, Jessica reached in and fished out the object. She stared at it, puzzled. *I thought I threw this away.*

"What is it?" Lisa asked. She peered over Jessica's cupped fingers.

"I . . . I don't know." Jessica unrolled the chain and let the pendant dangle. "I found it hanging on the car door handle when—"

"Jesus, Joseph, and Mary!" Sharon bolted out of her seat as though she'd been goosed, and her mug crashed to the table. She clutched her hands to her breasts while hot coffee did an acrobatic loop in Lisa's direction.

"Mama!"

"Sharon!"

Lisa dodged the scalding arc and toppled over in her chair. Coffee splattered onto the floor, barely missing her.

Flabbergasted, Jessica dropped the pendant and rushed around the table to Lisa, who was already clambering to her feet.

"Mama, what's wrong with you?" Lisa demanded. In a wobbling stance, she tossed back her disheveled hair, then righted her eyeglasses, which had been knocked askew.

Sharon seemed oblivious to the surrounding bedlam. Her chubby face had taken on a waxen appearance, and she nervously scanned the distance between Jessica and the table. "W-where is it?"

Jessica took a step toward her. "What, Miss Sharon? What's wrong?"

Sharon stumbled back, shoving her chair aside with the back of her knees. "That—thing!" Sharon cried. "Where is it?"

"Mama, what the hell's the matter with you?" Lisa asked, a worried pitch in her voice.

"You mean that necklace?" Jessica asked, and hurried over to where she'd been sitting. She found the pendant on the floor near a leg of the table and picked it up. "This?" She held the pendant out to Sharon.

"Whoa, Jesus," Sharon wheezed. "W-where did you get it?"

Jessica drew her hand back, puzzled by Sharon's

panicked reaction. "On the door handle of the rental—"

"It can't be the same one," Sharon said. Her eyes filled with tears, and she shook her head. "It's just—just not possible. It can't . . . I gotta go to the bathroom!" She spun about suddenly and dashed out of the room.

"Mama!" Lisa threw Jessica a frightened, questioning glance, then took off after her mother.

Within seconds, Jessica heard a door slam and water running. She held the ornament up by the chain, and the curiously shaped pendant fell limp. Jessica frowned. Why would a broken necklace cause so much fear? She touched the point of its peculiar shape, and a sense of familiarity tingled through her.

"What was that all about?" Lisa's voice startled Jessica and chased the sensation away. "I couldn't get her to tell me anything."

"I . . . I don't know."

"Well, it's got something to do with that." Lisa walked over to her and put a timid hand under the pendant.

"I could swear I've seen this before," Jessica said. "Strange thing is, I didn't feel like that when I first saw it."

Lisa flicked the pendulum with a fingernail. "It looks like a big teardrop."

"Yeah."

"Whatever it is, it has Mom freaked out, Jess." She tossed a sentinel glance over her shoulder. "You'd better get rid of it."

The creak of a door prompted Jessica to shove the

pendant into her pocket. She and Lisa exchanged a quick nod, then headed for the kitchen.

Sharon emerged from the hall a few minutes later, her feet scuffing across the floor like she couldn't raise them. Her red, puffy eyes darted from Jessica to the dining room.

"Don't worry, Miss Sharon, I put it away," Jessica said, and headed for the sink. "Why don't you sit and rest for a while? I'll get you a glass of water." A sudden thought made Jessica do a double take at the window over the sink. *The man from this morning!* She'd forgotten about him after her visit with Todd, and she wondered if the embossed handprint was still there. She didn't think this would be a good time to bring it up, however.

"No water," Sharon said dully.

Lisa pulled a stool away from the snack bar and signaled for her mother to sit. "Catch your breath at least."

Ignoring the invitation, Sharon opened a utility drawer and removed a pack of cigarettes with a pink Bic lighter stuffed in its cellophane wrapper and an ashtray. She shook out a cigarette, lit it, then inhaled deeply. "My nerves," she said, as though having to explain the need for the habit. Her voice quivered around thin plumes of smoke. "Sorry."

"Mama, what was that all about?" Lisa asked. "What had you so scared?"

"That thing," Sharon said matter-of-factly.

"But why would an old necklace frighten you?" Jessica asked.

Sharon studied Jessica and took another drag on her cigarette, this one pulling the burning paper halfway up to the filter. She blew smoke at the ceiling. "It happened before you were born," she finally said. "Shit, I can't believe I'm doing this."

Jessica saw Lisa arch an eyebrow in surprise at her mother's use of the mild profanity. Sharon rarely used anything stronger than *doggone*.

Leaning against the kitchen counter, Sharon puffed on the cigarette again, then stubbed it out in the ashtray. "I promised Roberta I would never tell."

Jessica's fingertips went cold at the mention of her mother's name.

"We were just kids, and we kinda made a bet that one of us would chicken out before we'd go through with it." Sharon paused for what seemed an eternity, then said, "I wish we would have." Her chest heaved visibly. "Chickened out, I mean."

Lisa quietly lowered herself to the floor, sat, and pulled her knees up to her chin. She watched her mother closely.

"What happened?" Jessica prompted.

"Your mama was pregnant with you then." Sharon's eyes settled on a distant vision. "We went to this, uh—this gris-gris person—a man—to see if you were going to be a boy or a girl. It was a joke really. One of our friends—I don't think you've ever met her. Bertha Sonnier?"

Jessica shook her head, more in disbelief at what she was hearing than lack of recognition in the name.

"She told us he was good at telling the future. That he could even tell a pregnant woman if she was going to have a boy or a girl. They didn't do those ultrasounds back then, not like they do now. So we went, just to try him out."

There was another heavy pause while Sharon lit a second Parliament. Lisa and Jessica glanced at each other but remained silent.

"It was weird," Sharon continued. "Beyond weird. I remember there was a little black boy there who wouldn't leave your mama alone. He kept wanting to touch her stomach. The boy's mama—I guess she was his mama—was a real strange one. She never said a word to anybody the whole time we were there, but when that boy finally *did* wind up touching Roberta's stomach, the woman flipped out, went completely berserk."

"Why? Did the boy hurt her?" Jessica asked.

"No, he didn't hurt your mama," Sharon said, then quickly folded an arm across her chest and took a drag on her cigarette. "But that thing did."

"That metal thing?" Lisa asked.

"Yeah, the one Jessica's got, or . . . or one just like it." Sharon lowered her head, seemingly embarrassed by what she had to say. "That gris-gris man put it over Roberta's stomach, and it started swinging." She let out a regretful chuff and wiped her nose with the back of a hand, the cigarette dangling precariously between her fingers. She watched indifferently as ashes fell to the floor. "We should've left then and there, but we didn't. Everything went wrong after that. That necklace, or whatever you want to call it, actually jumped out of the man's hand, and the point of it stuck in Roberta's stomach."

Jessica gaped. "You mean the man tried to stab her with it?"

"No," Sharon said, looking at her calmly—too calmly. "It just did it by itself."

"Oh, come on, Mom," Lisa said incredulously. "How could that be?" She stood up and walked over to Sharon. "Look, you said it was weird in there, right? Maybe you were so freaked out, you didn't see—"

"Oh, I saw," Sharon said. "You'd better believe I saw. Scared me so bad I pissed my pants." She thumped and mashed the cigarette in the ashtray for a long time before turning back to Jessica. "Let me see it."

Jessica placed a hand over her pocket. "I don't think—"

"No, Mom," Lisa said quickly. "Not if it's going to upset you like before."

Sharon gave Lisa a reassuring pat on the arm, then held out a hand to Jessica. "I *want* to see it."

Reluctantly Jessica dug the pendant out of her pocket and held it out to her.

Sharon chewed on her bottom lip, then gingerly picked up the chain. "It's got to be the same one," she said. "Looks too damn much like it for it not to be. But it's been so many years . . ." The iron bulb twirled and swayed lazily. Sharon shook her head thoughtfully. "Went right for her stomach like it was trying to get to you or something. Lord, I can still hear the sound it made when the old man pulled it out of her." She sniffed and dropped the pendant back into Jessica's hand. "I took her to the doctor after that. Luckily it hadn't gone in too deep."

Stunned by Sharon's confession, Jessica watched her walk stoop-shouldered to the stove and pick up a kettle. She sensed the woman had more to share but was biding her time to find the right words.

Sharon carried the kettle to the sink, but instead of filling it with water, she placed the kettle on an adjoining counter and turned to Jessica. "I think something else happened to your mom that day," she said. "I'm not really sure what, but she was never quite the same afterward. I think it messed her head up really bad. She started having a lot of . . . well, problems with her nerves and everything." Fresh tears filled Sharon's eyes. "I've always wondered if her problems were God's punishment for what we did—you know, going to that man in the first place."

Lisa went up to her mother and hugged her. "That's silly, Mom."

"Yeah, but the old people used to say—"

"What old people?" Lisa asked.

"Old people, like your grandmother."

"You mean you told this to Grandma?"

"Oh, I didn't tell her what we did," Sharon said. "I just asked her if she knew of any gris-grises. I made it sound like I was only curious, but what I really wanted to do was find help for Roberta. She was getting worse—in her head, and I thought if her having gone to that gris-gris man caused her problems, maybe bringing her to a different one might fix them."

"What'd Grandma say?"

"I thought she'd have a stroke right then and there. She made me swear never to go near one. Said they were dangerous, and that their hoo-doo followed people home and could even trickle over to their children if the hoo-doo was strong enough." Her eyebrows suddenly shot into twin peaks. "Holy saints, I'd forgotten all about that children part. Jess, first your mom—Todd—what if my mama was right?"

"Oh, come on, now!" Lisa scolded. "You can't be serious! Jess, don't you even listen to that mess, you hear?"

Jessica didn't answer. She stared at the pendant in her hand. The foggy sense of familiarity she'd felt from it earlier was becoming alarmingly clear. She now knew who the boy in Sharon's story was, and she was as certain of his identity as she was of her own name. The boy was the man in the window, the voice in the thicket, the one who called himself Eli. And somehow he was tied not only to this pendant but to her. The surety with which Jessica felt that made her consider whether there might be some validity to what Lisa's grandmother had said.

When she finally looked up at Lisa and Sharon, they were staring at her intently. "What if—and I'm saying *if,*" Jessica said to Lisa, "your grandmother was right?"

Lisa's mouth dropped open. "How can *you* of all people believe that's possible?"

Sharon pursed her lips and turned back to fill the kettle with water.

"Just what if?" Jessica asked, ignoring Lisa and posing the question to Sharon. "If something did follow Mom home, and it somehow got transferred to Todd"—*and to me*, she thought—"do you think it can be reversed, Miss Sharon?"

Sharon gazed out the kitchen window, letting the water overfill the container. "I don't know," she answered quietly.

Lisa threw up her hands. "Would you listen to the two of you?" She stormed over to her mother, grabbed the kettle, and slammed it down on the stove. "The both of you sound like—"

The kettle pitched to the floor with a loud *thonk!*

Sharon gasped as a stream of water sloshed across the back of her shorts and legs.

"I didn't do it!" Lisa declared.

Jessica hurriedly scooped up the kettle and was settling it back on the stove when an ear-piercing shriek stopped her cold. It came from the hallway, and she knew by Lisa and Sharon's bewildered expressions they heard it, too.

The three women stood frozen for a second, then, like sprinters at the sound of a starter gun, they collectively ran for the hall.

A crash that carried the intensity of a thousand windows breaking at once erupted from Lisa's bedroom. Sharon pushed past them and headed in that direction. Lisa scrambled to her mother's side.

"Don't go in there!" Jessica warned.

Despite her warning, Sharon flung open the bedroom door, and both Daigle women immediately stumbled backwards in a coughing fit, clamping their hands over their nose.

"It smells like rotted fish guts in there," Lisa said, her voice muffled behind her hand.

Sharon gagged, then nodded in agreement.

With her heart galloping to her throat, Jessica crept up to the doorway and peeked inside. She saw nothing but the murky shadows of the daybed and bureau. The smell was definitely there, however, a mixture of decayed flesh and ammonia that for some reason didn't leak out into the hall. It was as if the bedroom had been vacuum-packed in rot.

Suddenly another crash erupted from the room, this one shaking the house. A tortured moan followed, and it rapidly escalated to an almost unbearable volume.

Lisa and her mother grabbed on to each other and ran for the kitchen.

"Jessica, get away from there!" Lisa shouted.

"Oh, God, Jess, come on!" Sharon cried.

Jessica glanced toward her friends but didn't move. She refused to be chased away this time. This wasn't like before when she'd thought a few of her mental screws had stripped. Sharon and Lisa were witnesses as well. She had to get to the bottom of this or she *would* go crazy.

"What the hell are you doing?" Lisa yelled from the end of the hallway. Her voice barely penetrated the rising decibels of the moan. Sharon no longer stood beside her, and Jessica assumed she had escaped either to the kitchen or out of the house altogether.

Now or never, Jessica thought, then gritted her teeth and thrust a hand around the door frame and felt along the nearest wall for the light switch.

"Come on!" Lisa begged.

Feeling the plastic nub of the switch, Jessica pushed it up. Nothing happened. She pressed it down, then flicked it up again—still dark. In the time it took her to even think about toggling the switch again, something cold and rubbery grabbed her hand, holding tight, and the moaning turned into shrill laughter. Jessica screamed and locked her feet and free hand against the doorjamb to keep from being pulled inside by her captor.

The putrid air thickened and filled her lungs. She coughed and gagged and braced her body against the door. With a hard yank, she jerked herself free and landed in the hall on her back.

"Jessica!" Lisa pelted down the hall toward her.

"Get outta my way, Lisa Clare!" Sharon appeared in the hallway entrance, holding a fistful of the dried palm fronds she normally kept tacked to the kitchen doorpost.

Lisa stuttered to a stop and whirled about to face her mother. "What do you think you're doing?" she shouted over the maniacal laughter.

"If the priest's blessing on this stuff is strong enough to protect the house from bad weather, it damn well should be strong enough to handle this!" Sharon proclaimed. Then she charged down the hall, waving the branches in front of her.

"Mama, no!" Lisa cried.

Sharon reached the bedroom door before Jessica could even sit up. Holding the fronds up in the air, she made the sign of the cross, then raked and crushed the leaves between her hands. Sharon pitched the mulch into the dark room, and the laughter abruptly died. A rush of frigid air burst into the hallway, and light immediately filled the bedroom.

Sharon stood motionless in the doorway, her hands still raised.

"Mama?" Lisa's voice sounded unusually loud in the paneled hall. She hugged herself, then swayed as though her feet were planted to the floor. "Mama?"

When Sharon didn't respond, Jessica picked herself up and, laying a hand over the pain in her lower back, walked over to her. She peered into the room, where the older woman's gaze remained fixed, and her hand dropped to her side.

"Would ya'll get the fuck away from there?" Lisa whispered loudly.

Normally Jessica would have lit into her friend for using serious profanity in front of her mother, but she let it go this time. It just didn't seem to be that big a deal as she and Sharon watched crushed palm fronds float and swirl in figure eights around the bedroom.

Chapter Twenty-four

Todd knew something had gone terribly wrong. He also knew it had involved him. He just couldn't recall what that something was. He remembered seeing Jessica somewhere and recalled someone putting fresh bandages on him. Other than that, his mind was a lint trap, collecting nothing but fuzz.

Turning over on his side, Todd watched moonlight filter through the window slats from his cot. He thought about the visit he'd had from the balloon man, that big white face with the crooked mouth. And he thought about death and how badly he wanted it. If only the assholes here would leave him alone and stop trying to rescue him. Todd didn't want to be rescued. He wanted out of life.

Laughter trickled in from outside his room. Not funny laughter, but crazy, like in a movie with a wicked witch. He heard grunting and shouting, continuous squeaks from rusted bedsprings, and the slap, thump of a mop being pushed across tile.

Restless, Todd rolled over on his back and stared at the ceiling, wondering how many people had slept on this cot.

He thought about Jessica again and how scared she had looked. So, so afraid. She'd left in a hurry, too. Maybe she couldn't stomach being around him anymore.

"Who could?" a crisp voice said from inside Todd's head. "You're a maggot." The voice was solitary, which was a morbid relief to the shrill cacophony he'd had to endure up to now.

He rolled onto his side again and tried to remember what Jessica had talked about—something about Jake. Todd's eyelids grew heavy as he pictured the boy running and laughing for a football—on some green lawn—too long ago.

"You're not worth the trouble anymore, faggot," the crisp voice said in disgust.

Todd cleared his throat and pulled his knees up to his chest. The stinging in his groin made him adjust his position slightly. He listened to the dark.

Someone has to make sacrifices in this world. There isn't much time left until all the commies take over, and then where will we be? Someone has to stop them. I could go back to school and get a degree in engineering. Then I could build a bomb that would take care of all of them. I could invent stuff. Where is the balloon man? I hope he doesn't come back.

Todd's mind went blank for a few seconds then: *Jessica's hair looked dull, like she wasn't getting enough vitamins. I've gotta talk to her about that. She's gonna get sick if she doesn't take care of herself. She's gonna get zits with all that stress.*

Sleep captured Todd's last thought and brought him quiet. The muscles in his legs twitched as his body relaxed. He exhaled heavily, and his breathing soon took on a deep, steady rhythm.

"Hey!" a voice shouted in his ear.

Todd's eyes flew open, and he flipped onto his back and thrust out his hands protectively. A naked man stood beside him, his body sleek and hairless from head to foot. His eyes looked like those of a rat—dark, beady, and bulging.

"Wake up, sleepyhead," the man chirped sarcastically. His breath smelled of pine and rotting fish.

Todd coughed from the stench and closed his eyes.

"No, no, no sleeping now. Time for your medication."

Todd opened an eye and frowned. A naked male nurse? He opened the other eye. The man carried nothing in his hands. No med cups or syringe.

"You have been sleeping entirely too much," the man said, wagging a crooked finger at him. "And we must do something about that." He grabbed Todd by the hair and yanked him upright. Then the man's slick, bald head began to swell and blanch. It grew to the size of a large balloon, and the mouth quivered its way to a vertical position.

"Oh, master, we knew you'd come!" Voices suddenly congregated in Todd's head like zealous converts at an altar call. "Maikana! Maikana!"

Todd shuddered and squeezed his eyes shut tight.

Please, God, please, God, please, God, make the balloon man go away!

"Look at me!" the balloon man roared, the stink from his breath so strong it felt like spikes driving up Todd's nostrils.

"I said look at me!"

Trembling, Todd opened his eyes. The white face was almost on top of him now, eyes over eyes, mouth over mouth. Todd knew if he opened his mouth to scream, he'd suck in the poison coming from that noxious, vertical chasm and suffocate. He clamped his teeth together and mashed his lips shut tight.

The balloon man shook Todd by the hair, then released him. He took a step back and raised a fist. "You have procrastinated long enough! If the intent of your indolence was to bide time until the arrival of that woman, then you are an even greater fool than I suspected. She will never have you. You are mine! Do you hear?" The rat eyes moved in swift circles, making Todd dizzy. He shut his eyes again and wished the horror away.

"You *will* look at me!"

The head of the cot heaved up, then the whole bed flipped over on its side, tossing Todd to the floor. He landed on his stomach, and pain blasted through his groin. He crawled as quickly as he could to the corner of the room, where he cowered.

"Who—who are you?" Todd cried.

The white head bobbled, and the fist dropped. "Did you not hear them calling me in worship? Are your ears failing you? I *am* Maikana, far beyond any hallucination your warped mind might conjure. I am the author, the alpha and omega, of your every thought. You are mine and always have been! *This*," Maikana said, somehow tapping on the inside of Todd's forehead, "will always be mine! Do you hear and understand me now, you cowering bungler?"

In a flash, Todd's hands were jerked to his sides, and the beady eyes glared at him, demanding an answer.

"Y-y-yes," Todd stammered.

Maikana cocked his head, and a pointed, quizzical expression flicked across his face. "Humans are extremely ridiculous, you know. There are millions like you, were millions before you, and there will be millions after you. What logic is there for one to believe I could possibly be stopped? Why, the numbers alone prove my invincibility. And why, pray tell, should my work be halted? My charge is but to bring a taste of the unusual to those deserving. I would think anyone would find it invaluable to have no other responsibility in their miserable little lives save for the ramblings of their twisted minds. Yet they still complain. They all complain." The vertical mouth opened wide, and a wheezing laugh fell from it. The head swayed contemplatively from side to side. "Did you know that your sweet, nurturing mother was a favorite of mine?"

Todd gaped at the figure.

"Oh, yes. She was for years. Isn't this lovely? A family affair." Another chuckle vomited from the mouth. "But, of course, clinicians believe this mental condition to be"—the voice took on a radio announcer's drama—"genetically predispositioned."

Todd took advantage of Maikana's musing and scooted farther away until his back pressed against a wall. "What do you want from me?" he mumbled. *If I pluck my eyes out, I wouldn't have to see him anymore. I should have done it sooner, when I had the chance. I would still be able to hear him, but it wouldn't be any different than the other voices, and I wouldn't have to look at his face.*

"You are my special prize, my special one. Someone so delightful and treasured that I must keep a very close eye on you. A very close eye, indeed." Maikana paused, then taunted seductively, "Go on, sweet boy, pluck them out. Let me watch your fingers dig out those gelatinous beauties. Let me hear the rip as they tear away from muscle."

Nearly paralyzed, Todd struggled to shrink back farther, to become part of the wall.

The rat eyes looked amused. "You actually think that self-mutilation will rid you of me or bring you redemption?"

Todd threw an arm over his eyes.

Maikana's chuckle echoed through the room. "I do get so much pleasure from watching the likes of you. Now, look at me, you neurotic idiot! I will not allow you to rob me of the pleasure of your misery."

Peeping over the folds of his pajama shirtsleeve, Todd prayed silently. *Please, God, let me die. Please, please let me die!*

"Are you deaf as well as stupid? Or is your stupidity the result of your deafness? There is no one to save you. You have indeed been forgotten and are now but another troublesome responsibility for this humble place." There was a soft chuckle in

Todd's left ear. "Sweet, sweet, useless boy. Know that I will be with you always, even after death. I will make certain your family's family knows me well, and they will most assuredly think of you as I seduce them heart and soul."

"Yes, you will! You will!" the voices in Todd's head chorused.

At the mention of family, Todd saw Jessica in his mind's eye, and a surge of anger blasted through him. He threw his arms down and shouted, "No! You won't touch my family! I won't allow it!"

Laughter exploded from Maikana. "You will not allow it?" he mocked, his head rocking back and forth in merriment. Suddenly, he glared fiercely at Todd. "You will kneel to me!"

"Fuck you!" Todd screamed. He stood up, his body shaking. "You leave my family alone!"

Maikana's eyes bulged from his head. They pushed outward from the sockets, stretching on what looked like thick cords of mucus until the eyeballs were only inches from Todd's face. Maikana cooed, and the eyes changed from ratlike to reptilian. Abruptly, they snapped back into their sockets with a labored *thwap!*

"After all I've done for you," a woman's voice whined from Maikana's mouth. Todd recognized the raspy sound immediately. It was his mother's voice. "You ungrateful little shit. After I suffered the tortures of hell to give birth to you, and this is the thanks I get? You'll be the death of me, Todd Allen, the death of me. That's what you want, isn't it? For me to die? I can do that, you know. I can take the pistol in my nightstand and shoot my brains out, and it would be all your fault."

Todd's heart hammered painfully in his chest, and he fell to the floor. He slapped his hands over his ears.

"I work my fingers to the bone every day, and for what? I never wanted kids. You were a mistake, both of you were. If it hadn't been for you, your father would still be with me!"

Todd cried out and crossed his arms tightly over his chest. He rocked frantically. His eyes locked onto Maikana's face, but his mind saw his mother's. "Maammaa," he wailed. "Maammaa!"

Maikana's head contracted to its original size and, with a wobble, settled between the shoulders of his naked body. The rat eyes returned. "Stop whining, fool," he said sharply, "and pay attention."

Todd snapped his mouth shut.

"Let this serve as your last warning," Maikana said. "All you have suffered thus far is nothing compared to what I am capable of rendering. Should *they* come to you, you must not allow them to touch you. Do you understand? *Especially* the woman. If you allow her near you, I will make certain she receives a thousand times your torture—as will her son." With that, Maikana vanished, leaving nothing behind but the smell of decay.

Tears streamed down Todd's cheeks, and his body convulsed with the fury of his rocking. He felt nothing but hollow desperation. He stared straight ahead, unblinking, as three words tumbled over and over in his mind.

Enough is enough.

Chapter Twenty-five

Jessica had no sooner coaxed Sharon away from the bedroom door than the woman grabbed her arm and muttered, "Listen!"

A low, faltering, clacking sound reached Jessica's ear, and Sharon's grip tightened on her arm.

"What now?" Lisa asked, her body visibly trembling. She'd reluctantly joined her mother and friend to watch the frond parade, which was still in full swing.

The three women pressed tightly together and peered down the darkened hall.

"My sewing machine," Sharon said. "It's coming from the sewing room."

Jessica pulled away from the huddle. "Both of you stay here while I go check it out."

"No," Sharon said sternly. "You go, we go."

"Have ya'll lost your minds?" Lisa asked. "Let's just get the hell away from here!"

Sharon parked a fist on her hip. "This is *my* house, and I'm not going to let nothing or no one chase me out of it."

"What are you going to do, Mama? Fuss and shake your finger until it goes away?"

"Look, young lady—"

While the two women argued, Jessica edged down the hallway to the sewing room. As she crept closer, the door whispered open. Her breath quickened, and she balled shaking hands into fists. If anything intended to grab her this time, she wanted to be ready.

Gathering what little courage she had left, Jessica forced herself across the threshold, then came to an abrupt standstill, scarcely able to grasp what lay before her.

A pale green light bathed the ten-foot-by-ten-foot room, heightening the surrealism of its contents. Sharon's sewing machine sat on a folding table against the back wall. The old Singer model droned on while its heavy tailoring needle pumped and clacked away furiously. Sitting in front of the table, on a worn-out ottoman, was a black boy of maybe three or four. His body was semitranslucent and covered in rags. He hummed an off-key tune and, from the movement of his shoulders, it appeared to Jessica he was working something with his hands.

To the right of the boy stood two carts. One held scraps of multicolored fabric, various pattern guides, pincushions, and scissors. The assorted sewing paraphernalia tumbled about freely like someone was scrounging through them. The second cart, a foot shorter than the first, had two shelves, both filled with fashion magazines that stacked, fanned, then reshuffled themselves.

Instead of being frightened, Jessica felt oddly drawn to the ineffable sights, especially the boy. She took a tentative step forward, and her mind issued a sharp distress signal, warning her to get away while she could. Jessica ignored it and cautiously pressed on, urging one foot in front of the other, slowly, so slowly.

The boy twirled around on the ottoman and looked up at her.

Jessica gasped. The boy had a man's face, which was covered with gaping sores that ran across both cheeks and the right side of his nose. His dark brown, reptilian eyes blinked rapidly.

The boy-man smiled broadly, revealing tiny white teeth. Then he said in a child's singsong voice, "My mama makin' me sumpin'. Sumpin' new to wear 'cause I been good. But I gots to give this back to you first." He held out his small hands, which were draped with a white linen cloth. Something squirmed beneath the covering, and the boy stretched his arms out farther, offering it to her. His eyes changed rapidly to black, innocent orbs. "You can takes it," he said cheerfully.

As he spoke, the stirring about on the plastic carts settled into silence, as did the clacking from the sewing machine.

Drawn into the boy's gaze, Jessica inched closer, and the hideous face transformed from gangrenous to smooth, young and small. His innocent features summoned her closer still.

Whispers of movement from beneath the cloth captured Jessica's attention. A hand, with fingers so small they looked webbed, fell from the bottom of the drape. Her heart thudded loudly as the minuscule hand twitched, then hung limp. As though hypnotically persuaded, Jessica's hand extended toward it.

Suddenly, a bolt of lightning struck just outside a nearby window, and its brilliance blasted the pale green light from the room. A monstrous clap of thunder trailed quickly behind, and it sent tremors through the floor. The boy wobbled like he was sitting on a slippery log. Just when Jessica thought he would fall over, the boy stood up and pulled his covered hands to his chest. With a sad expression, he turned from her and walked away. His body moved effortlessly through the ottoman, through the sewing table, then finally through the wall, where he vanished without a trace.

An inscrutable surge of panic struck Jessica full in the chest, and she cried out, "No, wait! Come back!"

At that moment, Lisa burst into the sewing room, her eyes wild. "Fire! It's on fire!" Without further explanation, she grabbed Jessica by the arm and pulled her from the room.

They sped through the house to the living room, where Sharon stood with a fire extinguisher aimed at a smoldering television set. A decoupage of white, clumpy foam covered the wall behind it.

"It's out," Sharon said breathlessly. "Lightning must've struck it."

As though heralded, another crash of thunder sounded, and the living-room lights flickered. Rain began beating against the windows, and the house creaked as strong gusts of wind bludgeoned its walls.

"We'd best hurry and get the kerosene lamps before the lights go out for good," Sharon said. She looped an arm around the extinguisher and hugged it to her.

"Screw the lights," Lisa said. "We just need to get out of this house."

Sharon lifted a defiant chin. "I am *going* to find my kerosene lamps, and I don't want to hear another word about it." She turned on her heels and marched from the room.

Jessica didn't want to hunt for kerosene lamps. Now that she knew they didn't have a blazing inferno to deal with, she wanted to go back and find the boy. He'd said he had something to return to her, and although she'd caught only an obscure glimpse of what he had hidden beneath the cloth, Jessica felt an inexplicable desire to reclaim it.

Lisa had other plans for her, however. Still holding tight to Jessica's arm, Lisa muttered a few choice expletives and dragged her along after Sharon.

An explosion of sounds detonated from the kitchen archway as soon as they reached it. Pounding, crashing, banging, slamming, a clamor worthy of a cerebral meltdown. But it was the sight that greeted the women that stopped them cold.

Every cabinet door in the kitchen flapped open and shut with repetitive ferocity. Between swinging intervals, plates and bowls, cups and saucers flew from shelves and crashed to the floor. Pots with mismatched lids clanged together in grand style. Drawers opened and closed, intermittently tossing forks and knives, serving spoons and teaspoons across the room. The strip of fluorescent lights above the sink flickered from white to pale green.

"Oh, God," Sharon cried.

"Oh, fuck!" Lisa said.

Jessica stood in stunned silence as every burner on the stove ignited, shooting blue-white flames to twice their normal height. The water faucet turned off and on while the gooseneck spigot jerked from left to right. The pantry door flew open, and canned food and jars were indiscriminately tossed out. Canisters of flour and sugar pelted the snack bar and showered the room in cloudy white puffs.

"We're fuckin' outta here!" Lisa shouted, then turned to Jessica. "Where're your keys?"

Jessica blinked.

"Car keys, dammit, you're parked behind me!"

Snapping to attention, Jessica jerked a thumb over her shoulder. "The living room, my purse—"

Lisa dashed off in that direction without another word.

Sharon moaned. "Oh, God, oh, Jesus. Jess, what're we gonna do? What do we do?"

The tormented look in Sharon's eyes lit a fuse of anger in Jessica. She didn't understand what was going on or why Sharon and Lisa were suddenly involved. But she sure as hell planned to find out.

Taking Sharon by the shoulders, Jessica gently turned her away from the kitchen and nudged her into the dining room.

"Stay here," Jessica said firmly.

Sharon paled. "Where're you going? Jess? No! Don't go—"

Jessica stormed back to the kitchen with her fists clenched at her sides. "What do you want?" she screamed into the chaos.

A cookbook whipped past her, and she swatted at it.

"What?" she demanded.

From behind the snack bar came a raspy chuckle. Without warning, the boy from the sewing room hopped into view. He wore his boy face.

"I gots to give it back to you," he said, smiling sweetly. His voice carried over the dissonance as clearly as an organ playing in an empty church.

The cloth he'd carried earlier was now tied about his neck, bandanna style. He held out his hands, but this time what he offered Jessica lay exposed. The squirming, mewing fetus shivered in his palms.

Jessica drew in a sharp breath, instantly remembering her dream. "No," she murmured. "Don't, please—"

The smooth, young face immediately darkened. His eyes bulged, then sank into their sockets until they disappeared. A voice, deep and wet, bellowed from him. "By the process of elimination and the laws of retribution, your lineage is no more!" With that, the small fingers wrapped around the fetus and squeezed hard.

"Stop!" Jessica lurched for the boy, whose hands now dripped with blood.

"No!" Sharon's shout preceded a flying tackle that sent Jessica sprawling to the floor.

In that instant, the kitchen door burst open and the boy was sucked from the room in a cyclonic whirl of wind and rain. The door slammed shut behind him, and the culinary cavalcade abruptly ceased.

Sharon rolled off Jessica, and they both sat up quickly, breathing hard.

Within seconds, Lisa came running pell-mell into the kitchen. "I've got the—" She skidded to a halt. Her mouth dropped open, and her eyes cut a swift path from her mother to the backside of the kitchen, where they locked. Her nostrils flared. "Shit," she muttered.

Jessica scrambled to her feet and tracked Lisa's gaze. Sharon followed suit.

Across the kitchen door, written in large, blood-red letters, read a simple command:

HURRY

Chapter Twenty-six

Eli trudged through the downpour with his head bowed and his arms wrapped around his chest. The pellets of rain felt like sparks of fire against his flesh. The pain only served to remind him that the window of opportunity he had with the woman was nearly closed. He worried that he might not be able to accomplish what needed to be done.

He moved slower, much slower than he had that morning, his energy level all but gone. His thoughts seemed no more than a random jumble, which concerned him greatly. Eli couldn't discern anymore if Maikana was influencing the mind clutter or if it was his own body preparing to shut down. It all felt the same. The last thing he wanted now was confusion. He feared it might cause him to hurt the woman instead of help her.

As Eli reached the thicket at the end of the street,

a sad calm settled over him. He lowered himself to the ground, crawled beneath the brush, and found the tire iron he'd hidden there.

Exhausted, he pulled the rod to him, then slowly rolled out of the thickest section of bramble. When he found enough clearing for his head, Eli sat up and drew his knees to his chin. The rain still found him through the tent of leaves, but at least the torrent was deflected. He lowered his head, flinching as raindrops plopped onto his back. Each drop felt hot and cold at the same time, and they reminded him of pattering showers over the swamps. How the rain stirred the muddy waters and filled the air with a musky, yet fresh, scent that had always made him feel warm inside. Eli wondered about how different things felt and looked and smelled when it was the last time they were to be experienced.

The leaves fluttered and scratched against his face and arms, and Eli considered a place where nothing could be felt at all. He thought about all the people who'd come to the end of their days and wondered if they'd felt the same things he felt now. Were they saddened they would never smell color again? The green of the leaves that left a tingling in the nostrils or the silver of the rain that cleared it?

Clutching the metal rod, Eli swatted a tangle of branches and weeds beside him. He didn't know whether to feel sad or angry.

He closed his eyes and thought of his mother. He could recall only one memory of her that brought him comfort. It was a scrap of a memory, barely there. Maybe it had been a dream instead of an actual experience—something he only wished would have happened. Either way, the thought of a boy lying across a swayback porch on a hot summer night, wakened by his mother as she stroked his hair and cooled his face with a wet cloth, soothed him. That memory, or dream, always seemed to have a short shelf life, only holding in his mind for as long as it took him to draw a few breaths. Then it would drift off to some other place, as it was doing now, where it would wait for another special time, usually a hard time, a lonely time, before it would return.

One person who always came readily and frequently to mind was Johanson, and Eli called him up quickly. He wondered what Johanson was doing right this moment and whether the old man was even thinking about him at all. He imagined himself sitting in Johanson's boat, the murky water slapping against the aluminum sides. The vision came to Eli's mind so vividly he could almost feel the rays of sunlight beating against his face.

Johanson would be listening carefully to his predicament, offering no advice until asked. And if, when asked, no advice came readily to mind, he'd start lazily stroking the water with a paddle until some came.

Eli wondered how he would even explain this situation to Johanson. What question was there to pose that *could* be answered? He would die if he didn't get to the woman, and probably die if he did. Where was the question in all of that?

Eli could hear the faraway slap and swirl of the paddle in the water . . .

"Dare ain't no question," Johanson would decide. "Jus' what is and what you got to do. And if you got to do somet'ing, den do it wit' all you got. Utterwise, you ain't about nuttin'. You be nuttin' more den a slug on a rock, takin' up space. And de good Lord didn't make you to be no slug."

"But I afraid ah dyin'."

"We all gots to."

"Don't make no difference to me. I still be afraid."

The paddle would be pushed through the water with harder, deeper, longer strokes.

"Yep, I'm supposin' I would be, too."

And that would be the end of that. Short and to the point.

Eli stuck out his tongue and let rainwater fall against it. It tasted cool and promising, like rain always did after a hard, dry spell. But he knew there was nothing really to be promised now. His time was just about over, and that was all there was to it.

He dragged himself out of the bushes and stood, holding the tire iron at his side. No fresh revelations turned him one way or the other. He had to hurry and get this over with, like Johanson would have said—do it with everything you have. Do it hard, do it fast, get it over with. Then what will be, will be.

Eli hoped he had enough time left to do just that.

Chapter Twenty-seven

"W-when did that happen?" Lisa sputtered, pointing the knob of her chin at the writing on the door.

"Just before you got here," Sharon said. She peered nervously about her war-torn kitchen. "I think the—the boy wrote it in blood."

"What boy?" Lisa asked, her voice turning shrill.

"The one from the sewing room," Jessica said.

Sharon's head snapped in her direction. "You saw him in there? When?"

"Earlier. When you were putting out the fire—"

"Wait just a goddamn minute," Lisa said. "Who are ya'll talking about? *What* boy?"

"I don't know who he is," Jessica said. "Only that he—"

"Oh, I know who he is," Sharon blurted.

Jessica and Lisa looked at her expectantly.

"It was him." Sharon wrung her hands. "The boy

I told you about, the one that touched Roberta's stomach."

"There's no way it could have been him, Mama," Lisa said, frowning. "He'd be thirty-nine, forty years old now, not a boy."

"I'm telling you it was him," Sharon insisted. "It was!"

As impossible as Sharon's statement sounded, Jessica felt truth in the woman's words. The revelation seemed to add another jagged piece to the growing, macabre puzzle inside her. Although not enough pieces had been collected yet for Jessica to identify the puzzle's picture, its disclosure felt imminent.

A crash of thunder startled Lisa, and she jumped. "Shit—whatever—forget the boy. I've got the car keys, let's just go." She cast a reluctant glance toward the kitchen door. "That—that way, I guess. It's closer."

Lisa quickly waded through broken plates and dented pots with a determined set to her jaw. When she reached the door, she grabbed the knob as though she intended to yank it off. After a few frantic twists and pulls, she yelled, "It won't open!"

Jessica hurried to her side. "Let me try." She quickly dried her palms on her slacks, then took hold of the knob. It wouldn't even turn.

"The front one," Sharon called, signaling them out of the kitchen. "We'll go out the front."

As the three women rushed through the house, the tempest outside gathered strength and rattled every window they passed. Overhead, the rain sounded like marbles pummeling the roof.

When they reached the living room, Jessica detoured to the phone while Sharon headed for the front door. Lisa parked herself between them, watching anxiously.

Even before Jessica picked up the receiver, she had a feeling the line would be dead. It was. She depressed the disconnect button, then released it and listened again.

"Anything?" Lisa asked.

"No."

Lisa threw her hands up angrily. "Do I look surprised?"

"The rain must've made the wood swell up," Sharon said, tugging on the front door, " 'cause this one isn't opening either."

"You mean we're trapped?" Lisa asked incredulously.

Jessica dropped the receiver into its cradle, then went to a window and peeked past the sheers. Jagged swords of light illuminated the neighborhood, and she saw trash cans and roof shingles zip across lawns. She pressed a hand against the windowpane. It vibrated beneath her fingers.

"Screw this," Lisa said. "We're getting out of here even if it's through there!" She pushed Jessica aside, ripped the sheers away from the window, and released the lock bar on top of the sash. Then she pulled up on the lower sash, straining until her face turned red, but the window refused to budge.

Blam! The sound of a heavy crash rolled toward them from the back of the house.

"No way, you sonofabitch," Lisa shouted at the window. "You're *gonna* move!" She grabbed a metal magazine rack that rested near the recliner and dumped the newspapers tucked inside it onto the floor. Holding the rack in both hands, she swung hard and rammed it into the window. The rack bounced back without so much as cracking the glass. Lisa swung again, producing the same results—none.

Sharon, pale and sweating, gave up on the front door and hustled over to her daughter. She snatched the bent rack from her. "Give me that." With a loud grunt, Sharon lifted the rack over her head, turned sideways, then hammered it into the windowpane. The only thing that broke was the rack.

Claps of thunder shook the house, and the lights flickered twice, then went out, pitching them into utter darkness.

"Stay together," Jessica said firmly.

She heard the magazine rack clatter to the floor, then Lisa call out, "We're over here, where're you?"

"Here."

"Keep talking so we can find you."

"Here—here—here—" Jessica felt a hand smash her left breast.

"Shit, sorry."

An impromptu chorus of grating, scraping, thumping noises erupted nearby, and Sharon and Lisa sandwiched Jessica between them.

"What the fuck's that?"

As though in answer to Lisa's question, lightning emblazoned the room, revealing an aberrant ménage à trois. The coffee table now sat atop the sofa, and the recliner, which had tilted over, butted up against both.

Sharon let out a thin squeal and made a hasty sign of the cross. Lisa slapped her hands over her eyes.

Jessica waited for the next lightning strike to cut through the darkness, then broke away from the panicked women and ran to the front door. She gave it a hard tug, but it still wouldn't open.

Suddenly the house lights stuttered, on—off—on.

"Hurry, let's try another window before they go out again," Lisa said, then took off with Sharon trailing close behind.

Jessica followed them into the dining room and saw Lisa promptly grab hold to one of the split-bottom chairs near the table and throw it at the dining-room picture window. The chair bounced off the window, leaving it intact, then collided with the table and splintered.

"Fuck, fuck, *fuck!*" Lisa threw a kick into the air.

"The bedrooms," Sharon said. "We can try—"

A deafening *rip!* sent all three women racing toward one another. A roll of thunder pounded through the house.

"Hail Mary, full of grace—" Sharon prayed aloud.

Thumping, pounding, then an explosive shatter sounded from the living room.

"This is enough!" Jessica yelled, and began moving them en masse in that direction. She felt like a Pavlovian experiment or worse, a rat trapped in a shoebox, and she refused to be either. There *had* to be a way out of this house. She just had to find it.

"No, no, I don't want to go in there," Sharon cried. "I don't want to see anymore. I—I've got a headache. I need to go lie down. I need to . . ."

They cornered the entrance to the living room, and Sharon gasped so hard she choked. The coffee table now stood on end near the recliner, and the sofa lay on its back. A gaping hole sat in the middle of the television screen.

As Jessica gently thumped Sharon on the back, trying to help her catch her breath, the front door flew open and slammed against the inside wall. A blast of wind and rain raged through the house.

"Yes!" Lisa shouted triumphantly. She grabbed her mother's arm. "Come on, come on, it's open!"

Sharon inhaled sharply, then pulled out of her daughter's grasp. "My purse—in the kitchen. Gotta get my purse."

"Mama!"

"I need my purse," Sharon cried. She turned to Jessica, her eyes filled with terror and tears. "My stomach medicine's in there. I can't go without my medicine. My doctor said—"

"Get the fuck out of this house!" Lisa's scream pierced through the bawling wind, and Jessica and Sharon looked back in alarm.

A man, dressed in ragged, rain-soaked clothes that clung to his thin body like a second skin, stood in the living-room doorway. His face was little more than a mangle of waterlogged flesh and gristle. And from his hands swung a long, black, metal rod.

Chapter Twenty-eight

The sound of cannon fire shook Todd from his sleep. He bolted upright in bed, puzzled, trying to remember where he was. He heard spattering sounds against the window, like tiny pebbles were being tossed against it. *Rain,* he thought. *Just thunder and rain.*

The cannon suddenly exploded again, and his room filled with a crystalline radiance that made him squint. In that instant, a pencil-thin streak of violet light shot out from between the window slats. It targeted the plastic chair resting against the wall opposite Todd and melted it on contact. Another blast of thunder immediately followed, and Todd's cot vibrated beneath him. He scrambled off the bed and hobbled to the far corner of the room, where he squatted, and covered his nose against the stench of burnt plastic.

Cries of alarm rose from somewhere out in the hall.

Todd watched in awe as the cot began to quake more violently, metal legs thumping and bumping against the floor. It finally flipped over on its side. Springs groaned and pinged as it wrenched itself in half.

Get out, get out, get out! Todd thought. *Gotta get out of here!* But even in his terror, Todd knew there was no place for him to go but right where he was. His room door was locked at all times, so even if he reached it there would be no escape.

Without warning, the mangled cot slid across the floor and slammed into the wall now splattered with molten plastic.

The doorknob began to rattle loudly, and Todd gasped with relief. Someone had come to save him!

"Help!" he yelled, afraid to get up from his corner. "I'm here! Over here!"

The knob rattled louder, and someone hammered on the door as though attempting to break it down with a fist. Lightning shattered the room's darkness and summoned a clap of thunder even louder than the one before. Cries from patients in rooms flanking his turned into petrified shrieks.

"Hurry!" Todd shouted.

The door burst open, and the air immediately grew heavy and smelled of sulfur.

Todd scrambled to his feet and lurched for the door. Just as he made the threshold, a blast of wind threw him back into the room, tossing him on his butt. Wind whipped vehemently about the room as though a colossal fan had been switched on. It pulled

Todd's hair straight back from his head and pasted his pajamas to his body. Struggling to his feet again, he strained against the whirling fury. He managed to move forward only two or three inches before he lost his balance and fell.

Abruptly the rush of wind died.

Todd lay on his side, stunned. He barely had time to collect his breath before a low, guttural groan quickly caught his attention. With a thudding heart, he turned toward the sound.

A slim, dark-haired woman stood just inside the doorway, facing the plastic-smeared wall. Even in profile, Todd recognized her immediately. He sat up, wanting to laugh and cry at the same time.

"Jess!"

Slowly she turned to face him, and Todd's mouth dropped open in horror. The right side of her face was nothing more than bloody pulp. A gelatinous substance trailed along the right side of her neck and onto her shoulder. Blood matted her hair and dripped along the front of her blouse. Nothing remained of her eyes but the sockets that once held them.

"N-no," Todd whimpered. "Oh, J-Jess."

The sound of his voice seemed to give her direction, for she shifted slightly to the left, then inched toward him.

Todd whimpered again and scooted backward.

She stepped closer. Her mouth opened, and a gurgling sound escaped. " 'Most time, Toddy," she said. " 'Most time." She smiled, revealing blood-soaked teeth. Blood spilled over her bottom lip, and she slurped it back into her mouth like thick soup.

He groaned with nausea.

"It'll be quick, Toddy. Real quick. You'll never know what hit you." The crimson grin broadened across the lopsided face. "I promise."

Although Todd suspected his brain of melding phantasm with reality at times, he felt no doubt about the validity of the threat standing before him. His mind didn't know where to slot the monstrosity, however, for he sensed this to be no dream, no hallucination, and definitely *not* his sister.

"Just hold still, okay? Just hold still." She crept toward him on tiptoe, slowly, carefully, like someone trying not to wake a sleeping child. As she drew nearer, she lifted her arms and reached out for him in earnest.

Todd scrambled backward and screamed, "No!"

She came to an abrupt halt, and in the time it took Todd to realize he was now trapped between her and the wall at his back, the face changed from Jessica's to the slick, white bulbous features of the balloon man.

A gray tongue slipped out between full, thick, vertical lips, and it wagged at him seductively. " 'Most over," it teased, and began to move toward him again.

Shivering uncontrollably, Todd pulled his knees to his chest and wrapped his arms around them. There was nothing he could do but watch as it came closer, ever closer. Death was but a few feet away now, and as much as he had desired it only hours ago, at this moment, Todd feared dying more than he had feared anything else in his life.

" 'Most over, Toddy!"

Todd rocked his body from side to side and began to take long, deep breaths to stretch his lungs. If he was going to die, then he wanted his last exhalation to be huge, and he wanted it to carry the name of the one person who'd ever really given a damn about him. The one person whose love he never doubted. The one person he'd trade every happiness he'd ever known just to see once more.

And as the balloon man leaned over for him, Todd lifted his head, filled his lungs one last time, then shouted, "JESSICAAAAA!"

Chapter Twenty-nine

Sharon's shriek hung in the air like a parachute caught in a northeaster.

"Get outta here!" Lisa shouted, and scrambled for the crumpled magazine rack. She grabbed it and pointed the bent frame at the man threateningly.

Jessica stood paralyzed, her heart a captive timpani. She couldn't believe it. Finally, in the flesh, without cover of window screen or thorny bush, in plain view for anyone interested to see, stood the man who had called himself Eli.

Lisa inched forward, thrusting out her weapon. "I said go, you ugly fuck! You deaf? Need me to unplug your goddamn ears for you, mother—"

"Wait," Jessica said.

The rack drooped, and Lisa turned to her, gawking. "*Wait?*"

Sharon whimpered and crossed herself again

while the wind lashed through the room and sent discarded newspapers flapping about in every direction.

"*Wait*?" Lisa repeated incredulously.

Jessica ignored her and took a step toward Eli. "What do you want from me?" she asked.

Eli blinked slowly. His eyes were red and nearly swollen shut. They wept a thick yellow gunk that refused to be washed away by the rain. "We gots to hurry," he said, his voice weak and barely audible above the raging gusts.

"It's you that'd better *hurry* your ass out of here," Lisa countered, jabbing the air with the twisted rack.

Jessica held up a hand to silence her.

"We gots to hurry," Eli said a bit louder. "No more time—you brother—most over." A fierce blast of wind and rain shot through the house and nearly knocked him over. His eyes squeezed shut, and what remained of his face wrinkled in pain.

"What about my brother?" Jessica urged. "Who are you? What do you want with him? What do you want with me?"

The wind calmed slightly, and Eli's chin dropped to his chest. He stood so motionless, for a moment Jessica thought he'd fainted standing up.

Gradually Eli looked up, and his lips quivered. "Now be de time," he said, and squared his shoulders. "You gots to take care ah him. You brother. And I gots to help."

A shrill wail ripped out of nowhere, and the window they'd tried to escape through earlier exploded, making everyone duck.

"Hurry, don't gots no more time!" Eli wailed, motioning to Jessica.

As though prodded into action with a hot poker, Sharon jumped in front of Jessica. "Nobody's going anywhere with you, mister. Now, get out of here!"

Eli squinted at Sharon. "I knows you," he said, his voice ominous.

Sharon stumbled back.

"I knows you," he repeated, and glared down at her.

"Well—well, I don't know you," Sharon shouted. "So get out of here before we call the police and have you—"

"I can hold it?" a boy's voice burbled from Eli's mouth.

Sharon's face turned ashen. She shook her head. "No," she mouthed. Her eyes searched for Lisa, then Jessica. "No!"

A horrendous crash resounded from the back of the house, and the lights went out again. Lightning flashed, backlighting Eli's emaciated frame, and Jessica saw him drop the tire iron and grasp the door frame as if his life depended on it.

"Hurry to you brother, now!" he shouted hoarsely. "Go NOW!"

Sudden whirring, motorized sounds turned Eli's eyes into slits. He groaned loudly, pitifully, and doubled over as though he'd been gut-punched.

The whirring intensified, and in the time it took Jessica to blink Eli back into focus, he was gone.

Chapter Thirty

"Let's go!"

Jessica heard Lisa's command, but the only action she seemed capable of was gaping at the empty doorway. Her brain parroted Eli's words again and again. *Hurry to you brother—hurry to you brother.* Each time she'd seen Eli, his messages about Todd had grown more urgent but no less choppy and confusing. What did this man have to do with her brother? And why had he been so insistent that she get to Todd right away? How *could* she get to Todd now? It was the middle of the night. She'd barely managed to see Todd during regular hospital hours. There was no way they would let her in to see him this late. And even if by some miracle they did, what was she supposed to do? Eli had told her to take care of her brother, to help him, but how? With what?

Another cerebral message prodded Jessica, suggesting that she pinch herself so she'd wake up and this nightmare would be over. Then she'd be back in Memphis, sitting up in her own bed with Frank snoring beside her.

"Jessica!" Lisa pinched her on the arm.

So much for waking up.

Lisa shook a set of keys at her. "I'll unlock the car. You get Mama." Without waiting for a response, she took off for the front door and all but dove through it.

Jessica wet her lips, which seemed to crank her legs into motion. She hurried over to Sharon, who stood glassy-eyed and silent in the middle of the living room, and took her by the hand. She followed Jessica like a reluctant child out of the house and into the deluge waiting for them outside.

Two steps into the yard, Jessica found herself sloshing through ankle-deep water.

"My house!" Sharon cried, suddenly pulling up short. The rain quickly flattened her hairdo and pasted it to the sides of her face. "Look at my house!"

A huge pecan tree, which shaded the east corner of the Daigle property, had been seared in two. The larger half jutted up from the roofline of the house. Remnants of the decorative window boxes floated across the lawn, and two front windows were shattered.

"It's destroyed," Sharon sobbed. "My poor, poor house."

"Get in!" The back door of the rental car swung open, and Lisa waggled a hand at them. "Come on!"

Jessica nudged Sharon gently. "It'll be all right,

Miss Sharon, don't worry. Just get in the car now, okay, honey? You're getting soaked."

The woman balked, then stumbled along as Jessica led her to the car.

Once Sharon was safely tucked inside the vehicle, Jessica darted for the passenger's side, and a lightning bolt ripped a seam through the night. The ground rumbled beneath her feet, and as the thunder rolled into silence, she heard someone call out to her.

"*JESSICA!*"

Jessica whirled about. "Todd?"

"*JESSICA!*"

Her ears burned with the echo of her brother's voice. Even through the howl of the wind and patter-splat of the rain, it came through clear and scared and sounded as though he stood only a foot away.

"*JESS, HURRY!*"

"Todd!" Jessica screamed into the storm. She turned in halting circles, looking for him, knowing he couldn't possibly be there. "Todd!"

A car horn blew impatiently.

"What's the matter with you?" Lisa shouted from a crack she'd made in her window. "Get in the car!"

"It's Todd," Jessica shouted back.

"What?"

"Todd, I heard Todd!"

"Get in the goddamn car, Jessica!"

Jessica stood in the downpour, listening a moment longer. "Todd?" she whispered.

When no one answered, she squeegeed her face with a hand and waded through the water to the other side of the car.

"*Jessicaaaaa . . .*"

Jessica's heart and instincts jolted with the sound of the fading, frightened cry. She opened the passenger door and hurriedly slid inside. "Go to Municipal," she said to Lisa, and slammed the door shut. "Todd's in trouble. I've got to get to him—now—just like Eli said—right now."

Jiggling a key in the ignition switch, Lisa glanced at her. "Municipal? Todd? Hold up—who's Eli?"

"The man who was in the house."

Lisa sat back, abandoning the key. "Hamburger face?"

Jessica tapped the dash impatiently. "Just start the car already."

"You think Todd's in trouble because of what that freakazoid said?"

"No," Jessica snapped. "Because I heard him."

"Who?"

"Todd."

Lisa frowned. "When?"

"Just now, outside. Now, can you stop with the fifty damn questions and go?"

Lisa swiveled about, glancing through the car windows. "You saw Todd?"

"No, dammit, now go!" Jessica reached over and twisted the key in the ignition. The engine whined, sputtered, then stalled.

"Gimme that before you break something," Lisa said, and swatted Jessica's hand away. She turned the key in the ignition and the starter clicked, but the engine remained mute.

A crack of thunder sent a rattling shiver through the car.

"Hurry . . . please," Sharon said from the backseat, her voice small and quivering.

"We're trying, Mama." Lisa clenched her teeth and tried the key again. "Gotta get the car started first."

"Jess, you drive," Sharon said anxiously.

"Mama, the driver won't matter if the car won't—"

"Jessica's supposed to drive!" Sharon shrieked.

The car engine suddenly sputtered to life, and Lisa threw the gearshift into reverse and floored the accelerator.

The rental shot out of the driveway and back-swerved onto Sylvia Street. Lisa hit the brakes, then slapped the gearshift into drive. The car coughed, then blasted forward.

"Be—be careful," Sharon said, and gripped an armrest.

Two-foot waves fanned out on either side of the vehicle as Lisa plowed down the center of the road.

As they neared the first intersection, Jessica said grimly, "Take a right on Main."

"Not a good idea," Lisa said, gripping the steering wheel tightly. Rain cascaded over the windshield in sheets, making the wipers virtually useless. "Westside of Main's got that dip in the road by the railroad tracks, and there's probably three feet of water in it right—"

"Take it anyway," Jessica demanded. "It's the shortest way to Municipal."

Lisa punched the steering wheel with the heel of a fist. "Jessica, look at this storm! I can't see my hand in front of my face. I can't even make out the edge of the road to watch for ditches. Every goddamn thing's flooded! How in the hell do you expect us to make it all the way to that hospital?"

"Lisa Clare, do what she says," Sharon said sternly. "If Jessica says go to Municipal, you go."

Lisa tossed a bewildered look over the seat at her mother, then peered at Jessica. "The two of you want to fill me in?"

"I already told you," Jessica said, staring straight ahead. "Todd." She threw a finger at the windshield. "Stop!"

Lisa slammed a foot against the brake, and the car fishtailed, then jerked hard to the right. There was a sharp crunch of metal against metal.

"Sweet Mary of Mercy!" Sharon cried.

The car rocked to a stop, and Lisa threw up her hands and scowled at Jessica. "That stopped enough for you? What? I thought you were the one all piss-bent on hurrying."

Jessica nodded at the octagon-shaped sign now bent over the hood. "Stop sign."

Lisa exhaled loudly. "See what I mean? I didn't even see the damn thing." She put the shifter into reverse and backed up slowly. A screech vibrated through the car as the hood pulled away from the metal pole. "Shit, I can't even see the crossroad." Lisa set the vehicle back in drive and tapped the accelerator. The back end of the car fishtailed slightly, and she hit the brakes again. "I can't do this! It's suicide!"

"*JESSICA!*"

Jessica bolted to attention at the sound of Todd's voice.

"*JESS—PLEASE—HURRY!*"

In one fluid motion, Jessica yanked up on the door handle, shoved the passenger door open, and jumped out into shin-deep water.

"What are you doing?" Lisa shouted.

Jessica cupped her hands around her mouth and shouted as loud as she could into the wind. "Todd!" If she could hear him, then maybe he would hear her. "Todd!"

"Jessica!" Lisa and Sharon were both yelling from the car.

"Todd!" Jessica called again, then listened intently. When she didn't hear a response, panic galloped up her spine and threatened to send her racing off on foot for the clinic.

Instead, she rushed around to the driver's side of the car and pulled the door open. "Move," she demanded, already shoving her body against Lisa's. "I'm driving."

With no more than a stunned expression, Lisa scooted over to the passenger's seat.

Jessica glimpsed at Sharon's reflection in the rearview mirror. "You okay?"

"Yes," Sharon said, looking oddly relieved.

"Good. Both of you put on your seat belts," Jessica warned, and gripped the steering wheel until her knuckles turned white. " 'Cause come hell *or* high water, we're getting to that clinic." She punched the accelerator, clueless as to how she would get into the hospital once they got there, but not caring.

"I'm coming, little brother," she whispered. "I *am* coming."

Chapter Thirty-one

By the time Jessica turned into Municipal's parking lot, the rain had finally slowed to a drizzle, and she felt on the brink of a nervous breakdown. It had taken them nearly an hour to travel the twelve miles between the Daigle house and here. Street flooding and downed tree limbs had caused her to detour repeatedly and rarely allowed her to reach speeds higher than fifteen miles an hour. Not a great response time for someone hell-bent on getting to her brother.

"Why're you parking way back here?" Sharon asked.

"Because there's no other lot," Jessica said, flexing her stiff fingers away from the steering wheel. "This is it. You have to take a sidewalk to the—"

"Look!" Lisa said as the car's headlights cut a bright swath across the back of the clinic.

Jessica hit the brakes and the car slid to a stop. There was no mistaking the man now pinned in the glare of the headlamps. Eli stood leaning against the brick building near a glass exit door about sixty feet away. He turned sideways, away from the light, and hunched his shoulders.

"What the hell's he doing here?" Lisa asked.

"Oh, this is not good," Sharon muttered, and wiggled to the edge of her seat. "Not good at all."

Jessica threw the gearshift into park. She wasn't surprised to see Eli. In fact, the moment she spotted him she sensed that somehow he would be the avenue she needed to get into Municipal. What did puzzle her, however, was how he'd managed to get here at all. It would have taken a healthy person much longer to hike the twelve miles than it had taken them to drive it. Eli seemed barely capable of standing. How could he have possibly made a trek that long in so short a time?

Keeping one eye on him, Jessica unbuckled her seat belt. "Stay put. I'm—"

"No way, kiddo. You're not going this one alone," Lisa said, and she was out of the car before Jessica could stop her.

"Lisa Clare, you get back in here this minute!" Sharon cried. "Jess, make her come back!"

Jessica hurried to open the driver's door, but it felt cemented to the frame. Refusing to waste time by fighting with it, she swiveled around on the bench seat and scooted toward the passenger door, which was still open. It banged shut before she reached it.

"Oh, Lord, Lord, Jess, I can't get out. The window won't even go down!" Sharon slapped a palm against her window repeatedly and shouted, "Lisa Clare, you listen to me and come back in here this instant! Jess, do something!"

In one quick scan, Jessica caught sight of Lisa standing near the hood of the car, hands on hips, threatening to skin the rest of Eli's body if he didn't leave them alone, and Sharon in the throes of a panic attack in the backseat. Jessica hit the automatic window buttons set in the front door panels and heard them whine, but the windows remained motionless. Riding on impulse, she immediately jammed her feet against the passenger door, bent her knees, then leaned over and grabbed the door handle. She whispered a hasty "Please, God," then yanked up on the handle. The lever moved, and Jessica stuck the toe of her tennis shoe beneath it to hold it in position, then shoved hard against the door with both feet.

Every tendon and muscle burned as she strained to straighten her legs. Gradually the door squeaked open a few inches—then a bit farther—a little farther still. When she finally had her legs stretched out to full length, Jessica hastily dropped her feet to the ground and was about to do a tuck and roll when the door slammed back against her left shoulder. It continued to urge itself shut, pinning her between it and the door frame.

Jessica heard Sharon yelling her name and tried to call out for help, but her lungs didn't seem to contain enough oxygen to push the words past her lips.

"Hold on!" someone shouted, then Lisa's face suddenly appeared in Jessica's line of sight. Locking her fingers around the lip of the door just above Jessica's shoulder, Lisa said sternly, "Push while I pull." Then Lisa tugged on the door, leaning back for leverage. Jessica gritted her teeth and pushed, already feeling some of the pressure ease from her shoulder.

"Try now," Lisa commanded.

Hunching forward, Jessica strained against the narrow opening until she popped free. She landed on her side in the flooded parking lot.

"Ya'll wait for me!" Sharon yelled.

"C-can't," Lisa said, still clinging to the door. Her feet began to slide across the wet pavement. "Can't hold it."

Jessica struggled to her feet in time to see Sharon dive for the front seat, then do a belly bust between the headrests. In that instant, Lisa let out a loud whoop and the passenger door swung shut, smashing her fingers between layers of steel.

"Jesus!" Lisa bellowed, and her knees buckled.

Jessica lunged for her friend and looped an arm around her waist to hold her upright. With her free hand, she quickly ran a finger along the edge of the door, searching for the slightest crevice with which to latch on to. There wasn't one.

Sharon's terror-stricken face appeared in the back passenger window, and she beat on the glass with a fist. "Open it, open it, her hand! My baby's hand!"

"G-get it—J-Jesus, m-my f-fingers." Lisa slumped against Jessica, and her head lolled back.

"No, no, breathe, honey. Come on, hang on." Jessica eased Lisa against the car, then pulled up on the door handle with both hands. It wouldn't budge. Jessica yanked harder, her fingertips numbing. "Help!"

she shouted, and threw a desperate glance toward Eli. "Help me get it open!"

He cocked his head slightly to one side, then leaned over and picked up the tire iron lying at his feet.

Lisa groaned loudly, drawing Jessica's attention back to her. "J-Jess, s-stop p-p-pulling. You're just—just pissing it—" Lisa's eyes rolled to full white, and she slumped into a heap, both arms suspended awkwardly over her head.

Sharon shrieked, and the car began to rock with her frantic efforts to get out of the car.

"Don't just stand there, goddammit, do something!" Jessica glared at Eli, then zeroed in on the tire iron in his hand. "Use that! Pry the door—"

"You don't got no time for dat now," Eli said calmly. "It won't let you do nuttin' wit' her anyway. Leave her."

"I can't just leave her!" Jessica screamed.

"You don't got no choice. If we don't gets to you brother now, we lose. Hurry—now."

Jessica let go of the door handle and hovered over Lisa, who was still out cold. "I can't!" she insisted. "She could lose her fingers if I don't do something."

"You gonna lose you brother if you don't COME NOW!" Eli's voice inflated to a booming roar. Then, without warning, he spun about and swung the tire iron into the glass door, shattering it.

Jessica gasped and waited for an alarm to sound. None did.

"Come now!" Eli demanded.

A blast of wind suddenly detonated behind Jessica

and shoved her away from the car and toward Eli. She had to run to keep her feet in sync with the momentum of her body.

As Jessica neared him, worries of Sharon and Lisa faded. The force that physically compelled her forward seemed to encapsulate her thoughts, focusing them in one direction. She *had* to get to Todd.

Ducking beneath icicle-length glass shards, Jessica followed Eli into the building, where he led her down a long corridor awash with light from the car's headlamps to a heavy wooden door that signaled its end.

Eli motioned for her to stay back, then raised a hand and splayed his fingers. Immediately, strips of wood began to rip away from the door like giant banana skins.

Jessica glanced nervously over her shoulder. Though they were at the very back of the building, far from the reception area, she was sure the vehement tearing and ripping sounds would summon a security guard from somewhere. But the corridor remained empty, and when she turned back she found the door had been literally stripped open.

Eli walked nonchalantly over the debris, tossing wood scraps aside with his metal rod. Jessica tagged along mutely, as though what had just happened was the most natural process in the world. After the last couple of days, a Sasquatch could jump off a rooftop doing the merengue, and she'd probably just toss him a quarter tip. There just didn't seem to be much shock value left in anything anymore.

Chapter Thirty-two

Russell Trahan was not excited about being on night duty. Not that he wasn't a company man by any means. But he'd set up a date with Marilyn Forrestier, the new cashier from the Piggly Wiggly supermarket, for tonight and had had to cancel it at the last minute. Mr. Godwin, Municipal's administrator, had called him and asked if he'd fill in for Mike Williams, the regular night orderly, who had come down with the flu. Russell reluctantly agreed, then phoned Marilyn to cancel their date. She'd hung up on him.

With his feet propped up on the reception desk, Russell flipped halfheartedly through the latest edition of *Sports Illustrated*. He'd made rounds an hour ago, making certain all thirty-three patients were tucked in for the night. The storm had frightened a few of them, especially old Mr. Hargroder, but Russell quickly settled him down with a Twinkie from his own supper sack. Once that had been done, he'd had nothing left to do but double-check door locks. The rest of the night would be spent fighting sleep.

Fifteen minutes into the magazine, Russell's eyelids drooped and the glossy pages began to blur. He yawned, dropped his feet to the floor, and sat up straight.

Man, it's going to be a long night, he thought.

He was in the middle of another yawn when he heard a faint scratching sound. He clamped off the yawn and cocked his head, listening. The scratching grew louder.

Geez, he thought with disgust, *they need to do something about the rats in this place. This one sounds as big as a dog!*

Russell quietly swiveled his chair to one side and stood. The noise seemed to be coming from somewhere deep in the walls, but he couldn't tell exactly where. He tiptoed around the reception cubicle and tried to hone in on the sound.

Without warning the scratching turned into a *bang! rrrip!*

Russell jumped back, startled. "That definitely ain't a rat!" he said shakily. It sounded like someone tearing through a wall with an ax at the back of the building.

Rrrip!

Flustered, Russell ran back to the cubicle, wondering if he should call for backup. But backup for what? He really didn't know what he was dealing with yet. Maybe he should check it out first, get a handle on what was going on before calling anyone.

While he debated, the banging, ripping, chiseling sounds escalated in volume.

Russell chewed on a thumbnail. What if he went back there and found out the patients had congregated for mutiny and decided to destroy the place? What would he do then? He could possibly take on one or two, but *not* thirty-three.

He spat out the masticated nail and shook his head. It couldn't be the patients. There was no way for them to get past the lockdown system on their room doors. And if by some miracle they did somehow manage to get out of their rooms, each corridor entrance that led toward the back of the building had a solid-core door with dead bolts attached.

As rational as that seemed to Russell, the question still remained. What the hell was going on back there? If you took the patients out of the equation, that left outsiders, and who in their right mind would be trying to break *into* a mental hospital?

Russell scooped up the receiver, then held a hovering finger over the number pad, not sure whom he should call first. He had always been instructed to immediately contact the administrator in case of an emergency. But 911 was only three numbers away. Mr. Godwin's was seven. It took the police department only fifteen minutes to get here; it took Godwin thirty-five.

He jabbed the number 9 and was about to tap in a quick 1-1 when he realized the demolition racket had stopped. Lowering the receiver from his ear, he listened intently and heard a faint titter, then a louder giggle that seemed to come from behind the hall access door.

Puzzled, Russell hung up the phone. "Who's out there?" he called.

Another giggle. This one high-pitched, like that of a child.

"You better answer me!"

Silence.

"Whoever's playin' games back there, this ain't funny!" Russell shouted.

A snicker, then a guffaw.

"Okay," Russell mumbled angrily. "You want funny? I'll show you funny." He pressed the button that deactivated the lock on the west hall access door. When he heard the buzzer, he spun around to rush the door but wound up tripping over his own feet.

Russell felt himself falling in slow motion, face first, over—*glass?*—six-inch slivers of pointed, razor-sharp—*glass?*—glass. Questions about how the shards got there never entered his mind. What he did think about was: Why couldn't he move his hands out in front of him to break the fall? And who had been laughing at him? And who was going to watch over the patients now?

The last thought that entered Russell's mind before the glass penetrated his eyes and sliced through his brain was that he'd never know what it felt like to kiss Marilyn Forrestier's thin, pink lips.

Chapter Thirty-three

Although Eli's pace slowed as they meandered through the halls of the clinic, Jessica still struggled to keep up with him. Her equilibrium felt off, and she had to trail a hand along the cinder-block walls to keep balanced.

She was about to ask Eli for the twentieth time if he knew where he was going when he made a sharp right at another intersection, then came to an abrupt stop. Jessica stumbled to a halt behind him.

The new passageway was wider and longer than the previous ones and well lit with rows of fluorescent lights. Though the walls and floor contained the same ascetic blend she'd seen throughout the rest of the building—gray cinder blocks and worn, gray-speckled tile—the atmosphere felt different. It felt charged with an energy Jessica couldn't identify, a raw, naked dynamism that frightened and angered her at the same time. The air smelled different, too, like condensed sweat instead of the peppermint-laced Lysol she'd grown accustomed to in this place.

Eli trudged forward, holding the tire iron out in front of him like a divining rod. It bounced gently from side to side, occasionally pointing ahead toward a group of flat-paneled, wooden doors that faced one another from opposite sides of the corridor. Even from seventy feet away, Jessica could easily make out the white, stenciled numbers and letters that labeled each door. The ones on the left ran in sequence from 1A to 6A, and the ones on the right, 1B to 6B.

Jessica's internal radar zeroed in on those doors, and her heart gave a sudden, erratic flutter. Todd was here, in one of those rooms. She felt it as surely as she felt the nausea now rising in her throat. She stopped and swallowed hard to keep the wave of queasiness in check. The floor seemed to sway beneath her feet. She leaned against a wall to wait out the vertigo, but it only intensified, and before she knew it, Jessica found herself stumbling about like a drunk whose feet couldn't find purchase. Her vision wavered, bringing Eli in and out of focus. He walked on ahead, widening the distance between them, but he appeared to be having as much difficulty holding steady as she. It was then that Jessica realized the vertigo had nothing to do with her dizziness. The floor *was* moving, and it was quickly turning into an aquatic roller coaster.

Horrified, she dropped into a crouch and rode the speckled tile and concrete as it heaved and fell. The hall rapidly filled with the sounds of cracking, buckling concrete, patches of tile rupturing with an explosive *pop!* The shriek of twisting metal caused

Jessica to glance up, and she saw the numbered doors begin to bulge and push away from their rigid jambs like swollen bellies. Eli stood between them, balancing against the riptide of tile, his back still to her. He seemed unaffected by what was occurring around him.

"Which one is he in?" Jessica shouted over the din, sensing Eli already knew where to find Todd. She struggled to her feet and fought to find a rhythm in the rolling floor so she could stay upright. "W-where is he?"

Eli snapped a look over his shoulder, and Jessica gasped and nearly fell over again. Eli's eyes wept a frothy purulence, and his teeth were bared and clenched. Bright red slashes striped his cheeks. He turned away from her again, and the movement caused his moldy shirt to clamp against his body, revealing the outline of his backbone. It looked like a serrated rope, ready to burst from his flesh.

Slowly, Eli lifted his arms above his head and in a loud, clear voice said, "She here now, Maikana. Lets him go—you finished!"

The decree ushered in an explosive report as many of the fluorescent lights overhead detonated in their plastic sheaths. While the hallway fell into a smoky gloom, door pins from 2B flew out of their hasps and stuck like bayonets in the opposite wall. The door ripped open, taking the lock with it, and a loud, long scream erupted from inside the room.

As the voice of the screamer receded, the door to 6A fell out of its frame and dropped with a resounding crash to the floor. A laughing, shrieking woman ran out of the room and, without breaking her stride, rammed headfirst into a wall. An audible *snap* abruptly killed the laughter, and the woman collapsed in a heap. Jessica recognized her as Terri, the young woman she'd met in the commons area who had insisted she give her a cigarette.

Fearing her brother might be the next one to come flying into the hall totally unhinged, Jessica cupped her hands around her mouth and yelled, "Todd!"

Eli looked back at her and casually pointed to 5A as if to say, "He's in there. Can't you see that?"

With no further preamble needed, Jessica took off in that direction, tripping and falling every other step. "Todd!"

By the time she reached 5A, Jessica was drenched in sweat and her arms were badly scraped and bleeding. She collapsed against the door, about to call for her brother, when a hand clamped down on her shoulder and roughly pushed her aside. Jessica fell to the floor just as the door to 5A split open, bursting from the middle. Wood shrapnel flew in every direction, with the largest shank piercing the center of Eli's chest. A look of shock swept over his face, and he dropped to his knees, the tire iron clattering to the floor.

"No!" Jessica scrambled on hands and knees to Eli's side. "Get up," she cried. "I don't know what to do. What am I supposed to do?" She pressed a hand against his back, and her fingers sunk into him like he was made of sponge.

Eli groaned, then his head whipped back and his eyes fixed on her, ablaze with fury. "You cannot help him, you asinine whore, he is mine." He swung at her with a fist, and Jessica threw herself backward.

"Dead or alive, all of you will be mine. I will make certain of it."

"Get away from me!" she screamed.

Eli laughed wildly, then grabbed the spear in his chest and twisted it. The howl of pain that erupted from him wrapped around Jessica with such force, it felt like thorns pressing into her flesh. Eli fell over on his side, silent, his expression a frozen mask of disbelief. And the undulating floor immediately grew still.

Jessica shivered, her emotions roiling. In a matter of minutes, Eli had gone from saving her life to threatening it. She didn't know what to make of that—of him. She nudged his leg with a foot, and when Eli didn't move, she stood up and cautiously stepped over him so she could peer into 5A.

Eli had been right. This was Todd's room, but the man standing in the center of it scarcely resembled her brother. His eyes were glassy and wide, his pajamas torn and dirty, and he was systematically pulling out clumps of hair from the top of his head.

"Todd!" Jessica hurled herself across the threshold and abruptly crashed into—*bars?* Though the impact of cold, hard steel had kept her from entering the room, Jessica couldn't see anything but an open threshold.

Stunned, she righted herself, then braced an arm tightly against her side and charged the opening again. This time she bounced off the barrier as though she'd collided with a sheet of rubber and wound up sprawled across the floor.

With a growl, Jessica jumped up and threw herself against the obstruction again. Just as before, she ricocheted off and tumbled over on her back.

Groaning, Jessica slowly rose to her feet. Her pant legs were ripped in several places, and her arms were covered with blood. She stumbled to the threshold and pressed her hands against the unseen obstacle, watching her brother. "Oh, Toddy, please stop. Please."

Without pause or the smallest acknowledgment of her presence, Todd continued to yank hair from his head. The right side of his scalp was nearly bald.

Jessica slid down to her haunches and sobbed. Her mind felt as fragile as an eggshell, ready to shatter with the slightest nudge. From what part of hell had this whole, implausibly horrific nightmare come from and why had it come to them? How could she help Todd if she couldn't even get to him? How could any of this possibly be real?

A sharp pain suddenly registered in Jessica's right calf, and she looked down to see Eli's hand grope blindly for her leg. His fingernails raked across her skin. With a wheeze of panic, Jessica dropped to her butt and pedaled backward, kicking at his hand. "Leave me alone! Don't—don't touch me!"

Eli's body convulsed, and the shaft that impaled him rattled against the floor. His head jerked back to a brutal angle. "The t'ing," he said, his voice a bare whisper. "Where—where be—the t'ing?"

"Shut up! Shut up!" Jessica cried. "I'm not listening to you anymore. You're a liar!" She held her hands over her ears and pulled her knees to her chest.

"You gots to cross him over," Eli said, his voice soft and pleading in her head.

"Stop it! Shut up!" Jessica began to beat her forehead against the cinder blocks to drown out his voice.

"He gonna die."

Blood trickled over Jessica's eyelids, but she paid it no mind. She concentrated on the thumping and ringing in her ears. *No more voices,* she thought, and banged her head harder. *No more nightmare, no more responsibility. No more Jessica.*

"Where be the t'ing? No more time—no more."

I'll make this whole ugly thing go away. That's what I'll do. I'll just make it all go away, and nothing will matter anymore.

"Jessica Lynn, you stop that this minute!"

The command startled Jessica immobile.

"Look out, Jessica! Move!" The voice sounded like Sharon's.

Detecting a presence nearby, Jessica slowly turned her head to the right and saw Eli looming over her. The spear waggled obscenely in his chest as he raised his arms over his head. The tire iron was clamped between his hands. She just stared up at him and wished he would hurry and kill her and get it over with.

"Jessica!"

Numb, Jessica barely had the energy to shift her head toward the voice.

Sharon stood at the end of the hallway, her hands braced against the wall, feet straddling two piles of flooring debris. Stumbling up beside her was Lisa. She had one hand cradled, and her mouth was agape.

"The pendant, where is it?" Sharon asked, her voice sounding to Jessica like a desperate echo from a seashell.

Without answering her, Jessica looked up at Eli and felt a sudden rush of air as he swatted the rod in her direction. It missed her by inches. She blinked.

"Jessica, move!"

Jessica glanced over at Sharon curiously.

"Where is it, Jess? Where's the pend . . . *oomph*!" Sharon fell with a thud over a pile of rubble.

Jessica giggled, and another swoosh of air circled her head. "It's in my pocket."

"Take it out," Sharon yelled. "Take it out!"

Whoosh—whoosh.

"Look out!" Lisa cried.

"Jessica Lynn, you look at me right now," Sharon demanded.

Jumping to attention like someone had slapped her awake, Jessica blinked rapidly.

"Take out the pendant!" Sharon screamed. She was bent over on hands and knees, maneuvering like a crab, trying to get to Jessica.

Whoosh—whoosh—whoosh.

The sound of pummeled air made Jessica lean back in alarm.

"For God's sake, take it out!"

Jessica shoved a hand into her pocket and drew out the metal ornament. It was fiery hot to the touch and glowed brighter than any one-hundred-watt light-bulb. Her mind snapped back sharp and focused.

Whap!

The tire iron struck the cinder blocks just above Jessica's right shoulder. She caught Eli pulling back for another strike.

"Now throw it! Throw it at him!" Sharon shouted.

Jessica quickly threw the pendant at Eli without question, but wondered what damage such a small object could do to a maniac with a steel rod.

The chain snagged on the tire iron, wrapping around it as it swooped down in an arc. Missing her once more, Eli bared his teeth, lifted the rod up high, and aimed for the top of her head.

"Don't!" Jessica blurted.

Eli's shoulders suddenly slumped, and his face collapsed into wrinkles of perplexity. He dropped his arms, and the pendant slipped from the tire iron as it tumbled from his hand.

Jessica caught the ornament before it hit the ground, and immediately hurled it at him again. Her heart sank as it flew over Eli's head.

"Sharon, Lisa, get out of . . ." Jessica's mouth fell open as she saw the pendant stop in midflight, then circle back to Eli. It whirled above his head, leaving a thin trail of black smoke. Eli cocked his head as though listening intently.

The chain pulled taut as the ornament twirled faster and faster. When it finally became an unrecognizable blur, the pendant fired like a bullet into the top of Eli's skull and Jessica heard it bore through the man's cranium cap. Eli's scream was cut short as his body jerked and contorted, then crumpled to the floor.

"No!" a monstrous bellow vibrated the air, and the walls shook with its power. The doors to 1A, 3A, and 4B flew open, and the corridor immediately filled with a brilliant white light.

Suddenly encapsulated in the radiance, Jessica was overcome with a need to expand her lungs, to suck in as much of the light as possible. Giving in to the compulsion, she held her arms out at her sides, closed her eyes, and drew in a long, deep breath that made her body tingle. An intense heat began rolling through her body. It traveled from head to foot and back again before culminating in her fingertips. She was left warm and vibrant and filled with an indomitable sense of wholeness. Her mind screamed rebirth, and although she didn't understand the fullness of what was happening to her, she savored it.

Gradually Jessica opened her eyes, and she wasn't surprised to find she'd levitated six inches off the floor. She glanced over at Sharon and Lisa, who were gawking up at her.

"Sweet Mother Mary," Sharon breathed.

"Holy shit," Lisa mumbled.

Jessica smiled, then simply thought the word *down,* and her body gently lowered to the floor. She immediately turned to Todd's room and pressed her hands against the transparent barrier. It dissolved beneath her touch.

She entered the room, and Todd dropped his hands from his head and stared at her fearfully. Jessica took a step toward him, and he quickly moved away from her.

"They're all gone, *mon beau frere,*" she said, and was astonished by the sound of her own voice. It was deeper, richer, and carried a French accent. "They can't hurt you anymore."

Todd's bottom lip quivered, and tears slid down his cheeks.

Jessica moved closer to him. "I promise with my whole heart and soul, I would never hurt you."

His shoulders twitched as she neared.

"Let me touch you and help you. Let me take your

suffering away." The words sounded like an old prerecorded tape playing in Jessica's head. They felt familiar and comfortable, like she'd used them a million times before.

A spark of hope flickered in Todd's eyes, then died quickly. He turned his head away from her.

Jessica raised her hands slowly. Her fingers felt hot and charged with a strong electrical current as they neared Todd's head. He whimpered when she finally placed her fingers over his ears and the pad of both thumbs on a spot between his eyes.

In that moment, the room and institute disappeared from Jessica's sight and she found herself standing alone in a garbage dump. The odor surrounding her now was putrid enough to turn the strongest of stomachs, but she inhaled deeply. For her, the smell was like radar. It would help her find the treasure she sought.

Three piles of rubbish were stacked at least forty feet high, with their collective circumferences covering the length of a football field. Jessica walked steadily around the first mound, previewing black fungus growth on old paper sacks and boxes. A fresh collection of mud lay heaped alongside an old winter coat. Plastic bags and crumpled paper gave way to mice and roaches that scurried into hiding as she walked by. There were children's toys, old and crippled, tossed among the debris. Jessica spotted the rusted handlebars of a tricycle poking up from a mound of mildewed clothes, and she recognized it as the bike Todd had gotten for his second birthday. The price of it, back then, had caused a monstrous fight between her parents. A jack-in-the-box, with the clown head missing, rested sadly atop a mashed carton of maggot-infested Chinese food. Jessica had always hated the surprise attack of that damn toy. She remembered the nightmares that springy, painted face had given Todd as a child.

Sniffing deeply, she turned toward the second pile of refuse and circled back to the front of it. There she found an old Frigidaire toppled on its side with flies congregating around its tightly sealed door. Placing a foot against the edge of the refrigerator for leverage, Jessica pulled the door open wide.

A desperate sucking in of air came from the confined space, and the sound drew a smile to Jessica's lips. She held out a hand. "You don't have to hide here anymore," she said softly. "There's nothing left to be afraid of. I promise."

A small hand, the size appropriate for a seven-year-old, reached anxiously for her. Jessica took it and gently pulled the young boy close to her. Her arms wrapped around him gently. "I promise, Toddy. I promise."

Holding her brother tight against her, Jessica led him away from the garbage, the infestation, and the filth of memories past.

Todd was still in her arms when her mind registered they were back in room 5A. With a sigh of contentment, she kissed a tear from Todd's cheek and smoothed his hair, which had turned cotton white. Then Jessica Lynn Guidry LeJeune smiled broadly into her brother's shining, happy—whole—brown eyes.

Chapter Thirty-four

Jake LeJeune thought the deserted parking lot of Olin's Furniture Store made for a perfect pump and jump site. It didn't have parking bumpers like most lots. The concrete pad was open, flat, and wide, excellent for pumping out the new, twenty-two-inch, fire-engine-red Apache bicycle he'd gotten for his birthday.

The jumps would be done from a portable incline that he and his buddies had spent most of the morning putting together. The ramp was supreme: a four-foot-long by three-foot-wide plywood board, braced by elk blocks that sent the offshoot to a record height of three feet.

Jake pedaled faster, circling the ramp and surveying the local competition.

A couple of yards away, Billy Thompson sat astride his one-year-old, black ten-speed with his arms crossed over his chest. He always kept a pack of Marlboro cigarettes rolled up in his shirtsleeve so all the kids would think him cool. Jake had never seen him smoke one, but he figured if Billy's mom ever caught him with that pack of smokes, his hide would wind up anything but cool. With or without cigarettes, however, Billy was thin and tall for a soon-to-be sixth grader, which made him light on his bike and serious competition.

Whipping around the lot in a cloverleaf, red-faced and sweating a river, was Chad Stillen. Chad rode a puke-green Schwinn with bulky handlebars that looped back to the rider like a girl's bike. He didn't have a snowball's chance at the jump, and everyone knew it. The guys just let him hang out with them because his dad owned a Big Burger franchise, and they usually got to eat there for free. Chad was going to be a sixth grader like the rest of them, but his bulk made him look like he belonged in high school. Most of the kids left him alone because of his size—until they discovered that any confrontation usually sent Chad running away in tears.

Last on the competitors list was Evan Mitchell, and there was little doubt the guy would get priority jumping rights. The long-haired Hanson look-alike rode a sleek Silver Arrow that had two disk reflectors set in the spokes of each bike wheel. Evan had been responsible for getting the materials for the ramp from his dad's construction site, and he made sure everyone remained well aware of his prominent connections. As major contributor to their ramp project, Evan took the liberty of establishing the first rule for the afternoon's event: no helmets allowed. This made Jake nervous. He knew if his mother found out about the rule, she'd have a cow. Fortunately she was still out of town and, the last Jake had heard from his dad, not expected back until Sunday. Still, to be on the safe side, he'd have to make sure each of these guys gave him a spit-shake oath to never tell.

Confident that he had about as good a chance as any of them in making a good, clean jump, Jake quickly fell into formation.

The boys rode around the ramp, discussing the speeds they would need to reach maximum projection. They had about five hundred feet of acceleration distance before hitting the ramp, enough if they pedaled hard and fast. Chad was chosen to mark the distance of each landing, then Billy would mark Chad's distance when it was his turn.

"Line 'em up," Evan barked, his face stern and drawn. He whipped his bike around, making his back tire squeal. "You got the chalk?" he called out to Chad.

"Got it." Chad held up a large piece of sidewalk chalk.

"No cheatin', ya hear?" Evan said.

Chad threw a hand out as though to bat Evan's words away. He paced off a couple of feet from the side of the ramp, then squatted down low.

"I'm first," Evan announced. "Remember, no shoutin' or yellin' 'til I make the jump. It'll make me break concentration. If anybody does it, I'll have to jump again. In fact," he added with an authoritative smirk, "if anybody does make me mess up, they'll be thrown out of the club."

Jake wiped sweat from the side of his face. "What club?"

"The jump club, stupid," Evan said.

"I didn't know we were a club," Billy said.

"I just made us one," Evan said, then pedaled toward the end of the lot.

Billy and Jake looked at each other briefly, rolled their eyes, and backed away from the ramp.

Evan circled the end of the lot twice, then braked. He adjusted his sunglasses, then pushed off on his bike and headed for the incline. He stood up and hunched over, his legs pumping furiously while his body rocked from side to side.

Jake had to force himself to stay put as Evan flew by. He wanted to jump out and scare a little humility into the guy for acting like a jerk, but he decided against it at the last minute. There was no stopping the wide grin that danced across his face just from thinking about it, though.

"Shiiiit!" Evan yelled as his bike hit the ramp, flew across the board, then catapulted high into the air. He was still standing on the bike pedals when the back tire hit the concrete. Leaning forward, Evan managed to force the front wheel down and stay on the bike as it landed.

Chad raced to the point of impact and marked a two-foot-long chalk line.

"Man, that was awesome!" Evan whooped and yelled as he pedaled back to his friends. Not one of them said anything when he pushed his sunglasses up over his head with shaky hands. "That was the ultimate, the majorist bomb." Evan's eyes lit up like flares. "Go on, Jake the Snake, your turn."

Jake hated when the guys called him that. Why couldn't he have a cool name like Brandon, or even Evan? You couldn't think of much to rhyme with Evan.

"I'm going next," Billy said, already unrolling the cigarette pack from his sleeve. "Hold these for me, Jake. Don't wanna mash 'em." He handed the already mashed pack to Jake, pushed his bike off with one foot, then pedaled lazily to the edge of the lot. He eyed the ramp and rode nonchalantly toward it.

"What're you doin'?" Evan snorted. "You're not going to make the jump at that speed."

"I wanna check the ramp," Billy said, circling his bike to the back of the elevated slab of plywood. He leaned over and studied the elk blocks beneath it. "They're startin' to slide," he announced.

"What a pussy," Evan said. He shoved the kickstand down on his bike and stomped off to investigate.

While the two boys readjusted cinder blocks, Jake leaned back on his bike and stretched his legs out in front of him. A breeze tousled his hair, and he folded his arms across his stomach and gazed up at the cloudless sky, letting the wind cool his face. He thought about something else his dad had told him, that his mom would be bringing Uncle Todd home with her, and that he would be living with them for a while. It had been some time since Jake had seen his uncle, but he remembered how funny the man was, how easily he laughed, and how he never once talked down to him just because he was a kid. Adding another person to the house would crowd things up a little, especially the bathroom, but Jake figured it might be pretty cool having him around anyway.

"Hey, dream boy." Billy whacked Jake's shoulder hard as he rode past him. "Wake up and watch how this is really supposed to be done." He leaned hard to the left, then to the right as he made a semicircle around the lot. After coasting a few feet, Billy took his hands off the handlebars.

"Quit hotshottin' and do the jump," Evan shouted at him.

Billy lifted the middle finger of his right hand and waved it at Evan like an injured worm. He grabbed the handlebars and started pedaling. His style was different from Evan's. It was harder, faster, and contained no fear. Leaning his bike left, then right, Billy gained momentum while his feet drove the pedals into spinning blurs. He sat on the seat and straightened the bike only inches away from the ramp, then hit it with a loud "WHOA!"

Within seconds, he was airborne and overshooting Evan's chalk mark by at least two feet. Billy whooped in triumph. The expression on his face abruptly changed from glory hound to terror, however, as his bike tilted forward, flipped, then crashed to the ground with him beneath it. Billy's scream echoed across the parking lot.

Jake raced to Billy's side with Evan close at his heels. Chad followed up the rear, but immediately froze like a wide-eyed mannequin as soon as he got a good look at his injured friend.

"My arm," Billy cried, rolling from side to side. Below his right elbow, Jake noticed a jagged piece of bone poking through the skin.

"Oh, man," Evan said in awe. "The bone's stickin' out his arm."

"Don't just stand there," Billy yelled. "Get help. An ambulance, the fire department, somethin'!"

"Right, help," Evan said, already running back for his bike. When he reached it, he slapped the kickstand up with a foot and shouted over his shoulder, "Ya'll stay with him while I go get my dad!" Not waiting for a response, Evan pushed the bike into a running start, then hopped onto the seat and took off.

Billy moaned loudly, and Jake knelt beside him, unsure of what to do. He'd had some first-aid training while in the Cub Scouts last year, but nothing that addressed anything of this magnitude. He studied the wound, surprised there wasn't a rush of blood squirting from it. In fact, there was very little blood at all. Even more surprising to Jake was his own reaction to the wound. Instead of being grossed out by the injury, he wanted to touch it.

"Does it hurt bad?" Jake asked.

Billy moaned again. "Like a sumabitch. My bike—how bad is it?"

Jake glanced over at the tangled handlebars, the crooked seat, and the twisted front tire. "Not too bad," he lied.

Billy gave a little nod, then closed his eyes and began to cry.

Jake flinched, pained by his friend's sobs. As they grew in volume, a soft voice suddenly whispered in Jake's right ear, *"Stop his suffering, now. Stop the suffering."*

Puzzled, Jake peered up at Chad, who stood a few feet away. "Huh?"

Chad blinked but offered no other response. His gaze remained fixed on Billy's arm.

"Touch him, Jake."

This time Jake recognized the voice as female, but one unfamiliar to him. He swiveled about on the balls of his feet and looked around the lot. There was no one else around.

"Stop the suffering."

Jake frowned. Now the whispery voice seemed to be coming from his own head. At a loss and becoming a bit frightened, he turned back to Billy. The boy still had his eyes closed but was no longer crying. His face held a grimace of intense pain.

"Touch him. Stop his suffering. Now."

This time the sound of those words sent a warm flush washing through Jake's body. It started at the crown of his head and rolled toward the soles of his feet. It made his ears ring, and seemed to transform the desire he had earlier to touch Billy's wound into an overpowering, do-or-die necessity.

Overcome by compulsion, Jake reached for Billy's disfigured arm and wrapped a hand around the bone fragment. He immediately felt a vibrating heat flow from his palm and fingers.

Billy's eyes flew open, and he cried out in pain. "What're you— Stop! Stop!"

Jake paid little attention to his friend. He stayed focused on keeping his hand over the wound as Billy tried to wiggle free. The resonating heat suddenly increased to twice its original intensity, and Jake instinctively gave the wound a little squeeze.

Billy let out a horrified shriek, then abruptly fell silent. His eyes went wide with amazement. "It—it ain't hurtin' no more," he exclaimed.

Releasing his grip, Jake sat back on his haunches.

"I mean, it ain't even hurtin' a little bit!" As though needing to prove his point, Billy touched the bone still poking through the flesh of his right arm with a tentative finger. "See?" He shook his head slowly in disbelief, then gazed up at Jake. "How—how'd you do that?"

Stunned himself, Jake only shrugged. He didn't have a clue how.

"Man," Billy said excitedly, "when you grabbed me like that, I thought you'd gone nuts and . . ."

As Billy rambled on, Jake studied his hands. He lightly tapped his tingling fingertips together and thought of his mom. This must have been what she felt the few times she'd touched him between the eyes when he'd been very sick or in pain. He wondered why, if he now possessed the same ability as his mom, he hadn't felt led to touch Billy between the eyes. Why directly over the broken bone?

Jake chewed his top lip thoughtfully and gazed across the parking lot. He had a million and one questions, and sensed it would take longer than his lifetime to have them all answered. From the moment he had touched Billy Thompson's arm, Jake had felt much more than electrified heat. He'd felt realigned, repositioned, inside. And that change in him seemed so large and significant, Jake couldn't quite wrap his mind around all of it yet. He sensed two things to be elemental, however. The first was that this realignment meant to alter his life forever, and the second—it would change the world.

Jake closed his eyes with the weight of that insight. *Come home, Mom*, he thought. *We have a lot to talk about. A lot to talk about and a lot to do.*

He slowly opened his eyes again, and the world looked exactly as it had a moment ago. The sky remained blue, Billy still chattered away with a broken arm, and Chad stood glued to the same spot as before. Yet Jake felt a twinge of sadness. For him, bike races and games, the overall simplicity of childhood, had already begun to fade into a past lifetime. He knew nothing would be simple anymore.

He had inherited a gift, one he never asked for, but one he would be required to share with many, many people.

Hurry home, Mom. Please, hurry home.